"Wild [and] delightful."

—*PopSugar* for *Burn It All Down*

"Side-splitting."

—*Shelf Awareness*, **Starred Review,** for *Burn It All Down*

"Hilarious."

—*Booklist* for *Burn It All Down*

"Just the summer read you've been craving…a fiercely funny novel."

—*Real Simple* for *Burn It All Down*

Praise for Nicolas DiDomizio

"Filled with charm, hilarity, sweetness, and swoon, *The Gay Best Friend* is an absolute MUST-READ. DiDomizio deftly creates characters that are as lovable as they are deliciously flawed, and I am officially obsessed with this book."

—**Lynn Painter**, bestselling author of
Mr. Wrong Number, for *The Gay Best Friend*

"*The Gay Best Friend* is fun, frothy, and full of feels. With characters so messy they seem like people you've known your entire life—you know, the ones you simultaneously want to shake some sense into and hug the stuffing out of. It's the perfect beach read."

—**Xio Axelrod**, bestselling author of
The Girl with Stars in Her Eyes, for *The Gay Best Friend*

"Outrageously witty and incisive! *The Gay Best Friend* captures all the kinetic energy of a '90s Julia Roberts film and queers it. A perfect summer read that reminds us: putting yourself first should never be a second thought."

—**Timothy Janovsky**, author of
Never Been Kissed, for *The Gay Best Friend*

"Equal parts hilarious and heart-wrenching, *The Gay Best Friend* is not to be missed. It explores the complexities of love, friendship, and our capacity for forgiveness with sharp, emotional detail. In Dom, DiDomizio has created an unforgettable character to root for and relate to. I loved every page."

—**Annette Christie**, author of
The Rehearsals, for *The Gay Best Friend*

Also by
Nicolas DiDomizio

The Gay Best Friend

nearly
wed

NICOLAS DIDOMIZIO

sourcebooks
casablanca

Published by Sourcebooks Casablanca, an imprint of Sourcebooks
P.O. Box 4410, Naperville, Illinois 60567-4410
(630) 961-3900
sourcebooks.com

Cataloging-in-Publication Data is on file with the Library of Congress.

Printed and bound in the United States of America.
VP 10 9 8 7 6 5 4 3 2

For all the romantics

"Every human motive is in the end a yearning for companionship, and every act of every person on this planet is an effort not to be alone."

—Joel Derfner, *Swish*

"Under the shell, the lobster is little more than jelly-soft flesh and floppy organs."

—Trevor Corson, *The Secret Life of Lobsters*

prologue

A BRIEF HISTORY OF MY DELUSIONAL OBSESSION WITH LOVE AND MARRIAGE

By Ray Bruno

It all started about three decades ago. My parents would try to lull me to sleep each night with the traditional bedtime stories my older sister had loved—*Goodnight Moon*, *The Little Prince*, that one picture book about the cookie-eating mouse who won't stop asking for shit—but the only thing I ever wanted to "read" before bed was their wedding album.

Jim and Janice Bruno's Special Day: August 31, 1981.

I can still picture it. The ivory-colored cover was thick and padded, with an oval cutout in the middle to display the happy couple's official wedding portrait. It was all so eighties: two giddy young newlyweds perched atop a grand staircase, the train of my mother's puffy white gown spanning exactly eleven steps (this was how I learned to count to eleven), and my gruff father in the only tux he's ever worn, looking suspiciously like Sonny Corleone in the opening scene of *The Godfather*.

The pictures on the inside were even more ridiculous.

An army of hot-pink bridesmaid dresses at a mile-long head table, a cake higher than Willie Nelson, and so. Many. Mustaches. One dance-floor candid shot in particular featured exactly thirteen of them (this was how I learned to count to thirteen).

But while the album itself might have been dated, the love story my mom told as she flipped through its pages was timeless.

She talked about my father as if she were still the smitten young waitress she had been the day they met—when he marched into the Clam Shell for a cold beer after twelve hours of hauling lobster traps, locked eyes with her from across the bar, and expertly captured her heart.

"The luckiest catch of my whole damn life," he used to say.

"First of all, he reeked of herring chum," Mom would joke. And then she'd beam. "But it was love at first sight. He made me molt."

Her usage of *molt* instead of *melt* was an extremely Bruno choice of words. Everything was a lobster metaphor in our house.

And I must admit, while the typical expression of lovers making each other melt is cute and all, molting is a far more romantic concept. It's the process by which lobsters shed their old shells so they can grow into newer, bigger, better ones. It's also the only time their reproductive organs are exposed and unprotected enough to mate. Growth and vulnerability—the ingredients of lasting love.

"I knew immediately that he was the One." Mom was intent on acquainting me with every cliché in the book. "We had an undeniable spark."

As if all of this wasn't enough to turn me into a hopeless

romantic, we also lived in the town of Seabrook. The only thing our Connecticut shoreline community was known for more than its lobstering industry was its couples tourism.

The jewel of Seabrook is the Earlymoon Hotel, a sprawling waterfront resort famous in New England for its "earlymoon" vacation packages. A honeymoon before the wedding. Every summer, engaged couples flood the resort's private beaches to escape the stresses of wedding planning—shedding their old, single selves and basking in the excitement of their forthcoming new identities as halves of married wholes.

Molting.

These getaways have always been billed as the key to approaching your wedding day on the right foot, with a clear mind and a strengthened bond. In Seabrook, it's not about something borrowed or something blue. It's about time spent at the Earlymoon Hotel. Even my parents had a stay there before their wedding—a gift from my mom's wealthy uncle—and they lived less than six miles away from it.

"That place is magical," Mom would tell me, actively feeding the beast. "Every time I drive by it, I fall in love with your father all over again."

It wasn't long before I started telling anyone who'd listen all about my future earlymoon, my future wife—a hilarious detail when you consider the fact that I was a little boy *obsessed with wedding culture*—and our future marriage.

By the time I was twelve, I was routinely asking my best girl friend to make and renew a pact with me: If neither of us was married when we reached the (apparently geriatric) age of twenty-eight, we'd marry each other.

This was the exact plot of *My Best Friend's Wedding*, because of course that was my favorite movie at the time. I dreamed of walking in Dermot Mulroney's shoes one day—engaged to Cameron Diaz, with Julia Roberts scheming for my heart behind the scenes. (Not just one bride, but a backup too!)

It's sad that I forced myself to identify with the role of Straight Groom when Rupert Everett's character of Gay Best Friend was right there, but I wanted love and marriage—not a lifetime of chirping sassy quips from the sidelines. Plus, you know, it was the nineties. It would take me (and society) several years of evolution before I started to view my gayness as less of a curse and more of a gift.

I eventually outgrew the straight element of my fantasies, but the fixation on marriage persisted.

When I finally came out of the closet at twenty—the same age my parents were when they met—all I wanted to do was find a husband. It was 2008 and gay marriage had just been legalized in Connecticut, something I thought was a fortuitous coincidence at the time, but really wasn't much of a coincidence at all. I could have come out before then, but I didn't. Something in my subconscious needed marriage to be on the table first.

Flash forward to 2015, when I was working in New York City as a staff writer at a trashy clickbait website and living in Hoboken with my boyfriend, Byrd Corson, another staff writer at another trashy clickbait website. On June 26th of that year, the Supreme Court's federal legalization of gay marriage blew my heart wide open.

Byrd and I had only known each other for a year, but that didn't matter to me. There was something in the air that day. And I had a deadline coming up! My twenty-eighth birthday. I excitedly proposed to Byrd via text message moments after the ruling was announced on CNN.

Regrettably, he said yes.

I immediately began researching every photographer in the tristate area, determined to obtain a storybook wedding album of my own, and we moved through the rest of the planning process at lightning speed.

The festivities took place on a frigid day in January (the only month we could afford) and flew by in a manic blur. It didn't feel great to rush the one major life event I'd staked my entire sense of identity on since birth, but somehow this felt like the only way to make it happen. Almost like I knew deep down that if we'd taken our time—if we'd indulged in an earlymoon, for example—one of us might've come to our senses and called the whole thing off.

When our album arrived a couple months after the wedding, I experienced actual chest pains as I relived what should have been the happiest day of my life.

None of the pictures looked...right. There was no grand staircase, no militia-sized wedding party, no Willie Nelson cake. It was painfully clear from our body language that we were neither present nor in love—just stiff and forced, consumed with trying to project an image of perfection. There was no trace of that giddy look in my parents' eyes on the cover of their album.

No molting.

This was a difficult reality to accept because I had tried so hard to select a husband with whom I'd be compatible. I held out on getting serious with anyone until I found a man who made it past all my very specific dating app filters: age (mine), location (mine), career (mine), hobbies (mine), interests (mine). I'd have to get along with my clone, right?

But while Byrd and I had everything in common on paper,

something was off between us in the flesh. We had no spark. It was more like a gas burner that wouldn't light; it ticked and ticked, but the flame eluded us. I mostly pretended I didn't notice.

Byrd took the opposite approach. It was only a matter of months before our marriage descended into a nonstop cycle of fighting followed by silence followed by resignation. Lather, rinse, repeat, until he eventually admitted to cheating on me with one of his exes. We made a half-hearted attempt to work it out for a few weeks, but Byrd was done. He filed for divorce right before my twenty-ninth birthday.

The punch line? My clone-husband cited irreconcilable differences.

Of all the shame I've carried in my life, my divorce has weighed the heaviest. I had been so consumed with being a young groom that I never considered how humiliating it would feel to be a young divorcé. A failure at the only thing that had ever mattered to me.

Beyond the standard amount of post-divorce embarrassment, I had to face the fact that it was a gay divorce. I had always judged incompatible straight people who rushed into marriage purely for the sake of being married. For half of college and most of grad school, in fact, my entire personality revolved around my opinion that they took their rights for granted—treating vows as if they were merely words to say and not promises to make. I had sworn I'd be different. The fact that I had to *win* the right to marry was supposed to guarantee I'd be different.

And yet.

"I'm such a joke," I lamented to my parents during a trip home after the papers were signed. "How did I let this happen? All I've ever wanted is what you two have."

My father clicked his tongue in pity and sized me up. "You try too hard, kid. You think I ended up with your mother because I spent years trying to force her into existence? I never even thought about getting married. It just happened when it was supposed to happen." He paused before offering his go-to solution for all my problems: "You should be more like your sister."

I scoffed. "Stef is obnoxiously anti-love."

"Yet somehow she's in a happy marriage," Dad marveled. "It was easy for her to find a husband because she never wanted one in the first place."

"Is this supposed to make me feel better? Because all it's doing is making me resent my only sibling."

"I think what your father's trying to say," Mom interjected, "is that maybe you should use this as an opportunity to focus on yourself. You're young! Don't worry about getting married. Just live your life."

This is all very easy for you two to say, I thought to myself. *You have no idea what it's like to be a single gay man in the special circle of hell known as modern-day Manhattan.*

But I followed their advice nonetheless. Tossed my wedding album into a bonfire in their backyard on Thanksgiving night. Deleted my dating apps and pitched every editor in the city until I finally got hired at a reputable publication that didn't make me cringe at the sight of my own byline. I moved into a studio apartment. My weekdays were spent focused on my new job, weekends with friends and family. I got lonely often, but I learned how to sit with the feeling and let it pass, which it always did. By the time I turned thirty, I nearly believed that happiness without marriage might actually be within the realm of possibility.

But then.

On a random weeknight under the bright lights of the raw bar at Grand Central Station, I met him. We were seated elbow to elbow on adjacent barstools—slurping down a dozen oysters each—when he gently poked my shoulder.

"They only gave you eleven," he remarked. A painfully handsome stranger with warm brown hair and the subtlest cleft in his chin.

I flinched—way too dramatically—at the unexpected attention, coughing through a flame of Tabasco in my throat. "I'm sorry?"

His deep-brown eyes widened. "You alright? Too much heat on that one?"

"I'm fine," I replied. "I love heat. I just swallowed it wrong."

"Nothing worse than swallowing it wrong," he said through a playful smirk. "Hate when that happens."

I scanned the restaurant in disbelief. Was a hot man flirting with me? In the wild? It didn't seem possible. As delusional as I'd always been about romance, I had given up on the idea of an old-fashioned meet-cute a long time ago—after I accepted my sexuality and determined that my chances would always be limited to gay bars and the internet.

"Same," I said, at a loss for a witty comeback. I had nary a quip in the arsenal. Norah Ephron had failed me. "It's a very unpleasant sensation."

I decided to douse my next oyster in even more hot sauce, due to some weird impulse I had to prove just how much heat I could take. But instead of the usual quickie Tabasco shot, the entire contents of the mini-bottle poured out at once.

The oyster was fully drenched, but I raised it to my mouth anyway—as if the bloodbath was entirely intentional—because what other choice did I have at that point?

"Wait," the hot stranger protested. "Please don't eat that."

"Trust me," I assured him. "I have a high tolerance."

"For...plastic?" He pointed at the tiny Tabasco cap that had fallen off and landed at the lip of the oyster shell.

"Oh." How did I not notice that? This man had me flustered. "So that's why it was coming out in a geyser-like fashion."

He laughed without breaking eye contact. My typical instinct around strangers has always been to avoid eye contact entirely, but his eyes were so...warm? Generous. Undistracted. It was physically impossible not to meet them with mine.

I leaned in. "Are your eyes always so..."

He cocked his head as he waited for me to find the word. Suddenly the thought of saying something like *warm, generous,* or *undistracted* out loud made me full-body cringe.

"Open?" I improvised.

Open?

"Well, yeah," he answered. "Unless I'm sleeping. Or blinking."

He was still smirking, still looking right at me, and I couldn't remember the last time a person had given me such undivided attention.

"Even during graphic kill scenes in horror movies?" I asked. "I always shut mine for those."

"I can handle a little blood," he said. "I'm a doctor." He kept talking before I could ask what kind. "Did you hear what I said earlier? They shorted you an oyster. There are only eleven on your plate..."

This threw me for a loop. "You just randomly happened to notice I have exactly eleven oysters?"

"My train's delayed," he explained. "And I'm a compulsive counter when I'm bored. Can't stop myself from counting up everything in sight."

This threw me for an even bigger loop. "Your solution for boredom is to...observe your surroundings? What about your phone?"

Now he was squinting at me. The crow's-feet around his eyes paired with a general air of maturity suggested he was a good decade older than me—well outside the narrow age range I would've selected on a dating app—but this didn't feel weird. It felt comfortable.

"I generally don't use my phone unless I have to answer a call or send a message," he replied. "You know, phone things."

"Were you, like, cryogenically frozen in the early two-thousands and just thawed out this very evening?" I asked. "No offense."

"None taken," he said. "What gave me away? The knee-length cargo shorts and Abercrombie graphic tee?"

I couldn't suppress a grin as I glanced down at his perfectly pressed ensemble—navy slacks and a stretch oxford button-down. "Touché."

"They actually gave me thirteen oysters," he added. "So if you don't mind accepting raw shellfish from a total stranger, we could restore equilibrium without disrupting the bartender. She looks slammed."

He paused, smiled, extended a hand. "I'm Kip."

I glanced at our respective platters and thought of the eleven steps on the grand staircase. The thirteen mustaches on the dance floor.

Kip.

"Nice to meet you," I replied as my muscles relaxed, my heart swelled, my shell cracked. The molting had already begun. "I'm Ray."

monday

1

~

F iona Apple," Kip whispers.

My body convulses as I release a shriek so piercing I'm surprised it doesn't trigger a nearby car alarm. I'd thought I was alone in the foyer.

"You're going to give yourself a heart attack one of these days," he continues, entirely unbothered. Even if I had triggered a nearby car alarm, he still wouldn't have flinched. Kip Hayes doesn't have a jumpy bone in his body. "You need to relax."

"*You* need to stop sneaking up on me," I tell him. "Paula Cole."

We're doing that thing where we randomly greet each other with names of iconic female artists who have played the main stage at Lilith Fair at least once in their careers. It's an admittedly ridiculous bit that started early in our relationship, when I tried to prove to Kip that even though I was a child in the nineties (while he was in high school and college), I was just as clued into pop culture as he was. Probably even more so.

"I'd hardly call that sneaking up," says Kip. "I was especially sure to address you gently."

"Fiona Apple is an aggressive choice," I retort. "Gentle would have been Sarah McLachlan."

He flips me a lighthearted middle finger, which is basically our love language. His body looks so good in its current attire (light-weight running shorts and a Nike tank) that I can't *not* touch it right now. So I pull him into a hug and brush my lips against his.

We make out for a few moments before he steps back and chuckles to himself.

"You were in such a trance when I came down," he says. "Admiring the new tree again?"

His eyes crinkle in amusement at my passion for home decor, something he could never be bothered to give a shit about. This is a man who once returned from a weeklong medical conference and didn't notice I had *entirely new kitchen countertops* installed in his absence.

"I was," I admit. "I'm just so glad we found something to fill the space."

This vaulted foyer has been a huge pain in my ass since we moved out to the suburbs last year—the most formidable design challenge in the whole house. The previous owners had filled it with a heinous credenza and an antique pendulum clock that somehow looked haunted, so they were no help when it came to inspiration. I left it empty for months after the rest of the rooms were furnished, hoping the right piece would reveal itself in time.

And then it did. I was at Crate & Barrel a few weeks ago when an enormous faux olive tree caught my attention. I'd never thought of myself as an artificial-tree-in-the-foyer kind of person, but this tree spoke to my soul. It was freakishly realistic and reminded me of our trip to Tuscan wine country last summer, a destination I'll never forget because it's where Kip surprised me with his proposal.

"Don't you just love it?" I ask Kip as I gesture toward the earthy weave of branches and leaves floating above us. "I know you love it. Even though *you* don't know you love it, like, on a conscious level, I know that somewhere, deep down, this tree has made your life complete."

"I do love it…" He playfully squeezes my ass. "But only because it makes you so happy."

The feeling of his hand over my boxer briefs riles me up. I wrap my arms tighter around him and gesture toward the staircase. "Morning quickie?"

"I wish," he says. "You know I gotta hit the pavement if I'm gonna get my run in and make it to work on time."

"Just be late," I suggest, fully aware that Kip would rather eat glass than compromise his punctuality. He's the rare primary care physician who spends ample time with each patient while also ensuring he never keeps the next one waiting, and it all starts with him getting to the office an hour early each morning. "You're about to be on vacation."

"Where we can have all the morning sex we want," he promises. "Besides, you have to get moving, too. If you wanna beat Monday-morning traffic—"

I cut him off with a sigh. "Tell me again why I agreed to go to Seabrook two full days ahead of our check-in?"

"Because you haven't seen Stef since three Christmases ago," he reminds me. "It'll be good for you two to spend some quality time together."

It's not that I don't miss my sister—I do. It's just that I hate being away from Kip. Life feels off-kilter when he's not around, like I'm missing an essential organ. I'm sure there's a therapist out there who would say this metaphor suggests an unhealthy level of attachment to my significant other, but I'd be inclined to say this hypothetical therapist is full of shit. I just love my man. I sleep better when he's next to me.

"I do want to reconnect with her," I admit. "I'm just so eager to kick off our earlymoon. It's going to be the best week of our lives, you know."

"How could I forget? You've only told me about a million times since we got engaged." He kisses my neck before adjusting his shorts and heading for the door. "See you in an hour, my love."

‿

I head upstairs to the master suite and throw a week's worth of beachwear into the suitcase Kip left splayed out in the closet for me. Then I shower with the water as close to boiling as possible, in an effort to psych myself up for the solitary drive to Seabrook. I honestly can't remember the last time I've spent three hours in a car without Kip behind the wheel.

He gets back from his run right as I'm prepping my pre-trip breakfast.

"Shit," he exclaims as I approach him in the foyer. "I forgot to grab the mail, and I just took off my shoes." A pause as he tunes his ear toward the hum of the microwave coming from the kitchen. "What are ya heating up?"

"Oatmeal," I answer. "And don't worry about it. I just put my shoes on. I'll go get it."

He flashes a thank-you smile as I push the door open.

A haze of humid morning air drifts into the foyer, and then— wait a minute—holy shit—*what the fuck is happening right now*—a literal *bird* flies in with it. Directly into the brush of my Crate & Barrel olive tree!

"Oh my God!" I shriek—even more piercingly than when Kip startled me earlier. There is a wild animal in our home. Just making itself comfortable among the polyester leaves and silicone kalamatas. "Kip! There! Is! A! Bird! In! Our! House!"

He straightens his posture as he assesses the situation.

"Stay calm…" He peers at the bird through the leaves and suppresses a grin, almost as if he's amused by the fact that our home is under attack. "We'll get it out."

"Should I shut the door?" I understand the door would need to remain open for the bird to let itself out—which would be my preferred method of resolution—but I'm also terrified of its friends/family/colleagues following it inside. "Or leave it open?"

The bird replies by taking flight. The sound of its probably diseased wings *flap-flap-flapping* in an enclosed space is so loud, so unnatural, that it triggers my loudest shriek yet.

"Do something!" I plead. "You're a doctor!"

"What does that have to do with anything?" Kip says through a snort. "You want me to write the bird a prescription?"

"YES!" I shout. "A prescription for Get-the-Fuck-Out-of-Our-House!"

"He probably just needs a little nudge…" Kip takes his tank top off and attempts to use it as a flag to direct the avian terrorist toward our doorway.

But the bird is terrible at taking direction. Instead of flying *out*, it flies *up*, directly into the frosted-glass chandelier I picked out from West Elm last year—and you know what? This bitchy little finch has excellent taste in home finishes, I'll give it that.

"I'm shutting the door!" I exclaim. The outside air has me feeling far too vulnerable to a repeat invasion. "But how do we get this thing *out* of here?"

My shirtless fiancé rubs his chin in thought and then just starts laughing to himself.

"You gotta admit," he cracks, scratching at the hair on his chest. "This is kinda hilarious."

"Babe," I tell him. "I'm fully open to laughing about this situation once it's resolved and our home returns to a state of peace. But until then, we have to figure out how to get this bastard out of here before it shits all over the place! Birds do that when they're nervous."

"Awww," he says. "I feel bad for him. He must be so scared."

"Yet another reason why we must get him"—I'm interrupted by more *flap-flap-flapping* as the bird migrates from one light bulb to another—"the *hell* out of here!"

Kip takes an assured breath as my hysteria spiral continues. "I got this, babe. Let me think—"

He's cut off by the sound of the microwave beeping from down the hall.

"Your oatmeal's ready," he cracks.

"THAT'S NOT HELPFUL."

My elevated tone prompts the bird to flap away from the chandelier and return to the olive tree, triggering yet another shriek from me and another laugh from Kip. "This is just like that Alfred Hitchcock movie—"

"*Psycho*?" I ask. "Because your nonchalance about this travesty is Norman Bates-level absurd."

"I was actually talking about *The Birds*. You know, the one where—"

"I KNOW WHAT HAPPENS IN *THE* FUCKING *BIRDS*!"

He laughs again and grabs me by the arm. "Babe. Stuff like this happens all the time, trust me. I promise we'll get it out. Everything will be fine."

I know he's right, but still. How does one get a bird out of a home? I try to think back to any experience or memory that might be useful in this situation, and what I come up with is that one episode of *Friends* when a pigeon flew into the apartment and Rachel caught it with a spaghetti pot. "Should we sacrifice one of our Calphalons?" I ask.

Kip scrunches his face. "One of our what?"

Of course he wouldn't know our pots by name. "The stainless-steel cookware set we got from Williams-Sonoma last year."

He scrunches his face even more. "Your solution is to cook the bird?"

"It would be to catch it!" I open my arms and put an invisible lid on an invisible pot. "Like a trap."

He waves the suggestion off. "I have a better idea."

He whips his tank top against the tree branch where the bird is currently perched, causing it to flutter back up to the chandelier and *me* to emit my eightieth shriek of the morning.

"My bad," Kip says.

The bird swoops down from the chandelier and is now headed directly toward us.

"Babe," I cry as I brace myself to be pecked to death. "Baaaaabe!"

But the bird doesn't attack. It bypasses us entirely and lands softly on the base of the olive tree—the lowest altitude it's dared to tread throughout this entire saga.

Now that it's within reach, Kip snaps into action.

He immediately throws his tank top over it—like a ninja—and the poor thing jerks and jerks but can't manage to spread its wings beneath the weight of the sweaty fabric.

I suddenly realize that I've been terrified of a probably six-ounce finch this whole time.

Kip squats down and gently scoops up the bundle with his hands, holding it tight as the bird squirms. "I won't hurt ya, little guy," he whispers. Then he turns to me and says, "Screw shoes. Open the door."

My pulse slowly returns to normal as Kip steps barefoot onto our front porch and down into the driveway.

"One…" He starts to count as he unfurls the tank top. "Two…"

The bird takes flight immediately upon three.

I can finally breathe again as it disappears into the summer sky.

"See?" Kip yells back at me. "I told you it would be fine."

Of course he did. And of course it was.

And that's why I can't wait to marry him.

He checks the mail while he's outside—his broad shoulders glistening in the morning light—and shoots me a playful wink from the street.

And now I'm back to being helplessly turned on. Displays like this really underline Kip's hotness, which only increases the deeper he gets into his forties. He's fit but not ripped, with a natural strength that comes less from pounds of weight lifted and more from years of life lived. His hair has just enough gray in it to be reasonably described as salt and pepper, and his facial features are so rugged it's almost cruel.

And the best part is that he's so *secure* in this hotness of his. Unlike the exes of my twenties, who were always posting thirst traps and fishing for likes, Kip has no social media presence at all. I'm the only person in the world with this view.

Well, me and our next-door neighbors. One of whom Kip appears to be greeting at the moment. "Good morning, Mr. McClackey."

"What in the Sam Hill is going on in your house, Dr. Hayes?" McClackey says. I can't see him from this angle, but his voice is as Grampa Simpson-y as ever. "I could hear that roommate of yours screaming all the way from my shed out back."

I resist the urge to sprint outside and shove my tongue down Kip's throat, both to scandalize the old jerk and to set the record straight (or gay, as it were) once and for all. Mr. McClackey insists on clinging to his assumption that this house is Kip's heterosexual bachelor pad and I'm just some rent-paying acquaintance. I've never had the chance to correct him—mainly because I consistently park in the garage to avoid the risk of neighborly small talk altogether—and Kip's past attempts have always been for naught.

"My apologies," Kips yells across the yard. "It's been an eventful morning."

He waves McClackey off and saunters back inside. My hero returning from his mission to save both our home *and* its winged intruder.

"All this chaos was for nothing," he says through a teasing grin. "Mailbox was empty."

And then we burst into a shared fit of laughter.

"What the hell just happened?" I ask, struggling to catch my breath.

"You summoned a bird into our house with that tree you love so much," Kip teases.

"I wouldn't have *had* to if you'd remembered to check our empty mailbox to begin with," I tease in return. "Seriously, though…" I throw my arms around him and dig my fingers into his back. I don't even care that I'm showered and he's all run-sweaty; there's nothing better than being tangled up with this man. "What would I ever do without you?"

"That is a terrifying question." He gently bites my lower lip. "Luckily, you'll never have to learn the answer to it."

2

⁓

'm in a grimy rest-stop bathroom off the Merritt Parkway, exorcising a venti cold brew from my bladder, when my phone buzzes with a text from CeCe Wilson—my editor at *Appeal*.

So I just devoured your piece! she writes. I know you only sent it as a joke, but I kinda love it? Totally vintage Ray Bruno. And explains so much about you. LOL.

Shit. I hope I didn't give the wrong impression by actually sending her the personal essay she facetiously pitched during our Zoom meeting last week.

I had fun writing it, I respond once I'm back in the parking lot. Because I did have fun—so much fun that I couldn't resist sharing it with her. But please don't get any ideas. You know there's no way we're publishing this thing.

CeCe came up with the idea—"A Brief History of My Delusional Obsession with Love and Marriage"—after a reader wrote in to complain about me. Something about how my celebrity divorce coverage feels less like the snarky lifestyle content *Appeal* is known for and more like the gloomy climate reporting of a stodgy newspaper.

I suppose the article in question was a little melodramatic.

This is a devastating blow to the institution of marriage and the concept of love in general, I had written after an Oscar-winning actress announced her split from the director husband she'd been with since the early nineties. The number of decades-spanning Hollywood marriages has rapidly deteriorated in recent years, and this latest casualty doesn't inspire much hope for the future. If this couple—the prototype for a generation!—could fail, one must worry about where the future of matrimony is headed altogether. We can only hope that both parties find healing during this difficult time, and that the aftershock of their breakup doesn't lead to a ripple effect throughout the industry.

"I hate to say it, but…" CeCe had squinted as she'd pulled up the reader's email. "AssEatingGremlin921@hotmail.com is right. I know the hyperbole is mostly a shtick with these posts, but still. Your secondhand heartbreak for these famous bitches can be a major buzzkill."

"Because divorce *is* a buzzkill," I'd explained. "It's a tragedy! Basically like death, but worse."

I was joking, but I also slightly meant it. I had a brush with death as a child—severe anaphylaxis after an asshole bee tried to *My Girl* me at the beach—and that temporary physical trauma was nothing compared to the protracted mental anguish of my divorce.

CeCe laughed. "You know what I'd just love to read from you? A brief history of your delusional obsession with love and marriage. Can you write that for me? Please?"

I knew she didn't actually expect me to write it, but the thought of doing so poked at something buried deep within me. I used to write stuff like that all the time. My early love of words was cultivated entirely on websites like Myspace and LiveJournal—social media platforms that allowed my angsty teen ass to craft and publish an endless stream of navel-gazing blog posts all about me, me, me.

By the time I got my first digital media job in 2012—at a millennial "news" start-up called *Microphone*—writing about myself had become my bread and butter. Overly confessional personal essays were routinely going viral back then, and my bosses clung to the trend in an attempt to reach the soaring traffic numbers set by their investors.

Some of my colleagues balked at the directive to write about our private lives, but I was happy to oblige. I filed thousands of words about my experiences as a hopelessly romantic gay man in desperate search of a husband. Awkward first dates, messy hookups, my shit show of a marriage to Byrd—nothing was off the table.

I told people that I wrote about myself because I wanted to make readers feel less alone via the transformative power of testimony (LOL), but that was only a small part of it. Mostly I was just self-absorbed and desperate for attention. Writing the posts in the first place was a direct result of the former, and sharing them was my attempt at satiating the latter. Likes, comments, and follows were my primary source of validation—proof that I wasn't a worthless piece of human garbage. Proof that I was special, even, and my special life was being witnessed.

But then I started seeing Kip, which changed everything.

"I almost called this whole thing off," he'd told me on our first official date, a week after our chance meeting at the oyster bar. "Not that you don't seem great—you really do. I'm just not sure you and I would be a good fit in the long run. I'd hate to waste your time."

I couldn't believe he was being so direct with this information. I'd felt that way about plenty of prospective partners before, but I'd never admitted it to their faces. I always just did the millennial thing: gave a canned excuse about being "super-busy right now" and saved my true feelings for the internet.

"Oh." I cleared my throat and pretended not to be crushed. I had kind of already married Dr. Kip Hayes in my head during the period between our meet-cute and first date. "I thought we hit it off the other night…"

"We did," he said. "But I'm a very private person—"

"Me too!" I chirped. Apparently my instinct around him was to say literally anything I thought he wanted to hear—even if it was a massive crock of shit.

Kip flashed a *yeah, right* smirk. "I Googled you, Ray Bruno…"

"Ahhhh." I shrank five sizes in my barstool. "Of course you did."

I had Googled him, too, but all I found was official doctor stuff—the website of the private medical practice he worked for and an abundance of glowing Healthgrades reviews—which only made me more eager to see him in real life again. To solve the mystery of who he was outside of work.

Kip proceeded to tell me why he valued his privacy so much. He was recently divorced himself (from a woman) and still taking baby steps out of the closet. But even back when he was in a postcard straight marriage, he still always had a strong aversion to unnecessary attention.

"I don't need my patients going online and finding evidence I have a personal life," he said. "And the whole concept of social media doesn't much appeal to me anyway. I'd rather live my life than worry about documenting it for some nebulous audience of 'friends.' If someone is an actual friend, they'll already know what I'm up to."

His philosophy made sense—reminded me of my family's attitudes toward social media, actually—and forced me to question what I was really getting out of being Extremely Online in the first place. Certainly not the clarity or contentment that Kip seemed to possess.

"Social media can be a great way to find community," I attempted. "Connecting with like-minded people, bonding over shared passions…"

"I guess that's true," Kip admitted. "Is that what *you* use it for?" The man could see right through me.

"I am exceptionally attracted to you," I redirected. I figured if he could be so straightforward, I might as well give it a shot as well. "What if we keep hanging out—no pressure—and I promise never to post anything about you?"

He raised an eyebrow. "Ever? Even if it doesn't work out?" A pause. "Even if it *does* work out?"

I put a hand on my heart. "No matter what."

He exhaled, looked up at the ceiling, then right into my eyes. "I am exceptionally attracted to you, too…" A smile spread across his face. "Fuck it. I'm in."

Our attraction grew from there—wild and unruly—like ivy spreading across the sides of an old building. It wasn't long before I started sleeping over at his West Village apartment, sometimes spending entire weekends tangled up in bed with our phones shut off from Saturday morning all the way through Sunday night. I hadn't felt that carefree, that *present*, since I was a child. It was such a liberating reprieve from the endless spiral of self-analysis I'd fallen into as an adult.

I kept my word to Kip about not posting about him.

And the more time we spent together, the less compelled I felt to post so much about myself, too. I wanted to save everything for him—someone who actually mattered—because the feeling that came from being seen by Kip was a million times better than the empty validation that came from being just another character on the internet.

By then I was working at *Appeal*, writing a column about my misadventures as an under-thirty divorcé, but thankfully CeCe wasn't as committed to the first-person industrial complex as my previous bosses were. She'd said when she hired me that she didn't care what I chose to write about, as long as I had fun doing it. Apparently she'd read all my work at *Microphone* and could easily clock when I was truly enjoying an assignment versus when I was just churning out clickbait to meet traffic quotas.

"You suck at faking it," she'd said. "Which is what makes you so great."

It helped that there was zero pressure from leadership to chase clicks; *Appeal* had recently pivoted to a paid subscription model, and they had a devoted built-in audience.

So when I told CeCe that I wanted to cool it with the oversharing, she was supportive. We put our heads together over the coming months and formulated what eventually became my current beat: a blend of pop culture reporting, elevated celebrity gossip, and marriage/relationship trends—all subjects that are *very* me, but not *about* me.

Which is why I know CeCe won't expect me to turn this personal essay into an actual article. She'll just appreciate the glimpse into her favorite staff writer's Hallmark-addled psyche and then return to our regularly scheduled programming.

My phone buzzes with another text as I prepare a playlist for the second leg of my drive to Seabrook.

I know you'd never publish something like this, CeCe writes. But you know what I do think would be a fascinating subject to explore? The whole "earlymoon" thing. Do people really do that? A honeymoon before the wedding?

It's literally why I'm off this week, I reply. Remember?

Oh, right, CeCe writes. Guess I just assumed it was a weird "you" thing.

I might take offense if it weren't so true. It does sound like something I would make up on my own. Like how I suggested Kip and I get "engagement butt-cheek tattoos" rather than rings, since

I knew we'd eventually be exchanging wedding bands anyway. (We ended up going with engagement *watches* instead, mostly because Kip scared the shit out of me with a story about a patient of his who once contracted hepatitis from a botched tat job.)

It's definitely not just me, I shoot back. Google it! My hometown is the earlymoon capital of the world.

I crank my car's AC and continue building my playlist—lots of nineties Metallica and Mariah Carey (I love a good yin/yang journey)—until CeCe chimes in again.

So I just Googled it, she texts. And not to sound like an SEO hag or anything, but I'm noticing a major deficit in these search results. It's all tourism guides and social posts...

Dammit. I completely set myself up for this. She's gonna ask me to publish something about my time at the Earlymoon Hotel. And the worst part, I realize, as I monitor her text bubble at the bottom of my screen, is that I *want* to.

I have an idea! she continues. What if you do a feature about the hotel? Interview some couples, give us the scoop on what this earlymoon situation is really all about.

It's immediately apparent that this is a horrible idea. I want to be *present* on my earlymoon—not working.

Love the concept, I text back. But I can't. You know I'm off until next Tuesday!

You could work on it after you get back, she insists. I'm not a tyrant.

Fair, but still. Knowing I have to write about my trip would cast a shadow over the entire thing. I'd be thinking about the story the whole time—brainstorming ledes on the beach, tapping notes into my phone between sunset beers.

And as tempting as it is to use my title at *Appeal* as an excuse to strike up conversations with fellow hotel guests—I could talk to people about their relationships all day long—the only relationship I should be caring about during my earlymoon is the one between me and my future husband.

You could frame the piece around your own earlymoon, CeCe continues. And then zoom out and highlight the experiences of the other couples there. Carrie-Bradshaw-circa-*SATC*-season-one vibes, you know? OMG. This is sooo you. I literally just got chills. I feel like your spirit is moving through me.

I have to hand it to her—the woman knows how to dangle an irresistible pitch in front of my face. Except for the part where she's suggesting that I frame the entire story around my own experience. She knows me better than that.

Why couldn't I focus solely on the other couples? I ask her.

And an internal question for myself: Why am I even entertaining this conversation in the first place?

Because you're an earlymooner yourself, she replies. And you're actually from Seabrook, which is worth mentioning to readers.

Me: That's a valid point.

Why did I just say that? I need to be shutting this conversation down. If not because of my own reservations, then because of the ones I know Kip would have. He's not quite as private as he was when we first met—he's obviously out of the closet at this point—but he still doesn't understand the millennial impulse to overshare. My typical end-of-vacation Instagram posts are already flirting with his tolerance limit for public exposure; a full-blown feature in *Appeal* would irk him to no end. And that's the last thing I want to do before our wedding.

Especially when agreeing to my wedding plans—two hundred guests and all the traditional fanfare—was a big enough compromise for him in the first place.

So that settles it.

This whole idea is a nonstarter.

Just give it some thought, CeCe texts before I can shut her down for good. I know you'd have a lot of fun with this.

3

As I meander through the center of town, I'm distracted by an abundance of new storefronts I've somehow never noticed before: all twee little gift shops called "Seabrook [*insert random shit here*] Company."

So far I've strolled past the Seabrook Tea Company, Seabrook Candle Company, Seabrook Olive Oil Company, Seabrook Peanut Butter Company—and it's barely been half a mile. I know I haven't visited much since my parents moved away, but damn. This place is a far cry from the Seabrook of my youth, back when the center of town was all bait stores, Italian ice stands, and souvenir shops.

But one thing that thankfully hasn't changed is the Clam Shell. Even after all this time, the high-pitched creak of its wooden screen door is the most familiar sound ever.

Ditto the omnipresent whiff of fried seafood and melted butter in the air.

"Sister!" I exclaim as I spot Stef at a high-top in the corner, directly below a neon Budweiser sign. She's clearly started drinking without me—there's a half-full pitcher of beer on the table—and I'm glad. Conversations with Stef are always easier when there's a slight buzz between us.

"Broski."

"You look great," I tell her as I settle onto my barstool. She's wearing cutoff jean shorts and a Nirvana tee, with her dark hair pulled into a low pony through the back of a weathered Red Sox cap. "I'd never guess you've been hauling traps all day."

By contrast, our father used to come home from a day on the water looking (and smelling) like the Creature from the Black Lagoon.

"I showered at the gym," she explains curtly.

"Oh. Right."

Aaaand we're already out of things to talk about. It's so strange: in my head we're still as close as we were growing up, but then we see each other in person and I'm reminded of how much adulthood has driven us apart.

"So how was the catch today?" I attempt.

"Next subject." She slugs the rest of her beer down and signals the waitress for more, thank God. "Another pitcher of Coors—and a pint glass for my little brother—thanks."

"Why don't you wanna talk about it?"

Stef cocks her head and launches into an impression of our father. "You never ask a lobsterman about his catch—what's-a-matter with you?"

Her delivery is so dead-on, I almost feel like he's here with us. "You really are Dad in a wig. It's uncanny."

"And you're Mom with a penis," she says, her voice returning to its typical Janeane Garofalo deadpan.

"Please." I nearly gag. "Those two words should never be said in the same sentence."

"Which two, exactly?"

The new pitcher arrives and we immediately start pouring. I can't remember the last time I drank Coors Light—a beer made for drinking twelve beers at a time. With Kip, it's always just one or two craft IPAs, sipped slowly and intentionally, savoring both the flavor profile and the moment.

"So...what's new?" Stef asks me. "Other than the fact that you've decided to slum it with the villagers for two nights before your honeymoon excursion."

There's a kernel of sincerity behind her sarcasm that troubles me. Stef has never understood my decision to leave Seabrook and pursue a life beyond lobstering, but her choice of words just now makes me wonder if she resents me for it.

I lean forward. "First of all, you of all people should know it's an *earlymoon*. The wedding isn't until the end of August. Which, by the way, you and Lenny still haven't RSVPed to—"

"We're both having the filet. Obviously."

"And second of all," I continue, "I want us to have fun these next few days! When's the last time we really had time to hang without our spouses?"

"Kip's not your spouse yet."

"You know what I mean," I huff. "Are you okay? What's your deal?"

Stef exhales. The hardness in her expression softens just enough to let a glimmer of vulnerability shine through. "It's been a long day. With my sternman out sick and Lenny visiting his parents up in Maine, this is already shaping up to be the week from hell."

"Why don't you take tomorrow off?" I suggest. "I know Dad worked twenty-four/seven, but you don't have to do *everything* like him."

"That's not an option. That's never..." She seems like she wants to say more, but stops short. "I don't wanna talk about lobsters. Let's talk about literally anything else."

"Fine." I knock back some more Coors and summon a subject

change. "What's the deal with all these new shops? Seabrook Tea Company and all that?"

"Let's see," Stef says. "The tea place is run by the Walkers. The candle place is the Cassaras. The olive oil place is the Healys…"

What the hell is she talking about? These are all the families we grew up with—fellow lobstering clans.

"Ralph Cassara has a side business making candles?" I ask. The idea sounds just as absurd as our own father becoming a candle-maker (or a tea or olive oil merchant). "What in tarnation?"

"It's mostly Brenda," Stef says. "These businesses were all the wives' ideas. I'm sure if Mom and Dad didn't move to Florida, Mom would've convinced him to open a stupid little specialty shop of their own."

"Please. You know they were all in on lobstering."

"So were the Cassaras. So was everyone else in this town…"

And then it surfaces. A memory from before our parents retired—Dad complaining about his once-booming catch shrinking to unsustainably low levels, the lobster population fleeing the ever-warming Connecticut coast for the cooler waters of New Hampshire and Maine. I don't know much about climate change, but even I can infer that the situation probably hasn't improved in recent years.

So that's it. Business is bad. This is why Stef has been on edge tonight—and come to think of it, probably for a while now.

"So when did this happen?" I ask. "All these shops?"

Stef scratches her neck. "Most of them have been around for a few years."

"Huh."

"I wouldn't expect you to have noticed," she says. "What with you being sequestered in Kip Land and all."

I know Stef hasn't always been Kip's biggest fan—they're basically two different species—but *sequestered in Kip Land?* She's making my relationship sound like some kind of fucked-up hybrid of prison and theme park.

"What is that supposed to mean?" I ask.

"That you don't care about anything other than Kip." Her inflection is somewhere between neutral and bored. She doesn't think she's saying anything controversial, just stating the obvious. "Your entire existence revolves around him."

"He's my fiancé," I counter. "Of course he's my main priority in life…"

Stef hiccups. "Main priority? Or *only* priority?"

"Main priority," I repeat. "I have plenty of other stuff going on outside of my relationship."

"Like what?" Stef challenges. "Name one thing."

"I…" Shit. This is hard. "Oh! I recently purchased the most gorgeous faux olive tree for our foyer."

"I'm going to pretend you didn't just say that," she says. "I'm being serious with this question. Just name one thing."

Being put on the spot makes my mind go blank. I can think of exactly zero non-Kip things happening in my life. But then again, I'm deep in the throes of planning a wedding. Why shouldn't my life revolve around him right now?

"See?" Stef says. "You can't think of anything. Before you met Kip—"

"Before I met Kip, I was miserable. Remember?"

"At least back then I knew what was going on with you. You used to tell me everything—and even when you didn't, all I had to do was check social media or your latest *Microphone* article to get up to speed. Now the only type of information I can expect to glean from your articles is shit like, I don't know, when Kris Jenner had her last period."

"August 2, 2011," I remind her. "And how could I have *not*

reported on that? Kris handed me the exact date in a phone interview! It's the best scoop I've ever gotten."

Some people might be impressed that my job occasionally
involves such exposure to famous people, but Stef couldn't possibly
care less about that kind of stuff. Which I suppose means I should
be touched that she still bothers to read my work at all.

"I just want you to be happy," she says. "You've always been
such an open book, and then Kip came along—"

"It's called growth," I explain. "You should be happy that I'm
not oversharing on the internet like I used to. I only ever did that
because I craved attention, you know."

"I won't deny you've always been a massive attention whore,"
she cracks. "But writing about yourself was about more than that.
It was a creative outlet for you. And then you just gave it up to make
Kip happy."

I can see why Stef would draw this conclusion—and I'd be lying
if I said Kip's aversion to attention didn't factor into my decision to
give up personal writing—but what she doesn't understand is how
deeply unhappy I was back when my entire life was fodder for the
anonymous trolls of the internet. The praise I received from genuine
"fans" of my work paled in comparison to the vitriol hurled at me
by the hordes of *Microphone* hate readers whose sole motivation
for visiting the site was to channel all of their latent discontent into
weaponized mockery toward the staff writers.

"I'm a million times happier with Kip—and with my work at
Appeal—than I was back then," I tell my sister. "I'm really surprised
you can't see that."

"Mostly what I see is you jumping into a marriage that's destined to be creepily similar to Mom and Dad's."

It was only a matter of time before she brought them up, especially given our current location. Stef has always hated how Mom

mythologizes this restaurant as the birthplace of their fairy-tale love story.

"Jumping?" I ask. "This isn't Byrd and me, Sis. And not for nothing, but Mom and Dad have the best marriage of anyone I've ever known. I'd be thrilled to have what they have. It's all I've ever wanted."

"I'm painfully aware of that fact. I was your older sister throughout all of the nineties." Stef empties the pitcher into her glass. "We need more Coors. And we should probably order some food, too."

I eagerly nod in agreement. Both because I'm hungry and because I'm hoping that the introduction of some fried clam strips will redirect this conversation toward something more pleasant and sibling reunion-y—gossip about our cousins or a shit-talking sesh about our high school nemeses or something—anything but this needless interrogation about my future marriage.

Stef goes to the bar in order to save the bartender-slash-waitress a trip.

I get a text from Kip in her absence: Sheryl Crow.

Joan Osborne, I reply.

How's it going in Seabrook? he writes. Just got home from work. Miss you.

My entire body smiles. Just the thought of him fills me with comfort and—ironically, given that I'm currently in my actual hometown—a sense of home. If this were any other Monday night, we'd be curled up on the couch watching *Jeopardy!* right now. My happy place.

At the Clam Shell with Stef, I text back. And I miss you more!!! REALLY can't wait for you to get here Wednesday.

Enjoy your sibling time, Kip replies. Text me before bed. Love you.

"I get up for two seconds and you're already texting him." Stef plunks back down at our table with a fresh pitcher in one hand and two empty side plates in the other. I consider challenging her assumption that it's Kip I've been texting, but since it happens to be correct, I don't say anything. "You are *so* Mom."

"Would that really be such a bad thing?" I ask.

"Yes," she says. "Because contrary to the years of brainwashing she subjected you to, she and Dad do not have a healthy marriage."

"Are you on drugs? They're obsessed with each other."

"That's the literal definition of codependency."

Stef sits up straighter, as if I've just proven her point for her. And maybe I kind of have. But honestly? I'd rather be overly attached to my partner than completely indifferent. *I'd die without you* is a sentiment that underpins countless love stories through the ages. *You're great but I'd also be fine on my own* sounds more like the opening line of a breakup song.

"There's nothing wrong with needing someone."

Stef ignores my defense. "Who even *is* Mom? 'Jim Bruno's wife' is the only identity she's ever bothered to claim—even more than being our mother. Her entire world revolves around Dad and what he wants."

"Or maybe she just happens to want the same things he does."

"The woman has a Cinderella complex," Stef counters. "And she'll do anything to keep her Prince Charming. Such as move to Florida, despite the fact that she's always said Seabrook is her favorite place in the entire world. Dad just calls the shots and never meets her halfway."

Maybe Stef has a small point here. It was a shock when our parents broke the news of their move to Orlando five years ago. I'd always assumed they were Seabrook lifers.

"Even if that's the case for Mom and Dad," I say through a shrug, "it has nothing to do with my relationship. Kip always meets me halfway."

Stef clicks her tongue. "Really? I'd love a recent example."

My mind goes blank again. "What is it with you and examples?"

"Just give me one."

I groan, feeling defeated. But then I think of something big. "The wedding! Kip wanted to do city hall, but instead we're doing two hundred guests in the Hamptons."

It took months of convincing—and I can tell he's still somewhat uncomfortable with the idea of turning our love into a full-blown circus (his word, not mine)—but he eventually caved because he knows how important it is to me. If that's not meeting someone halfway, I don't know what is.

"And what'd you have to give up to get him to agree to that?" Stef asks.

The true answer is an announcement in the Vows section of the *Times*—CeCe knows the editor and had guaranteed us a spot—but I'd rather not give Stef that kind of ammunition.

"Nothing," I lie instead.

She pins me with one of her older-wiser-sister looks.

"Just a *New York Times* wedding announcement," I quietly admit. "Not a big deal."

Stef's eyes go wide. "You got in at the *Times*? You literally sobbed when they refused to run a profile on you and Byrd."

"That was a blessing," I remind her. "And it's fine. Kip didn't want thousands of readers of the country's biggest and most influential newspaper poring over details about his personal life. It's a small price to pay for my literal dream wedding."

"Are you sure he's out of the closet?" Stef asks. "Because…"

"*Of course* he's out."

The fact that Stef would even ask a question like this goes to show just how long it's been since we've had a proper conversation. She must think Kip is still the semi-closeted enigma he was during the early months of our relationship.

He and I sometimes clashed back then due to the vast disparity of our outness levels, but I tried to be as patient as possible. He had to move at his own pace and comfort level; coming out wasn't nearly as easy for him at thirty-nine as it was for me at twenty. His decades-long performance of straightness had been so effective that he didn't have the luxury of relying on people's assumptions. He had to *tell* everyone in his life. And without the assistance of social media, coming out was less of a grand announcement and more of a daily chore. One he hated doing and often avoided. But he did eventually get there.

"Kip's outness isn't an issue at this point," I insist.

"I'm not asking if he's out to friends and family," Stef clarifies. "I mean, like, is he out to his dentist? His barber?"

"I'm sure people just assume," I say. "He's probably mentioned me to them."

I realize as I say it that I'm now lying for the sake of winning this argument. I haven't thought about it until just now, but I'm positive Kip's not going around gushing about me during his biannual teeth cleanings. But I don't think it's a gay thing. I can't imagine he ever gushed about his ex-wife, either. He's just not someone who feels the need to share his life story with his dental hygienist.

"No one would ever assume Kip is gay," Stef says through a snort. "And I'm allowed to say that because people assume I'm a lesbian every day…" She pauses. "Let me ask you this. Does he kiss you in public?"

I squirm in my seat. PDA has always been a fraught subject for me and most gay men I know over the age of thirty-five. Straight couples can kiss and hold hands all day without anyone so much as blinking at them, and in theory I believe gay couples deserve the same luxury. But in practice? I've never been fully comfortable kissing a man outside of spaces like gay bars or private parties. I have too many early gay memories that involve getting stared at or taunted or worse. One time my college boyfriend and I held hands on a side street in New Haven—by all accounts a liberal city—and got an empty Sprite can hurled at us from a moving vehicle while the driver mocked us with slurs.

So as unromantic as it is, Kip's anti-PDA policy has never bothered me. It saves me the trouble of having to confront my own hang-ups on the matter.

"We're just not one of those PDA couples," I tell Stef. "And neither are you and Lenny, by the way."

"That's fair," she concedes. "PDA is disgusting no matter who's engaging in it."

She pauses and looks me directly in the eye for several seconds. "You know what? I'm sorry. I know Kip is a good guy. I guess I'm just having déjà vu to the last time you got married. I want to make sure it's something you really want this time and not just, I don't know, a resigned compromise based on your long-standing fear of dying alone."

The circumstances around my two marriages couldn't be more different, so I find it hard to believe she truly feels concerned about me repeating history. It almost makes me wonder if this conversation has actually *not* been about me this whole time.

"Is that why you married Lenny?" I ask. "As a resigned compromise based on your long-standing fear of dying alone?"

"Oh please." The sincerity in her voice leaves as quickly as it came. "I'd *prefer* to die alone. I'm hoping Lenny bites it first so I can have some wild single years in retirement. I'll be the sluttiest octogenarian in the nursing home."

The sarcasm is off-putting, but I remind myself that's just how Stef is. There's no way she'd actually prefer to die alone in a medical facility rather than at home, spooning with her husband, like that old couple in bed at the end of *Titanic*. I'm pretty sure that's how everybody wants to go. (Minus the iceberg.)

"I love that journey for you." I play along. "But Kip and I are going to die on the exact same day, when he's a hundred and I'm ninety…"

Stef coughs. "You're sick."

"…and then we'll be cremated together. And our ashes will be mixed with potting soil and planted in a biodegradable urn before eventually growing into a whimsical olive tree on the idyllic campus of a storied New England prep school—"

"Please stop," Stef interjects.

I continue just to annoy her. "And every year on August 31st— our wedding anniversary—two students will randomly pick and eat a pair of olives from the same branch, and these olives will make them fall madly and irreversibly in love with each other, creating an invisible string that tethers them together for life, thereby ensuring that *our* love lasts eternally, through the love of others, for generations to come."

Stef stares at me, stone-faced, for several moments. "You know what's terrifying? I honestly can't tell if you're joking or not."

"I'm obviously joking!" I take a swig of beer for effect. "An olive tree would never survive in this climate."

Our food arrives before Stef can express any further disgust.

The edge between us gradually wears off as we split a massive fisherman's platter—all the golden-brown whole belly clams, scallops, shrimp, and calamari we can eat. Kip would never order something like this—he's always telling his patients to ditch fried food, and he refuses to be a hypocrite—so I make sure to savor the taste while I can.

"I'm just glad you're happy," she eventually says. "That's all I want for my little brother."

"Gee, thanks, Big Sis." I put a hand on my heart. "I'm glad you're happy, too. With Seabrook and lobstering and everything... It's really awesome how you're keeping the Bruno legacy alive. I know Dad's proud of you."

She holds her breath for a moment before responding. I almost detect a flash of worry in her eyes, but it's replaced with a nonchalant gaze before I can tell for sure.

"You know me," she says. "Living the dream."

4

My childhood bedroom hasn't changed at all. The space is now a spare room for Stef and Lenny's overnight guests, but it's still adorned with all the mass-produced home decor I picked out in high school—mounted nautical accents, vintage shipping labels in faux-weathered frames, and a hanging rope mirror facing the bed.

It's way too busy for my current tastes, but all things considered, I think my adolescent design choices have held up in a way that would make Joanna Gaines proud. I was never one of those "band posters and friendship collage" kids. I was a basic-bitch-in-training with an addiction to strip-mall stores like HomeGoods and Pier 1 Imports—the pinnacle of design in my teenage mind.

Needless to say, I didn't have many friends in high school.

Mostly I talked to college guys online—occasionally hooking up with them in dorm rooms and back seats—only to hate myself for it later. I wanted love even back then, but I settled for casual sex because I was still closeted and at least sex was something close to true intimacy.

Actually? "Settled for" isn't quite accurate. I hadn't yet learned hookup culture's silent code of detached indifference, so I'd always try to turn sex into something more—incessantly texting and calling and showing up on campus—but I only succeeded in making guys think I was either a deranged stalker or a pathetic joke. I once asked a UConn sophomore to be my boyfriend and he literally laughed in my face.

"I think I'm developing feelings for you," I'd said in my best adult-character-in-a-nineties-rom-com voice. "Why don't we try to make it work?"

Cue the hysterical cackling, until he caught his breath and horror swept across his face.

"Oh, shit, wait. You're serious?" Meanwhile, he'd been inside me just fifteen minutes earlier. "Um. I think you should leave."

Scenes like this were not uncommon in my youth.

And they would always fling me into a depression, which I'd address via addiction. Not to drugs or alcohol, but to home fragrance products and textured wall art. I lived my life like a Bath & Body Works three-wick candle in the wind. Did everything I could to conjure feelings of the home I might someday build with a man who deemed me worthy of building one with.

Hence the thick wooden oar with the phrase *Live, Laugh, Lobster* hand-painted across it in red cursive that's still mounted over the bed eighteen years later.

A quiet laugh escapes my throat as I plop down on the mattress, feeling a rush of gratitude for my current set of circumstances. Thank God none of those disposable guys of my youth actually gave me what I'd thought I wanted. The life I ended up with as an adult is a million times better than the one I dreamed of as a kid.

I pull out my phone with the intention of sending Kip a goodnight text, but my earlier chain with CeCe grabs my attention first.

The phrase "vintage Ray Bruno" jumps out. As does the "I know you'd have a lot of fun with this" that she ended the conversation on.

I'm reminded of Stef's rant at the Clam Shell earlier. Her

accusation that I've given up a key piece of myself—my favorite creative outlet—for the sake of my relationship.

I suppose I can admit she's partially correct about that. I don't know when (or if) I'd have stopped writing about myself if Kip hadn't expressed such a strong issue with it on our first date. But I do know that even if he *had been* comfortable with it—or even if I was single right now—I'd still never want to return to the extreme levels of self-disclosure I'd trafficked in during my *Microphone* tenure. That didn't make me feel good.

CeCe's earlymoon idea wouldn't be anything like that, though. It would be a sourced, reported feature, with my personal experience serving as a small point of entry to the experiences of others. No oversharing or attention-seeking—just good old-fashioned lifestyle writing. The kind of work that tons of reputable journalists have published over the years—very Sunday edition of the *Times*.

And speaking of the *Times*, Stef was right that I've always dreamed of documenting my love story in the national paper of record. I had given that dream up for Kip's sake, but maybe this can be a consolation prize. A way to shout about our love to the world—just once— and let all of *Appeal*'s readers know that I'm no longer the disaster twentysomething I was back when I used to write my dating column.

I know Kip won't love that I'm writing about him on a public platform, but I also can't imagine he'll totally freak out over it. Especially if I let him read the first draft—which I'd be sure to do—thereby giving him the chance to eliminate any particular words or details he doesn't want turning up in search results when patients Google him.

And as for being present on the earlymoon? That's probably not as big a deal as I'd initially thought. We have almost a full week to be present. A few hours talking to hotel guests will barely be a drop in the bucket. Kip always takes an hour each morning to run anyway— the perfect window for me to conduct some research over coffee.

A wave of certainty washes over me.

I can do this.

I fire off a text to CeCe before I can change my mind—Count me in on the earlymoon story!—and then make a call to Kip while I still have my nerve. If I don't tell him about this decision before I go to bed, it'll feel like a secret when I wake up.

"Hey, babe." His voice is like a massage for my entire nervous system—instantly soothing. I melt into the saggy mattress and close my eyes. "You caught me just before I was hitting the hay. Wild night with the sister?"

"I guess you could say that." I decide to omit the part where she grilled me on Kip's suitability as a husband. That'll make for a better story to tell in person, over cocktails. "We had a lot to catch up on. I didn't realize how long it had been since we've hung out."

"See? I knew going up early would be good for you."

It occurs to me that I should have told Stef about how our sibling bonding time was all Kip's idea. If she's right and I am "sequestered in Kip Land," it's not because he asks me to be. It's a choice I make for myself, because "Kip Land" is the most comfortable place in the world.

I glance at the faux-antique anchor hanging on the wall across from me and feel a sharp sense of longing for the home I've made with him back in Westchester.

"She seemed a little…" I start, not sure where I'm going with the statement. I haven't really sorted my thoughts on her yet. "Less carefree than usual. I think work has been rough or something."

"That's a bummer," he says. "Is there anything we can do to help?"

It's admirable that his first instinct is always to offer help, but Stef would never accept such a thing. And I'm still not sure if she even needs it. Our conversation was so focused on me that it's possible I misread her situation entirely.

"She's fine," I assure him. "So listen. I talked to CeCe today—"

"On your week off?" he says.

"I know, I know. She and I have no boundaries." I leave out the part where I'm mostly okay with it. CeCe's my boss, but she's also one of my best friends. "Anyway, she pitched a story that sounds like it'd be really fun. It would be about the resort."

Kip yawns. "What resort?"

"You know..."

What was I thinking, accepting this pitch? Those Coors Lights must have severely clouded my judgment. Because now that I have to tell Kip, it's obvious he'll be against it. I've already been testing his limits for months with the wedding planning; I don't need to test them even further with something like this.

But now that I've brought it up, it's too late to reverse course.

So I swallow my worry and hope for the best. "The Earlymoon Hotel."

Kip clears his throat. "What about it?"

"Well..." I stammer. "Just a lifestyle piece about the whole 'earlymoon' concept. Tell the stories of some couples..."

"Which couples?"

My vocal cords aren't quite ready to say the words *you*, *me*, or *us* just yet—so I start by leaning heavily on the interview angle. "Whoever's willing to talk to me. I was thinking I'd email the owners and see if they can connect me with people. My dad used to supply lobster to the resort back in the day, so I'm sure they'll be open to helping me out. They'll probably appreciate the publicity, really, now that I think about it."

"You're gonna be working during this trip?" Kip never gets angry, but he does get annoyed on occasion. My chest stings at the realization that this is one such occasion. "I'm confused. You're the one who's been talking about how special this trip is to you, you've been looking forward to it your whole life, and all that. And now you're gonna be working? I could have saved my vacation days—"

"No, no, no. I'm not gonna be working!" I insist. "Maybe a few interviews here and there—during your runs—but it won't be *work*-work. I didn't even pack my laptop. CeCe's not expecting me to start writing until after we get back."

He takes a few measured breaths. "I guess that's not so bad, then."

"Not at all," I tell him. "I'm really excited about the potential with this one. To feature a landmark from my hometown and tell several real-life love stories at the same time…"

My voice trails off as I get lost in the possibilities.

"Well, in that case, thank CeCe for me." His voice is back to its usual state of calm, which floods me with relief. "I love when you're working on a story that really matters to you. It's been a while."

Stef was totally off the mark with her concerns earlier. Kip doesn't just meet me halfway—he meets me *all* the way. Granted, I'll still need to tell him about the personal angle when he arrives on Wednesday, but I've already kept him up too late tonight. The important thing is that he knows there will be an article.

"Thanks for understanding." I stare at the popcorn ceiling for a moment and imagine Kip lying on our bed doing the same thing, staring at the wooden beams of our master suite. We both breathe into our phones for a few moments until the breaths turn into yawns. "Let's get some sleep. I know you still have one more day of work before joining me in paradise."

Kip chuckles quietly. "I love you."

"I love you, too. Good night—"

"Oh, wait, one more thing." His words come out rushed—like he just realized he left the oven on or something—a millisecond before my thumb ends the call. "You're not gonna write about *us* in your story, right?"

tuesday

5

~~

'm startled awake by a flood of artificial light.

"What the hell?" I rub my eyes and catch a glimpse of my Carhartt-clad sister in the doorway. Her posture is so stiff and drill-sergeant-like that I nearly expect her to blow a whistle and demand I drop and give her twenty. "It's the middle of the night!"

"It's quarter to four," she says. As if that's not the middle of the night. "I'm sorry to do this, but I need your help."

My vision is still blurry due to the brightness of the light bulbs in here. They've gotta be at least eighty watts each—an abomination. And a stark reminder why my personal rule at home is nothing above forty, soft-white only.

"Can I sleep first?" I ask. "And help you later?"

She purses her lips. "We gotta be at the dock in twenty."

And then I notice the giant pair of rubber overalls draped over her forearm. My entire body groans as I realize what's happening.

"Please? You're my last resort." Her posture slumps. I don't think I've ever seen her like this—dejected, asking for help. "My sternman bailed again, Lenny's still in Maine, and I could really use a first mate. It won't be a long day! Just seven or eight trawls…"

I think of Kip's words last night—before his bedtime curveball—when he wondered if there was anything we could do for her.

Apparently there is, and it involves me jumping on a lobster boat for the first time in over fifteen years.

But if it gives my sister some relief, I suppose it's worth it.

I stretch my arms over my head and force myself to sit up. "It's been forever since I helped Dad out on the boat. You're gonna have to—"

"I'll tell you what to do." A relieved smile stretches across her face as she throws the overalls on the bed, the rubber landing cold and slimy against my chest. "And you can borrow some of Lenny's clothes."

Fifteen minutes later we're cruising down Summerland Road, the air in Stef's beat-up Dodge Ram smelling like a pungent blend of black coffee (our fuel) and fish guts (our bait).

I crack a window and stick my head out into the predawn air for some relief. A road sign for the Earlymoon Hotel—four miles away—serves as a reminder that Kip and I will be unpacking our bags in a private suite just thirtysomething hours from now.

Which is followed by the much less pleasant reminder of the hole I dug myself at the end of our conversation last night. I don't know if it was the way he phrased the question, or if I was just afraid to open a can of worms when he was clearly tired, or if it was just that he caught me off guard. All I know is that I reflexively told him what he wanted to hear—*of* course *I won't be writing about us in the article*—and the call was over within seconds.

So now I either have to tell him the truth or tell CeCe I'm scrapping the first-person element. Tug at my future husband's boundaries or avoid them altogether.

"Sorry if I came off as anti-Kip last night," Stef says.

"No worries." Given my current predicament, I do understand how she might have doubts about our compatibility. Kip and I are opposites in many ways, and sometimes our philosophical differences make us vulnerable to this kind of friction. But we have something deep and primal in common—an inherent connection to each other—that always offsets any misunderstandings in the long run. Stef just hasn't spent enough time with us in person to realize that. "I think you just need to get to know him a little better. Maybe at the wedding you can spend some quality time together."

Stef laughs. "At the wedding? You guys are gonna be caught up be in a whirlwind of wedding shit."

"Oh. Right. Duh." This coffee clearly still hasn't kicked in. "After the wedding, then, for sure."

I take a moment to consider the whirlwind she's talking about. The ceremony, the pictures, the reception. The first dance—a public display of affection I had to negotiate with Kip at length. He wanted to eschew the tradition altogether, ostensibly on account of his two left feet, but I knew there was a fair amount of internalized homophobia at play. A quickie first kiss at the altar is one thing, but two grown men slow dancing for an audience is a much more extended performance of gay love.

I challenged his reluctance by explaining how important it was to me that we honor our love with all the same silly celebrations that straight couples never think twice about. If they can make a spectacle of their love for a day, why shouldn't we?

He offered the counterargument that gay people should be allowed to create their own rules and traditions, which is a notion I agree with in theory, but not when it comes to me and my wedding. Anything less than the whole nine yards, I argued, would be a self-loathing compromise based on a fundamental sense of inferiority.

Kip laughed and made a joke about how my brain has been poisoned by the wedding industrial complex.

But eventually I wore him down. In fact, I scheduled us for a private slow-dance lesson this Friday at the Earlymoon Hotel—one of the many prewedding activities offered in their deluxe earlymoon package.

"You ready to get your hands dirty?" Stef asks as she pulls into the marina.

"Definitely not." I shiver with an adolescent memory of the time I went out with my father and forgot to bring the gloves he'd bought me especially for lobstering. He made me work a full day anyway, and the spiky bones in the fish bait left my hands so mangled and swollen I couldn't use them for days. "Please tell me you have an indestructible pair of gloves onboard."

Stef laughs. "Lenny's got extras. I'd hate to jeopardize your career as a hand model."

I flip her a middle finger. "This pose is my specialty."

We step out into the crisp air and head to the dock with gear from Stef's truck bed in tow, gravel crunching beneath our feet. It's still dark, and the reflection of the marina's FUEL sign glimmers against the black water. Stef's boat—named *Xena: Warrior Princess* (and she wonders why people think she's a lesbian)—is docked first in line at the jetty. It's impossible not to notice she's one of only three lobster boats in the entire harbor.

"Is everyone out on the water already?" I ask. "The last time I went out with Dad, I could've sworn there were more stragglers than this."

Stef shrugs. "There are no other boats, Broski. We're the first ones here."

"You mean…?"

"Yep." She throws her hands up. "This is Seabrook's entire lobstering industry."

Damn. So it's even worse than I'd assumed.

But I'm not gonna exacerbate the situation by acknowledging

it. Instead I'm going to be the optimistic younger brother who gives her hope.

"More for us to catch!" I chirp.

Stef warms *Xena* up and we're steaming out to sea within minutes. My role for now is to prefill bags with bait so we have something to reload the traps with later. The stench is vile even in open air—I'd kill for a gas mask (or a Bath & Body Works three-wick) right now—but my dad's voice in the back of my head stops me from complaining. Suddenly I'm seventeen again, mindlessly transferring the chum from buckets to bags in a repetitive, steady, machinelike motion—like an assembly-line worker or a Keebler elf.

We're barely a mile away from the shoreline when Stef starts to slow down.

"First line of buoys comin' up!" she yells from her captain's perch. "Need you on the gunwale!"

I place my current bag down and head over to her. She's got a maze of GPS and radar screens in front of her—way better technology than I remember Dad ever having—and a further rush of memories rises in me. The way he would whistle along to Tom Petty behind the helm and yell "haul, pick, bait, set" at Stef and me between songs, the closest thing he ever had to a mantra.

"What color?" Dad's buoys were always a recognizable blend of maroon, white, and three shades of green, but it occurs to me I don't know Stef's signature.

"Fluorescent yellow and neon purple," Stef answers, which nearly makes me crack up. Those don't sound like her at all. "Can't miss 'em."

She stops the boat when we get to the buoys. "I'm gonna have you measure. Any bugs less than three and a quarter, you gotta throw back. More than five, throw back. V-notches, throw back. Eggs, throw back. Got it? Nothin' but keepers in the tank at the end of the day."

Her rapid-fire delivery stresses me out at first—it's freakishly Dad-esque—but then she hands me an aluminum lobster gauge and I feel well equipped for the task at hand. I throw her a fake army salute. "Yes, ma'am."

She pulls up the line and slams a trap against the gunwale. She doesn't even glimpse its contents before sliding it directly at me.

"Open 'er!"

I do as told—opening the trap comes back as easily as riding a bike—but there's one problem. There's nothing in it. The bait has barely been touched.

"Sis?" I yell. "When were these set?"

"Couple days ago," she answers. "Why?"

"No reason." I stack the trap behind me and tell myself it's an aberration. I won't stress Stef out yet; surely the next one will be full of keepers. "Ready when you are!"

We go through the entire twelve-trap trawl—haul, pick, bait, set—and I've thrown back approximately ten bugs (Bruno-speak for lobster) and kept nine. Stef hops back to help set the freshly rebaited traps, and we're off to the next trawl.

The rest of the day goes by like this, and the catch is consistently disappointing. I'm starting to understand why my parents retired early.

But what about Stef? She still has a couple decades of work ahead of her. She's happy when she's lobstering, but she's happiest when she's got a healthy catch. I can't imagine what this constant cycle of scarcity is doing to her psyche—not to mention her bank account. There's no way she's turning a profit after all the overhead costs of fuel, bait, gear, and maintenance.

Eventually we're on the last trap of the last trawl. This one has six whole bugs in it, but the gauge forces me to throw half of them back. I band the claws on the remaining three, toss them in the keeper tank, and rebait.

Stef whips around to reset the line of twelve traps stacked on the deck. I step aside to let her do her thing, but as she slides the next one toward the water, I feel a sudden tug on my ankle.

Oh. Fuck.

My foot is barely an inch away from being caught in the rope.

My stomach drops and my mind races as I realize I have mere milliseconds to save myself from being dragged hundreds of feet underwater with the traps. How the hell could I be so careless? Of all the things I'd remembered today, somehow I'd forgotten about the horror stories Dad used to tell of lobstermen who met their demise in freak accidents just like this.

"Shit!" I try to yank my foot out, but lose my balance and land right back in the danger zone.

"Ray!"

Before I know what's happening, Stef grabs me by the waist, lifts my 180 body weight off the deck, and throws me against the captain's door.

"You trying to get killed?" she huffs. "*Christ!*"

The trap zips down the deck and off the boat as if possessed by an underwater demon.

I heave a sigh of relief. "Thanks for saving my life, Sis."

She punches my arm. "Don't make me do it again."

⌁

We're filthy and foul-smelling when we arrive back at the house, so the first thing we do is disappear to our respective bathrooms for scalding-hot showers.

The second thing we do is obtain a pair of ice-cold beers from the garage fridge.

"You did alright out there today," Stef says. She's out of her

Carhartt garb and curled up on our childhood couch in gym shorts and a tank top. "For a city boy, at least."

"City boy?" I take a swig of Coors Light. This one tastes better than all the beers we drank last night combined. This one was hard-earned. "I was literally born and raised here. And Kip and I don't even live in the city anymore. We bought a house in the suburbs last year, remember? You still have to come visit."

"I've never gotten an invite."

Is it true that I've been there for a year and still haven't invited my sister over? It seems impossible, now that she's sitting across from me after we've spent the past twenty-four hours together... But no. She's right.

"You have an open invite," I attempt. "You know that."

"How would I know that?"

I should've known better than to bullshit my sister.

"Fair," I admit. "Well, we'd love to have you and Lenny visit for a weekend. We can play a round of golf. And there are tons of great restaurants and shopping..."

She gives me an air-cheers with her Coors Light and the room falls silent. Everything in here is exactly as it was when the house belonged to our parents—the same wooden paneling, tile floors, water-stained ceilings—and I wonder if Stef has ever considered a gut renovation. For someone who purports to believe our parents' marriage was so unhealthy, she doesn't seem to have a problem living the exact life they did.

But I'm glad. Stef living here means I'll always have a home in Seabrook to come back to—the luxury of a living time capsule. It occurs to me now that I don't take nearly enough advantage of it. Kip and I really should visit more often.

"What would you have done if Mom and Dad sold this place to someone else?" I ask Stef.

She shrugs. "I mean, Lenny and I rented that apartment on Wharf Road forever. We'd probably still be there. Or who knows—maybe we'd have moved to Maine by now."

I do a double take. "Maine? *By now?*"

Her face assumes a no-nonsense glare. "You saw the catch today."

"It wasn't so bad." My instinct for optimism is difficult to squash, even when it takes the form of denial. "We got a ton of keepers…"

"Ray, come on."

"So that's your plan? Leave Seabrook?"

"Eventually," she says. "Lenny's parents are still lobstering up there—territory's been in their family for generations and we'll be shoo-ins when they retire. The situation around here is only gonna get worse, and we're not one of these couples that can just stop fishing and open up a gift shop."

"But you can't *leave* Seabrook," I protest. "Mom and Dad already did—"

"So did you," she reminds me. "You don't *really* care about this, do you? It's not like you ever come up to visit."

She's got me there. But that's only because I just assumed Seabrook—and Stefani—would always be here. It never occurred to me there'd be an expiration date on my ability to come back. "I've been meaning to visit more, though, after the wedding. Kip's only been here a handful of times! We spend so much time with his family upstate…"

"I'm aware. It's why Lenny and I stopped bothering with the holiday invites."

I slump against the chair. "Define 'eventually.'"

Stef's brow raises. "Huh?"

"You said the move would be happening 'eventually,'" I remind her. "What does that mean in actual years?"

Something in me needs the answer to be at least five or so—far enough away that I don't have to worry about it anytime soon, and with enough time ahead for Kip and me to develop a new tradition of coming up for a few weekends each summer.

Stef bites her lip. "I shouldn't have even mentioned it. I'm sure it won't be for a long time. Lenny's parents don't have plans to retire anytime soon."

"Good."

"Don't worry about it." She laughs to herself while heading to the garage for another beer. "Seabrook will always be Seabrook. Maybe it won't have lobsters—or me—but your beloved Earlymoon Hotel isn't going anywhere."

wednesday

6

T he reservation's under Hayes," I tell the guard—his name tag says Horace, and somehow it fits—from the driver's seat of my Subaru. "Kip Hayes."

Horace glares at me, reaches a hand through the window. "ID?"

Shit.

"He's my fiancé," I explain. "We're arriving separately…"

"Ray Bruno?"

Oh. Right. Of course Kip included my name on the reservation—he never forgets stuff like that. He's not like me when it comes to logistics, which is to say flighty and careless (and occasionally a hazard to myself and the general public).

I pull out my driver's license and hand it to Horace, who then hands me back a five-day parking pass to hang from my rearview mirror.

"Alrighty then," Horace chirps. Now that he knows I'm a legitimate guest, his demeanor has done a perfect backflip. "Just follow this road straight through the first few holes of the golf course, past the spa complex, and right up to the valet in front of the main hotel." He flashes a winky smile as he flicks a switch by his desk. "Welcome to paradise."

The front gates whoosh open, sending me into a trancelike state.

I've passed this entrance a million times before—it asserts itself in big, stone letters right off the shoulder of Summerland Road—but the other side of it has always been expertly obscured by a thick combination of trees, fences, and vegetation.

When I was a wide-eyed kid listening to my mom's fairy-tale retelling of her earlymoon, I imagined the inside to be something like Oz. A Technicolor dreamland with an emerald castle on the horizon, an omnipresent sense of magic—and perhaps a flying monkey or two—in the air.

When I was an angsty teen hooking up with douchey college guys, I imagined it to be something like a northern Mar-a-Lago—obnoxiously manicured, plastered in gold for no reason in particular, and generally overhyped. Not to mention unattainable, especially if I ever wanted to come out of the closet.

When I was twenty-seven and engaged to Byrd, I finally just Googled pictures of the place. I'd circled back to the dream of a storybook marriage by then, and I figured an earlymoon would be the perfect way to guarantee it. But as I glanced at the Earlymoon Hotel's website, I realized two things: (1) It was basically just a standard—massive, but standard—New England beach resort, and (2) it was way out of our internet-writer price range. Byrd and I could barely afford a modest wedding—let alone a honeymoon—let alone a bonus early honeymoon.

As I drive through the resort's main road right now, I realize my mother was right all along. It's like I'm not in Seabrook at all.

And the pictures really don't do it justice. The fairways are greener than any I've ever seen—and Kip and I have played nearly every public golf course in the greater metro area—almost like the rolling hills of Ireland as depicted in the 2007 Hilary Swank vehicle *P.S. I Love You*. Even the fescue looks like it was painted into the scene by Bob Ross himself.

The landscaping gets even more impressive the closer I get to the beach—vibrant flower beds, lush sand dunes, and towering beach grass soar against an endless vista of blue sky and bluer waters.

And then there's the main building, which somehow manages to look like both a mega-hotel and a quaint inn—four stories of Cape Cod-style shingled gray siding, clean white trim, and panoramic balconies. I can actively feel my organs relax as I open my car windows and breathe in the fresh salt air.

This is going to be an amazing week.

The valet takes my car and I saunter into the grand lobby, where the front-desk clerk hands me a key and alerts me that my fiancé has already checked in. This is physically impossible—Kip texted an hour earlier and said he still hadn't gotten on the road yet—but I'm so eager to get to the room that I don't bother to correct her.

I take the elevator to the fourth floor and float through the hotel's clean hallways on a cloud. The past two days haven't felt anything like a vacation—especially given the reality check about my sister's current situation—but now I'm in full leisure mode. My mind overflows with excitement over the possibilities of the week ahead. Days in the sun, on the golf course, at the spa, on the beach. Nights in the hot tub, at the cabana bar, in our hotel bed.

Not a care in the world.

I swipe the key to our suite and drop my bags on the floor once I'm inside.

This room—awash in soft, natural sunlight—is yet another thing that puts the pictures to shame. Reflections of water glisten across the ceiling and walls, thanks to a pair of enormous windows that frame the entrance to our private beachfront balcony. There's a strong "sleeping quarters on a yacht" vibe to the decor, but I can't imagine a room on any ocean vessel feeling quite this spacious. There's a linen sectional in one corner and a down-draped

California king in the other, with a vaulted ceiling that seems to stretch to heaven. A dresser against the side wall displays an array of welcome goodies—including a bottle of Veuve Clicquot on ice, which I don't remember ordering, but which has my mouth watering nonetheless.

I snap a few pics of the room and send them off to Kip: Get your ass over here or I'm drinking this champs without you! Natalie Merchant!!!

I throw my phone on the bed and head out to the balcony, where I'm immediately greeted by the gentlest summer breeze and a chorus of seagulls in the distance. The sensory perfection of this experience is honestly starting to get ridiculous at this point. I'm almost ready for a flaw—any flaw—just to prove this is still real life.

The beach outside stretches for what looks like miles, with lounging couples dotting the sand every fifty yards or so. The Earlymoon Hotel is adults only, so there's not a child in sight, thank God. (I love kids as much as the next person, but let's not pretend they aren't notorious vacation-ruiners.)

I get the sense that part of what makes this place so special is that they've figured out the perfect guest-to-beach ratio. The hotel is big, but it's only four stories, and the size of our room suggests there probably aren't very many rooms in total. Given the seemingly endless amount of land and space on the property, I can't imagine the resort ever feels crowded—or just normal levels of occupied—even at full capacity. Couples must feel like they have the grounds to themselves most of the time.

I slide into a lounge chair and close my eyes, facing the sun. The heat on my cheeks brings about a revelation:

I can't do the earlymoon article.

Interviewing couples about their trips sounded like so much fun at first, but that was before I got here and fell under the spell of relaxation in the air. Even if it's just an hour each morning, that's an hour I could spend in bed with Kip or out on this balcony with the brilliant sunlight.

I open my eyes and observe the first couple in my line of sight—a dainty redhead in a blue bikini and a brawny bald man in matching swim trunks—which raises another point. Even if I wanted to talk to them, why would they want to talk to me? I'm technically a journalist (even if I never actually feel like one), and I'm pretty sure most people find journalists annoying at best.

But most of all, there's Kip.

The way he ended our phone call the other night made it clear that he wouldn't be comfortable with even the most innocuous mention of his name in *Appeal*, and even if I could talk him into it, that in itself is a form of work I don't feel up to in this environment.

Especially when I've already put so much work into getting him on board with my wedding plans. I feel guilty enough as it is for pushing him *that* far out of his comfort zone.

At one point during my nonstop campaign against his city-hall wishes last year, I swear he almost even teared up. (And Kip is obviously not a crier.) He was talking about how his first wedding was a dream for his ex-wife, but a nightmare for him—apparently he'd felt like "a bug under a magnifying glass" the entire time—and he said didn't want to go through that again. I promised he'd feel differently at *our* wedding, given that our relationship is actually based on true romantic love, but still. I felt so bad for him that I immediately offered to kill the Vows piece as a compromise.

It wouldn't be fair for me to backpedal on that compromise now.

I need to text CeCe with this change of heart, so I head back inside to retrieve my phone. This time, I stop to look at the spread on the dresser and realize there's a handwritten note tucked between the ice bucket and the champagne flutes. From Kip:

Surprise! Decided to leave early and do my run here instead of at home. Don't start drinking this champs until I'm back!!! Love you.

A wave of gratitude swells in my chest. If I weren't already certain about my decision to kill the article, this clinches it. If Kip's starting our trip out on this thoughtful and romantic note, there's no way I'm gonna counter it with my selfishness.

Can't do the earlymoon piece, I text CeCe. We'll think of something just as good when I'm back next week. Promise!

She texts back immediately. What? Why? I already sold SZ on it!

SZ is code for Sub Zero, our private nickname for CeCe's boss—Subina McCue—*Appeal*'s ice queen of an editor in chief.

I'm sorry!!! I write back.

Before I can elaborate on my apology, I'm distracted by an echo of Kip's voice coming from what sounds like the balcony. I zip back out there and immediately spot him down on the beach. He's sweaty, shirtless, panting, and randomly engaged in conversation with that couple I had just been creeping on moments ago.

"You had the right idea," the bald man is saying. "Primary care sounds like a cakewalk compared to the shit I gotta deal with in cardiology. I'd kill to just order blood work and write scripts all day. You know what I had to do to get this week off?"

"It's not *just* blood work and prescriptions," Kip says through a laugh that I can tell is fake and annoyed.

"Just joshin' ya." The man playfully slaps his arm, and Kip seems to relax. "Kip fuckin' Hayes!"

"Jake fuckin' Meyers!" Kip mimics back.

"What are the odds I'd run into you here, man?" Jake asks. "Haven't seen ya in…at least a decade. How've you been? How's Annie?"

"She's..." Kip clears his throat, catches his breath. "We're divorced."

"I'm so sorry," the bikini-clad redhead chimes in, putting a hand over her left boob. "I'm Lucy, by the way. Jake's fiancée."

A redhead named Lucy? I'm instantly obsessed.

Kip nods. "Nice to meet you. Congratulations."

"We're here on an early honeymoon," Jake explains. "*This one* convinced me it was a good idea."

Lucy slaps his arm. "Babe! It's called an *earlymoon*. It's what this place is known for."

Jake chuckles and then addresses Kip. "Is that why you're here, too, then? With Wife Number Two?"

"Actually, uh..." Kip stammers. "No."

Jake cocks his head.

Kip looks around—but not *up*, where I'm currently crouched by our balcony railing like a soldier on enemy lines—and releases an uncomfortable laugh. "I'm just here with...a buddy of mine."

Jake cocks his head even more.

My head? Currently somewhere between spinning and crashing. Violently.

"We didn't realize it was a couples place," Kip continues. "Thought it was more known for the fairways." He throws his hands up and forces a laugh. "That'll teach me not to do my research before booking my next golf trip."

The lies are rolling so easily off his tongue at this point that I barely recognize my own fiancé. He's a stranger, a ghost, a figment.

A fucking *buddy*.

7

It's generally believed that relationships are best in the beginning, thanks to the excitement of the chase, the high of infatuation, the endless possibilities—all that shit.

But for Kip and me, it was a little more complicated. Our relationship has never been more difficult than it was during our first year together.

Our chemistry was off the charts from day one, but so was the weight of our collective baggage. It would've been hard enough just dealing with the two recent divorces between us, but then there were the hurdles of my insecurity and Kip's closetedness.

The former was exacerbated by my parents' decision to leave Seabrook shortly after Kip and I met. This shouldn't have been devastating to me as a twenty-nine-year-old adult with my own life in New York, but I had leaned on family heavily during the aftermath of my divorce.

I took the train to Connecticut nearly every weekend back then, eager to escape the harshness of the city, and spent all my free time watching sports with my dad, shopping with my mom, getting drunk with Stef, that sort of thing.

It wasn't that they offered me some kind of grand emotional therapy; it was more the mindless familiarity that I found so comforting. My family could be counted on to never change, which I valued more than ever after seeing how quickly Byrd was capable of flipping on me barely a year into our marriage. He was supposed to be the exception to all the flighty, noncommittal, shallow guys I'd cyclèd through in my single years. If he could change so easily, I had little reason to think the city had anyone left to offer me.

So when my parents abruptly moved away that fall, I became even clingier than I normally would've been in the face of a promising new romance.

"I'm terrified of losing you," I remember admitting to Kip one night as we spooned between rounds of sex. He was the big spoon, so I was essentially speaking to his nightstand, which somehow made it easier to disclose all of the fears I might've otherwise had the sense to keep hidden. "You can have any guy you want. You don't realize it yet, because you've been passing as straight your whole life. But now that you're starting to come out, it just seems so unlikely that you'd *choose* me…"

My voice trailed off before landing on a line of self-sabotage. "Maybe we should end it now. I'm, like, five minutes away from being irreversibly in love with you…and I don't think I'll be able to handle it when you realize how much better you can do."

He took a few breaths directly into my ear, and at first I couldn't tell if they were frustrated or affectionate.

"I find it hard to believe it can get any better," he whispered. "What makes you think I'm not terrified of losing *you*?"

"Trust me," I said. "That's not something you have to worry about."

He squeezed me tight, and I'd never felt so secure.

But after breaking the honesty seal that night, such episodes became all too frequent.

Most of the time things were easy between us, but sometimes

I'd get this uncontrollable itch to test him. He was always so willing to provide evidence he loved me that I became addicted to collecting it. Showing him pictures of the hottest men on earth to see if he'd admit he found them attractive (he always insisted I was hotter), texting him when I knew he was out with friends (he always responded), drunk crying for no reason until he'd cradle me and rub my back (which he always did with the patience of a saint)—needy shit like that. I knew it was a bad look—and that I was too old and ostensibly mature for such behavior—but the enormity of our love brought out the messy teenager in me. It was embarrassing. I couldn't help it.

Meanwhile, when we weren't together, he was busy doing the work of coming out. Having heart-to-hearts with his childhood best friends, college buddies, and basketball league teammates. Awkward phone calls with family members, both immediate and extended. Everyone was surprised but supportive, and several people expressed sympathy that he'd ever felt the need to conceal his authentic self to begin with.

It was all so anticlimactic that I began to wonder why he hadn't considered doing it sooner. I understood that being a member of Generation X meant he was raised in an even more homophobic social climate than I was—my nineties childhood was at least a little more accepting of gayness than his eighties childhood—but still. Kip was so strong and confident in every other area of his life; it seemed strange he couldn't muster the courage to flout society's norms until he met me.

The more out of the closet Kip became—the more people other than me knew he was gay—the more afraid I became that some imaginary man would swoop in to steal him away.

Someone older, better-looking, more successful than me.

Someone more like Kip himself.

"You're the one who's been pushing me to come out," he said to me during a particularly heated conversation on the topic. "And now you're worried I'm gonna leave you because of it?"

He had me there. I was so eager for him to come out—so he could acknowledge our relationship to the people in his life, and also for his sake, so he could finally know the freedom of living openly—that I hadn't expected the potential side effects.

"I'm a hypocrite," I admitted. "I'm sorry."

He pulled me in toward him. "What do I have to do to prove to you that I'm here to stay?"

I barely took a moment to think before spitting out an answer: "Introduce me to your parents."

Kip had been telling me stories about them for months at that point, enough for me to deduce that he valued their approval and wouldn't introduce someone to them unless he truly believed it was rock-solid. One of the reasons he'd stayed in his unhappy marriage for so long, in fact, was because he didn't want to disappoint them by tarnishing the Hayes name with something so human as a divorce.

Introducing me to them as his boyfriend would be the ultimate expression of commitment.

"You *want* to meet them?" he asked. "You do know they're… nothing like your parents."

Mom and Dad had welcomed Kip into their house months prior with a few magnums of cheap wine and a giant platter of baked ziti, while Dr. and Mrs. Hayes preferred to host guests at their country club in upstate New York. Presumably with normal-sized bottles of expensive wine and a full gourmet menu.

"*Of course* I want to meet them," I said. "I want to know everything about you—especially where you came from. I'm sure I can charm them."

Kip pondered the request for several days, until he eventually sealed the deal with a kiss. "Let's do it."

We planned a skiing getaway at their upstate house that winter. As the date neared, I started to get nervous about my promise to charm them. My exes' parents all adored me—I had barely any friends growing up, and had therefore learned to schmooze adults at an early age—but the stakes felt higher with Kip's family. I loved Kip so much more than I'd ever loved any ex. I worried that if his parents somehow didn't like me, he might start to look at me through their eyes and decide I wasn't the best fit after all.

The fact that we were indeed doing dinner at their club only added to my anxiety. I'd known a number of rich kids in college and had eventually learned how to interact with them, but the dinner location made the whole thing feel very much like Jack Dawson getting invited to the first-class wing of the *Titanic*. I couldn't stop thinking about all the possible rules of etiquette I might break by way of ignorance.

"Just be yourself," Kip advised. "They'll love you."

So I was—and they did.

By the time cocktail hour ended and we settled into a table in the dining room, I felt supremely comfortable in their presence. Kip had always billed them as this kind of untouchable royalty, but I'd found them to be incredibly down to earth. Dr. and Mrs. Hayes—who insisted I call them Marshall and Viola—were endlessly interested in my work as a relationships writer, and even more intrigued by my family's history of lobstering.

"There's nothing better than a good crustacean," Marshall said as the lobster he ordered arrived at the table. His voice was like Kip's but scratchier, his hair like Kip's but grayer—a sneak peek of Kip's future form. "We owe a great deal to the good fishermen of the world." He raised his scotch glass and proposed a toast. "To the Bruno family."

We all clinked glasses.

"I'm just so glad Kipling introduced us to you," Viola told me. She had big Jane Fonda energy, which is to say we shared an immediate connection. "We were shocked when he told us…you know…"

"Mother," Kip interjected.

She cut her son off with a casual hand. "But I couldn't be more pleased that he's with such an interesting young fellow. Marshall and I are proof that opposites do indeed attract, you know. What with him being a doctor and me being an artist."

I raised an eyebrow. "An artist? Kip didn't mention that."

"Watercolors," she said. "I'll show you some of my work back at the house." She paused. "I was hoping I'd pass some of my creativity down to my son, but alas. He is his father through and through."

I smiled. Kip had told me early on that his career path was entirely influenced by his father's. My heart broke a little for him at first, as pop culture had conditioned me to assume this meant Kip had some kind of buried creative passion that he was forced to squander in order to secure Daddy's approval, but that couldn't be further from the truth. Kip has nary a creative bone in his body, and following in Dr. Marshall Hayes's footsteps was always his dream just as much as (if not more than) his father's.

Viola looked at her husband and son and sighed with contentment. "Dr. and Dr. Hayes. My boys."

"Kip's a good egg," Marshall said.

Viola turned to me. "Did Kip tell you what our last name would've been if his father hadn't changed it?"

"Viola," Marshall said. "We don't need to—"

"I haven't told him yet," Kip said through a laugh. "Please do the honors, Mom."

Viola's mouth curved into a devious smile as she took a sip of chardonnay and prepared for story time. "Marshall and I weren't married yet, but we'd been together a while... Gosh, I suppose it was 1973. He was just finishing up medical school. And out of the blue, he comes home one night and tells me he's gone and legally changed his last name to Hayes!"

I couldn't help but laugh along with her. Both out of politeness and because it was so strange to think that Marshall would go to such an extreme to assert his individuality. I wondered if it was because he was estranged from his parents, but Viola's lighthearted delivery made me feel like it couldn't have been that serious.

"What was it before?" I asked.

"Haze!" Viola answered. At first I thought she was just saying "Hayes" again, but then she spelled it out for me. "H-a-z-e. And let me tell you, I was furious! I'd been looking forward to being *Viola Haze* for years by then. Had my signature all ready to go and everything." She hit Marshall on the arm. "Then this one goes and takes away my Z."

"I was starting residency at Yale," Marshall explained. "I couldn't walk around with a name tag that said *Dr. Haze*. Patients would never have taken me seriously. It sounds like the name of a comic book villain."

Which is exactly what would've made it so awesome, I thought but didn't say.

"You're welcome, son," Marshall said to Kip. "I did it for us both."

Viola tossed her napkin at him. "He wasn't even born yet!"

I laughed along with the table, but it struck me as so sad that Marshall did the name change not to assert his individuality, but rather to erase it. I suddenly had a deeper understanding of why Kip had never given himself permission to come out when he was younger. It would've been very un-Hayes-like of him.

After the entrées wcrc finished, Viola ran into some women from her ladies' golf league and joined them at the bar for a nightcap. Marshall, Kip, and I migrated to the cigar room.

"I'm glad you're happy," Marshall told his son as he lit up. "That's all that matters."

Something about the way he said it—and the vibe between them at that moment—made me realize there was a whole-ass iceberg beneath the statement. I later learned from Kip that his father's initial reaction to his coming out was far from supportive. (Viola? She was *thrilled*.) Apparently Kip had to explain himself at length before Marshall accepted that his forty-year-old son wasn't just going through a post-divorce identity crisis.

"Thanks, Pops…" Kip blew a puff of smoke into the air and then smiled at me. "I've never been happier."

And then some random man walked in.

"Marshall," he said. "Haven't seen you in a dog's age!"

"Alistair." Marshall stood up and gave the man a firm handshake. "Good to see ya, old pal." He grabbed Kip's shoulder. "You remember my boy, Kip?"

Alistair nodded. "Of course, of course."

Marshall then gestured toward me, right as a gust of cigar smoke to the lungs triggered me into a violent coughing fit. Kip had warned me not to inhale, but the only thing I'd ever smoked was weed and apparently it was a habit.

"This here is Kip's…" Marshall cleared his throat. My stomach sank as I realized what was about to happen. "Skiing buddy Ray. They're hitting the slopes this weekend."

I turned to Kip—expecting to at least exchange a couple of undercover *you-believe-this-shit?* glances—but he was busy nodding, smiling, playing along.

Kip apologized later that night, explaining that he didn't want to make a scene by challenging his father in front of his "old-fashioned" club friend, and I mostly understood. It wasn't like I wanted him to jump onto the table and go all "I'm here, I'm queer, deal with it" on the entire cigar room—but still. I hadn't realized how easy it would be for him to throw himself—and me—back into the closet for the night. I swore he had made more progress than that. It stung to learn he hadn't.

But that sting was nothing compared to the sting I feel right now—five years, a house, and an engagement later—as I realize just how much progress he's yet to make.

8

~~

You're here!" Kip says upon finding me in our suite. "I just did a few laps around the perimeter, and this place is incredible. I honestly can't believe all this is right here in Seabrook."

He goes in for a hug. Normally I wouldn't mind getting some of his sweat on me, but right now it makes me recoil. "Babe, you're dirty. I'm clean. *Hello?*"

"Fine, fine." He throws his hands up in surrender and scans my face, then the room, laughing as he spots the discarded Veuve cork on the dresser. "You fucker—I knew you'd start without me." He picks up the nearby bottle. "Wait. Is this empty?"

A burp rises in my throat because yes, it is. After I overheard my fiancé refer to me as nothing more than a "buddy" fifteen minutes ago, I had no choice but to slug back as much alcohol as possible.

Maybe it shouldn't have bothered me so much. I'd be a hypocrite if I said that I've always made it a point to be out and proud to every person I come across on the street. Sometimes it is absolutely easiest to just let someone assume straightness and keep it moving.

But this guy wasn't a random stranger. He wasn't even some "old-fashioned" country club friend of Kip's father. He was someone Kip clearly has a personal history with and who asked point-blank if Kip was in a new relationship. Sure, it would've been a little uncomfortable to correct Jake's assumption that Kip was here with "Wife Number Two," but certainly not apocalyptic. He could've just said, "Actually? Husband Number One." And then Jake would've raised an eyebrow, maybe expressed some shock, before ultimately saying, "Good for you, man!"

And that would've been that.

Instead, he's thrown us into the closet during what is supposed to be the most romantic week of our lives.

And to think I was so close to writing an article about us. Kip couldn't even acknowledge my existence to a long-lost acquaintance, and I was over here ready to gush about him to thousands of monthly *Appeal* subscribers.

"I was thirsty," I say in my best I'm-definitely-not-upset-about-anything voice. There are a million other words on the tip of my tongue, but I stop myself from letting any of them slip free. I want to at least give Kip the chance to explain himself on his own terms.

"I can see that." His brow scrunches. "You okay?"

"Why wouldn't I be?"

He shrugs, drops his shorts, heads toward the bathroom. "I'm gonna take a quick shower, then wanna do lunch? I'm ravenous. We have lots of options. I passed by several different bars and restaurants on my run."

So he's not planning on telling me about the encounter with Jake and Lucy at all.

He must simply be hoping we don't cross paths with them this week, or that if we do, he'll be able to quickly introduce me to them by first name—no label attached—and rush us out of the conversation. Given the fact that we never engage in PDA, he probably figures they'll have no reason to suspect anything.

Kip turns the water on and starts humming "Levon," his go-to shower song, as if he hasn't a care in the world. And in spite of everything, I can't help but smile at the echo of his baritone. His singing voice is objectively bad, but the energy behind it is adorable.

Maybe I should just let it go. Pretend I never overheard the conversation at all. I'm not exactly mad at *him*, anyway. I'm just... mad at the situation. Mad at myself. I've clearly missed something over the past few years.

Most of the time, Kip and I are around people who know us. We're always eating at the same restaurants, drinking at the same bars, golfing at the same courses, with the same rotation of friends, family, neighbors, and coworkers. Kip hasn't needed to explicitly come out to someone in forever. At some point he must've decided his work was done—there was no more need to confront whatever kernels of internalized homophobia might have still lingered in his system after all the initial heavy lifting was over.

And it's not like our daily lives are colored by secrecy and shame. Far from it. Our love isn't plastered all over social media, but it's strong and it's real. We're happy in our own little world together.

But what if that's not enough?

What if I hadn't been so willing to kill the *Times* announcement in exchange for my dream wedding?

That question alone presents the fundamental difference between us in a glaring light. I want to shout about our love from the rooftops, and Kip wants to keep it just between us. To the extent that he has just actively lied to someone about who I am—and what I mean—to him.

The fact that he could casually do so during a time like this makes me wonder if it's a habit of his. It's like Stef asked me the other night: How out *is* he, really?

There's no question that everyone who knows us as a couple— everyone in his life who truly matters—knows he's gay.

But what about all the people who don't matter? Is he going

out in the world each day presenting as a straight man, even when explicitly asked about his relationship status? What's he gonna do once we're married and sporting his-and-his wedding bands? Just let everyone assume I'm Wife Number Two?

We need to hash this out.

Even if I choose not to say anything, Kip will easily clock that I have something on my mind, and he'll ask me about it soon enough. Better to bring it up and see if we can resolve the issue before lunch. Hopefully Kip will explain that his answer was a mindless slip, and that he's in fact not in the habit of erasing our relationship for all the side characters of his life.

I guzzle a tall bottle of spring water from the minibar to clear up some of my champagne buzz. By the time Kip stops singing and turns the shower off, I'm ready for a mature and levelheaded conversation about my concerns.

But then he steps out of the bathroom naked, excited, with a look in his eyes.

Having been deprived of this view for the past two nights, it doesn't take me long to catch up to his level of excitement. For all the differences between us, one thing we've always had in common is a passion for each other's bodies.

It started from day one.

Kip is a stickler about getting at least eight hours of sleep, but during the first year of our relationship, sleep went out the window entirely. There was something so natural and strangely innocent about sharing a bed with him. It was nothing like the sex I'd had with past hookups or even serious exes—all verbal and practiced and, more often than not, rough. Sex with Kip was sloppy and unrehearsed—the kind of sex you can only have with someone who genuinely fascinates you.

While Kip eventually got his sleep cycle back on track, this instinctive hunger for each other has remained intact over the years—even now that our bodies have long been memorized by each other and our moves have become predictable and routine.

This might sound like the most boring sex life ever to some people, but to me, it's perfect. Safe. Home.

Kip creeps forward and helps me out of my shirt. "Let's kick this vacation off right."

I relax into his touch, my worries quieted by a more urgent horniness.

But then I have a flash of a memory—or not a memory, really, but a feeling—of those early months.

One way I used to justify Kip's reluctance to come out was with the old cliché that "no one needs to know what we do behind closed doors." It's a sentiment that I generally agree with—it's not like I need Kip's med school friend to see what we're doing *right at this moment*—but it's also one that has contributed to more than a small amount of gay erasure over the years. Used by the kinds of people who want to present as tolerant and accepting, but deep down harbor a belief that gays are still deviants whose practices shouldn't be acknowledged out loud. Straight people can walk around with kids—effectively tiny human-shaped billboards saying, "We fucked to make this!"—but just the slightest intimation of gay sex can sometimes be enough to make even the most well-meaning allies cry TMI.

"You seem distracted," Kip says. "You sure you're alright?"

"Yeah, yeah, here." I guide his hand below my waist, muting my running thoughts before they kill the mood. "Just shut up and touch me."

He hesitates for a moment, like he might challenge my answer, but he lets it go the second his fingers are wrapped around me. "If you insist."

He kisses me hard, I kiss him back harder, and we both melt into the raging, invisible force that has always connected our bodies to each other so fervently.

This.

This is the only thing that matters—the most natural, certain, and *right* feeling in the world.

The rest is just static.

The rest has nothing to do with us.

The rest can figure itself out later.

9

⌣

Kip and I snag a table at the Gull's Nest, one of the resort's more casual beachfront dining options. We each order an IPA called Sip of Sunshine, which couldn't be a more appropriate name for our current situation. We're out here dressed like swimwear models—Kip in a plain white cabana set from Brooks Brothers, me in loud Hawaiian trunks and a tank from Kenny Flowers—drenched in sunlight and enveloped in an ever-present shoreline breeze.

Kip raises his glass and smiles. "To us."

Everything in me wants to reciprocate and continue with the day as if that whole balcony moment never happened. This setting is so perfect, our love so nearly perfect. Do I really need to throw a wrench into the mix by demanding an explanation for why he downplayed our relationship to someone he's probably never going to see again after this week?

"To us," I say back—and mean it.

Maybe instead of confronting him directly, I can just...nudge him. Initiate a few minor acts of PDA. I'm sure the people at this resort won't be fazed, and perhaps then he'll come to the realization on his own that it's silly to be so wary of claiming our relationship in public.

I reach across the table and massage his hand for a moment after we toast.

He pulls it away and coughs into it.

"So how's the article going?" he asks. "Any thought on how you're gonna approach our fellow earlymooners?"

"It's…" Instead of telling him that I canned the piece shortly after arriving at the hotel, I make a mental note to text CeCe that I've had yet another change of heart. Maybe writing about our trip—about our love—could be just the thing to crack his shell. "I'm going to shoot the owners an email and drop my dad's name. I'm hoping they'll be more willing to talk to me that way, given the personal connection."

"I can't imagine they'll be opposed to the free publicity," Kip says. "And how are you gonna find couples to interview?"

His jaw twitches just a little as he asks that last question. I wonder if it's because he's worried I'll somehow start talking to Jake and Lucy.

"I'll ask the owners if they have any leads," I respond. "Or I can just stalk the bars and creepily approach the least intimidating patrons."

"The bars? You said you were just gonna work on this during my runs. No one's gonna be drinking first thing in the morning."

"I mean I'll ask them at the bar," I clarify. "Then schedule interview time over breakfast."

"You really think people are gonna be open to this?"

"Some will be," I assure him. And myself. "Some people hate the idea of talking to journalists about their personal lives, but others jump at the opportunity. Remember that piece I did about Jack and Jills a few years ago?"

"Coed bachelor-bachelorette parties," Kip confirms. "That was a good one."

Kip had suggested a joint bachelor party at one point—a Jack and Jack—but I lobbied hard for the earlymoon instead. And of course we didn't for a second consider separate bachelor parties. Both because I've always found the tradition so unromantic—all those "end of freedom" connotations—and also because our lives are way too entwined to even make the concept work. Kip might be able to have a weekend away with his buddies, but most of my friends are simply the other couples we hang out with. (Unless you count CeCe, who probably would've loved nothing more than to drag me out for a night of partying, if only for her own amusement.)

"It's not gonna be a heavy lift," I tell Kip. "You'll barely know I'm doing any interviews."

He sips his beer and nods. It occurs to me that by not telling him about my intention to mention our own trip in the article, I'm being dishonest. And while floating the idea seemed like a potentially disruptive move during our phone call the other night, it now strikes me as the lesser evil to confronting him about the whole Jake-Lucy thing. So maybe this can be the first step toward addressing the elephant in the room.

I take a deep breath. "CeCe had an interesting idea. She suggested I use our experience as a framework for the story. You know, like, open with a little bit about us and our relationship, why we're doing an earlymoon, and then zoom out into reporting on the rest of the resort..."

Kip bites his lip. "You said the other night that you weren't gonna write about us."

"I wasn't going to," I improvise. "But then I thought about it, and I probably should disclose to readers that I'm from Seabrook, you know? And that I've always been fascinated by this place—"

"No."

"No? That's it? You're not gonna even hear me out?"

"You already know how I feel about this kind of stuff. I don't like having my private life out there like that—"

"It's just a wedding trend piece," I counter. "It's not like I'm gonna be writing about your dick size." I pause. "Not that you'd have anything to be embarrassed about even if I did."

"Still! You'd be writing about our relationship."

I take a slug of beer and shoot Kip an accusatory look. "Are you out to your barber?" I ask.

He scoffs. "What are you talking about?"

"Are you out to your dentist?"

He scoffs again. "My—"

"What about Mr. McClackey?" I wasn't prepared for the image of our crotchety old neighbor to storm into my head right now, but alas. All those times he's referred to Kip and me as "roommates." I'm suddenly unsure if they're truly the result of McClackey's narrow-minded assumptions or Kip's active misdirection. "Have you ever really tried to tell him the truth?"

"Who cares about what McClackey thinks?" Kip asks. "Or what anybody thinks, for that matter."

"You must," I tell him. "Otherwise you wouldn't have such a problem with me writing this article."

The waiter swings by and drops off a large platter of oysters on ice. "Can I get you anything else for now?"

"Two more beers," Kip and I say in unison.

Silence unfurls between us as we take in the sight of our appetizer. Every time we order from a raw bar, at least one of us brings up a memory from the night we met at Grand Central Station. The further along we get in our relationship—the more we feel like we've known each other forever—the more that meeting feels like it was either a miracle or fate or some combination of both.

Because honestly, what were the odds? So many things had to

happen in just the right way, at just the right time, in order for us to end up sitting on those two stools at that moment. What if our trains hadn't been delayed? If there had only been one open stool? If they hadn't mixed up the number of oysters on our plates? Or what if I'd never moved to New York in the first place? The list of rhetorical questions could stretch all the way back to our respective births.

"Meeting you was the best thing that ever happened to me," I tell Kip. "All I want to do is acknowledge that in my work."

He squeezes a touch of lemon over the oysters. "I get that, babe. And I'm trying. That's why I agreed to a wedding ten times the size of the one I wanted…" He pauses. "You *know* I hate being the center of attention."

"Which is totally fine. You *not* being an attention whore is one of the many things I love about you."

As I say it, I realize just how much I mean it. Kip's aversion to the limelight—the fact that he's able to generate self-esteem without the help of external validation—has always been incredibly attractive to me. Aspirational. It almost makes me feel like a hypocrite for trying so hard to get him to agree to this article.

But it's not like I'm asking him to create a full-blown social media presence. I'm just asking for permission to publicly acknowledge the fact that we're together.

"Oh, shit." Kip's face creases in concern as he looks at me. "Don't freak out… Don't move…"

I immediately know what he's going to say. We've enacted this scene a hundred times before in various outdoor dining scenarios. "Fuck. A bee?"

"On your neck," he confirms.

Every nerve ending in my body freezes in terror as the realization dawns on me:

I forgot to pack my EpiPen.

And this fucker chose to land on my *neck* of all places. I can only imagine how much faster my throat will close up when the venom is injected so closely to it.

"Is it gone?" I say breathlessly, my hands glued to the edge of the table. "Is it gone? Is it gone? Is it gone?"

Kip's face flushes with concern. "You forgot your EpiPen, didn't you? Babe! I thought we talked about—"

"I know! I just forgot. It was chaos in our house when I was packing. That stupid bird flew in and distracted me."

"For someone who's so terrified of getting hurt, you're pretty careless when it comes to protecting yourself."

"I have *you* to protect me," I explain. "You're a doctor! Is it gone?"

He shakes his head. "Stay calm. It has to fly away eventually."

As if inspired by Kip's words, the bee buzzes off of me and lands directly on his side of the table. I rocket out of my chair like it's made of knives, and Kip smacks the bee with a drink menu, killing it immediately upon impact.

My hero.

I exhale in relief as I return to my seat, suddenly feeling giddy at having evaded death. "You could get canceled for that, you know."

He laughs. "Don't remind me about *that* saga."

The saga he's referring to is an article that nearly got me fired from *Appeal* a few years ago. I pitched it to CeCe as "an impassioned bee takedown," a satirical essay about how humans should just eradicate the species altogether, for the sake of myself and everyone else who's deathly allergic to them.

Bees serve no practical purpose on this planet, I'd written. All they do is terrorize and kill—like Michael Myers! Except worse, because they're tiny and have wings. What have bees ever contributed to humanity and/or the environment? Literally nothing.

CeCe loved it—despite the fact that *Appeal* has never been known for its satire—and we published my unhinged rant with the inflammatory title "Against Bees."

And then it went viral. Thousands of readers thought I was being serious—as if I somehow managed to get a job writing for a national media outlet without being aware that bees serve a critical environmental purpose (to say nothing of their honey production)—and my inbox was soon flooded with long-winded explanations of how the entire United States agricultural industry would collapse without the essential crop-pollination that bees provide. *Appeal* leadership eventually got involved and had to slap a flag on the post clearly telling readers it wasn't meant to be taken seriously.

"I didn't *want* to kill the bee," Kip says. "I do feel bad about it."

"But you knew it was either him or me, so you did what you had to do."

"Exactly," he says through a laugh. "Now let's move inside. I don't want another close call."

"No!" I insist. "This is the Earlymoon Hotel." I gesture out across the balcony railing, down to the perfect stretch of beach below. "Look at how beautiful it is out here. We can't let the threat of bees thwart our capacity for alfresco dining."

He chuckles at my phrasing. "It doesn't look like there are any others buzzing around, so…fine. But if we do see another one, I'm *forcing* us inside. Your health is far more important than 'our capacity for alfresco dining.'"

"I love you," I tell him. "So much."

"I love you, too." Kip's shoulders relax just a little as we fall into a comfortable silence, slurping oysters and soaking up the sun. Eventually he says, "What if you write about us in the article but don't actually mention my name?"

"What do you want me to call you?"

"I don't know," he says through a shrug. "Just…"

"Mr. Big?"

He rolls his eyes. "You could just say, like, 'my fiancé,' or something."

I could, but that would make it sound like I'm hiding something. Not to mention the fact that constant repetition of the phrase "my fiancé" would be a total pain in the ass—both to write (that damn accent) and to read. Especially if I want him to have any kind of meaningful role in the story.

"Why are you so protective of your Google results?" I ask.

"Because you can't erase them," he says. "They're there forever."

I cock my head. "You have seen *my* Google results, right? Literally the first thing that comes up is an old *Microphone* post called, 'It Happened to Me: I Got Stung by a Jellyfish and Forced My Boyfriend to Pee on My Leg, but Instead of Curing the Sting, All It Did Was Activate His Latent Watersports Fetish.'"

"Of course I remember that one. I almost canceled our first date because of it, remember?" Kip laughs. "Why were your headlines at that place always so damn long?"

"SEO keyword targets."

"Ah. Right."

"Which is exactly why it would've so been nice to replace that with a *New York Times* Vows profile," I tell him. "The *Times* easily ranks higher in search than *Microphone*… It would've been my new top result."

Kip takes a breath but holds back his response.

"What if I refer to you by first name only?" I ask. "My fiancé, Kip, a doctor…"

"I don't know," he says. "How many doctors named Kip are there in the Westchester area? My identity would just be a few clicks away."

"Trust me. Readers do not give enough of a shit to do that kind of research. But even if they did, why would it matter?"

He finishes a sip of beer and leans back. "It's complicated. You know, I have my dad and my family to think about. They're always referring patients to me. Not to mention my *existing* patients..."

"So what if they find out you're gay?" I ask. "This isn't 1982."

Kip splashes some Tabasco on an oyster and slugs it down. I follow suit while waiting for him to formulate a response.

"I admit it," he finally says. "I still have some work to do with"—he throws his hands out—"being more open. You know that. Sometimes you forget that up until I met you, I moved through the world as the straight guy everyone always expected me to be. It takes effort to upset that expectation, and sometimes it's just easier not to."

He sounds apologetic, almost like he's trying to clear his conscience of the whole Jake-Lucy thing without actually telling me about it in the first place.

Now would probably be a great time to tell him I overheard the conversation myself—put it all out there, have the fight, clear the air before it grows into a secret—but he keeps speaking before I can interject.

"But it's more than that," he says. "People on the internet don't *know* us. And if you only go by what's written in black and white, it just doesn't seem like we make any sense. All your old blog posts and articles... *I* think they're adorable and hilarious because I know you. But it's all very young and messy and not the kind of thing my name should be associated with. I have to maintain a certain image of credibility."

The implication behind his words stabs me in the chest. "So it's not your gayness you're ashamed of. It's just me. Like, as a person."

"I didn't say that."

"You didn't have to."

"Ray..."

"What if I was a person your father respected? What if I was ten years older and had a better-paying job and had never posted all about the fucked-up exploits of my teens and twenties on the internet? Would you have agreed to the *Times* announcement then? Would you be agreeing to the earlymoon piece now?"

"Babe, I don't wanna fight. Come on." He lowers his head, sighs. "You know what? Fine. Just mention me by first name. That's fine."

This doesn't feel at all like the victory I'd thought it would.

"Can I kiss you?" I ask, leaning in. "Right now? Publicly?"

"Now you're just being petulant."

I slam back against my seat. "Right. Petulant. Because it's so bratty to want to kiss the man I'm going to marry in two months."

We both release long, frustrated sighs. I can tell he's just as disappointed as I am that we're starting our vacation off on this note. It's unlike us—one thing we've had in common ever since our first fight is the fact that we both hate fighting—and it's all my fault for thinking now was the best time to spring the idea of a personal essay on him for the first time in the history of our relationship.

I slurp down another oyster and try to quiet my frustration. I don't want this to turn into a huge thing. Every time Kip and I fight, I become paralyzed with the fear of losing him. It's irrational—he's done everything to prove he's all in on our relationship, not least of which was proposing marriage—but my track record haunts me.

My relationships prior to Kip were all so dysfunctional that each and every fight had the potential to turn into *the* fight—the one that ended it all. And even if they didn't end things, they'd still be generally excruciating. Byrd, for example, was so stubborn that he'd stay mad for several days after even the most inconsequential disagreement, which was torture for me as someone whose impulse is to resolve conflict as quickly as possible.

Kip also has the impulse to resolve things quickly—not because he's afraid of losing me but because he's a logical person and doesn't believe in wasting time and energy on silly arguments—but his method is different. While I need to talk, talk, talk about every detail until we're back on the same page, he simply needs an hour or two alone. After decompressing, he's always quick to both offer and accept apologies.

But he needs the alone time first.

Which, considering how limited our time at this resort is, really sucks.

"Why don't we split up for a bit?" he says. Calm and measured and right on cue. "I saw their golf course has a range attached. I could stand to hit a few balls before we play this weekend. And maybe you can get a jump start on research for your article..."

Even though I knew this was coming, I can't stop myself from trying to protest. The thought of being abandoned by him right now—*here* of all places—activates a storm in my chest. "I don't want to get a jump start on my article. I just want to—"

"I'm not abandoning you," he says, literally reading my mind. "I just feel like we both need a second to pause and think."

I consider protesting further, but it's clear he's already made this decision for the both of us.

"Fine," I choke out. "Fine."

"Dinner." Kip flags the waiter and tells him to charge the meal to our room. "We'll get things back on track at dinner."

10

A thought washes over me, repeatedly, nastily—unlike the very pleasant saltwater waves currently washing over my feet—as I stroll the beach alone.

Kip is ashamed of me.

That's what he meant when he talked about his "credibility" being compromised by my name popping up in his search results.

Why does he care so much about something he barely has any control over?

Just to torture myself, I plop down into the sand and pull out my phone to Google him.

The first hit is the professional bio at his practice's website.

Kip Hayes, MD, has been caring for patients out of our midtown office since 2009. Dr. Hayes obtained his undergraduate degree from Columbia in 2001, his medical degree from Weill Cornell in 2005, and completed his residency at Yale New Haven in 2008. Board-certified in family medicine, Dr. Hayes is passionate about helping patients reach and maintain optimal health.

Below is a picture of him in a white coat—light-blue oxford and navy tie peeking out underneath—looking so impossibly friendly I wouldn't be surprised if they used this picture in a promotional brochure for antidepressants.

Both the bio and the photo serve as stark reminders of just how differently we exist in the world. He's a forty-five-year-old physician numerous patients trust with their lives. Of course he doesn't want them to know the person he's chosen to spend his life with is a messy millennial blogger whose primary contribution to society is deeply unserious internet content about celebrities and sex toys.

For a brief moment I imagine an alternate universe where Professional Kip—*Dr. Hayes*—is actually proud of both me and his gayness. That version of Kip would probably have wanted us to get engagement rings, purely so he could gush to all the nurses about how lucky he is that I said yes to his proposal. He'd probably be all over social media. A hot gay doctor dispensing free medical advice? He'd be a TikTok celebrity. I could already see the viral clips of him in scrubs (even though he never wears scrubs), smizing at the camera as he talks about the crucial difference between LDL and HDL cholesterol, casually dropping references to his lovably wacky young fiancé.

"If you aren't following Ray's work on *Appeal* yet, what are you even doing with your life?" he'd ask his followers. "Last week he ranked all of Taylor Swift's exes based on what kind of cereal they'd be! Jake Gyllenhaal was Apple Jacks. Calvin Harris was Grape Nuts. Joe Alwyn was Kashi! My future husband is a genius."

I snap out of the daydream upon the realization that I'm not imagining an alternate version of Kip so much as I'm imagining an alternate version of *myself* if I were Kip. I've heard what Kip has to say about social-media-famous (or *any* famous) doctors before. He thinks they're all narcissistic hacks. If they truly cared about medicine, they'd be performing research and caring for patients, not gazing at their own reflections in smartphone cameras.

It's a fair point, even if it does discount the possibility that some doctors actually do use social media for good, to educate people who might otherwise not have access to basic healthcare.

But if Kip feels this way about medical professionals on social media, what does that say about how he views *my* career choice?

Maybe he's never truly taken me seriously.

I know he loves me, but there must be a part of him that believes he knows—or perhaps even *is*—better than me. How could he not? He has a decade on me.

Sometimes I'll think back to myself a decade ago and cringe at what a mess I was, but then I cut my past self some slack knowing that I still had so much to learn back then. So when I see a twenty-five-year-old do or say some dumb shit, I try to cut them some slack, too.

It's quite possible Kip views me with some version of this same filter.

Perhaps there's always been this imbalance between us that I willfully ignored because on some level, I liked deferring to him as the adult in the relationship. Maybe the safety I've always felt from him is simply the result of me handing him the keys and letting him make all my decisions for me.

As I stand up and head back to the hotel, my mind wanders to a memory from that first date of ours—the one when he told me he'd Googled me and nearly ended our relationship before it began.

We both showed up to the bar directly from work that night, which meant he was in pressed slacks and a fitted dress shirt. Meanwhile, my ensemble consisted of ripped jeans and a vintage Shania Twain graphic tee.

I immediately wished I'd taken CeCe's advice of changing into something less juvenile before the date—"This guy sounds like an *adult*-adult," she'd advised—but for some reason I insisted on being myself.

Kip tensed up upon seeing me—probably questioning every life choice that had led him to that moment—but he seemed to relax after a few sips of pale ale. Soon enough the conversation was flowing as easily as it had during our unexpected oyster meet-cute.

"You don't have a passport?" he asked me at one point, incredulous, after I explained to him that I'd never traveled internationally before. The word *passport* wasn't even in my family's vocabulary. My father was a third-generation lobsterman. Once the Brunos settled in Seabrook, they never left.

"I never even traveled by plane until a few years ago," I added with a shrug. "My childhood was just very local yokel, you know?"

The waitress delivered our meals just then—a sad-looking fillet of grilled salmon for him, a mouthwatering burger with a fried egg on top for me.

"Speaking of egg yolks," I said. "Have you—"

I cut myself off upon noticing a look of confusion cross Kip's face.

"What?"

"We weren't speaking of egg yolks."

"Yokel..." I realized as I said it that, despite my brain having always envisioned the word *yokel* having a yolky connotation, the words actually have nothing to do with each other. "Well, it sounds yolk-adjacent."

Kip chuckled and shook his head. "I guess I see the logic there."

"I was just trying to segue into asking you if you've ever had a burger with a fried egg on it," I said. "Have you? The combination is truly life-changing."

"Can't say that I have."

"Aha!" I said. "So I've never traveled internationally, but *you've* never had a burger with a fried egg on top. When it comes to who's more worldly, I'd say we're just about even."

He laughed. "It's a little harder to see the logic on that one."

I took a huge bite.

"At my age," Kip said, "and with my profession, all I see when looking at that is a clogged artery."

I put the burger down, as it suddenly tasted like edible death.

He cleared his throat. "Sorry! I'm not judging your dinner selection. You're young—your body can certainly handle the occasional indulgence. Please, please, eat."

I opted not to tell him that my burger consumption was far more than occasional.

"I'm gonna be thirty in a month," I said. "You're...what? Thirty-five?"

"Forty," he corrected me. "In two months."

So we officially had a decade between us. I had suspected a somewhat significant age gap from the moment we met, but something about hearing it confirmed out loud was fascinating. Given the life experience and pedigree he had on me, I would've expected to feel so intimidated by his presence—out of place and out of my depth.

But instead I felt completely comfortable. While nothing about us made sense, somehow I felt we had something invisible in common. In a way I couldn't (and still can't) articulate, I detected an overwhelming sense of sameness beneath the surface.

"So you were born in, like, the seventies?" I asked him.

"The very *late* seventies," he said. "Don't age me even more."

"You're one of those Gen X people," I teased.

"And you're a dreaded millennial," he said. "I'm pretty sure we should hate each other."

This was back in 2018—before Gen Z came along and made us both feel ancient.

"I'm actually quite jealous of you," I told him. "It must have been so awesome to be a teenager in the nineties. And to be in *college* in the nineties! I loved everything about that decade—the movies, the music, the—"

"You were just a little kid," he interjected. "You couldn't have loved it that much."

"I was old for my age," I insisted. "My favorite television show was *Ally McBeal*."

"The dancing baby?" He raised an eyebrow. "I've never seen an episode."

"First of all, the baby was a very small plot point in season one. The show itself was about a hapless young lawyer's neurotic search for love," I told him. "See? I'm far more of a nineties expert than you."

"Impossible."

I sat up. "Name three artists who've performed at Lilith Fair."

"Seriously?"

"I'll go first: Tracy Chapman, Lisa Loeb, Sheryl Crow."

"Good ones," he said through a smile. "Um. Let's see. Sinéad O'Connor...Natalie Merchant...Tori Amos—"

"Wrong! Tori never played Lilith."

"What? That's impossible. She *had* to have."

"You'd think so," I said. "But she didn't. Google it."

He did. And then he laughed and threw a hand up. "Alright, alright, you win."

"Thank you."

"Touring feminist folk festivals aside, you know what I loved most about that decade?" he said. "The lack of technology. That was the best part."

"So that's why you're not on social media," I replied. "Because you're a Luddite."

His eyes lit up. "You Googled *me*, too? I'm touched."

"And I found absolutely nothing of value," I complained. "It's like you don't even exist outside of your identity as Dr. Hayes."

He nodded in satisfaction. "That's how I like it."

"Are you a serial killer?" I asked. "Oh my God. A serial killer with a medical degree. This is not going to end well for me and/or my organs."

Kip nearly spit out his beer. "How does me not being on social media make me a serial killer?"

"Because that's how cases are solved. Social media activity offers more clues than just about anything else. The fact that you eschew it altogether is highly suspicious."

I hoped he could tell I was joking, so it was a relief when I got a chuckle out of him.

"I just think people don't value anonymity enough," he said. "All I've ever wanted was to help my patients at work, build a comfortable home, have fun on weekends. A normal life. But these days it's like everyone wants to be famous for no reason, like everyone thinks their life is more interesting or remarkable than the next person's. It honestly strikes me as a sickness." A few moments of silence passed before he followed it up with, "No offense."

"Just because I share every embarrassing detail of my life online doesn't mean I think it's remarkable!" I protested. "And I don't want to be famous."

It was somewhere between a truth and a lie. When I was a pop-culture-obsessed kid back in the nineties, yes, I definitely dreamed of fame and fortune. I had all the classic fantasies that friendless gay kids have: the rags-to-riches, geek-to-chic transformation, showing up to my high school reunion via private helicopter like Alan Cumming in *Romy and Michele*.

But at thirty? I wasn't delusional. I just wanted to stay employed and continue getting paid to write. Sure, I occasionally got a rush of dopamine when one of my blog posts or tweets would go viral, but...well, okay. Maybe a part of me did still want to be acknowledged more than the average person.

"I didn't mean to sound judgmental," Kip offered. "I've read quite a few of your articles. Once I got sucked in, I couldn't stop. They're really entertaining." He paused. "I would venture to say that you actually *are* more remarkable than most people. Any fame of yours would surely be warranted."

If he had proposed marriage right then and there, I would've accepted.

"Which article was your favorite?" I asked.

"Hmmm." Kip blushed. "Probably that one about the time you passed out while getting blood drawn, and then almost dropped the casket while you were a pallbearer at your great-aunt's funeral later that morning. That post had me laughing out loud on my lunch break. I'm so sorry for your loss, by the way." He paused. "The next time you get blood drawn, try to drink half a gallon of water beforehand. That's what I advise my patients with difficult veins. It'll help the blood flow more easily."

I smiled as I pictured him sitting in his office with a Tupperware salad, reading my words on his computer screen. "Thank you for the free medical advice. Did you also read the one about when I had to give a urine sample but then accidentally spilled it all over the floor before I could screw the lid on?"

He cracked up. "You really don't have a great track record when it comes to lab work."

We went back and forth on a few more of my articles—some he'd read, others he said he couldn't wait to look up on his train ride home—and although I pretended to be embarrassed that a potential suitor had so much access to my life history, I secretly relished the idea of capturing his attention with my stories. It struck me as magical that someone like him could enjoy reading the work of someone like me, evidence that opposites do indeed attract under the right conditions, with the right words.

"You owe me one," I told him toward the end of the night.

Kip's brow scrunched up in curiosity.

"An embarrassing story," I said. "As much as I loved hearing about your semester in Spain and your big poker win in Vegas, I feel like the humiliation factor is severely imbalanced now that we've talked about so many of my articles."

"That's fair," he admitted. "I suppose I just don't get embarrassed easily."

I shot him a blank stare.

He smiled sheepishly. "I guess my divorce? That has probably been the most embarrassing experience of my life thus far..." His voice trailed off. "Hold on. Let me think of an actually funny story. I don't mean to freak you out by bringing up my divorce."

"I'm not freaked out."

Having been fresh off my breakup with Byrd, I could relate to the feeling of being ashamed. I hated that my judgment was revealed as being so poor that I made a lifelong vow to someone I couldn't even last a year with; hearing Kip allude to his own experience with divorce actually made me feel like we had some unexpected common ground.

"I'm still recovering from my own divorce," I continued. "How long were you and your ex-wife together?"

Kip sighed. "Over twelve years. She's an incredible person. I loved her so much—as a friend, at least, which was enough for me for a while."

"It was?" I asked.

"It was," he said. "There were so many years where I was able to compartmentalize, put my sexual desires in a box, forget about them, and we were *happy*. We lived a great life out on Long Island for most of my thirties. My parents were so proud, even if they sometimes nagged us about starting a family."

As he spoke, I remembered one of the only other results that came up in my Google search of him. An image from some hospital charity gala on the Upper West Side. He and his ex-wife in formal wear—tux for him, black cocktail dress for her—smiling beside a champagne fountain. *The Foundation thanks Dr. Kip Hayes and his wife, Annie, for their generous donation.*

And now he was at a divey English pub in Midtown, swapping stories with a gay blogger in aggressively ripped denim and Shania Twain fan apparel.

"If you don't mind my asking…" I started.

"Why'd we break up?" he finished for me. I nodded, and he continued. "We both just ran out of steam. She knew I was gay before I ever admitted it to her—or even myself. How could she not know? She'd had boyfriends before me, and I wasn't nearly as sexual with her as they'd been." He cleared his throat. "The closer we got to forty, the more I think we both had the same revelation. She wanted to be with a man who actually wanted her, and I wanted to be with a *man*, period."

There was a vulnerability to the way he spoke that made me feel for both him and Annie, even though I couldn't quite relate. I had dreamed of being in a straight marriage as a kid, but that dream went up in flames the second I hit puberty and realized how powerless I was against my raging desire for dick. Even as I tried to tame it during my adolescent years in the closet, deep down I knew it was a futile endeavor.

The fact that Kip *was* able to tame it for his entire adult life thus far struck me as both an incredible feat of willpower and also the saddest thing I'd ever heard.

"Do you still keep in touch?"

He shrugged. "Not anymore. She kept the house, already has a new guy living with her. I moved here to the city. She forgave me, but I have to live with the fact that I ate up years of her life. It was very selfish. We had some fun together, but I wasn't being honest with her about who I was. I'll probably always feel terrible about it."

"You weren't being honest with yourself," I offered. "It's not like you were being actively malicious."

"Of course not," he conceded through a wistful sigh. "I suppose it all worked out as well as it possibly could have. I'm glad she's happy now."

I raised my pint glass. "To Annie."

Kip's head tilted. "Are we seriously about to toast to my ex-wife? I must admit I didn't have this on my first-year-of-gay-dating bingo card."

"Okay, yeah, that was weird of me." I lowered and re-raised my glass. "To you, then. May your life only get gayer from here on out."

As our relationship developed over the coming weeks, months, and years, I grew to love the way our lives were two entirely different gay movies. Mine was a lowbrow romantic comedy; his was a prestige drama about the metaphorical closet. (He'd be played by an A-list straight actor, who'd inevitably win an Oscar for the role. I would for sure be portrayed by an obscure gay comedian who screams a lot.)

Our differences eventually became my favorite thing about us. Our strength. He was a lover of stability and routine, and I was someone who *wanted* those things but oozed chaos, and together we achieved a happy medium. He had years of life experience on me, but I had years of *gay* experience on him. So we took turns being each other's teachers. He taught me about golf and fiscal responsibility; I taught him about bears (burly hairy gays), otters (skinny hairy gays), giraffes (tall gays), and the importance of quality lube.

Looking back on the past six years, our differences have brought us together far more than they've ever driven us apart.

And yet here I am, alone during our earlymoon, Googling him from the beach while he practices his swing at the range.

11

I still have a couple hours to kill before meeting Kip for dinner at the resort's steak house, and I don't feel like sulking anymore. Not on the beach, not in our room, not anywhere.

So instead, I opt for the cabana bar up on the second patio level, which overlooks the massive pool on the first patio level and the beach below that. (The back of the hotel is essentially a never-ending staircase of waterfront resort clichés.)

I signal the bartender and order a piña colada with a dark rum floater—not my go-to vacation drink, but rum always hits me quickly and I need these two hours to speed by in a blur. Mainly so Kip and I can hurry up and squash our fight before it festers and grows into something malignant.

I realized down at the beach that I've already gotten what I wanted anyway—he agreed to let me write the article using his first name—so now I just need to reset the energy between us. Apologize for losing my temper and threatening him with a public kiss. Give him a chance to assure me that he's not ashamed of me—or himself—and that his preoccupation with keeping a squeaky-clean online footprint is merely some residual brainwashing from his uptight father. Maybe he'll even admit to calling me a "buddy" to Jake and Lucy, and explain that he only did it because he was caught off guard by seeing someone from so far back in his past.

This trip can still be the earlymoon of my dreams.

"Here you are, mate." The bartender—a randomly Australian beefcake whose name tag says Lance—slides me my drink. I twirl the rum floater around with the drink's paper umbrella before he chastises me for apparently breaking some kind of rule. "Next time I'll just mix it in for ya." He flashes a smile. "Cheers."

I thank him for the frozen alcohol and begin inhaling it through my straw. The icy sweetness rushes to my head in a tsunami-like fashion.

And then my phone buzzes with a text from CeCe.

Feel free to ignore me, she writes. I know you're on vaca! But Sub Zero has been breathing down my neck since I told her you canned the piece. She loved the idea so much she wants me to assign it to a freelancer, so this is your last chance to change your mind before someone else gets an all-expenses paid trip to the Earlymoon Hotel.

Oh. I'd totally forgotten to fill CeCe in that I've already changed my mind. But now it looks like that was a good thing.

Wait, I text back. Does this mean I can now expense my trip if I say yes?

That's exactly what it means, writes CeCe. You're welcome.

Kip will love this. He doesn't have a problem being the primary breadwinner in our relationship—we split our mortgage based on a relative percentage of our incomes—but he always gets excited when my job involves free shit. It's one of the only career perks he's never experienced firsthand, save for the occasional hospital pen or pharmaceutical-company swag bag.

Consider my mind changed, I write back.

I knew it! she replies. Okay. I'll let Sub Zero know and let you go back to making love with your future husband. Mwah!

A few seats down from me, a couple giggles over a pair of margaritas. I creep on them from the corner of my eye—he's rubbing the small of her back as she rests a hand on his thigh—and feel yet another tsunami-like rush in my head, this time of jealousy.

It's not that I have some intense urge to engage in that kind of thoughtless PDA with Kip, but something in me does want it to at least be an option. The look in his eyes when I suggested we kiss at lunch earlier made his feelings toward the matter crystal clear, which makes me wonder what's going to happen at our actual wedding.

He knows we'll be expected to kiss at the altar—and several times throughout the reception—and yet the thought of doing so in any other context seems to induce pure terror. Is it because he feels like he'll have more control over an environment made up entirely of our friends and family—no risk of undercover homophobes in the room? Or is it just because a wedding is a setting in which PDA is automatically understood as not just appropriate, but required?

But then what about the first dance?

Kip and I have attended more weddings than I can count over the past several years, and we haven't slow-danced at a single one of them, the ballads always serving as an unspoken cue to either go pee or fetch another drink from the bar. It crushes my heart a little each time it happens, but I can't blame the pattern entirely on Kip. I'm always hyperaware of the fact that weddings are full of the friends and family of whoever invited us, and statistically speaking there's usually a good chance that at least a few people would be scandalized by two dudes slow-dancing. And even if they weren't, just knowing about the possibility of such people being in attendance is enough to take all the fun out of it for me. I'd worry we were making a spectacle of ourselves during a time that should be all about the bride and groom. I realize these concerns are total bullshit, but they're bullshit that I've somehow internalized nonetheless.

I take another sip of colada and look away from the couple, catching sight of a sign behind the bar announcing the resort's upcoming Lobster Fest, this Sunday night at the grand pavilion.

JOIN US FOR A MAGICAL NIGHT OF LOBSTER, COCKTAILS, AND DANCING AS WE CELEBRATE THE EARLYMOON HOTEL'S FIF-TIETH ANNIVERSARY! BEACH ATTIRE OK, BUT SHIRTS AND SHOES REQUIRED.

Maybe (probably) it's the rum hitting me, but I decide to inter-pret the timing as a sign from the universe.

Kip and I will attend the event, where we'll throw aside all of our hang-ups and hit the dance floor for every slow song—regardless of how many guests might stare. I already have our private lesson scheduled for Friday, so it's perfect. Lobster Fest will be a low-stakes chance for us to rehearse our new moves. (Not that I'm exactly sure what "moves" to expect to learn that I hadn't already picked up eighteen years ago at prom, but I am looking forward to figuring out exactly where each of us should put our hands.)

"Are you waiting for someone?"

The voice comes from behind, and then its owner plunks down in the stool next to me. An amber-haired beauty I instantly recognize from my balcony eavesdropping moment earlier—Jake's fiancée, Lucy.

"Or can I sit here?" she asks.

I nearly choke on a chunk of pineapple as I attempt a verbal response, so instead I answer with a curt smile-and-nod combo.

"Thanks," she says, then orders a strawberry daiquiri.

Her presence compels me to bury my face in my phone, which is still open to my text chain with CeCe. If I didn't know who Lucy was, I'd definitely use this as an opportunity to strike up a conversa-tion, feel her out, see if she might be interested in being quoted in my piece. But since I *do* know who she is, I need to guzzle the remainder of my piña colada and get as far away from her as possible. My penchant for oversharing intimate details of my personal life with women I meet and become instant besties with at bars is a dangerous liability right now.

I take a vigorous sip through my straw and nearly wail from the brain freeze.

Lucy giggles beside me. "You okay, Sparky?"

I flash a tight-lipped smile and give her a thumbs-up as she receives her daiquiri and takes a similarly vigorous sip.

"Christ! That's cold." She squinches her face tight and slaps her head. She looks exactly like a young Debra Messing from this angle, despite sharing a name with the most iconic redheaded sitcom actress of all time. (Although some people—by which I specifically mean myself and most gay men born between 1970 and 1989— might argue that Debra is an equally iconic redheaded sitcom actress.) "I should've learned from your mistake."

Shit. She's trying to make small talk, and I'm running out of evasive nonverbal responses. Also inconvenient is the fact that I *want* to talk to her. She is fully Grace Adler in my mind at this point, and the rum in my system has me eager to assume the role of Will Truman.

"They should call it brain *squeeze*," I attempt. Crickets. "Because, you know, it really feels like someone is squeezing your brain…" Attempting to say something insightful has made it painfully apparent that I'm more buzzed than I'd thought I was. "Whereas to actually *freeze* a brain, I imagine, it would take some time. Think about how long it takes for a tray of ice cubes."

Lucy half laughs. "Are you okay?"

"I may have had some rum," I admit. "Hi. I'm Ray."

"Nice to meet you, Ray." She crosses her legs in my direction and extends a hand. Her nails are shiny and flamingo pink. "I'm Camille."

I acccpt her handshake and nearly begin saying, "Nice to meet you, Lucy," until my brain catches up to the fact that she definitely gave me a fake name just now.

Unless this isn't Lucy? But no. I remember the hair, the bikini—which is still mostly visible under her sheer white sarong—the voice. This is one hundred percent Lucy.

But I have to pretend her name is Camille, for some goddamn reason.

"So what brings you to the Earlymoon Hotel?" Lucy-Camille asks me.

I consider my answer for a moment before deciding on complete honesty, mainly because the knowledge that she's actively spinning her own web of lies is giving me anxiety on her behalf. If she asks too many follow-up questions, I'll just have to think of some creative way to conceal Kip's identity.

"Here on an earlymoon with my fiancé," I tell her. "And I'm a writer. Doing a story on the hotel for *Appeal*."

"Shut up!" she says. "I love *Appeal*. My sorority house had a subscription. I used to devour every issue from cover to cover when I should've been studying."

This makes me like her, because I used to be the exact same way back when *Appeal* came in glossy magazine form. Even though they'd already transitioned to a digital-only model by the time CeCe hired me, landing a job at such an iconic media brand felt a little like winning the lottery (minus the, y'know, money).

"Do you still read it?" I ask, because how amazing will it be if it turns out she's a fan of my work? I sit up a little straighter, preparing myself for a shower of praise.

"I've never bothered getting an online subscription," she says instead. RIP to my ego. "Their paywall is a bitch."

"It's worth it! You should sign up."

"Perhaps I will." She twirls a lock of hair and leans toward me. "So tell me about this fiancée. Where is she right now?"

I burst out into a full-blown cackle. Lucy-Camille's daiquiri must be stronger than it looks. I haven't been mistaken for straight in years.

"What's so funny?" she asks.

"Nothing," I explain. "Just that my fiancé is a man. I'm gayer than a Fig Newton."

"Oh." She sounds disappointed. "I should've known a straight man wouldn't write for *Appeal*." She pauses and collects an errant thought. "What's so gay about Fig Newtons? My grandmother loved Fig Newtons."

"I dunno," I admit. "It just feels like a gay cookie, spiritually."

She holds in a laugh. "And what would you say is a...spiritually *straight* cookie?"

I pause for a moment before landing on the obvious answer. "Nilla wafers."

"My grandmother loved those, too!"

I clink my colada against her daiquiri. "Cheers to Grandma. A sexually fluid cookie icon."

We share an awkward laugh, and then Lucy-Camille's energy seems to deflate even more than it did previously. I worry that I've killed her buzz by conjuring memories of a dead relative, so I scramble to change the subject.

"To answer your earlier question," I say. "My fiancé is currently clearing his head at the driving range. Day One of our earlymoon and we've already had a small fight."

Why I felt the need to spill these details to a stranger who won't even trust me with her true identity is beyond me, but my impulse to overshare gets the best of me.

Lucy-Camille makes a pouty face. "I'm sorry. What was the fight about?"

I shake my head. "The article, I guess? He didn't want me to mention him in my work—never has. My editor even has a connection at the *New York Times* Vows section, and they were going to do a whole profile of us, but then K..." I cut myself off upon remembering that she met Kip earlier today and knows his actual name. "My fiancé squashed the piece! So I don't know. I always figured stuff like this was just because he's a super-private person, but lately I kinda feel like it's more that he's ashamed of *me*, specifically. Like if I was a buttoned-up doctor like him, he'd have no problem telling the world about our love."

Fuck. I probably shouldn't have mentioned that he's a doctor if I want to keep his identity shrouded in mystery.

I expect Lucy-Camille to perk up and tell me that her fiancé is a doctor too, but she doesn't. Instead, she says, "That's so weird. You'd think he'd be proud to have such a creative husband! *Appeal* is a legitimate publication."

"Thank you!" I say. "He *should* be proud of me."

I realize after I say it that I'm not giving Kip nearly enough credit. Because I know he's proud of me and my work. He doesn't gush about it to a ton of other people, but he always tells *me* how much he loves my articles. He still reads them on his lunch break; I know because we often talk about them at dinner.

"Have you always been a DC?" Lucy-Camille asks.

"A what?"

"Doctor chaser," she says.

"God, no." The idea that I could've sought Kip out for his profession is truly laughable. Not only because neither of us did any seeking in the first place—the universe simply threw us together—but also because prior to Kip, I'd never have considered being in a relationship with someone in his line of work. Growing up in a lobstering community like mine, doctors weren't husbands or family members or even friends—they were mythical authority figures you'd see when you had a problem that needed to be solved. Like the Wizard of Oz, except in scrubs and/or a white coat. (That, or they were tourists.) "I always thought I'd end up with someone more like myself. My first husband was a writer."

She raises an eyebrow as she looks me up and down. "You're divorced?"

I offer a sheepish smile and search for a subject change. I'd rather not get into a whole thing about Byrd.

"What about you?" I ask. "Are you a...DC?"

Lucy-Camille laughs. "Well, my fiancé *is* a cardiologist..."

"So you're also on an earlymoon?" I ask. "I should ask you some questions for my article."

I'm not quite sure if I want her to say yes or no. On the one hand, it would be great if I could ride our rapport into a few spicy pull quotes. On the other hand, I'd be quoting a woman who I know is actively lying about her identity. Even for a lighthearted story like this (which I doubt *Appeal* would bother to thoroughly fact-check), that sounds like fairly shitty journalism.

But maybe if we get deep enough into this conversation, she'll eventually tell me the truth.

Lucy-Camille plays with her left earlobe as she digs for a response, and I notice that all the fingers on her left hand are bare. No engagement ring.

"I'm sorry," she finally says. "My situation is too complicated to speak about on the record. I would need several more of these in my system"—she waves her half-empty daiquiri in the air—"to even speak about it *off* the record."

A part of me wants to encourage her to drink up, because I couldn't possibly be more intrigued by what I'm becoming increasingly convinced is the double life she leads. But the other part of me feels like I should distance myself from her entirely. Clearly she's got a lot going on—and could possibly be a con artist—and I have enough issues of my own to deal with right now.

"That's fair," I concede. "Totally understand."

She swivels her barstool slightly away from me. We quietly sip our respective frozen drinks for a few moments. The couple across the bar continues their giggling, seagulls caw in the distance, and the resort's sound system plays "Escape (The Piña Colada Song)" by Rupert Holmes at an audible yet inoffensive volume.

I feel weird with how we ended our conversation, so I attempt to fill the space with a painfully cheesy observation about the song's lyrics. "What the hell is going on in this song? I mean, honestly, who *likes* getting caught in the rain? And I find it so sad that this couple was literally out there trying to cheat on each other via personal ads, and when they realized what they were doing, no one was even mad?"

Lucy-Camille tosses me a polite fake-chuckle. "Maybe they were never monogamous to begin with. Maybe they had some kind of understanding."

"No way," I scoff. "The entire song is based on a *mis*understanding. Their communication style was just totally fucked up."

Lucy-Camille contemplates this for a few sips. Then the sipping turns into sucking—extremely vigorous sucking—until there's not a drop of daiquiri left.

"I gotta run," she says. "It was nice chatting with you… What was your name again? I'll look up your stuff on the site."

"Ray Bruno."

"Right. Ray. Got it." She jumps down from her stool and adjusts her sarong. "Good luck with the article."

She saunters away before I can even wrap my head around what just happened.

"Was she with you?" the bartender asks as we watch her disappear into the hotel. "She didn't pay for her daiquiri."

Aha! Maybe she *is* a con artist.

"She's not with me," I tell him. "I'm here alone."

That last sentence echoes in my mind long after it leaves my lips, until it eventually becomes a pit in my stomach. I'm here alone. Lucy-Camille's presence was such an effective distraction that I'd almost forgotten it's the first day of my earlymoon, and I'm here. Alone.

Dinner can't come soon enough.

12

The hostess leads me to a table by the window overlooking the beach, where Kip is already seated in the chair facing the inside of the restaurant. Whenever there's a choice between a good seat and a shitty one, Kip always volunteers for the latter. This reminder of his selflessness instantly relaxes me.

"Fiona Apple," he says as he stands and grabs the side of my waist.

"You already used her this week," I remind him with a playful smirk. "Emmylou Harris."

And then he gives me a quick kiss on the mouth. Right in front of the hostess—who smiles approvingly—and this entire dining room full of fellow earlymooners. There's a small pang of self-consciousness in my chest, but it's drowned out by my appreciation for the gesture Kip is making.

"Holy shit," I marvel as I take a seat. There's a bottle of Sancerre in an ice bucket on the table—which explains why his lips tasted like wine—and I pour myself a glass. "That was an unexpected but very welcome greeting."

Kip's face is ablaze with adrenaline. "I'm gonna be honest with you. That was extremely uncomfortable for me. My heart is racing right now."

"You kissed a boy," I tease, resisting the homosexual urge to sing the next few words in a full-on Katy Perry voice. "And you liked it." I gesture around at the restaurant. "And! Literally no one in here gave a shit."

He laughs.

"Thank you for making an effort," I offer a bit more sincerely. I'm sure he cased this place while he was waiting for me—scanning the dining room for Jake and Lucy-Camille—but still. It's clear he gained some perspective during his alone time. "I know that was a big deal for you."

"I thought about what you said earlier," he says. "And you were right. We're getting married in two months. I'm gonna need to get comfortable with a certain amount of PDA."

He bites his lip and then covertly points to a straight couple two tables down whose tongues are currently so deep in each other's mouths I'm surprised neither of them have induced vomit yet.

"But not that much," Kip adds. "That is where I draw the line." He pauses. "If I'm being technical, the line is actually much further back than that." Another pause. "Basically, the line is what we just did."

"That's fine by me," I assure him. "It's not like I want to approach anything near"—I tilt my head toward the tongue twins— "whatever that is."

He smiles. "I'm glad we're on the same page."

I'm also glad, even if there are other matters we're still not entirely aligned on. The main one being his characterization of our relationship to Jake and Lucy-Camille, but I can't bring myself to mention that at this point. A full day has passed, which means it's already crossed into "why didn't you say anything?" territory— which means it's already a secret—and besides, it's unclear what Lucy-Camille's real name even is. Clearly this isn't a situation where transparency reigns.

So I commit myself to enjoying the moment instead. Kip and I clink our glasses, place our orders, and talk about our plans for the week.

The food is cooked to absolute perfection. We each get the steak and lobster tail, which the waiter informs us is from Maine. It's probably an unremarkable detail to most, but for me, it's a pinprick to the chest. Both because it reminds me of Stef's plans to move there in the future, and because I'm old enough to recall when the Earlymoon Hotel exclusively served lobster caught right here in Seabrook.

I explain this to Kip, and he responds by asking, "How is your Pops? I feel like it's been forever since you called your parents."

All I can do is shrug. It's true that I don't talk to my parents nearly as much as I did before they moved to Florida, and I'm not sure exactly whose fault that is. On the one hand, I've always had a tendency to be so wrapped up in my relationships that I often forget about maintaining regular communication with my family. On the other hand, this is a quality that I've subconsciously picked up from observing their own marriage all my life. Back when my grandparents were alive, they always complained about my mom never calling them.

"He's fine," I tell Kip. "I'll call him next week. I wanna see if he's as worried as I am about Stef and her catch. It was brutal when I went out on the boat with her yesterday."

Kip frowns. "I'm surprised she's lasted this long, to be honest."

"She and Lenny are moving to Maine."

His eyes go wide. "When?"

"Not for a while." I realize she never gave me an exact timeline, but maybe if I say a long time out loud it'll come true. "Probably five years, at least."

"Wow," Kip marvels. "No more Brunos in Seabrook. It'll be the end of an era."

"She hasn't technically been a Bruno since she married Lenny."

"You know what I mean."

"Moving on," I attempt. "You haven't called your parents in a while, either."

Kip laughs. "I just spoke with them earlier."

"How *are* Marshall and Viola?"

"They're fine," he says. "Dad thinks this trip is a waste of vacation time. Mom thinks we should've made it two weeks instead of one."

I roll my eyes at this classic example of Hayes hijinks—each of his parents passing judgment on his choices in entirely opposite ways.

"I'm gonna have to side with Viola on that one," I admit.

Kip's smile flattens into a more pensive expression. "You know I'm not ashamed of you, right? My apprehension about all the online stuff is really just about work. It has nothing to do with *you*."

Given his timing, I can only deduce that the reason for his apprehension isn't exactly work itself; it's his father's perception of it. I've always known that Marshall was responsible for Kip's instinct toward conformity, but I hadn't realized until now how much of a blind eye I've always turned toward it. Marshall has come a long way since the night *he* introduced me as a "buddy" at his country club, but I could still easily see him advising Kip to keep his online footprint as clean as possible, if only for the sake of "the Hayes name." Surely he didn't go through all the trouble of changing its spelling only for his son to be publicly associated with the author of the 2015 *Microphone* post, "I Tried Six Different Prostate Massagers So You Don't Have To."

And you know what? Maybe that's fine.

Maybe our relationship has always worked so well *because* it takes place entirely offline.

My relationship with Byrd had been far too public to be healthy. Our two years together were exhaustively documented—in blogs and social media posts from both of our online personas—and that only added an extra layer of humiliation to the divorce. We'd made such a spectacle of our marriage that there was no way for our divorce not to be one as well. All I'd wanted to do was crawl into a hole during the initial aftermath, but I couldn't *not* post about it first.

Even before it all blew up—even when Byrd and I were at our happiest—the constant need to perform for an audience was tiring. If Byrd and I had been on vacation, at a dinner like this, both of us would be on our phones the whole time—taking selfies together, monitoring likes and shares, letting our food get cold as we snapped a million pics of it.

I don't miss any of that.

But still. It would be nice if Kip and I could find a happy medium.

Not even a medium, really.

Just...less of a paranoid fear about what would happen if my name *did* happen to pop up in a Google search of *Dr. Kip Hayes*.

As I contemplate this thought, I'm reminded of that picture of Kip and his ex-wife. The one that still shows up in his search results, from the hospital charity gala. Kip and I have been to a number of similar events in recent years—he donates to several causes—and yet we've never been professionally photographed together at any of them.

I asked him about this once, and he explained that he's always donated anonymously, as he thinks getting recognition for a donation undermines the spirit of giving in the first place. But Annie hated this policy—she put a lot of effort into her appearance at these galas and *wanted* to be seen on all the websites and newsletters—and was constantly pushing him to make a public contribution for once. That picture is evidence of the one and only time he relented.

And now it lives on forever.

As far as Google is concerned, they might as well still be married.

A part of me wonders if Kip realizes this.

I almost want to ask, but I don't want to sound like I'm accusing him of something. I don't want to think about any of this at all. So instead I think ahead—to an entirely different gala. The Lobster Fest taking place here at the hotel on Sunday night.

"There's going to be a big party here Sunday," I tell Kip. "An anniversary celebration at the grand pavilion."

He raises an eyebrow as he tops off our wineglasses.

"They're calling it Lobster Fest," I continue. "So we *have* to go. And we have that private slow-dance lesson on Friday, so the timing is perfection."

Kip's jaw twitches. "Why is it perfect?"

"Because we can practice our new moves there," I explain. "We've never slow-danced with each other, which, now that I've said it out loud, strikes me as truly absurd and incredibly sad. We have a lot of catching up to do before the wedding."

"We've slow-danced a bunch," he counters.

"I mean in public. Drunk in the kitchen at 2:00 a.m. doesn't count."

"I didn't realize the lesson was a confirmed thing," he says. "I thought it was just one of our options."

So the growth that compelled him to kiss me in this restaurant isn't quite strong enough to open his mind to the idea of a public slow dance. What I had thought was a leap of real progress was in fact just an impulsive dare.

"It's a *private* lesson," I emphasize. As if perhaps he'll be more open to the idea if he knows there won't be any spectators. As if I'm not also talking about how excited I am to have spectators just two days later. "Only us and the instructor."

"And who's the instructor?"

"I have no idea," I tell him. "Some trained professional."

Kip sighs in a cadence that distinctly reminds me of a child who's being told to eat more vegetables, even though he just choked down a full serving. "Would you be upset if we canceled the lesson?"

"We can't cancel the lesson." I try to sound as neutral as possible. The last thing I want is for this conversation to take a combative turn. "I prepaid…"

"I just wanna relax on the beach," he says. "Play some golf—"

"We have a tee time scheduled for Saturday," I remind him. "And all the time in the world to relax on the beach."

Our table goes quiet. I can tell Kip is feeling the same way I am—torn between pushing to get his way and wanting to avoid another argument.

"We can talk about it tomorrow," he suggests through a clenched jaw. "Let's just enjoy tonight."

13

~

"You know what, babe?"

Kip leans forward and flashes a sly smile. "What?"

I look into his eyes and feel so giddy that all I can do is laugh. It's been a few hours since dinner and we're finishing off yet another bottle of Sancerre at our high-top in the cabana bar, which has done wonders at shaking off the tension from earlier.

"Being on vacation is the best," I gush. "Isn't it just the best? We don't take enough vacations."

Another sly smile. "How drunk are you?"

"I have only the slightest of buzzes!" I protest. "I'm just saying, you know, look at this place…" I spread my arms out, directing his attention to our surroundings—the summer moonlight, the gentle waves. "If this were any other Wednesday night, you'd be at poker and I'd be…"

"Sitting at home waiting for me to get back from poker," Kip cracks.

"That's not what I do!"

"Really? So what did you do last Wednesday night?"

The truth is that I spent four hours meticulously deep-cleaning our oven while listening to a podcast about the making of *Notting Hill*…but it was less because the oven needed cleaning and more because, well, I was waiting for Kip to get back from poker.

"I don't remember," I lie.

"You're adorable," Kip says through a swallow of wine.

"I love you," I tell him. "I can't believe I get to marry you next month. It honestly feels like we're both getting married for the first time. I feel like neither of our first marriages counted."

He leans back in his wicker barstool and contemplates the suggestion.

"They didn't count," he agrees. "I was trying to be someone I wasn't. And so were you."

"Byrd knew I was gay."

Kip feigns a look of surprise. "He *did*?"

I playfully flip him the bird.

Kip continues. "I just meant that, based on everything you've told me about that marriage, it sounds like the whole thing was more for show than anything else."

Fair enough.

Even though Byrd was handpicked from a dating app specifically for all the qualities we had in common, I still never felt seen or understood by him. Maybe it was because so much of our story happened online—our first date didn't even occur until after several weeks of texting and social media stalking. Our digital selves fell in love before our real selves ever even had a chance to connect. And our real selves weren't nearly as compatible as we'd expected them to be.

"That whole relationship was just way too online," I admit.

"What's he up to these days?" Kip asks. "You never talk about him anymore."

"No idea." I blocked him across all platforms shortly before Kip and I met. Not because I'm in the habit of blocking exes, but because Byrd had a habit of sliding into my DMs every time he got drunk and lonely and thirsty for validation. It was exhausting having to remind him that *he* was the one who ended things. "I'm sure he's in another relationship by now... Maybe he got remarried. He was a serial monogamist like me."

I almost ask Kip what Annie's been up to since their divorce, but I already know the answer. She married an insurance guy and moved to the Boston area five years ago, where they immediately had a set of twins. It's always made Kip and me so happy that she ultimately found the happily-ever-after she deserved. Me because it was a win for *love*, and Kip because he'd never have forgiven himself if she didn't find someone else who was willing to give her the life she'd always wanted.

I raise my glass. "Here's to second marriages."

"To second marriages that feel like first marriages," Kip says with a wink. He finishes the Sancerre in his glass and adds, "Should we get a couple dirty martinis? Nightcap?"

"Did Jewel play the Lilith main stage in 1997?" I ask in response, meaning *duh*. "I'll go grab 'em at the bar."

The Australian bartender from earlier is still here, and he's absolutely drowning in orders.

A good three minutes passes before I get his attention, and then another two minutes before our drinks are finally ready.

As I walk back to Kip—slowly and carefully, as these martini glasses are filled right up to the lip—I nearly do a double take.

Two additional barstools have been pulled up to our table.

And they're occupied by Jake and Lucy.

Or Camille.

Or whatever the fuck her name is.

14

My entire body tenses as I approach the table with our martinis. And apparently so does Kip's. His facial muscles look like they're being held together by a rubber band, twisted and tugged in a thousand conflicting directions.

And then it snaps.

He shoots me a single pleading look—one I instantly interpret as *Please follow my lead and let me explain later*—before settling into a variety of fake smile I've only ever seen in his professional work portraits and old pictures of him and his ex-wife.

"Thanks," he says as I place his drink down. "Ray Bruno, this is Jake Meyers. One of my best buds from Cornell."

Jake raises his beer to greet me. "Nice to meet ya."

I settle into my stool and try not to think about the thick fog of unspoken chaos between the four of us. Jake thinks I'm Kip's golf buddy, Lucy thinks I think her name is Camille, and Kip thinks I don't know who either of these people are in the first place.

He must be dying inside, waiting for me to blow the cover on the true nature of our relationship any second now—either by calling him "babe" or making a comment about our wedding or making a nonsensical Lilith Fair reference or expressing a feminine trait of any kind, really.

But surely he has to know how ridiculous his cover story is. Two dudes at a romantic seaside resort for *several nights*—purely to play golf with each other? I mean, come on. He's gotta be planning to tell them the truth any minute now.

In the meantime, I'll just have to focus my attention on the martini I waited an eternity for. I take a massive swig, splashing half of it onto my chin in the process.

"You didn't tell us your golf buddy is a straight-up lush," Jake cracks and then laughs to himself. "I fuckin' love it, man."

There it is. The perfect segue for Kip to correct him.

Actually, he's my fiancé...

But instead Kip just laughs and shoots me another of those pleading looks—this time with a glint of desperation in his eyes. I try to ask myself what I would do if I hadn't already known who Jake and Lucy were going into this. Would I be picking up on Kip's subliminal message to play along? Or would I have corrected Jake on my own just now? I suppose it's impossible to know for sure. Especially when I'm this blotto.

Meanwhile, Lucy grabs my wrist from across the table.

"Hi!" she chirps as if we've never seen each other before. "I'm Jake's fiancée..." And then, fleeting but unmistakable, a pleading look of her own. "*Lucy.*"

I smile, nod, and sip my martini. The goal is to drain it as quickly as possible so I have a reason to get back up for a reprieve from this excruciating awkwardness.

Jake pats Lucy's thigh and addresses Kip and me from across the table. "So what's up with you guys? I've never taken a golf trip with less than a foursome. Just two dudes staying at a place like this...in this day and age... You know, everyone here probably thinks you guys are fucking." He launches into a *Seinfeld* impression—"Not that there'd be anything wrong with that!"—and then laughs at his own joke.

He's gotta be messing with us at this point, right?

He knows.

Kip has no choice but to respond with total honesty:

That is correct, we are indeed fucking—and wildly in love, engaged to be married, living a completely open life in Westchester that you've been oblivious to for the past six years because I'm a forty-five-year-old enigma.

But he doesn't say any of that. Instead he just clears his throat as Lucy slaps Jake's arm in admonishment. Meanwhile, I have no choice but to return to my binky (by which I mean vodka).

"Just bustin' your balls," Jake finally says. "I heard the course here is top-notch, fellas. Maybe I can get out for a round with you two one of these days—if the old lady lets me."

"Old lady?" Lucy says. "I'm twelve years younger than you, asshole." Okay, I love this woman. "And please *do* go! I'll be more than happy to take a self-care day. I've heard the spa complex here is a literal dream."

I shoot Kip a look. One that hopefully makes it very clear that while I might be willing to play along with this absurdity for a few late-night drinks, I refuse to spend eighteen holes of golf with this guy.

"I don't know if that's a great idea," Kip mutters.

"What? You're scared to get dominated like back in the day?" Jake taunts. Then he looks at me. "Ray, what's your handicap?"

I stuff my mouth with a martini olive and look the other way. Golf is one of my favorite activities, but I also suck at it. There's no way I'm admitting my handicap (which is north of thirty, stop judging me) to a guy like Jake.

Thank God Kip senses my discomfort and changes the subject.

"I can't believe it's been ten years since we've seen each other," he says. "How did we let that happen, man?"

Jake makes a face. "This is what happens when you don't have

Facebook. Until this morning, I legit thought you were still with Annie. Figured you had a couple kids by now..." He pauses. "What happened there? I could've sworn you two were lifers."

Kip takes a page out of my book, which is to say he goes head-first into his martini glass. After a moment he comes up for air and says, "Grew apart. You know how it is."

Jake lowers his voice. "Was she fuckin' around on you?"

Lucy slaps his arm again (something she's clearly quite used to doing). "Babe! That's so not—"

Kip replies with a curt *no*.

If I were still taking note of potential conversational openings for Kip to tell Jake the damn truth already—which I'm not, because they keep abounding and Kip clearly has no interest in seizing any of them—I might say this would be a great one.

Jake's mouth creeps into a smirk as he lowers his voice further. "Were *you* fuckin' around on her?"

"Drop it, man." Kip's voice takes on a note of stern finality, and I'm not gonna lie, it's kinda hot. "It was an amicable divorce."

Jake throws his hands up in surrender.

A breeze blows toward us from the water, prompting Lucy to wrap her cover-up around her freckled shoulders. I throw my head back for a moment, letting the air hit my eyes. The sensation wakes me up and heightens my buzz. If I have to be here with these people, I might as well try to have some fun with it.

"So!" I chirp. "When's the big day?"

"Last weekend of September," Lucy gushes.

"*Ours is the last weekend of August!*" is what I *want* to say—just to rip the Band-Aid off already—but I think better of it. Even if Kip is being wildly unfair to me right now, I wouldn't forgive myself if I drunkenly outed him over cocktails.

"That's wonderful," I say instead, keeping my voice low and

devoid of all personality—the best performance of heterosexuality I can muster. "How long have you been together?"

"Two years," Lucy answers. "Well, actually, gosh. We've known each other for four years. But Jake was a total dick for the first two. It was like pulling teeth getting him to commit to a relationship, let alone propose marriage."

Jake chuckles. "If I was such a dick, why'd you wait around?"

"I didn't," Lucy corrects him. "I was already with Peter by the time you came to your senses and said you wanted to get serious."

"Oh, right, Petey Boy…" Jake says. "I almost forgot about that little dweeb."

Lucy executes her third arm-slap in as many minutes. "He wasn't a *dweeb*. He was a nice guy."

"Exactly," Jake says through a cocky grin. "The last thing a woman wants is a nice guy. Am I right, boys?"

I recoil at the cartoonish display of bravado, but Kip does the opposite. He matches Jake's grin in a kind of telepathic high five. It occurs to me that his old closeted self must have been *such* an asshole. I probably wouldn't even recognize the version of him that existed fifteen or twenty years ago.

"There's nothing fuckable about a total wimp," Jake concludes. "A woman wants a man who will *take* her."

And then he has the nerve to throw his arm around Lucy.

She rolls her eyes but snuggles into his nook nonetheless. "You're such a caveman."

"And you love it."

Kip shoots me a please-don't-make-this-weird look, but I can't help myself from challenging him. He reminds me too much of the men I used to hook up with in my teens and early twenties—before I had enough self-esteem to know any better—and I regret never having challenged them on *their* bullshit.

"Plenty of women like nice guys," I say calmly.

Jake erupts into a fit of a laughter before looking at me and saying, "Oh. You're serious? Dude. Trust me. Plenty of women say they want a nice guy—but none of them actually mean it. They *love* assholes. It's just a fact."

I think about CeCe's husband, Connor, a nerdy software engineer who proposed to her via a custom app he developed specifically for the occasion. Or Stef's husband, Lenny, a lobsterman who often declares that his wife is stronger, smarter, and a better captain than he could ever be.

Jake is objectively wrong.

But he's clearly speaking from his own personal experience—which I don't doubt has involved getting plenty of ass in his day—so I acknowledge the morsel of truth in what he's trying to say: "I think you're only talking about your experience with a specific type of woman."

"Yeah," he cracks. "Hot ones."

I consider pulling up a picture of CeCe—an indisputable ten by any standard—but think better of it.

"For someone with a medical degree, you have such a simplistic view of how attraction works," I tell him, despite another one of those looks from Kip. "We're humans. Not lobsters."

"Who said anything about lobsters?"

Kip clears his throat. "Ray is from a local family of lobster fishermen…"

"Lobsters are simple creatures," I explain. "Males are divided into alphas—the dominant bullies who beat everyone up—and betas, the subordinates who just take the abuse. It's the female lobsters who initiate the mating process, but they only ever choose the alphas. They have to shed their shells to mate, which is a very vulnerable process, so they need to be sure their partner will protect them."

"And they mate for life!" Lucy chimes in. "I've always loved that episode of *Friends*, when Phoebe said Ross and Rachel were each other's lobsters." She cuddles up more closely to Jake. "So romantic."

I obviously love nineties sitcoms with a voracious passion, but that particular episode of *Friends* was a crock of shit.

"That's not actually true." I'm basically a mansplaining professor at this point, but for some reason I can't resist flaunting my useless knowledge. "They live together for some time while their shells grow back, but that's about it. Alphas have several partners. And if a female is ready to mate but only betas are available, she'll just wait around for the alpha to be done with his current partner. Basically, the betas just never get laid in their entire lifetime."

Jake cracks up.

"What's so funny?" I ask.

"You literally just proved my point," he says. "Humans and lobsters are the same. Which might explain why you're here with your buddy and not..."

"Alright," Kip interjects. "Let's change the—"

"Do you have any idea how much lower on the food chain a lobster is than a human?" I ask Jake. "Humans are complex, emotional, intelligent creatures." I shoot him a glare. "For the most part."

"I totally agree with Ray," Lucy says. "I'd hope we're a little more evolved than the crustacean I ate for dinner tonight. But I will admit..." She takes a sip of her daiquiri and hiccups. "Sometimes when I'm working out, I'll check out the guys at my Equinox. Sorry, babe! But I do."

Jake grimaces.

"And I gotta say," Lucy continues, "it's always the men with muscles who catch my attention the most." You know what? I'm starting to think Lucy might actually be a gay man trapped in a woman's body. "So maybe we aren't that evolved after all."

Jake instinctively flexes and checks out his own biceps. Kip continues his streak of awkward silence. I return my attention to my martini, but it's finally gone.

"I have to pee," I say quickly. "And then I'm getting another drink."

I don't bother asking if anyone else wants one.

15

As I dry my hands and exit the men's room, I'm immediately shoved back into it. Fight or flight kicks in for a millisecond—as if I'm being attacked in public at this highly secure and very sophisticated resort—but the flowery scent of Lucy's perfume quickly confirms that I'm merely being cornered by a drunk ginger.

"What the hell?" I ask.

She locks the door behind us. "Sorry! I'm just…"

"Engaged?" I suggest. "Not named Camille?"

"Thanks for not blowing my cover back there." She pulls her hair back and examines her face in the mirror. "Like I told you before, my situation with Jake is complicated."

I side-eye her from the closed toilet seat I've just settled onto. Something tells me we're gonna be a minute.

"And you're one to talk about honesty," she adds. "I looked up some of your stuff online, by the way—loved it. So fun."

My urge to interrogate suddenly takes a back seat to my ego's need to know more about her impression of my byline. "You Googled me? Really?"

"Of course," she says. "I especially loved your roundup of the best post-blow-job Listerine flavors. I did not expect to see *brown* take first place. What a plot twist. I didn't know people under the age of eighty even bought that one."

"It's the most effective at killing bacteria," I tell her. "Which, depending on whom you've just blown, can be of great importance—" I cut myself off upon realizing I've gotten very offtrack. "Why did you lie about your name earlier?"

"Why are you and Kip pretending to just be friends?" she counters. "I will say your man is very convincing. I'd honestly never guess." A pause. "You, on the other hand, with that whole lobster outburst…"

"That's because I'm not trying to convince anybody of anything! I haven't been in the closet since the Bush administration. Kip just threw me back into it for the night."

"Why? He's afraid of Jake's reaction?" She takes a moment to consider this. "I mean, sure, he's a total caveman. But he's not, like, violently homophobic or anything."

"Are you sure about that?" I ask. "Because if his views on women are any indication…"

"He's not that bad." She retrieves a tiny makeup bag from her purse and starts doing minor touch-ups. "And he's totally chill around my gay friends. Kip should tell him the truth. He'll be fine."

It occurs to me that Kip's jig is up anyway. There's no way Lucy won't tell Jake the truth the next time they're alone. They strike me as the kind of couple that likes to gossip about other couples for sport, and Kip's hidden sexuality would just be too good a nugget for Lucy to keep to herself.

A part of me feels relieved at the thought of her just putting it out there, but another part of me feels an impulse to protect Kip. Even if I do think he's being unreasonable in not telling Jake the truth, I still hate the idea of him being outed against his wishes.

Maybe I can bargain with Lucy—use my knowledge of her own dishonesty as leverage.

"Can you not tell Jake? Kip really should be the one to do it." With any luck, he's doing it right now, while they're alone at the table. "Let's make a deal. You don't say anything about Kip being gay, and I won't say anything about your secret identity."

"Blackmail?" A small laugh escapes her cherry lips. "You shady bitch. I love it! Deal."

Her laugh is contagious. I envy her ability to be so carefree, even in the face of what is clearly a heavy dose of relationship drama in both our lives.

The bathroom goes quiet, nothing but the sound of the overhead fan above us and the ever-present yacht rock pumping through the resort's sound system. As Lucy blots her face with a sheet of rice paper, I detect a flash of sadness in her eyes.

It's like she's looking in the mirror, yet doing everything she can to avoid actually looking at her*self*.

I'm dying to know what her story is.

"I just do this *thing* sometimes," she says—unprompted, as if she could sense all the question marks in my mind. "Put my engagement ring in my purse, flirt with a stranger, give him a fake name…"

"You were *flirting* with me?"

"That was the plan," she says. "Before we started talking and you told me you were gayer than a Fig Newton."

I laugh for a moment before the implication behind her admission catches up to me. "So you were looking to cheat on your fiancé *during your earlymoon*? This is supposed to be the most romantic week of your lives!"

Lucy rolls her eyes. "You sound like a pigtailed ten-year-old."

I ignore the diss and continue. "And where was Jake during all of this? Weren't you worried he'd see you?"

"Trust me, he's not the victim in our situation." Lucy lowers her voice. "He ditched the resort to go to Foxwoods—allegedly to cash out a sports bet he made the other day, but I'm sure he met up with a girl there. He's not a very good liar."

So this solves the mystery of why Lucy refused to speak on the record for my article. Which is for the best—a pair of cheaters actively embroiled in mutual deception is not the kind of couple I'm trying to highlight as the poster children of the Earlymoon Hotel.

"If you're both so unhappy, why are you getting married?" I ask.

"Who said we were unhappy? I'm happy enough."

"Happy people don't sneak around and lie to each other." I should be shutting this conversation down, but I can't help myself from defending the concept of love. "Especially during an early honeymoon."

"I love Jake," she insists. "He's not as big an asshole as he pretends to be. You should've seen him this morning at the pond over by the golf course. He was hand-feeding the ducks like they were little babies! Literally gave up half his sandwich. I mean, can you even?"

"But he cheats on you," I remind her. "And you cheat on him!"

"Oh, come on." Lucy squints at her reflection and plucks a rogue eyebrow hair. "It's not like I do it as a matter of habit—and I honestly wasn't looking for sex today. I just wanted to flirt a little. You know how it is. Don't you ever wanna sit next to something you know you can't have? Don't you ever miss that part of being single? The chase?"

"Not at all." Just thinking about all the chasing I did in my single years sends a shiver up my arm. "That's *why* I'm getting married. So I never have to chase anyone again."

Lucy glares at me through the mirror. "I call bullshit."

"Come again?"

"Do you love Kip?" she asks.

"More than anything in the world," I answer.

"You'd be lost without him? He's your everything? All that shit?"

"Yes," I proudly confirm. "All of it."

"Then you're just as much of a chaser as I am."

I'm inclined to challenge her on this, but she says it with such certainty that I can't help but give the idea some consideration. And you know what? Maybe I do chase Kip a little bit. I know he's mine, but there are parts of him that have still always felt somehow unattainable. I've been chasing him throughout our entire wedding planning process. If it *weren't* for all my chasing, we'd be getting married alone in a sterile courthouse on a weekday afternoon.

"Maybe you have a small point," I concede. "But still. I'd say your version of chasing is just a wee bit toxic, no? I imagine it'd be a lot healthier to just open up the marriage and call it what it is."

She laughs at the suggestion. "Have you *met* Jake?"

"Barely."

"He'd never go for something as nontraditional as an open marriage. He's too consumed with appearances."

"And you're seriously okay with this?"

Lucy rolls her head back, tugs at her hair, then stares into the mirror. Throughout this conversation, her face has gone from having a blurry late-night sheen to being perfectly in focus—all clean lines and a bright, dewy finish.

"It's complicated," she finally says. "Jake and I have a good life together. He's a handsome doctor... I want babies... And I'm not trying to be a *working* mother. So what if we mess around a little? It actually keeps things kind of interesting."

"'Interesting' is one way to put it." But really, the word that most comes to mind is *sad*. I can't help but think about what Stef said the other night at dinner, about marriage being a resigned compromise based on a lifelong fear of dying alone.

"That said," Lucy adds, "I appreciate you not telling him about our run-in. Our whole dynamic kind of hinges on willful ignorance. You know what I mean?"

I don't know what she means.

Or do I?

I'm certain our issues don't involve infidelity, but there's no denying I've chosen to ignore Kip's struggles with outness over the years. Every time I've opted not to correct Mr. McClackey, every time I've suppressed my instinct to show affection to Kip in public, every time I've watched him shrink around his father, I was making a decision not to confront this fundamental difference between us.

"Do you think our fiancés are having a similar conversation?" I ask Lucy, eager to get the hell out of this bathroom and see how Kip's doing.

"Jake's probably asking him a million questions," she says. "From what he told me earlier, he and Kip used to be really close."

"Then why haven't they stayed in touch?" I ponder. "Kip still talks to most of his med school friends."

"So does Jake," she says. "That whole Cornell crew—Cam Leonard, John Banks…"

"I know John." He lives an hour away from Kip and me; we have dinner with him and his wife, Liz, a few times a year. "I'm surprised *he's* never said anything to Jake."

Is it possible that Kip has sworn him to secrecy? Is it possible he's managed to remain *that* closeted right under my nose? I heave a disappointed sigh as I contemplate this.

"What's wrong?" Lucy asks.

"This whole situation is fucked," I groan. "Kip and I are getting married! He shouldn't be hiding our love from *anybody*—let alone someone he used to be good friends with. Sometimes I just wish he was more…open."

Lucy applies a finishing touch of gloss and smacks her lips. "I don't know what you're so upset about. Plenty of my gay friends would kill for a man like Kip."

"They'd kill for a man who won't even acknowledge their relationship in public?" I ask.

"He's got that raw masculinity," she says. "I've known you guys for five minutes and already I can tell that Kip is the strong, steady one, which gives you all the freedom in the world to be the mini-celebrity that you and every other Internet Gay thinks they are in their heads. There's no way you want him to be more like *you*."

Her shoulders perform a chipper shrug, as if she didn't just read me for filth. "I know you were judging straight people with your lobster metaphor earlier, but really, it applies to your relationship just as much. You're attracted to Kip precisely because of his alpha energy."

I've never thought of it like that, but Lucy might have a point. When I met Kip, I was indeed drawn to the unwavering confidence with which he carried himself.

But so much of that confidence is just a performance. An empty mask. Otherwise he wouldn't be so afraid to claim his sexuality—and me—with pride.

"He *is* weak, though," I tell Lucy. "If he weren't, we wouldn't even been having this conversation."

"Sure, I guess." She shrugs again. "But so is Jake. So am I. So are you."

I shoot her a puzzled look, because what is she even trying to say at this point?

"We're *all* weak in our own ways," she finishes. "What matters is how good you are at hiding it."

16

~

Lucy and I stagger our reentrances to the bar so as not to arouse suspicion in our fiancés, and the mere act of doing so ignites a wave of disappointment in my chest. It's the first night of our earlymoon. I shouldn't be sneaking around behind Kip's back with a woman whose entire relationship is built upon a foundation of willful delusion. This resort is supposed to be the most romantic place on earth.

Kip and Jake are laughing about something as I silently pass our table and head to the bar, avoiding eye contact. It's been entirely too long since I've had a drink in my hand.

As I wait for the bartender to notice me, a hand slaps my back. Kip's.

"I'm so sorry," he offers. "Can we go up to the room? I'll explain everything."

I release a breath. "Did you tell him the truth?"

"What?"

"While I was in the bathroom. Did you tell Jake the truth?"

"Well…no." His gaze self-consciously descends. "But I told him we're heading up for the night. So you don't have to say bye or anything."

And so I follow Kip back into the hotel, past the men's room

Lucy and I just camped out in, and up the elevators to the fourth floor. I huff and sigh every step of the way, just drunk enough to act like a petulant child, but not drunk enough to start airing my grievances out loud.

The last thing I want to do is have an argument in public.

The last thing I want to do is have an argument at *all*—especially one started by me—but something tells me it's unavoidable.

Back in the room, Kip throws the DO NOT DISTURB sign around our door handle and locks the security latch behind him. "Listen, babe..."

"*Buddies?*" I immediately hiss. "A fucking *golf trip?* At the Earlymoon Hotel? You realize how ridiculous that sounds, right? There's no way your douchebag friend bought that. It's so obvious that we're a couple."

I shouldn't be yelling at him right now—I can hear myself and I absolutely hate what's coming out—but I can't help it. While I understand on an intellectual level that Kip wasn't trying to hurt me, the part of me that got hurt anyway doesn't seem to give a shit. All I can think about is what this situation says about our compatibility, our future. I'm over here wanting to shout about our love to the world—or at least to the subscribers of *Appeal*—and Kip can't even bring himself to shout about it to one random asshole from his past.

"Do you have any idea how humiliating that was?" I continue. "To let him think that we're *so* ashamed of our relationship that we're lying about why we're here? I mean, honestly, Kip, we're getting married in two months. This is *absurd*."

Kip collapses onto the bed and groans, like I'm a fire he doesn't have the energy to put out. "I'm sorry, alright? It's complicated. I wanted to tell him the truth, but he just assumed we were here for the golf—"

"That's bullshit. You came up with that story all on your own."

He narrows his eyes at me.

"I heard you this morning," I admit. "I wasn't intentionally eavesdropping, but I could hear you from the balcony after your run. When you first ran into him…"

"You've had this information *all day* and didn't say anything?"

"Of course I didn't! This is our once-in-a-lifetime earlymoon. The last thing I wanted to do was ruin it by calling you out for throwing me back in the closet—"

"You? Throwing *you* back into the closet?" Kip says. "You honestly think this is all about you. That's… I don't know why I'm surprised."

"It is about me! It's about us. It's about you being ashamed of me. What'd you say earlier? You have to maintain 'a certain image of credibility.'"

Kip squeezes his eyes shut in frustration and makes a fist, both sure signs he's already hit his threshold for conflict and is about to shut this conversation down.

Three…two…one…

"I'm not gonna argue with you," he says, right on cue. "Let's just go to bed and talk about this in the morning, once we're sober and calm."

"Fuck you!" I shriek—Kip's dismissiveness combined with my drunkenness is a recipe for the absolute worst in me—and storm into the bathroom.

I slam the door shut, turn the water on, and slide down the back of the door until I'm fetal on the white bath rug. A surge of tears builds from my chest to my throat to my face, but I force them back down with all the strength I can muster.

I refuse to let the dam break loose.

Because if I spend the first night of our earlymoon crying on the hotel bathroom floor, what does that say about our future marriage?

17

It's almost comical how perfect our suite feels in the dead of night. Sheer white curtains gently drift with the ocean breeze flowing from our open balcony doors, waves crash in the distance—exactly like they do on all those meditation sound apps, except a million times better because the waves are real—and a soft glimmer of moonlight pours through the windows.

Paradise.

And here we are, wasting it, on opposite sides of the hotel bed. Angry and sad and disillusioned with everything this place is supposed to represent.

Or at least I am.

Somehow Kip has managed to fall asleep—evidence of his ability to compartmentalize, and therefore further evidence of how we might as well be entirely different species.

Maybe our relationship needs some serious work before we go through with getting married. Spouses are supposed to feel understood by each other, and that's clearly not happening here. Maybe all we've ever offered each other is physical pleasure and comfort.

But how could we go six whole years without realizing this?

It all just unfolded so naturally—especially in the beginning. We rode the wave of our lust and chemistry all the way into love and codependency, never stopping to look around and question the long-term compatibility of two people who are so fundamentally unalike. Maybe we didn't want to question it. Maybe we were afraid of the answers we'd pull up.

"You don't need to come out for me," I used to tell Kip in those early months. "I'm willing to wait until you're ready."

I wasn't full of shit when I'd said that.

I *was* that patient, and I didn't care whether or not he was out at that point, because the sensation of falling for him was so huge that everything I'd normally care about felt tiny by comparison.

"You say that now," Kip would reply. "But what if I'm never ready? I'm not as young as you. I'm used to living this way."

"It's not like you're old," I deflected. "We're basically the same age."

We weren't, of course, but I also didn't think our age gap was all that significant. It was above average, sure, but hardly a May-December situation. It wasn't like we fell into the sugar daddy/ sugar baby mold, an out-and-proud silver fox with his pool-boy twink. Those couples are staples of the gay community—there's a blueprint for how that whole situation works. Kip and I had something entirely different. Something that doesn't exist as a stereotype.

And we found a way to make it work. Year after year after year. It wasn't until he finally proposed that my latent obsession with marriage was reactivated.

Why did I have to insist on a traditional wedding, anyway? We both already had those with our exes.

But those weddings were built entirely on lies. I wanted Kip's and mine to be a chance at the real thing. The fairy tale I used to dream about as a kid.

That's why we're here at the Earlymoon Hotel in the first place.

I release a sigh as Kip continues to breathe peacefully across the bed.

The silhouette of his face in the moonlight makes me forget about our fight for a moment and just admire him. How am I even questioning our compatibility right now? I've never been anything but certain about this man. I quite literally can't imagine my life without him. Just because we have nothing in common doesn't mean we're not a good match.

I've already tried marrying someone with whom I had everything in common, and that ended in disaster.

It didn't even *begin* all that great.

Byrd and I met on Tinder, and our early text exchanges were more akin to a lengthy customer service survey than anything resembling flirting. That part was my fault. I was so convinced I needed a partner who shared all my core qualities that I couldn't resist digitally grilling potential suitors before wasting time meeting them in person.

When Byrd had confirmed that he was a writer, my age, and from a family of North Carolina farmers (I imagined this was the southern equivalent of being from a lobster family), I finally agreed to a first date.

"You're much easier to talk to in person," he told me over happy hour cocktails downtown. He wore a Bonobos button-down straight out of my own closet, and his sweepy golden-brown hair reminded me of leaves in the fall. "The way you texted, I couldn't tell if I was getting ready for a date or a job interview."

"Sorry about that," I said through a self-conscious smile. "I don't really date…"

He immediately called bullshit. "I've read your articles. They're literally all about your dating misadventures."

"So are yours!" I countered.

"I never denied it," he said through a laugh.

"Touché," I admitted. "What I meant is that I don't date for the fun of it. I more like audition potential husbands."

This was a direct quote from *Ally McBeal*, but it was accurate.

"Did you just quote queen Allison Marie McBeal?" Byrd asked. "I was obsessed with that show as a kid. Literally almost made me apply to law school." Byrd's mouth crept into a grin. "Honestly? Same. I don't date. I audition."

I twirled my straw around as butterflies rushed my essential organs. Meeting him was the biggest thrill of my life at that point. In retrospect, I realize it wasn't so much because we wanted *each other* all that bad, but rather because we wanted all the same things. I'd never experienced that before.

And so a whirlwind "romance" ensued. It was only a matter of weeks before we became mainstay characters on each other's respective Instagrams and blog posts.

I finally found the One! I wrote in one of my *Microphone* posts around that time. His name is Byrd Corson and he writes for one of our competitors (but here's a link to his byline anyway because why not? There's enough traffic for us all and I am SUPPORTIVE of my man's career!!!) and TBH I knew he was perfect for me when I used the word "husband" on our first date and he didn't run screaming. Wedding date TBD!

(Needless to say, this was before I started working at *Appeal* and learned how to write without sounding like I'd just snorted several lines of cocaine.)

While I was kidding about the whole wedding date thing, the legalization of gay marriage and our subsequent decision to impulsively tie the knot was barely a year away.

Which was just an utterly ridiculous decision. Because we already knew we weren't right for each other—even back during the whirlwind dating phase I wrote about in *Microphone*. I almost wonder if it was *because* we wrote about each other so much that we felt we had to make the relationship work, like we'd invested way too much of our identities into it for it to *not* lead to the marriage we both dreamed of.

But even though we both wanted the same thing, there was an essential chemistry missing from the very start. It was like we already knew each other so well that we were never surprised. Just annoyed. We'd read each other's blog posts during the day and have nothing to talk about at night.

And that's to say nothing of the insecurity that ran rampant between us.

"Who are you texting?" became a daily refrain in our apartment any time a phone vibrated. "Who are you texting? *Who are you texting?*"

We had no reason not to trust each other yet, but I think we did it because of some shared sense that we both *wanted* to cheat. Our sex life was a disaster from the start, and somehow we convinced ourselves it wasn't worth talking about. Maybe we both thought that getting married would change things.

It didn't.

We didn't even make it six months before Byrd finally answered one of my "Who are you texting?" inquiries with an ice-cold, matter-of-fact response: "My ex."

"Your ex?" I asked through a skyrocketing pulse.

"He's coming up to the city next weekend and wants to catch up."

Some partners might've been unbothered by such a proposition, but I think we all know Past Me was not that kind of partner. "And you told him no, right? Because you're married—"

"Just as friends," Byrd said. "Nothing more."

"Meeting up with an ex always leads to sex!" I said, instantly appalled at the fact that I'd undermined my argument by inadvertently rhyming.

Byrd rolled his eyes. "It will be fine, Dr. Seuss."

But of course it wasn't fine. When the eventual meetup happened, he didn't come home until three in the morning. And the funny thing was that I didn't pick a fight about it. I knew what had happened, and I knew what would happen if I acknowledged it.

This type of avoidance soon came to define our marriage.

But then we found ourselves in Seabrook a few months later—at my parents' house for a long summer weekend, roasting in bed due to broken AC—when Byrd's capacity for avoidance had burst all at once.

"It's so fucking hot in here," he grunted sometime around two in the morning. "I think we should get divorced."

I thought maybe he was talking in his sleep, but then he sat up and flicked a light on. He knew me too well to think I had ever managed to fall asleep in that rotisserie of a bedroom.

I pretended I hadn't heard him nonetheless.

"Let's just cut our losses," he said. "We're young. We can still start over—"

"This is heat exhaustion talking," I insisted as the walls closed in on us. A prison of shiplap and HomeGoods art prints. "We're not getting divorced! We agreed to work this out. We love each other."

"Why?" he asked.

"Why what?"

"Why do you love me?"

If I had had time to think about it, I could've come up with a whole list. Byrd had no shortage of objectively admirable qualities—he was kind, creative, smart—but in the moment, I couldn't come up with a single one. Because regardless of how great he was on paper, the simple truth was that I wasn't in love with him. If I had been, his cheating would've been a far more devastating blow—instead it was just another thing to sweep under the rug.

"Why would we have gotten married if we weren't in love?" I asked him.

"Same reason I slept with my ex," he said. "Poor impulse control." His back was stiff against the headboard, his gaze straight ahead at the dresser mirror, while my eyes remained fixed downward at the mattress. A tangled mess of sheets and thighs. "We moved too fast. That whole Supreme Court marriage decision... We were high on the idea of love."

I knew he was right, but it still felt like a betrayal. Our whole marriage thus far had been built on an unspoken pact *not* to admit we'd rushed into things. And now he was breaking it.

"What if we try therapy?" I pleaded. My palms were sweaty but my eyes were entirely dry—the lack of tears a sign that I was fighting for something I didn't even want. "It seems so silly to throw this away. We both want all the same things."

"I'm pretty sure that's the problem." Byrd released a long sigh. "We both *want* the same things, but neither of us can give them."

I knew immediately that he was correct. Byrd wasn't a knight in shining armor—and I sure as hell wasn't a knight in shining armor—and yet all each of us wanted was a knight in shining armor.

Or to put it in less dramatic terms, we needed partners who *did* have some level of impulse control. Partners who weren't afraid to take the driver's seat. Whereas Byrd and I were basically both fighting for the passenger seat, neither of us willing to put our hands on the wheel. Or even keep our eyes on the road.

It was a wonder we hadn't crashed and burned sooner.

I'm jolted back to the present moment by a salty gust of wind through the balcony curtains. A sense of gratitude washes over me as I realize how far I've come. I'm in Seabrook once again—except now in a wildly comfortable hotel room—this time with a man I know would never blindside me with a late-night proposition of divorce.

I wanted a partner who'd take the driver's seat, and I got it. Kip is a natural driver—someone who doesn't think twice about taking control. When we first started dating, I'd always ask him to pick the restaurant, and he'd text me back five minutes later with a location and reservation time. (Meanwhile, asking Byrd to pick a restaurant would devolve into an hourlong back-and-forth of indecision, culminating with melodramatic existential crises on both sides.)

I still remember the first time Kip told me he loved me. We were midway through a strip Scrabble game on the floor of my old studio apartment, and I'd just played MURDERER with a triple word score for thirty-nine points.

"I love you," he said through a wine-drunk grin, removing his white undershirt.

"Why?" I blurted out.

"Why?" he'd repeated. "What do you mean?"

"Why do you love me?"

I think a part of me figured that if this was the question that undid my relationship with Byrd, perhaps it could serve as a litmus test for the viability of my budding relationship with Kip. (Also, maybe I was a little nervous that the word that prompted him to confess his love for me was *murderer*. Was he trying to tell me something?)

He tugged nervously at the hem of his boxer briefs. "You're not going to say it back? Did I just make a fool of myself?"

"I love you, too!" I had thought that part went without

saying—I'd already been thinking and feeling the word *love* for weeks by then—but it was adorable that he needed to hear it out loud. "I'm not asking because I doubt that you mean it. It's just that these past couple months have been so surreal...and sometimes I have to pinch myself to know you're legit and not just some kind of cruel joke, you know?"

His lips bent into an understanding smile. "Trust me. I know."

"And I know why *I* love *you*," I added. "Because you're so brilliant, selfless, kind—"

"These are all very generic adjectives."

I punched his arm. "Let me finish. I love that you're so sure of yourself without ever being cocky. And how easy it is to be with you. I've never felt so safe with a guy. You have this aura of...certainty. The way you never second-guess yourself. The way you're the smartest person in every room we're in, but you never feel the need to prove it..." I was rambling by then, but I couldn't stop. "I feel like I can trust you in a way I've never felt I could trust anybody before. You're a rock-solid man, and I absolutely cannot believe you'd choose to be with a hot mess like me."

"You're not nearly as much of a mess as you think you are," he said. "And even if you are a little...messy...that's what I love about you. You embrace the chaos of life. You're not afraid to go against the grain."

"What grain?"

I'd never really thought of myself as much of a renegade. I've always had just as much anxiety about fitting in as the next person, and like most people I've ever met, I've always cared way too much about what people think of me.

"Like what you told me about your father," Kip said. "The way he expected you and your sister to get into lobstering because it's what your family has done for generations, but you chose to do something totally different than what was expected of you. I seriously admire that."

"Do you regret following in your father's footsteps?" I asked him.

"Oh, no, not at all. I've always wanted to be a doctor—thank God. If I *had* wanted to do something else with my life, I don't know how I'd have gotten the balls to go against his plan for me. Thankfully it was a non-issue."

I hadn't met Marshall yet, so I wasn't sure exactly what he'd been so afraid of. But having since gotten to know him, I can reasonably say that the man would have spontaneously combusted if his precious Kipling hadn't gone to medical school.

"Another thing I love about you," Kip continued. "The way you've been pushing me out of my shell." He gestured down at his bare torso. "I mean, look at me. Never in a million years did I think I'd be playing strip Scrabble on the floor of a studio apartment. To say nothing of the love you've stirred in me for the entire Lilith Fair canon. Did I tell you I listened to Shawn Colvin's entire *A Few Small Repairs* album on my commute the other day? A masterpiece. 'Sunny Came Home' was only the tip of the iceberg."

"Shut up!" I said. "That's an all-timer. Now we have no choice but to put it on."

As a symphony of folksy guitars filled the room, we rose to our feet and spontaneously began slow-dancing on the area rug.

"I get such a kick out of you," Kip cooed in my ear as we held each other close. "Careful! Don't step on my tiles."

I angled our direction away from the Scrabble board. "I'd never step on your tiles."

We shared a laugh and then continued dancing, just a pair of half-naked men swaying to the best of nineties chick rock.

He kissed me softly and then circled back to the words that had started this whole conversation: "I love you." Another kiss. "I love you, I love you, I love you."

My lips can't help but curl into a smile as I observe his sleeping face, now, all these years later. The funny thing is that, as much as he's always purported to get such a kick out of me, I get just as much of a kick out of him.

Especially in moments like these—when his typically composed energy is vulnerable, content, unguarded. There's an innocence to the way he sleeps that makes me want to protect him. Makes me want to heal whatever deeply buried wounds are responsible for his continued reluctance to be seen by the world for who he is. The way his heart raced after he kissed me at dinner? I want to kill whatever it was inside him that caused the racing. The way he instinctively told Jake I was just a friend? I want to kill the seed of shame that triggered the reflex.

I want to be *his* knight in shining armor for once.

If only he would let me.

thursday

18

I wake up to Kip's morning wood pressing against my hip, his thumb tracing my nipples, his lips kissing my neck.

"Babe," he whispers. "Rise and shine."

I can think of no better way to kick off the second day of our earlymoon than with an orgasm, but no. Glossing over fights with premature makeup sex never works. It needs to be at least somewhat earned.

"Can we talk first?" I ask. "Sorry…"

He rolls to his side of the bed and reclines against the headboard, forcing the blood away from his dick and back up to his head. "No, you're right. We should talk."

"I didn't mean to snap at you when we got back to the room last night," I offer. "You didn't deserve that."

He scratches at his chest as he considers this. A bath of morning sunlight pours through the curtains and onto his body, which makes every hair follicle seem to glow, which nearly makes me regret insisting on this conversation. We could be all over each other right now.

"I did deserve it," he responds. "It's not right that I lied to Jake. I swear it was just a mindless slip—nothing more."

"I know," I assure him. "And I know you hadn't seen each other in ages. I get how you might unintentionally revert to your old self around someone like that."

"That's exactly what happened," Kip confirms. "It just came out. And I regretted it immediately."

I place a hand on his thigh. "I was more upset because I hoped that if we ran into him when we were *together*, you'd course-correct and tell him the truth. So when we did run into him and you expected me to play along... I didn't see that coming."

"Neither did I," he admits. "I think a part of me was hoping for you to blow my cover the second you got back from the bar."

"I should have," I joke. If I hadn't eavesdropped in the first place, I probably would have, without even realizing it. "Lucy does know, though. I randomly met her earlier in the day, when I was at the bar and you were at the driving range. And then we had a stolen moment in the bathroom last night."

Kip's face goes wide. "Jake and I were wondering what took you two so long!" He looks up to the ceiling for a moment before his eyes land directly on mine. That impenetrable Kip Hayes eye contact. "Wait. You just *happened* to meet her? Or did you seek her out after you stalked us from the balcony? I know you."

"She approached me! I was sitting there first. Then she showed up and started making small talk, and I thought maybe I could interview her for my article...but of course that didn't go over well. Given how dysfunctional their relationship is."

"What do you mean? They seem happy to me."

Oh. Right. I almost forgot about the pact. I could break it right now—tell Kip all about the fake name, the flirting, the infidelity—but that wouldn't be fair to Lucy. And the last thing I need is for *her* to go rogue and tell Jake about Kip before Kip is ready.

"After Jake's whole 'women love assholes' speech last night?" I improvise. "A man like that is incapable of a functional relationship."

"He's always been like that," Kip claims. "But it's just a show. Deep down, he's a decent guy."

"So then you don't think it'll be a big deal when you tell him the truth?"

Kip's body tenses as he says, "I'm sure Lucy has already told him..."

"She hasn't. I made her promise to wait until you're ready to do it yourself."

"And you think she'll keep that promise?"

"I really do."

We fall into silence for a few moments. My mind searches for words that will help us get closer to a resolution, but I'm not even sure what I want that resolution to look like. We've both already apologized to each other, but it doesn't feel like enough.

Do I want Kip to text Jake right now and tell him the truth? Get it over with? Do I want him to kiss me in public again? Hold my hand? The more I think about it, the more I realize that what I really want is for Kip to never have lied in the first place.

For him to not be ashamed.

"Was Jake a homophobe back in the day?" I eventually ask. "Is that why your knee-jerk response was to lie to him?"

"Not really," he answers through a sigh. "I mean, yeah, med school was twenty years ago, so my buddies were *all* a little homophobic. But that's just how it was back then."

"I was in high school twenty years ago," I remind him. And myself. It's always jarring when we throw past dates at each other and compare notes on where we were in life—ten years doesn't seem like a big deal now that we're in our thirties and forties, but rewind just a couple decades and we were two people who would never even belong in the same room. "I remember what it was like all too well."

"Imagine what high school was like *thirty* years ago," Kip

counters. Less because it's relevant to this discussion and more because it's a habit. Every time we play the Who-Grew-Up-in-a-More-Homophobic-Society? game, he always has a trump card up his sleeve.

The room falls to silence again. Kip sinks further into the bed, his face casting a haze of disappointment over the crisp white sheets. I instinctively move closer and rub the back of his neck.

"I hope you know," he says, "I was disgusted with myself after I lied to Jake. I'm not ashamed of you. Or of us."

He takes a deep breath. "I thought about this a lot yesterday, and I realized I've always had this…reflex. When people I'm not close with ask me about my private life, I let them assume whatever they want. It's like I hate talking about myself *that* much."

"And people always assume you're straight," I think out loud.

He considers this. "A lot of the time, yes. But not always. Remember that *Appeal* holiday party a few years back?"

It takes a minute, but then it comes to me—Kip's first time meeting CeCe. At some point that evening, I made a comment about how Kip and I were both divorced. CeCe knew all about my first marriage by then—thanks to the thousands of words she'd edited about Byrd—but I had never written a single word about Kip, so she knew pretty much nothing about his past.

"Was your ex-husband *also* your 'clone'?" she asked him between slugs of cabernet. "Or is that just a Ray thing?"

I'd expected him to correct her—maybe crack a joke about how he used to have a beard (he was totally clean-shaven at the time, it would've been a hoot!)—but instead he glided past the misunderstanding entirely. "Definitely just a Ray thing," he said through a chuckle.

"Are you still on good terms with him?" she followed up. "Your ex-husband?"

Again I waited for a correction, a beard joke, anything, but again he just played along. "It was an amicable divorce, but we don't keep in touch."

Kip and I laughed about it on the way home—which now strikes me as strange, considering the heaviness of our current conversation—but I guess that's because *I* wasn't the one being erased in that scenario.

"That's just one of countless examples," Kip says to me now. "It's like I hate to upset people's expectations of me so much that I...just...don't."

A part of me has always known this about him—it's never clearer than when we spend time with his father—but hearing him put it in such direct terms nearly breaks my heart. I can't imagine how hard it must be to go through life trying to be everything for everybody.

"So is this why you've never corrected Mr. McClackey?" I ask. It's the last thing I want to bring up, but somehow it just comes out. I might need more practice when it comes to being the comfort*er* rather than the comfort*ed*. "Sorry—"

"Him again?" Kip cuts me off. "Who the hell cares what *he* thinks?"

Kip huffs and then shuts down, and now I feel like shit for letting McClackey—of all people—live rent-free in my head. Especially because I genuinely *don't* give a shit if he assumes we're just friends. It's more about what Kip's acceptance of that assumption says about our relationship.

"I still think that being a private person is a good thing," Kip finally says. "But I don't know... Yesterday made me realize there might be more to it than that. Maybe there is something wrong with me."

It's so unusual to hear him talk like this—expressing self-doubt, insecurity. Those are my things. Knowing that he's also capable of such emotions makes me want to take them all away from him and add them to my collection instead. Kip should never feel inadequate, because he never is.

"There is absolutely nothing wrong with you," I tell him. And then I wonder, "Why didn't you mention any of this to me yesterday? You know you can talk to me about anything."

"You shouldn't have to hear about this stuff..." He shifts his weight against the headboard. "I'm a forty-five-year-old doctor. I'm supposed to be the one of us who has his shit together."

His lips tremble as he finishes with, "But maybe I'm just a coward."

This conclusion makes my head spin, because that's the last word I'd ever use to describe Kip. All the things I'm afraid of—heights, failure, bees (and all stinging insects), silence, bats (and all nocturnal animals), being recruited for a flash mob, clowns, sitting in the emergency row on an airplane during an *actual* emergency, snakes, physical pain or discomfort of any kind, the list is endless, really, so I'll just stop here—none of them even faze Kip. When that bird flew into our house the other day? I knew he'd wrangle it without breaking a sweat.

Saving the day is what he does.

But what if what I've always perceived as his strength is just him being the person he thinks *I* want him to be? What if he's just as consumed with *my* expectations of him as he is with his father's? Jake's? The world's?

I sincerely hope not.

I want to be his safe space—not just another person for him to please.

"You're not a coward," I whisper as I reach back out and grab his hand. "You're the furthest thing from it."

Kip rubs his eyes before they can produce any tears.

"When I kissed you at dinner yesterday…" he starts and then his voice trails off, like his mind lost its grip on whatever the second half of that sentence was supposed to be.

"I know it was hard," I tell him. "Even I felt self-conscious."

Kip offers nothing but silence.

"You're not a coward," I repeat. "Maybe you still have some work to do to more fully honor your authentic self, but who doesn't? That doesn't make you weak. It makes you human."

Kip seems to untense ever so slightly at the assurance.

"And don't forget that you've already come a hell of a long way," I continue. "You're out to the people who matter. You literally proposed to me. If you'd told me six years ago that we'd be here on our earlymoon right now, I'd have been the happiest man in the entire world. I *am* the happiest man in the entire world. Because of you."

The question of Jake still hangs in the air, but at this point the only thing I care about is making Kip realize how loved and supported he is.

"Thanks," he finally says. "I love you."

"I love you, too," I tell him. "And you know what? *Fuck* Mr. McClackey—"

I cut myself off upon hearing how that sounded out loud.

"Actually," I clarify, "please don't."

His face relaxes at this. He even cracks a smile.

I seize the energy shift by jumping up and straddling him. "Okay! So here's the deal. It's the second day of our earlymoon, and we're going to have fun. No itinerary, no agenda, just a full free day to lounge on the beach. Or by the pool. Or both. I fully intend on drinking my weight in piña coladas."

"Those are pure sugar," Kip says, a sure sign he's returned to his normal form.

"This is the Earlymoon Hotel," I remind him. "There are no

limitations on sugar—or indulgences of any kind—in this magical haven."

"If you say so," he says through a laugh. "But first I gotta go for a run. And you have to go find someone to interview for your article."

The fact that his feelings about the article have turned from reluctant acceptance to legitimate encouragement makes me smile. He's making an effort. This is how he shows he cares.

"I'll head down to the restaurant to do some scouting," I tell him. "And then it's beach time." I lean forward and gently kiss him on the lips. "But first..."

Kip takes the hint, grabs my ass, pulls me in to him.

And then we're off to the races. Hands gripping, mouths roaming, bodies tangling, muscles contracting, making a mess of the sheets. Not care in the world besides giving each other as much pleasure as humanly possible.

Makeup sex really is the best when it's well earned.

19

One thing about me is that I fucking love breakfast. You wouldn't know it from my typical weekday-morning oats, but if I were on death row and had to choose a last meal, I'd request a hubcap-sized plate with every major breakfast staple represented: bacon, eggs, cheese, home fries (and/or hash browns and/or some other variation of breakfast potato), pancakes, doughnuts, sausage links, more bacon, waffles, sugary cereal, and you know what? Corned beef hash.

So my current location—the gourmet breakfast buffet in the main dining room—is basically heaven on earth.

Right before I came down here, I had a productive email exchange with the owner of the resort, who was very excited to hear about the article. (Possibly because I all but promised him a puff piece, who knows.) He's meeting me for a quick chat before he introduces me to a hotel guest he thinks will be the perfect interview subject.

I arrived thirty minutes early—so as to devour an undisclosed number of plates (fine; four) prior to our meeting—and I'm feeling Thanksgiving-levels of stuffed by the time he finds me at a table in the corner, wiping syrup from my mouth like some kind of cave-dwelling pancake troll.

"Ray Bruno?" says a dignified elderly man in Nantucket red pants and a flowy linen beach shirt. Spending decades as the owner-operator of an idyllic waterfront hotel has clearly done wonders for his longevity. "Arthur Adkins. Pleased to meet you."

I stand up and reciprocate his handshake. "The pleasure's all mine. Thank you for seeing me on such short notice."

"I'm just so delighted to have a travel writer in our midst once again," he says. "This place used to be crawling with 'em during the heyday of glossy magazines, but in recent years they've become just as scarce in Seabrook as...well...lobsters."

The reminder of my sister's vocational predicament stings, but I shake it off.

"I'm not exactly a travel writer," I admit through an awkward laugh. "More of a *love* writer."

"Even better!" He takes a seat beside me. "How is your father, by the way? I couldn't believe it when you told me you were Jim Bruno's son. Makes me feel older than Methuselah."

"He's doing great," I answer. "Retired. Florida."

"Smart man," Arthur says with a wink. "Please do give him my regards. He always had a bountiful catch."

He pulls a small pamphlet out of his pocket and slides it across the table. "This here is our origin story, which should cover the basics."

I scan the booklet, but it's all information I've already learned from their website. Arthur was a Wall Street hotshot back in the late sixties and early seventies, until one day he decided to leave the city behind so he and his wife could be by the ocean and actually enjoy life. They bought over two hundred acres of land in Seabrook, opened the Earlymoon Hotel in 1974 as a modest seaside inn, and as business grew during the seventies and early eighties, he gradually developed until it became the sprawling oasis it is today.

"I'd love to hear about this in your own words," I tell him. "What inspired the 'earlymoon' concept specifically?"

"Evelyn." There's a wistfulness to his voice that almost makes me sad I asked. "My darling wife, rest her soul. We were high school sweethearts, married just a few months after we graduated in 1963..." His voice trails off before he collects himself. "Ev was a spitfire—full of life, full of joy—and when she wanted something, she got it. I was putty in that woman's hands."

I lean forward in eager anticipation. Old-timey love stories are like crack to me.

He clears his throat. "She was terribly impatient, though. The summer after graduation, before our wedding, all she talked about was how she couldn't wait for our honeymoon. It wasn't going to be anything fancy—a road trip to Florida was about all we could afford—but that wasn't the point." He chuckles to himself. "Let's just say, back in those days, dating wasn't quite as loose as it is now. We had been looking forward to our wedding night from the moment we first kissed, sophomore year, in the gymnasium. She was a very eager girl... Am I being impolite? Let's just say that we decided to take an early honeymoon because we wanted to have a special experience before the wedding."

A sixties-era woman so horny she forced her fiancé to book an early honeymoon just so they could bone before the wedding? That is a queen in my book.

"That trip changed our relationship," Arthur concludes. "We just lay on the beach and played in the water and sat around our little rental cottage, but we broke through a wall I hadn't even known was there. I learned things about her that I'd never known, or even thought to ask."

"Where was the cottage?" I ask.

"Right here in Seabrook," he answers. "About a decade later, after I'd done well in banking, Evelyn and I just knew we had to come back here and build something special." He beams with pride while gesturing at the water view out the panoramic windows. "Our paradise."

"I'm so glad I asked you about this personally," I tell him. "You should talk more about Evelyn in the booklet."

Arthur's face turns crimson. "If you mention our own early-moon in the article, please try to use a bit more tact than I did."

I flash him a smile. "She sounds like an amazing woman."

"She really was." Arthur beams, then checks his watch. "Gosh, I've got to get going. The gentleman I wanted to introduce you to—"

He's interrupted by the sudden presence of a sloppily handsome, heavily tattooed man with broad shoulders and a dark-blond beard—someone who seems slightly familiar in a social media-ish way that I can't quite place. He has one of those looks where it's entirely possible he's Instagram-famous purely for being hot.

The man greets Arthur first. "Top of the morning, Mr. Adkins."

"Impeccable timing." Arthur stands and gestures toward me. "Joley Russell, this is Ray Bruno—the writer from *Appeal* I was telling you about. Ray, meet Joley. He arrived for his earlymoon yesterday. I believe you two will find you have quite a bit to discuss."

Joley rolls his hazel eyes in a way that tells me Arthur is saying this purely because we're both gay. I almost feel like I'm being set up on a blind date, but then remember we literally both have fiancés.

Arthur pats Joley on the back. "I'll leave you gentlemen to it!"

I push aside my collection of used buffet plates as Joley sits down. "Sorry about all these dirty dishes. There was a family of four sitting here earlier and they made a total mess."

(The fact that this is fully a child-free resort is neither here nor there.)

A dimple appears on Joley's cheek as he flashes a warm grin.

For someone with messy hair and a wrinkled tank top, his teeth are startlingly white. "Arthur tells me you're writing about couples at the hotel. I apologize, my fiancé couldn't make it. I'm an early bird, but he's a late sleeper. I'm sure he'd love to speak with you later on."

"Just you is fine." There's no way I'm gonna squeeze in an interview midday; Kip and I will be basking in the sun by then. "I'm just trying to get a few good quotes from anyone I can—think of this as a super-casual conversation. Have you ever read *Appeal*?"

"Not really," he admits. "I've...heard of it."

He shrugs in a way that causes his tank top to rumple, and I can't help but notice one of the tattoos underneath it.

"Is that a lobster claw?" I ask. "On your shoulder?"

He pulls it back to reveal the whole thing, which starts at the top of his chest. "Sure is. Pretty sick, right?"

I can't deny that it is. It reminds me of this phase I went through after my divorce, when I was close to getting something similar tattooed on my forearm, before Stef talked me out of it.

"Why would you get a lobster tattoo?" she'd asked when I showed her the sketch I was considering. "You hate lobstering. You haven't done it since you were a kid."

She was right, of course, but I really wanted to make a therapeutic statement with my appearance, and I knew I'd look terrible if I dyed my hair blond.

"Lobstering is the only thing I can think of that's really *me*," I had tried to explain.

"You left Seabrook the second you turned eighteen because it's so *not* you."

"True," I'd admitted. "But it's my roots. It's like how someone might get a tattoo of their country's flag or whatever."

She narrowed her eyes in skepticism, and I canceled the appointment later that day. A tattoo wasn't going to solve my real problem, which was unbearable loneliness. When you live in a big city after growing up in a small town, sometimes the things you hated about your old life become the things you miss the most. The things you cling to in an effort to differentiate yourself from the endless throngs of anonymous people who'd barely give a shit if you dropped dead in the middle of the subway tracks.

Joley snaps me back to the present by pulling his shirt over his head. "Here…you wanna see some of my other tats?"

Suddenly I'm sweating. Normally a shirtless stranger wouldn't induce such a reaction, but there's something about Joley's tone that makes the offer seem illicit. "No. No. It's fine. You can put your shirt back on."

"Are you hot?" he asks. "Need some water?"

"I'm fine," I assert through an uneasy laugh.

He lets the shirt fall back down over his tanned stomach—the only part of his midsection that isn't entirely covered in ink.

I clear my throat and search for a subject change. "How do you know Arthur?"

"Just met him yesterday. But we had been emailing a bit leading up to the trip. BJ—my fiancé—had about a million questions for the poor man." Joley rolls his eyes. "He's been unreasonably excited about this trip for weeks."

"So it was his idea to come here?" I ask, tapping a note into my phone.

"It sure as hell wasn't mine. BJ's one of those hopeless romantic gays." Joley makes a shoot-me-in-the-head gesture with his hand. Which is not very romantic at all. "His brain is totally poisoned by the Hallmark industrial complex. I guess he heard about this place from an old friend who's from the area."

I consider asking who the old friend is—Seabrook's year-round residents are a small-enough pool that I'd almost surely know the person—but then figure that "the area" probably doesn't mean Seabrook itself.

"So you'd never heard of an 'earlymoon' until he told you about it?"

"Nope. I didn't even want to do a *regular* honeymoon—or even a wedding reception, for that matter. All of these heteronormative traditions give me the creeps." He exhales. "But I caved. Beej really wanted this. And when I thought about it, having an *early* honeymoon struck me as unconventional enough to be worthwhile. Not just another pathetic parroting of the benchmarks associated with every basic straight couple in America. You know what I mean?"

Obviously I don't. All I've ever wanted in life was a relationship that "parrots" all the "pathetic" benchmarks of "every basic straight couple in America."

But I don't take offense. I've met Joley's type before—he's one of those "we need to do *everything* different because we're gay" gays, which I can respect and appreciate, but certainly don't relate to. As basic as it may sound, I genuinely believe that love is love. All romantic relationships have the same foundation at work—two people who want to feel seen, understood, and protected. And wedding traditions have been around for centuries for straight couples, so why shouldn't gay couples get the same validation, even if it is a little unnecessary?

"So are you and BJ not doing all the other stuff?" I ask. "Bachelor parties? A big wedding? A traditional honeymoon?"

"None of it," Joley says. "We're eloping to Vegas—Bennifer-style—next month. That was BJ's compromise for me. He's divorced, so he already got the whole wedding thing out of his system in his twenties."

"How old are you two?" I ask.

"Both thirty-five," he says.

"Huh." It's always a shock when I realize I'm not the only gay man to have been married and divorced by my mid-thirties. "Me too. I went through my own divorce at twenty-nine."

"Wow—I bet BJ would love to meet you. He's convinced he's the only thirtysomething gay divorcé in the entire city."

"New York?" I ask.

"Hell's Kitchen."

"And what do you do?"

"I cook," he says. "I'm the head chef at Chapman's, the steak house up on—"

"Seventy-second," I finish for him. Chapman's is one of Kip's and my favorite places in the city. Perhaps that's where I've seen Joley before. "Your food is amazing. The surf and turf, oh my God."

"Hence my lobster tat," he says. "I love a good crustacean."

"Wow," I marvel. "I suddenly feel like I'm interviewing a celebrity."

Joley blushes at the compliment, and shit. Does he think I'm flirting?

I shake the feeling out of my head and refocus on the task at hand. I need to ask him a good question. Something to elicit an article-worthy response.

"So what do you think of the resort so far? Even as a self-proclaimed nonromantic, have you fallen under its spell? Do you feel like being here is bringing you and BJ closer than you've ever been?"

"Not particularly," Joley deadpans. "To be frank, BJ's expectations are way too high. I mean, we had a decent fuck last night, but now he's passed out in the room and I'm down here alone…" A mischievous smirk spreads across his face. "Well, not exactly alone. I am talking to you."

My throat dries up as I attempt a response. I'm not sure what I was expecting Joley to say, but it certainly wasn't the phrase *a decent fuck* to describe the act of making love with his future husband.

His smirk grows into a laugh. "Let me guess. You won't be using that in the article?"

I suppress my own laugh as I tell him, "Probably not."

Joley straightens his posture. "How about this? The Earlymoon Hotel is the perfect place to prepare for a lifetime of wedded bliss. There's a feeling of seclusion and a sense of love in the air that makes me appreciate my fiancé in a way I never get a chance to during our hectic lives in the city."

I don't know whether to swoon or scoff. He's obviously being facetious—telling me exactly what he thinks I want to hear—but also: it's exactly what I want to hear. I take out my phone and jot down the statement verbatim into my Notes app.

"You're seriously writing that down?" Joley asks through another laugh. I'd be lying if I said it wasn't a somewhat contagious laugh—rough, but genuine. "Oh God. People are gonna think I actually meant it."

I fake a gasp. "You *didn't* mean it?"

He makes a jerk-off motion with his hand as I finish typing his words into my phone. Our table goes quiet for a moment, and I'm reminded that I just met this guy five minutes ago. And also that I have a fiancé whom I love very much, and so we really need to not be quasi-flirting right now.

Joley doesn't seem to share my concern, though.

He leans forward, lowering his voice as he says, "Can I ask *you* a question?"

"Um." I reach for my coffee cup and take a sip, even though it's been empty for a good ten minutes by now. "Sure."

"What are the terms of your relationship?" he asks.

I take another fake sip. "The...terms?"

"Are you open?" he clarifies. "Can you sleep with other people?"

It's a good thing these sips are fake, because I'd surely be spitting my coffee out right now if they weren't. While I can appreciate that all couples have their own uniquely valid ways of creating happiness—and there's certainly nothing wrong with the concept of a mutually agreed-upon open relationship—the term itself has always felt like an oxymoron to me. The whole reason I've been obsessed with relationships my entire life has been because I view them as a *closed* space between two people who love each other so much that they don't need anyone else.

This isn't to say I think it's impossible to be physically attracted to other people when you're in a relationship—I can't deny I was hypnotized by Joley's smile just a minute ago—but it is to say that I think true love is worth sacrificing extramarital sex for, if only as a gesture of loyalty and commitment.

"We are one hundred percent monogamous," I tell Joley, which feels like a good way to evade the slippery slope he's trying to get me to go down. "I'm like your fiancé. A hopeless romantic."

Joley slumps in his chair. "So. Boring."

"I take it you're *not* monogamous?" I ask.

"No, I am," he says. "Or I should be. I *will* be. After we get married."

I'm suddenly indignant on BJ's behalf. "But you haven't been thus far?"

"I love my guy," he swears. "But I don't see how me sleeping with other men contradicts that fact." He gives his lower lip an undeniably sexual bite. "Sometimes you just want a taste of something different. Especially after being with the same person for so long. And I mean, from a biological and evolutionary standpoint, it *is* human nature to want to spread your seed with as many partners as possible. Why try to fight it?"

"Because it's also human nature to feel possessive and insecure—not to mention inadequate—when your partner fucks someone else," I challenge. While Joley's argument may be true to an extent, my counterargument feels much truer. At least in my experience. "I could never put my partner through that. And I definitely wouldn't want him putting *me* though it."

I consider driving my point home by bringing up lobster mating habits again. While they might have several partners over the course of their lifetimes, when they do decide to mate, they do so monogamously until the several-months-long process is over.

But Joley rebuts before I have a chance to proceed.

"If a relationship is strong enough," he insists, "it can survive side flings without anyone's feelings getting hurt."

"And what happens when someone's side fling turns into love?"

"Simple. You don't let it."

"Love doesn't care if you want to 'let' it happen. It just happens."

Joley shakes his head in either disgust or amusement; I can't tell which. "You should put that in a song. Or better yet, one of those Valentine's Day cards for fourth graders."

I throw him a middle finger, then immediately dig my hand into my pocket when I realize how unintentionally flirtatious a gesture it was.

"Tell me something," Joley says.

"What?"

"Where's your fiancé right now?"

Something about his tone makes the question sound like an accusation, that I'm a hypocrite for suggesting monogamy works when it's my earlymoon and I've chosen to be here talking to Joley rather than having passionate morning sex with Kip. (If only he knew we just had some less than an hour ago.)

I shift in my seat. "He's on a run."

Joley leans forward, his smirk returning. "So your room is free, then."

"Free for what?"

I can't help myself from playing dumb, which I know on some level is just a ploy to get Joley to state his intentions out loud. Which is yet another unintentionally flirtatious move on my part, which makes me disgusted with myself. Someone shows me a single shred of sexual attention, and instead of shutting it down, I can't resist the reflex to tug at it? *Grow up.*

But that's easier said than done in the face of Joley's young, impulsive, bad-influence energy. He's acting like we're two high school kids who just snuck out of the house at 2:00 a.m. and met up in a moonlit old playground. No parents, no rules—the freedom to misbehave.

"A quick hookup," he says, his eyebrow raised, his voice matter-of-fact. "Whatever you're comfortable with."

Perhaps I wasn't prepared for him to be quite so direct with his answer.

This can't be happening. I haven't been propositioned for sex by a near-stranger in years—certainly not since I've settled into my life with Kip—and now it's happening at the *Earlymoon Hotel* of all places?

"We've already established that we both love our fiancés," Joley continues. "I'm just talking about a little fun. Something illicit and exciting, you know? Get the poison out of our systems before officially committing to a single penis for the rest of our natural-born lives…"

He reaches under the table and places a firm hand on my thigh in an effort to put me at ease. My mind reacts with indignation, but my body reacts with the beginnings of an erection.

Damn my penis and its lightning-fast refractory period. The

last thing I need right now is a deficit of blood flow to my rational brain.

Joley's hand travels further up my thigh, which doesn't help to quell the hardness growing in my Bermuda shorts.

"So?" he asks. "We don't have all day…"

I remove his hand from my leg with a burst of certainty.

Nope.

Nope, nope, nope, nope, nope.

I love Kip too much. I trust him and he trusts me, and there isn't a fleeting orgasm on this earth that would be strong enough to make breaking that trust worth it. I've learned enough to know that once trust is broken in a relationship, the relationship is over—even if you force yourselves to stay together.

So I jerk my leg away, sit up in my chair, and pin Joley with a stern look. "Come on, man. I just told you I'm monogamous. And you told me your fiancé is as well."

He cocks his head and pins me with a look that's less stern and more dude-you-were-*just*-flirting-with-me.

"Sorry if I gave you the wrong idea," I offer. "But I'm not interested. At all."

He throws his hands up in defeat. "I don't know what got into me. This is my honeymoon. Or earlymoon or whatever." He laughs uncomfortably. "I guess I just didn't expect to see any other gay guys here this week. Especially not any as handsome as yourself… and, well, it's basically a reflex at this point. Trying to initiate sex. Old habits die hard and all that."

He releases a frustrated sigh. "I'm sorry if I made you uncomfortable."

"It's fine," I assure him, even though it's not fine at all. Because now, even though I rejected his advances, I'm saddled with the knowledge that they existed in the first place. Which feels like a betrayal in and of itself. Just the conversation alone feels like a betrayal. How can I even begin to tell Kip about it? The second I get to the part where Joley propositions me, it becomes a confession. Kip isn't an insecure person—and I know for a fact that he trusts me—but still. It would only be natural for him to wonder if I led Joley on. If I flirted with him just enough to make him feel like he had a chance.

"Let's just pretend this conversation never happened," Joley suggests. "I'm sorry I couldn't be a better source for your article."

20

Shortly after I was hired at *Appeal*, CeCe assigned me a story about scientists who had conducted a pair of studies about the supposed link between genetics and cheating.

The goal of the research was to determine why romantic infidelity is such a common human behavior, despite the fact that our species is among the three percent of mammals that are hardwired for monogamy. After surveying a couple hundred participants (and analyzing their DNA), they concluded that it all comes down to two factors.

The first is the dopamine receptor gene, which regulates how much dopamine (an essential pleasure hormone) is released after sex. This gene comes in two variants—long allele or short allele—and apparently people who possess the long allele version are the cheating bastards of the world, because they're harder to please and more prone to risky behavior than their short-allele counterparts. The researchers' proof? Fifty percent of long-allele participants had admitted to being unfaithful in their romantic relationships.

Fifty percent!

Meanwhile, only twenty percent of short-allele participants had done the same. (Still a depressing statistic, but I can live with the idea that monogamy works out eighty percent of the time.)

The second factor was a hormone called vasopressin, sometimes known as the "cuddle hormone," which affects our capacity for trust and empathy. Participants with low levels of vasopressin also reported being cheaters at a higher rate than those whose vasopressin fell into the normal range. I don't remember the exact figures, but I do recall that one of the scientists literally injected vasopressin directly into the veins of a polygamist rodent (why do those two words together sound like a Reddit username?) and found that the rodent actually *started practicing monogamy* as a result.

"We can't publish this," I told CeCe. "These are hack studies!"

In reality, I had no idea whether the authors were credible or not. I just hated their findings. The idea that something as cruel as betraying a loved one's trust and then lying about it could be written off as a mere genetic predisposition flew in the face of everything I'd ever believed about love. And after having been cheated on by Byrd not even a year earlier, the last thing I wanted to do was promote research that could potentially absolve him of all the guilt I'd hoped he was drowning in.

But even if you take my idealistic view of love and my past bitterness toward Byrd out of the equation, I still believed the researchers were too simplistic in their approach.

They made no room for the fact that being a good partner requires a certain amount of mental strength and commitment beyond whatever your genetic makeup is—and *of course* it involves resisting certain hormonal urges. Life is all about resisting cravings. If I spent money or drank vodka or ate cake every single time the irrational part of my brain wanted to, I'd be an impoverished alcoholic with severe health problems. Sometimes the sacrifice (keeping it in your pants) is worth the reward (a healthy and loving relationship with a partner whom you can navigate the ups and downs of life with).

I explained all of these reservations to CeCe, and she'd responded, "It's just a study write-up, babe."

We ended up running the story with a silly headline ("LOL, Science Says Cheating Is Genetic and In Other News, Love Is Dead") and I moved on to the next assignment, but every so often I'll encounter a person who reminds me of those researchers' findings.

And today that person is Joley—clearly a long-allele guy with a severe vasopressin deficiency.

That, or he's just a terrible person.

Probably both. I don't know.

All I know is that he's not a reliable source for the article I'm trying to write about how this resort is the ultimate couples retreat. I thought it would be easy to find a few sublimely happy almost-married couples, yet so far the only two subjects I've talked to— Joley and Lucy—are both in severe need of relationship counseling.

So now that I'm back in the room, waiting for Kip to return from his run, I have to reconsider my options.

I could keep searching for sources, hoping that the next couple I land on actually seems to love each other.

I could go all in on the first-person angle and simply make it an essay about Kip and myself, but what would that even look like? "On our first day in this idyllic beachfront oasis, my fiancé told someone we were just friends..."

Or I could kill the piece altogether.

Before I can fully explore each scenario, my phone buzzes with a call from Stef.

"Broski," she says. "Whoa. I didn't expect you to pick up. Shouldn't you be frolicking on the beach with your beau?"

"He's out for a run," I tell her. "What's going on? Is everything okay? You never call me unless—"

"Everything's fine," she says. "I was just gonna leave you a voicemail. Can you stop back at the house before you head home from your trip? I was cleaning out our closets and found a box of your old crap from high school."

"Why are you cleaning out the closets on a random Thursday morning?" I ask. "Shouldn't you be out on the boat right now?"

"Day off."

"Since when do you take days off?"

"I don't know," she says. "Since today."

The line goes silent for a few moments.

"You don't sound nearly as happy as I'd expect you to during the trip you've been fantasizing about since you were in diapers," Stef says. "Everything okay?"

I'm surprised by how glad I am to hear her ask me this question. Normally I might deflect and tell her that the trip is every bit as magical as I'd always dreamed it would be, but instead I'm eager to talk through my worries with someone. Maybe she'll have some good advice on how to deal with the fact that my belief in the perfection of true love is actively crumbling beneath my feet.

"Kip and I got into a fight yesterday," I begin, "which wasn't how I wanted this vacation to start. We're fine now, but I've also been trying to interview some other people here—I'm writing an article about how this is Shangri-la for happy couples—and that's been a total disaster. Every couple I've met is so full of shit. One guy this morning literally propositioned me for a hookup before his fiancé woke up."

"Oh my God!" she squeaks before lowering her voice to an intrigued whisper. "Did you do it?"

"Of course not! I would never."

"Then what are you so upset about? If you guys made up from your fight, and you rejected that guy's advances, who cares about these other people's relationships?"

"It's the principle of it all." I step out to the balcony and survey the postcard scene before me—three tiers of patio and beach, a team of clean-cut resort staff in crisp white polos slinking around with trays of frozen beverages. Beyond them, an endless stretch of salt water and sky. "This is the Earlymoon Hotel. You know the stories Mom has always told us about her and Dad's time here. I wanted to capture *that* version of this place with my article. Not this mess."

I can practically hear her eyes rolling through the phone. "Bro. Come on. You're a thirty-five-year-old man. How are you still holding on to all that 'true love' bullshit she fed you as a kid? Her version of the Earlymoon Hotel has never existed. Her version of *her own marriage* has never even existed."

"What are you talking about? Yes, it has."

"The woman is delusional," she continues. "I love her, but come on. She and Dad have tons of issues."

"No they don't! They've been together for almost forty years. And when have you ever seen them fight?"

"You left Seabrook when you were eighteen," she reminds me. "I saw them fight plenty before they moved away."

"About what?"

"Umm…" She takes a breath. "Lobstering, money, retirement, Florida. Everything."

"All couples fight sometimes," I try instead. "But you can't deny they fight way less than most. Think about our childhood. They were always so happy together."

"Dad was barely ever around. He was always out on the boat," Stef counters. "Mom just constantly *talked* about how much she loved him. She was so obsessed with him and his approval that she barely even gave a shit about us. Her own kids."

"That's not true."

"Please," she replies. "You were starved for attention."

"And you weren't?"

"Not inordinately…" She releases a bored sigh, like there's nothing at all remarkable about this conversation. "I had my lobstering with Dad, which was more than enough parental connection for me. But you were stuck with Mom, and all she ever did was shove her Cinderella complex down your throat. The way she forced you to look at their wedding album… I mean, dude…"

"She didn't force me," I correct. "I wanted to look at it."

"That's not how I remember it."

"Well, it's the truth." At least I think it is. I remember having a strange obsession with the album, that much I know for sure. But I suppose the root of the obsession is up for debate. It's entirely possible my mother just kept force-feeding it to me until I acquired a taste of my own. "Whatever—it doesn't matter anyway."

Stef clicks her tongue. "I'd say it does. Not only did she program you to think you need a relationship to be happy, but she also programmed you to think the relationship itself has to be a twenty-four/seven fairy tale. And now look at her! She and Dad are sleeping in separate bedrooms down in Florida, you know."

"What? How would you even know that?"

"Lenny and I visited in February," she says. "They didn't try to hide it or anything."

A lump rises in my throat as I consider what this could mean. "Why would they do that? Are they getting divorced?"

"*That* would shock me," she says through an audible shrug. "They probably just like having their own space. Now that Dad is retired, you know, they basically spend every second together. And clearly their sex life has expired."

"Please never refer to their sex life again." It's a knee-jerk deflection, but I'm glad I went with it. Because to express what I'm truly feeling—something close to devastation—would only make me seem even more pathetic than I already feel.

The line goes quiet for a long time.

I forget about my parents entirely as my gaze fixes itself on a pair of women lying on the beach, their chairs staked right into the wet sand at the front of the tide. They seem to be on a different planet, making out as the water washes over their intertwined toes every few seconds in perfect rhythm. Like they're the only two people in the world.

Is that what I've been so upset with Kip about? Denying us the freedom to suck each other's faces in the sand while a bunch of anonymous resort guests watch from their balconies?

Something tells me that even if it were an option, neither of us are the type of people who'd take it.

And I know Kip established this morning that his reflex to play straight in front of Jake wasn't about me—but still. The fact that he has a habit of mirroring back to people what they want to see—which often is a straight, buttoned-up doctor—means that he *also* has a habit of erasing me from his life entirely.

And I can't help but wonder if he realizes that.

"Ray?" Stef asks. "Hello?"

I snap out of my lesbian-gawking haze. "Yeah. I'm here."

She sighs. "Listen, I'm sorry, okay? I didn't mean to piss in your Cheerios with all this. I just thought maybe it would help if you gave yourself some perspective. A marriage doesn't have to be some all-consuming romance-novel obsession. It can just be a marriage. The Earlymoon Hotel doesn't have to be some mythological love paradise. It can just be a hotel."

Now it's my turn to sigh.

"Stop being so obsessed with perfection and just enjoy yourself," she adds. "Or if you insist on being miserable, at least let me trade places with you."

"What's that supposed to mean?"

"It means you're at a five-star resort with your doctor fiancé," she says. "And I'm over here prepping my chum for tomorrow's catch."

21

~

It's a perfect beach day—all low tide, clear skies, and salty gusts of waterfront breeze. There's no one else within a hundred-foot radius of Kip and me, so I busted out the waterproof Bluetooth speaker and put on our favorite classic rock playlist. (There's only so much Lilith Fair Kip can take before he gets to choose the music.) Bob Seger sings about his night moves as we lay back in adjacent beach chairs with our eyes squeezed shut, soaking in the brilliant sunlight.

Stef's delivery might have been rough, but she told me exactly what I needed to hear.

I shouldn't be wasting time longing for this trip to be some kind of utopian love fest for the sake of an *Appeal* article; I should enjoy and appreciate the fact that I'm fortunate enough to be here with Kip in the first place.

I brush a hand through the hot sand and bask in the sensation as it pours between my fingers. The sand here is remarkably different than the sand at the other beaches in Seabrook—softer and cleaner and generally less threatening. My family and I used to go to the town's sole public beach (the one reserved for townies) all the time when I was growing up, and the condition of the sand there required beachgoers to wear those special swim shoes for protection. The dangers of jagged seashells, sharp rocks, or ciga-rette butts were never far off.

Nothing about this place feels like the Seabrook I grew up in.

Maybe that's why my mom always held it up on such a ped-estal. After hearing what Stef had to say earlier, I have to consider the possibility that Mom wasn't as happy as she always claimed to be. Maybe the hyper-manicured sheen of this resort represented the life she wanted—a version of Seabrook without all the flaws and messiness that made it a real place where real people live. Or maybe it represented the marriage she wanted—a version of my father who was more like a Prince Charming and less like a gruff lobsterman with a work addiction.

Maybe she romanticized her stay at the Earlymoon Hotel because it was one of the only times she had his undivided attention.

"I think they do something to the sand here," I think out loud, eyes still closed. "Like they purify it or something."

A few moments pass.

"What was that?" Kip asks as the music fades out.

Seagulls caw and waves crash in the gap between songs. I lower the volume so we can have a proper conversation.

"The sand here is really clean."

He sits up, digs his feet into the ground below him. "Yeah. I guess it is." His eyelids crinkle as he squints in my direction. "You alright?"

"Just thinking about my parents, how they had an earlymoon here back in 1981…"

"The Stone Age," Kip says. "I was three. You weren't even born."

Or maybe that's why she loved this place so much. Because their marriage was different before they had Stef and me. Maybe my mom romanticized the version of their relationship that wasn't complicated by additional mouths to feed.

"Stef called me this morning," I tell him. "She told me they sleep in separate bedrooms down in Florida. Can you believe that?"

"Jim and Janice?" Kip says. "No, I can't believe that. Your mom is so..."

"Outspoken about her love for my father?"

"I was gonna use the word 'obsessed.' But that works, too."

"It's unbelievable, right?" I ask. "But Stef and Lenny visited this past February and apparently they're just down there acting more like roommates than spouses."

"Maybe it's a health thing," Kip proposes. "Doesn't your dad use a CPAP? Could be too noisy for her."

"His snoring was too noisy for her," I correct him. "That's why he got the CPAP in the first place."

Kip leans across the sand and squeezes my shoulder, his hand providing a cool contrast to the heat of the sun. "Don't let this upset you. It doesn't necessarily mean they don't still love each other. And it's really none of our business either way."

"Yeah, no, I'm not upset." I remind myself of the promise I'd just made to myself—to appreciate the current moment. But it's still hard not to think about the possibility that the prototype I've always had for what constitutes true love is total bullshit. "I just feel like it's kind of nuts how my mom always talked about their marriage like it was the most perfect thing ever, you know? But now that they've been retired for a few years and they actually have to spend time together, they're already sick of each other."

"That sounds pretty normal," Kip suggests. "Wouldn't you get sick of me? Imagine if I didn't go into the office every day and you didn't have your job with CeCe. Maybe they just need some hobbies."

"I could never get sick of you." But of course, Kip is right. I'm the most codependent person there is, and even I can understand that any couple would tire of each other's company if they never had any time to themselves. "Even if I could, I would never let it get to the point of separate bedrooms. That's just a whole other level of—"

"Babe," he says. "Does it really matter? It's their life. It's their marriage."

"It does matter!" I protest. "It matters because…"

Because why? I let the question marinate for a few breaths until an honest answer rises to the surface.

"Because all my life, she sold me a lie," I explain. "And not only did I buy it, but I made it my entire personality."

"That's a little dramatic," Kip says through a laugh. "But alright. If that's how you feel, you should talk to her about it."

"You want me to call her? Like, right now?"

"It's probably more of an in-person conversation. Maybe after a few glasses of that cheap wine she loves so much."

"Barefoot…" I laugh as I think about the kitschy *Wine O'Clock* signage hanging over my parents' Formica Florida kitchen. And then it occurs to me that I've only ever seen it via FaceTime. "You know what? It's been four years since they moved, and we still haven't been down to visit them."

"Because every time I suggest it, you insist we use our vacation time to do something more romantic, just the two of us." He pauses. "Maybe you should go down and visit them. Maybe the real reason you're so upset over this is simply because you miss them. I know you and your mother used to be so much closer…"

"I used to be closer to a lot of people."

The unspoken part—that I let all my connections fall away once I found a man to throw myself into—hangs in the air between us. It's no one's fault but mine, but somehow it feels like I've just accused Kip of something.

"I remember," Kip says. "All the school friends and ex-coworkers on our wedding guest list, even though, for all intents and purposes, you've dropped them from your life entirely."

"Okay, way harsh, Tai. I still see them on social media. I still have a general idea of what's going on with them. Sometimes we talk. We'll always be friends, even if we never see each other."

Kip radiates skepticism from his beach chair, so I have no choice but to continue rambling. "You know how it is! It's impossible to maintain connections in this day and age. And I do still see some of my friends. We *just* played a round of golf with CeCe and her husband."

"That was a year ago," he quips. "And she's your boss."

"It still counts."

He laughs. "I'm just saying that when you really want to see someone, you find a way to see them. Look at me. I still see my buddies every week for poker. And you and I are always double-dating with John and Liz. And you know we see my parents at least once every couple months."

"That's because we live so close to them," I counter. "If we lived closer to Seabrook, I'm sure we'd see my parents all the time, too."

"You mean Florida."

"Oh. Right."

"Just admit it," he says through a sneaky grin. "You don't make an effort with anyone else because I'm the only person in the world that you care about."

"Right," I mock. "My entire world begins and ends with Kip Hayes."

As facetious as this exchange has become, I can't deny the truth beneath it. Although I never intentionally dropped the other people in my life, I certainly didn't continue making a strong effort to stay connected once things got serious between Kip and me.

But is that such a crime? I'm someone who functions best in a relationship—being single and having a wide net of family and friends was never enough for me. I've always craved the deeper connection of romantic love—that person you share everything with. I don't think there's anything inherently wrong with that. I know there are plenty of people who thrive on singlehood and independence, but aren't there just as many people out there who don't? Why else would so many of us bother with love and marriage in the first place? It's a perfectly human desire to not want to go through life alone.

Still, I can't help but wonder if yesterday's drama could've been avoided if my life wasn't *so* centered on Kip. Maybe if I had more of an individual identity, hearing him downplay our relationship to Jake wouldn't have been such a blow. I'm sure it would've hurt no matter what, but maybe it wouldn't have led me to question my entire existence.

"The wedding will be a chance to reconnect with people," I suggest, but Kip doesn't hear me. He's turned the music back on and his face to the sun.

I recline in my beach chair and run my fingers through the pristine sand once more. I grab a chunk of it and grip hard, determined to center myself in the moment and stop worrying about the future, but that only makes it slip through my fingers faster.

22

~

It takes a few piña coladas, but I eventually succeed in quashing my anxiety and living in the moment. This allows the afternoon to fly by in a blur of rum and sunshine—even Kip couldn't resist ordering a couple frozen mojitos from the resort's beachside cocktail servers—and soon enough we're back at the Gull's Nest, ravenous for seafood.

As the sun sets across the water and the sky turns a hazy shade of pink, I take a moment to breathe it all in. Gratitude washes over me like one of the waves against the bluffs. I can't remember the last time I've felt so content, so relaxed, so calm.

Which is why Kip throws me for a loop when, halfway through our appetizer of steamed littlenecks and pan-fried crab cakes, his face goes cold and he instructs me to *stay calm.*

"Don't move," he says. "There's another bee."

Normally I'd freeze in place as told, but apparently I've consumed enough alcohol to interpret the phrase "don't move" as something more like "evacuate your chair in a violent, jerking fashion."

All the couples in our vicinity immediately take notice of the towering homosexual frantically pacing amid the patio umbrellas.

"Ray! What are you doing?" Kip's voice is a tense hiss. "*That's* how you get stung—by freaking out instead of staying calm."

I survey our area for the bee—which I still haven't seen with my own eyes—and settle back into my seat upon determining that it's evacuated the premises.

And then it lands directly on one of our crab cakes.

"Just be still and let it fly away," Kip says. "It's getting late. The fucker's gotta retire for the night soon."

This time I actually do freeze in place, instantly sobered up by the visual threat of anaphylaxis.

You know? It's amazing how I can manage to be six feet tall, 180 pounds, with a thick dusting of facial hair, and yet. This tiny little arthropod has the power to fully hijack my nervous system and reduce me to the helpless seven-year-old I was back in the summer of 1995, the first time I ever got stung.

I was playing with buckets at the beach (the one with the crappy sand) when a wasp landed on my wrist. I swatted it away with my free hand, which pissed it off just enough to make an attempt at my life.

My skin burned and swelled as I burst into hysterical tears—under the false impression that the pain of the sting itself was going to be the worst of my problems—but my mom was distracted on the other end of the beach, eyes closed, facing the sun, Walkman headphones covering her ears. She was going through an intense *Men Are from Mars, Women Are from Venus* phase at the time (I wish I were kidding) and was known to be dead to the world when listening to the audiobook on cassette tape.

As I stumbled over to her beach chair, a deep sense of dread flooded my tiny frame. My entire arm was bright red, and I was winded after just a few steps. What was wrong with me? I'd seen Stef get stung by a bee the summer before, and she'd bounced back within minutes.

The next thing I remember is waking up at the hospital.

When it was explained that I was severely allergic, my child logic somehow convinced me that it was my fault. I knew I was different even back then—seen as somehow weaker than all the other boys my age—and so *of course* my body wouldn't be able to withstand a simple bee sting. I was defective. It was around that time I started fantasizing about being one of the lobsters in the tank on my dad's boat—a creature with a rock-hard shell of protection. Anything but my delicate, vulnerable, flimsy human skin.

"Ah! Shit!" Kip yelps me back into the present moment. He's sucking on the space between his thumb and index finger. "The bastard got me. Goddammit. That hurts like a bitch." He grabs an ice cube from his water glass and rubs it on the sting—a tiny red speck. "That's better."

A few swigs of mojito, and he's back to normal.

"Are you sure you're okay?" I ask.

He gives a thumbs-up. "You know me. This is actually good. Now the bee dies, my conscience is clean because *I* didn't kill it, and you don't have to worry about getting stung."

"You sacrificed yourself for me." I swoon, flooded with equal parts relief and gratitude and strong attraction. "That is the most romantic."

"I'm calling in an EpiPen first thing tomorrow morning," Kip says. "Clearly this place has a bee proble—"

His face tenses up again as he notices something behind me, and the relief leaves my system as quickly as it came.

"You've gotta be kidding me. Another one?"

"What?" He snaps out of it. "Oh, no, sorry…"

I whip my head around to the sight of a straight couple being seated a few tables behind us. The man has broad shoulders like Jake and the woman has red hair like Lucy—but they're not Jake and Lucy.

Kip exhales in relief.

"It's fine," I assure him. "Even if we do run into them, don't worry about it. I'll pretend to be your platonic golf buddy if I need to."

His eyebrows float up. "What? No. I can't ask you to do that."

"You just took a sting for me," I tell him. "It's the least I could do. And also, it wouldn't be fair to *you* if I forced you to tell him before you're ready. I can be mature enough to understand that your reluctance doesn't have anything to do with me."

I may be overstating my maturity just a tad, but I'm willing to shelve my concerns entirely until we're back home. Today was proof that we don't need to have it all figured out in order to enjoy ourselves on vacation.

"It really doesn't have anything to do with you," he says. "I love you. And I am *proud* to be with you. You're the catch of my life. I'm sorry if my personal issues haven't allowed me to fully express that to the world..."

"Fuck the world."

A vision of our wedding day flashes in my mind. Kip and I at the altar, two hundred friends and family members all watching with bated breath. Those are the people who matter—not some ex-friend from decades past who just happens to be at the same hotel as us.

"Speaking of the world," Kip says. "I forgot to ask. How'd it go this morning? Meeting the owner and all that?"

"Oh." I cough on a sip of water. (At this point, hydration is key.) "Uh—"

I'm interrupted by the arrival of our entrées. Seared bay scallops over a bed of spinach for Kip and a hot buttered lobster roll with a side salad for me.

"Did you get any good quotes for your article?" Kip goes on.

Somehow I've made it through the entire day without having to field any questions about what happened this morning. But now that I'm faced with one, I have the guiltiest conscience, which is just silly. It's not like I *asked* Joley to hit on me. It's not like I seriously entertained his proposition.

And it's not like Kip has any reason not to trust me. He's never been a jealous person. Hookups and exes and random internet gays used to DM me all the time at the beginning of our relationship—my inability to post about Kip on social media meant that they all assumed I was still single and DTF—and I wouldn't think twice about mentioning any of those to Kip. If anything, he was entertained and fascinated by such glimpses into what it was like to be an openly gay man in modern-day Manhattan.

But this feels different. It feels like something that would lead to more questions, which would then lead to the conversation feeling like an interrogation, which would then lead to me insisting that the exchange meant nothing—which is exactly what someone would do if it *did* mean something.

So I decide to give a very limited version of events instead. "The owner was super nice. He gave me this great story about how he and his wife went on an earlymoon in the sixties, mainly because she just couldn't wait to sleep with him. He tried to introduce me to another guest, but he didn't really have anything great to say about his fiancé."

"Oh," Kip says. "Bummer."

"I know, right? It's like… Why are they even here?"

"And she didn't have anything great to say about him either?"

I could correct his assumption that the fiancé in question is a woman, but instead I just stab at a cherry tomato in my salad. "He was having breakfast alone…"

I take another stab at the tomato, but it keeps bouncing away from my fork. "I'm hoping to have better luck tomorrow—with the number of couples at this place, I have to imagine at least one of them is blissfully in love and willing to shout about it."

friday

23

I f there's one quality of Kip's that has rubbed off on me over the years, it's his propensity for routine. Our lifestyle is a matter of clockwork, punctuated by various rituals at various cadences—from daily coffee to weekly meal prep to monthly bills to yearly weekend getaways—and I love all of it. There's something so comforting about maintaining a certain degree of predictability in an otherwise unpredictable world.

Even when we do deviate from our standard schedule and go on vacation, we still can't help but develop temporary routines for whatever environment we find ourselves in. Which is why I'm now back at the breakfast buffet while Kip goes for a run, and why our remaining mornings here will likely continue this way as well.

"You and your partner *must* attend," Arthur Adkins is saying. His silver hair glistens in the morning light as we sip coffee on the veranda. I ran into him at the omelet station a few minutes ago, and he insisted we take a moment to discuss Sunday's Lobster Fest. "Dinner, cocktails, dancing. My grandson is coming up from the city to DJ. It's sure to be a memorable soiree. Could be great material for your story."

This is true. I used to dabble in nightlife reporting in my pre-Kip days, and it's undeniably easier to get people to talk once they have a few drinks in them.

"We'll be there," I promise. "We have a slow-dance lesson with your on-site instructor later today, so we'll have some new moves to show off."

"Barbara! You will love her. She's a gem." He takes a thoughtful sip of espresso. "How did it go with Joley yesterday?"

"Great," I lie. "Thank you again for connecting us. I could use some additional voices in the piece, though, to round it out. You wouldn't happen to know of any other guests that might be open to talking to me? No worries if not. You've already done more than—"

"Say no more." Arthur stands up and scans the surrounding tables for fresh meat before landing on a couple that's just finishing up their meal. "I'll be right back."

He returns a minute later with a couple who introduce themselves as Mariah and Nicki, thereby confirming my suspicion that he's under the false impression that *Appeal* is an exclusively gay media outlet. But you know what? This is a gift. If there's any hope of finding a couple that's genuinely in love and obsessed with each other, it's sure to be found within the lesbian community.

And these women are gorgeous. Mariah's got a shiny mane of brown-blond hair, not unlike her pop diva namesake, and Nicki's sporting a tight buzz cut, which pairs beautifully with the gold hoops dangling from her ears, and—oh! I knew they looked familiar. They're the ones who were all over each other on the beach yesterday.

Arthur excuses himself as Mariah and Nicki take his place at the table, literally sharing a single chair. If they're experiencing any discomfort from unsupported ass cheeks, they don't show it. Both of them are simply beaming.

"This is so cool," Nicki says. Her voice is like a fruit smoothie: sweet and thick. "I love *Appeal*. I read it all the time at work. What section do you write for?"

My cheeks flush in anticipation of her disappointment. *Appeal* has some really good writers across all beats, and I'm not nearly as popular as any of them.

"Sex and relationships," I answer. "I'm Ray Bruno."

"Oh!" she says. "You did that series about Tom and Gisele's divorce, right? That was heart-wrenching stuff." She leans forward and makes a face at me—a blend of faux-pity and amusement. "How are you holding up?"

"It's been a difficult few years," I play along. "But I get a little bit stronger each day."

"Of *course* Nicki would know who you are," Mariah says through a giggle. Her voice is less like a fruit smoothie and more like coffee. Warm but with a kick. "So you're writing about couples at the resort?"

"I'm trying to," I explain. "I'm actually here on my *own* early-moon, but my editor thought it would be fun for me to write about the experience when I get back. I grew up in Seabrook, so I have a really deep reverence for this place. My parents had their earlymoon here. My mom has always described it as the most magical week of her life, and that's the kind of story I want to tell. But so far I haven't found any couples who really support my thesis."

"It's a good thing you found us, then! We are madly in love, and frankly I never want this trip to end." Nicki squeezes Mariah at the waist, catching my attention with her bright-blue fingernail polish. "I could stay here forever with my baby."

"Awww!" Mariah leans in to the affection and plants a kiss on her bride's cheek. "I love you so much."

"Last night was incredible," Nicki tells me. "A moonlit stroll down the beach, champagne and strawberries in the hot tub. Rose petals all over our suite. Every cliché in the book, and I don't care what anybody has to say, I love it all." She taps a nail against the

table. "I'll keep it real with you. I grew up in a humble neighbor-
hood with a strict religious family and didn't even *think* about
coming out of the closet until I was in my thirties. So to now be
in my forties, making a good living, all my hair chopped off,
staying at this bougie-ass resort with my future *wife*? I am one
lucky bitch."

Her earnestness makes me smile. It's a reminder that I too am
a lucky bitch. I'm here, with my future husband, against all odds.
Why do I keep undermining that fact with my constant efforts to
prove I'm a lucky bitch via my future wedding and the very article
I'm working on right now? Why can't I just let myself *be* a lucky
bitch without having to make a spectacle of it?

I push these questions out of my mind in favor of the ones I'm
supposed to be asking the couple in front of me.

"How long have you been together?" I ask. "What do you love
most about each other? What made you choose to take an earlymoon? Tell me everything."

"We've been together over a decade," Mariah volunteers. "Met
on a dating app when we were both living in Boston, but just got
engaged last year."

Over a decade! And they still couldn't keep their hands off of
each other at the beach yesterday. Or at the table right now, for that
matter. That feels like a win for love.

"I knew from the moment we met that she'd be my wife," Nicki
adds.

I tap a few notes into my phone. I'm not transcribing the entire
conversation, nor am I recording it, but I'm capturing just enough
to jog my memory later. And of course I'm jotting down the exceptionally quotable lines verbatim. Nicki's latest statement is exactly
the kind of canned yet heartfelt expression of love I hope to build
the entire piece around.

"We moved in together after six months," Mariah says. "Cue the U-Haul jokes. We just waited so long to get engaged because..." Her voice trails off.

"It was me," Nicki admits. "I wasn't ready for a long time. It's one thing to be in a gay relationship, but it's another thing to throw a party over it. Especially with my family. It had nothing to do with Mariah, but still. I was living a boring old hetero life before her, just because it was what everyone always expected of me. I had a lot of work to do to really accept *myself* at the beginning. And the idea of having a whole-ass wedding...putting a giant spotlight on my queerness? That terrified me for a long time."

If she weren't a petite Black lesbian with a buzz cut, I'd swear I was talking to Kip himself. The similarity between their coming-out journeys is encouraging—an indication that Kip's lingering issues aren't all that uncommon, and more importantly, they're surmountable.

Mariah rubs her thigh. "I know it did, baby."

"But now look at me," Nicki says with a wink. "I'm talking to a reporter about my big lesbian honeymoon!"

"Earlymoon," Mariah and I correct in unison.

We all share a laugh.

"I'll tackle the next question," Mariah continues. "What do I love most about my darling Nicki? Everything. She's the oldest of four sisters—practically raised them—and she's the most fiercely capable and protective person I've ever met. I feel safe with her."

This touches me, mainly because it's how I feel about Kip. Somehow he has big older-brother-who-practically-raised-his-siblings energy, despite the fact that he's an only child.

"Mariah is the most selfless person I've ever met," Nicki adds. "I work in finance, just totally soulless work, you know. I've had to hustle since I was a kid, so my only 'passion' is making money.

But Mariah? She saves babies. Like, for real! She's a NICU nurse... I mean, could the woman *be* any more nurturing?"

"Was that an intentional Chandler Bing impression?" I ask.

Mariah smiles. "*Friends* is everything to us—iconic nineties lesbian representation."

"Even if Ross was so problematic about it," Nicki chimes in. "Like, dude, your ex-wife doesn't want anything to do with your shriveled little Vienna sausage dick. Get over it."

I laugh while squirming at the image she's conjured.

"Moving on," Mariah says coolly. "We heard about this place from a friend. She came here with her husband a few summers ago and raved about how great it was to get away before the chaos of their big Greek wedding. And they're the happiest couple we know, so..."

"We booked it," Nicki finishes. "I never wanted a bachelorette party anyway. I want to celebrate getting married with my *love*—not with my friends. Bless them. But still. They'll all be at the wedding."

She shrugs and then turns to me. "What else do you wanna know?"

I stare at my half-eaten plate of breakfast foods for a moment until the perfect question surfaces. "What do you think is the recipe for a happy marriage?"

"I don't know about the *whole* recipe," Nicki says. "But communication is easily the most important ingredient. You can't keep secrets or hold feelings inside or hope your partner is gonna read your mind. Even if they're good at it."

An obvious answer, but true. Which might explain why I still feel a little weird about not mentioning the Joley thing to Kip earlier. What if we run into him later? Is my plan to just pretend I've never seen him before?

"An equally important ingredient is respect," Mariah adds. "Not just basic respect, either. It needs to be more like the 'highly respected' kind of respect. You know what I mean? Nicki is a goddess in my eyes."

Yet another sentiment I agree wholeheartedly with. There's no one's intelligence or opinion I value more than Kip's. As far as I'm concerned, he's the smartest man alive.

Nicki rolls her eyes. "I'm not that great. Sometimes Mariah holds me up as some kind of perfect person…which I'm not. I have flaws just like anybody else—"

"No, you don't." Mariah slaps her arm. "Except for your tendency to put ice cubes in your red wine. That's just unforgivable."

"I like it chilled!" Nicki protests. "Why should I deny myself just because some uptight wine snobs say I'm drinking it wrong? Screw that."

Mariah sighs. "I love you so much."

And then they abruptly start making out, creating a scene of same-sex PDA right here in the open air of the veranda.

But really, it's not a scene at all. No one around seems to even give our table a second look. I wish Kip could see them, lost in their love for each other and unbothered by the prospect of onlookers.

I consider clearing my throat to recapture their attention and get the interview back on track, but it's almost ten. Kip should be back from his run soon, and I'm determined to join him in the shower for a spontaneous morning quickie. If we accomplish nothing in the way of public romance, at least we can bat a hundred when it comes to making time for daily morning sex in our hotel suite.

"You two have given me plenty of great material," I tell them. "Thank you for taking the time to speak with me."

Their mouths detach for a moment.

"Here." Nick retrieves a business card from her purse and hands it to me. "In case you have any other questions. We're excited to be a part of this piece."

Nicki Jameson, Senior Portfolio Manager.

"I can't wait to read and share it far and wide," Mariah adds. "I'm so in love, and all I want to do is shout about it to the world!"

Same, I think to myself.

Even though I know it shouldn't matter.

Even though I desperately want it to be enough to just appreciate my love story for what it is—privately—the way Kip is so capable of doing.

Same.

24

~

Kip and I are meandering through the grand events pavilion on the west side of the resort, an indoor-outdoor oasis of weathered shingles and white trim, with rambling flower boxes peeking around every corner. The peonies and hollyhocks and pink roses are somewhat beautiful but mostly terrifying, because I know all that shit is just begging to be pollinated.

"I picked a hell of a week to forget my EpiPen," I joke.

"I picked a hell of a week to forget that you always forget your EpiPen," Kip jokes back. "But I got you, babe." He pulls a brand-new EpiPen out of his pocket and winks at me. "Called it in this morning. Picked it up while you were at breakfast."

My entire system floods with relief. I'd still have to go to the hospital if I were to get stung, but the EpiPen would at least buy us enough time to get there safely.

"My hero!" I gush. "What would I do without you?"

"I shudder to think," he cracks.

We take a left past a stairwell, even though I'm pretty sure we just went in a circle. My search for the Lovebird Studio, where our private slow-dance lesson is scheduled to kick off in five minutes, has been surprisingly difficult.

"Weren't we supposed to cancel this anyway?" Kip asks, a

hopeful lilt to his voice as we embark on another lap. "I'm an excellent dancer. I don't need a lesson."

This is a blatant lie. Kip is one of those around-the-house dancers: goofily twerking between rooms, popping, locking, doing the arm wave while loading the dishwasher—that kind of thing. But neither of us have any *real* moves to speak of.

"We both need this lesson," I tell him. "And it was a nonrefundable add-on. Don't you wanna be prepared for our first dance? We need to know where to put our hands and stuff."

"We already know where to put our hands *and stuff*," he insists. "We slow-dance all the time at home."

"Do we, though?" I counter. "Or do we just sway together while entangled in a tight embrace?"

And it's always a highly unserious endeavor, little more than an excuse to touch each other when we're in the kitchen waiting for the oven to ding.

"That's what slow-dancing is," Kip says.

"I think there's more to it than that," I respond.

He releases an irritated breath, and it occurs to me that he's serious right now. He doesn't want to do this, like, at all.

A part of me considers acquiescing to his request that we cancel, but a bigger part of me wonders if that would just further enable his patterns of avoidance. And haven't I already acquiesced enough? I gave up the Vows piece; I've been patient about this whole Jake thing. The least he could do is learn how to properly slow-dance with me.

"Please, babe?" Kip asks again. "Can we cancel this? I'll practice with you in our room, if you want. Taking a formal lesson just feels like too much."

"I just told you it's nonrefundable," I remind him.

"So what?" he challenges. "Sunk cost. Let's go to the beach. Let's actually enjoy this place—"

"I want our first dance to be perfect!" I kind-of-maybe snap. "Why are you waiting until right now—two minutes before the appointment time—to tell me you don't want to do this?"

"I've tried to tell you several times," Kip huffs. "You just didn't want to hear it."

"Can we talk about this after the lesson?" I squint at a directory sign poking out of one of the flower beds as we turn another corner. "Lovebird Studio! This way."

Kip grunts in frustration, but follows my lead nonetheless. I don't love the fact that we're going into our lesson with this tension between us, but maybe this is the only way to get him out of his comfort zone—by dragging him.

We both force composure as we step into the shiny studio.

Our instructor greets us warmly, a giant silk shawl draping from her open arms as she goes in for polite half hugs.

"Look what we have here!" she says. "You two gentlemen will be dashing grooms."

She reminds me of a cross between Dolly Parton and Diane Keaton, which is perfect. A part of me was nervous we'd get someone more like Sparky Polastri, the freakishly intense choreographer from *Bring It On* who screamed in everyone's faces about the proper technique for spirit fingers. Kip would've immediately shut down around a Sparky, but he'll be great with a Dolly-Diane. I can already tell he's more relaxed than he was twenty seconds ago.

All he needed was a nudge.

"So which one of you is Ray and which one of you is Kip?" she asks.

We introduce ourselves, and then she tells us her name is Barbara Eden.

This prompts me to do a double take, because she does look a bit like *the* Barbara Eden—star of the hit sixties show *I Dream of Jeannie*. Could it actually be her?

I shoot Kip an Are-we-really-about-to-get-a-dance-lesson-from-a-legendary-sitcom-actress? look, but he can't seem to read the expression, probably because he has no idea who Barbara Eden is in the first place.

Barbara taps at the iPhone in her hand, prompting the *I Dream of Jeannie* theme song to pump through the studio's speakers, and launches into a full-on belly dance. At which point I become distinctly aware that it's all a shtick.

"No relation to my namesake!" she proclaims, hips asway. "I just happened to marry a schlub named Frank Eden back in '72. Two husbands ago, but I'm keeping the name for life. Can ya blame me?"

I laugh, Kip laughs, and Barbara cuts the music.

"So let's begin!" she coos. "Tell me about yourselves: why you're here, what you most want to get out of this experience." She gestures toward a trio of yoga mats on the shiny wooden floor. "Here. Take a seat. Take a stretch."

"We're getting married in August," I start. "Big wedding in the Hamptons. Kip's a doctor, I'm an internet writer, and neither of us is naturally rhythmic. And we've never slow-danced."

"In public," Kip clarifies.

"With each other," I further clarify.

Barbara scrunches her face in confusion.

"We've done it in public with women," I further clarify, "but we've never done man-on-man."

And then I realize that it fully sounds like I'm talking about porn. And also that I'm not being entirely honest. I *have* slow-danced with a man in public before. At my first wedding, with Byrd. But as with everything else about our marriage, that feels like it didn't count.

"Basically we just wanna learn the basics," I finish. "Like where to put our hands and stuff."

Barbara nods. "I can help with that! What have you selected as your first dance song?"

"'Tougher Than the Rest,'" we answer in unison. "Bruce Springsteen."

She raises an eyebrow. "I don't believe I've heard that song in years. Most gay couples choose something a little more..." Her voice trails off. "Modern."

Her confusion doesn't surprise me. CeCe teased me relentlessly when I first told her about the choice. Something about how it's the wedding song of a schoolteacher and a cop getting shotgun-married at a VFW off the Jersey Turnpike circa 1987.

But there was no way we could choose anything else. "Tougher Than the Rest" has been with us since the very beginning of our relationship, ever since we took our first road trip together from New York City up to New Hampshire, listening to Kip's favorite classic rock station on Sirius XM.

When "Tougher Than the Rest" came on, which I had never heard until then, Kip reached across the armrest and linked his fingers through mine.

The lyrics were so simple and yet so precisely about us. It's not a song about first love or perfect love. It's a song specifically for people who've been married and divorced, people who understand that making a relationship work requires a certain toughness, a willingness to get hurt. The grit to stay committed when things inevitably get hard.

Feeling Kip squeeze my hand as Bruce sang about his stability—assuring his partner that he's not going anywhere—my heart soared. Every man I'd been with before Kip had a certain flightiness to them. An omnipresent sense that they were keenly aware of what else is out there—the better job, the bigger apartment, the hotter guy—and just might jump ship if the opportunity presented itself. Kip had already proven himself to be nothing like those guys, but his hand squeeze that day confirmed it. And in the years that have elapsed since, he's only continued to prove it more and more each day.

He is, without a doubt, tougher than the rest.

"It's very meaningful to us," I tell Barbara.

She pulls it up on her phone, which is connected to the sound system, and soon enough it's blaring through the studio. Kip and I exchange a look, and I get choked up thinking about our intertwined hands on that drive up north.

We execute a few basic stretches while Barbara absorbs the song, nodding along to the soft beat. Halfway through the second chorus, she bounces up from her mat and commands that we do the same.

"Let's get to it!" She grabs me by the waist and positions me directly in front of Kip. "Let's start with a basic step. This will be the foundation of your entire dance, and it's very simple."

She slowly circles us, pushes our shoulders down, and maneuvers our arms. Kip's right hand is placed just beneath my left armpit while my left hand rests below his shoulder. She draws our other hands together, halfway up.

The whole thing is very ballroomy and doesn't feel natural at all.

"In a traditional pairing, the man leads," Barbara says. "Of course, you're both men..." She strokes her chin for a moment. "Let's have Kip lead, given that he's a pinch taller. Is that alright with you, Ray?"

I have no idea what the difference is.

"Sure," I tell Barbara, hoping she'll be able to make this seem easy once the music starts.

She proceeds to guide us through the steps from behind

Kip—*left, together, left, tap, right, together, right, tap*—and I keep getting tripped up because the directions are actually the opposite for me. She then switches to a more generic phrasing—*one, two, three, four, five, six, seven, eight*—and I eventually get the hang of it.

We're just going from side to side at this point.

She puts the music on, and we do it to the beat, with Barbara guiding us in different directions. Kip's expression is blank—I get the sense that he'd still rather be anywhere else but here—but he's a natural at leading. His steps are firm, assertive, and easy for me to follow—backward, forward, back again, side to side, and back again, throughout the entire studio floor.

Even though it's a slow song, keeping up makes it feel fast.

Too fast.

I catch a glance of us on the mirror wall, and we actually look like we know what we're doing, but we also look ridiculous. Like we're cast members in *Bridgerton* or something, formally waltzing in a Regency-era ballroom. I know our kitchen slow-dancing isn't terribly elegant—and may or may not be riddled with vibes of early-aughts middle schoolers dancing to K-Ci & JoJo at homecoming—but it feels a lot more romantic than whatever this is.

"Okay, wait." I stop moving and address Barbara. "This feels too formal. Is there a less...extravagant version? Something that fits the song and our personalities more. Just a basic, romantic slow dance?"

She pauses the music and cocks her head.

"Ray's right," Kip says. "I'd rather not look so choreographed."

Barbara strokes her chin for a moment.

"Let's try a basic foxy," she eventually suggests.

She guides us into a pattern that involves far less footwork, but is still rhythmic enough to keep it from veering into K-Ci-&-JoJo-at-homecoming territory. Kip picks it up quickly, leading us with small steps back and forth within a limited portion of the floor.

"Excellent leading," Barbara says. "But you're both looking a little stiff." She gets behind me and pushes my shoulders down, then does the same to Kip. "Try to relax…"

"I feel ridiculous," Kip whispers into my ear.

"The gap between us feels big." I move closer and closer, until we're practically smooshed against each other. "How about this?"

Kip stiffens up even further.

"Gentlemen." Barbara sighs. "You're thinking too much. Just let go. Pretend I'm not here. It's just the two of you, leaning into your love." She sneaks up behind Kip and places a hand over his rib cage. "Take a deep breath in, Doctor. Now exhale."

I take a deep breath of my own as she starts the music up again. It's difficult to take her advice about letting go, because *thinking* about letting go precludes the act of *actually* letting go.

So I will myself to stop thinking altogether, instead focusing on the familiar feeling of Kip's hands, the subtle scent of his aftershave, the comforting presence of his body.

He continues to lead with perfect rhythm.

"There it is," Barbara exclaims. "You've got it! Just keep swaying."

Our fingers intertwine, and I instinctively press my chest against his.

His heart beats in time with mine, which I interpret as a sign that he's finally let his inhibitions go. I *knew* I could get him to come around.

I close my eyes and take him in. Gratitude swells in me as I think of all the reasons I love Kip—not the least of which is the fact that he *has* been so willing to humor me with all this wedding stuff—and the first word that comes to mind is *molting*.

We're vulnerable.

We're growing.

At least until Kip snaps out of his trance and jerks away from me like I'm made of fire. The music's still going, but there might as well have been a record scratch. I struggle to keep my balance as I stop moving.

"What happened?" Barbara asks. "You had it! It was perfect—although you may want to reconsider the interlocking of your fingers. That would make it very difficult to execute a turn or a dip..."

Kip looks like he's just seen a ghost. "I'm sorry. I just opened my eyes and saw us in the mirror and—"

He cuts himself off, his gaze ping-ponging all around the studio, from the walls to the ceiling to the front door, where it settles.

"That felt good, right?" I ask him, trying to drown out the voice in my head that's telling me I've finally done it: pushed Kip *too* far out of his comfort zone. "I think that's exactly the dance for us." I turn to Barbara. "No need for turns or dips. Nothing too fancy."

"Are you sure?" Barbara asks. "One well-timed turn can do wonders."

The thought of being twirled and/or dipped makes me physically wince. As much as I want us to have all the cheesy traditions straight people have at their weddings, some moves are just too dramatic in nature to attempt.

"I'd rather not," I tell Barbara. "What do you think, Kip?"

But he's still all tensed up, fixated on the front door.

Barbara follows his glance. "Oh. My next pupils must be early..."

And then I see them.

Right in the door's center window—poking their curious faces in from the hallway—Jake and Lucy.

25

Kip rushes us out of the studio so quickly we barely have a chance to thank Barbara Eden for her service.

"Jake," he says cautiously. "Hi…"

Jake's face is frozen in shock from his chin all the way up to his bald head. It's clear Lucy hasn't told him the truth, but now I almost wish she had. At least then he would be more prepared for this moment, giving it the nonchalant acceptance it deserves.

The nonchalant acceptance *Kip* deserves.

But instead Jake keeps narrowing his brow at us, opening his mouth to speak, and then going silent. He's a stalled car. The key's in the ignition but it won't start.

"Hi, boys," Lucy attempts. She looks more suited for a SoulCycle session than a dance lesson, in black stretchy shorts and a pink sports bra. "How'd you like the instructor?"

The question doesn't register at first because I'm so consumed with trying to gauge where Kip's head is at. But he's nothing more than a blank loading screen, waiting for his friend to say something, anything, to cut the tension.

"Her name is Barbara Eden," I finally tell Lucy. Maybe if she and I can get a low-stakes conversation going, the other two will follow our lead and we can all move on without acknowledging the gay elephant in the room. "Isn't that fun?"

"So fun!" Lucy agrees.

Jake clears his throat and finally seems to find some words. "I'm so confused..."

This snaps Kip out of his daze. He straightens his posture, places a tentative hand against the small of my back, and takes a deep breath.

"Ray is my fiancé," he says in his best let's-just-get-this-over-with voice. "We were just getting a dance lesson. For our wedding. Because we're getting married."

Jake stays frozen for a few more moments before abruptly snapping out of his own daze and overcompensating with exaggerated enthusiasm.

"Oh!" he stammers. "You guys are...uh... That's awesome, man! Holy shit, wow. I had no idea. But good for you, dude. I... That's awesome, man!"

"You already said that," Kip says through a patient smile. He's feigning an air of coolness, but I know this is killing him. Which means it's also killing me. "Thanks, buddy."

Jake coughs. "So...you're..."

Kip swallows a lump his throat. "Yep, I'm gay."

"Okay, Ellen," I crack—the requisite homosexual reaction to those three words.

Kip turns to me. "Huh?"

"Ellen," I repeat. "Her 1997 *Time* magazine cover..."

Crickets.

"When she came out of the closet," I add. "The headline was 'Yep, I'm Gay.' Remember? She was squatting in front of a plain white backdrop...wearing...shoes..."

"I do remember that." Lucy attempts to ease the awkwardness with a chuckle, but it feels canned and obligatory, like the *Laugh Now* sign just lit up at a sitcom taping. "Yes. She *was* wearing shoes!"

Jake follows with a laugh of his own, but it's not forced at all. It's more like one of those involuntary, awkward, I-am-unable-to-process-what's-happening-right-now laughs.

"Kip Hayes," he says to himself, "is *gay*."

Lucy slaps his arm. "Babe."

Jake turns to Kip. "So, like, what about Annie? What about that chick you were with before Annie? I mean. You don't *seem*—" He cuts himself off. "Sorry. I'm just trying to understand how this works…"

I can feel Kip's anguish beside me as he contemplates a response. I'm sure it was hard enough for him to say "I'm gay" out loud to someone who's always believed he was the quintessence of heterosexuality, so I imagine the last thing he wants to do is participate in an interrogation about it.

"I was in the closet for a long time," Kip says through a shrug.

"How did I not know about this?" Jake asks.

I'm getting a sense that his bewilderment is about more than just Kip. It's about his entire worldview being called into question. Somehow he's managed to go fortysomething years without ever meeting someone who challenged his preconceived notions of who's straight and who's gay.

"We haven't talked in ten years," Kip says. "It didn't occur to me to seek you out and tell you the second I jumped into my first gay relationship."

"Does everyone else know? The guys from school?"

"I really only talk to Johnny these days," Kip says. "He knows. And Cam, he knows too, I guess."

"And neither of them said anything to me!" Jake marvels. "This is the best-kept secret in Cornell history… Jesus."

Lucy grabs my wrist. "Do you know where the nearest bathroom is? I had one too many mimosas at brunch."

"Um…" I know I saw one at the entrance to the pavilion, but the fact that she's asking me specifically catches me off guard. "I think there's one—"

"Show me," she says. "Then we can give Jake and Kip a chance to talk in private."

There's a protective instinct in me that really doesn't want to leave Kip alone right now, but then he turns to me and says, "That's a good idea. I'll meet you by the entrance in a few."

—

Lucy pulls me into the men's room and locks the door behind us.

I perch myself on the sparkling-clean counter and ask, "Why do we keep ending up in men's bathrooms together?"

Thankfully, this one is immaculate. The air is fresh with the scent of eucalyptus, and the toilet looks like it's never come into contact with even a single drop of urine.

"I'm sorry," Lucy says. "That was just so painfully awkward out there."

"What *was* that? Has your fiancé never met a gay person?"

"Of course he has," she insists. "I told you he's great with my gay friends! He's just surprised."

My facial muscles twist with skepticism. "Surprised? Even after the other night?"

"Even after the other night," she says through a chuckle. "Jake is a brilliantly smart man and a great doctor. But he's not very perceptive in his personal life. He's much more interested in himself…"

"So he's a narcissist."

She considers this a moment. "Isn't *everyone* a narcissist?"

"I'm not!" I protest. Even though there are pages and pages of Google results from my past that suggest otherwise. "Kip's not."

That one's actually true—and part of why I love him so much.

Lucy smacks her lips in the mirror. "Jake will be fine. He just needs a sec to process."

"This is so silly. They're not even friends anymore. If it weren't for this trip, they probably wouldn't have ever seen each other again. And they probably won't ever see each other again after this."

"Maybe this is the universe's way of bringing them back together," Lucy muses. "Maybe we have some double dates ahead of us. You can visit us in the city. Oh! Oh my God. You guys should come to our wedding. We can seat you with John and Liz."

I shift my weight on the counter, which leads to catastrophe as I had no idea how close I was to the sink. Suddenly half my ass has fallen into it—causing the automatic faucet to start running—and I'm grabbing Lucy's shoulder for balance as my tailbone threatens to snap.

She graciously helps me regain balance. "You don't have to RSVP right now."

"Let's see how things go with Jake and Kip." I grab a bunch of paper towels to dry off my left ass cheek. "But sure. Maybe we could get together sometime. Kip and I never have any reason to go into the city these days. We miss it."

I don't really mean this—I love the fact that our lives have become so suburban and comfortable—but for some reason I can't stop myself from saying it. I feel like it's what Lucy wants to hear.

"Even if those two never want to see each other again," she adds, "there's no reason why you and I can't keep in touch." She hands her phone to me. "Here. Gimme your digits."

I toss my phone to her so she can do the same. As strange as this entire situation is, I am starting to enjoy these stolen moments with Lucy. They kind of remind me of college and grad school, back when I made more space in my life for friendship.

"It would be great to hang out *outside* of a bathroom one day," I joke as we accept our phones back from each other.

Lucy runs a hand through her hair and smiles. "You know what? I'd like to go on the record for your article."

This piques my interest. "Even though you and Jake low-key hate each other?"

"We do not!" she insists. "All that stuff from the other day, that's just our thing. Deep down, I am excited to marry him. And you know what? Yesterday was one of the best days ever for us."

This piques my interest even more. "How so?"

"Something about this place is bringing us closer," she says. "We played nine holes of golf in the morning, which is normally his thing, but it was so much fun. Then we did the couple's massage at the spa, which is typically *my* thing, but he loved it. He's always so tense, you know? I've never seen him as relaxed as he was on that massage table. It made him...*nice*. And then we had the best time at the swim-up bar in the pool.

"Him doing my thing with me, me doing his thing with him, both of us staying together for an entire day... I felt closer to him than I have in a long time. We always spend so much time apart that sometimes I forget we actually do love each other."

"Awww."

If I bury my knowledge of their patterns of deception, I have to admit she's giving me good material. The idea of an earlymoon as a prewedding escape for couples who are starved for quality time in their daily lives makes sense. And it's an interesting contrast to Kip and me. If anything, I'm starting to learn that one of our problems is *too much* quality time—at the expense of everyone else in our lives—to the extent that we take it for granted.

"I think I *will* quote you in the piece," I tell Lucy.

"Yay! I—"

She's interrupted by the sound of the door handle jiggling.

Followed by Kip's voice.

"Ray? Are you in there? Let's go."

26

Kip's energy is ice cold as we make our way back to the hotel. I'm dying to ask him a million questions, but he hasn't made eye contact with me once since we left the pavilion, and I know it's because there's a storm raging in his head.

"Babe," I finally attempt as we pass the cabana bar on the south side of the beach. "Are you okay? Can we talk about what just happened?"

"Let's just wait until we get to the room."

"But don't you think we should start talking about it now?" I ask. "That was a big moment back there... Are you okay?"

"I'm fine," he says in a definitely-not-fine growl. "I'll be fine."

I have to wonder if Jake said something to trigger him while Lucy and I were in the bathroom. Because shouldn't Kip be relieved right now? He got the difficult conversation over with, and now we can all move on.

"Jake seemed cool about it," I offer. "Once he got over his initial shock..."

"Can you drop this?" Kip says. "At least wait until we're in the room."

"But—"

"I just want to talk in private," he snaps. Then his voice pivots to a nasty sarcasm I don't even recognize. "Oh, sorry, I should explain. 'Privacy' is this thing where you actively choose to avoid attention. I know the term is foreign to you."

I could rebut with a comment about how people in this cabana bar couldn't give less of a shit about two anonymous homosexuals engaged in a lovers' quarrel, but that wouldn't help matters. He's pissed, and pushing his buttons while we're technically in public would only prove the point he just made, thereby pissing him off more.

So I back off and continue the trek in silence.

It's another postcard day at the resort—a blur of sun, sand, and water taunts my peripheral vision—and it kills me that we're now wasting another afternoon with this tension between us when we should be basking in our love. If an earlymoon is really supposed to be an indicator of a marriage's potential to thrive, it's starting to look like Kip and I might be screwed.

The second we get back to the room, he slams the door shut behind him.

"Sure you don't wanna close the security latch?" I ask. "Maybe throw up the DO NOT DISTURB sign? Just want to make sure this is private enough for you."

I'm disappointed with myself even as I say it. Just because he snapped at me earlier doesn't mean I need to snap back, but apparently my feelings were more hurt than I realized.

"Fuck you," Kip replies.

"What is going on with you?" I ask. "What did I do?"

He releases a long, frustrated sigh and paces around the suite. Housekeeping came in while we were out and cleaned up all the evidence of our stay thus far; the space is as tidy as the day we checked in. Nearly sterile.

"You made me tell Jake about us," Kip says. "I wasn't ready to do that."

"I didn't say anything to him! He just showed up at our dance lesson, and then you made the choice to tell him the truth."

"You knew I didn't want to take that damn lesson in the first place!" he argues. "I asked you so many times to cancel it, but you practically dragged me into the place."

"What is the big deal?" I prod. "You said you were planning to tell him yourself if we saw him again."

Kip finally stops pacing and collapses onto the linen sectional in the corner of our suite.

"You just don't get it," he says.

"Then explain it to me." I take a seat on the carpet, since the couch doesn't feel all that welcoming at the moment. "What did Jake say to you after Lucy and I left?"

"It's not anything he said," Kip huffs. "It's that I wanted to have that conversation on my own terms. I didn't even want to have it at all. I shouldn't be required to tell every single person from my past— including people I've consciously decided to *leave* in the past—every detail of my personal life."

This shit again? Why can't he understand that *not* having that conversation means completely undermining the validity of our entire relationship?

"Right," I huff back, "you'd rather just let them think you're someone you're not. Because that's *so* healthy."

"I'm not like you and everyone else in your generation," Kip says. "I don't need every Tom, Dick, and Harry to 'know' and 'see' me. If it's easier to let someone assume I'm straight, that's what I'm going to do. It's not always about some deep-rooted internalized homophobia or shame or whatever the fuck."

"He's not just some Tom, Dick, or Harry, though!" I challenge. "He used to be a good friend."

"Exactly!" He takes a deep breath and lets his arms fall. "We *used to* have a friendship. And the way he looked at me today, it was like our entire history was erased in a split second. The version of me that he knew just died right in front of us."

"That version of you was already dead," I remind him. "It's been dead for years."

"Not in Jake's mind. Now he's over there thinking he never really knew me at all."

"He *didn't* really know you!"

"Just because I covered up my sexuality doesn't mean I was a completely fake person. The person he knew is the person I was for almost forty years... And honestly? Sometimes I miss being that person."

"You miss being closeted?" I dig my fingers into the hotel carpet in an attempt to slow my heart rate. "You wish you never met me at all?"

"I didn't say that."

"That's the implication."

"I miss not being defined by my sexuality."

Defined by his sexuality? I can't even bring myself to justify that with a response. All I'm trying to do is get this man to acknowledge the existence of our relationship, not serve as grand marshal of the fucking New York City Pride Parade.

Kip rubs his temples as he searches for more words. "Listen, I am grateful for all you've done to help me accept myself and live more openly over the years. But at some point I have to be able to set my *own* comfort level with this stuff. And lately I've been wondering if—"

He cuts himself off and looks at me with the saddest eyes I've ever seen.

"If...?"

"If I just can't do this," he says quietly.

My throat constricts as I ask, "Do what?"

He extends his arms out and gestures at the space between us. "This whole performative *love* thing you want so bad. Our wedding…"

"Our wedding?" I repeat through the massive black hole that's suddenly opened up in my stomach. Even though Kip's words could very well mean he's trying to cancel it altogether, I can't even begin to acknowledge that possibility out loud. So instead I just remind him, "You're the one who proposed to me!"

"Because I love you!" Kip says. "Not because I wanted to turn our relationship into a fucking circus! Ever since we started planning this wedding, you've reverted into the attention-seeking hurricane you were before you met me. And it's gotten so much worse this week."

"So this is about the article?" I ask.

"Yes, it's… No."

"It's *not* about the article?"

"It's all of it," he groans. "It's about the fact that I said I wanted to do a small thing at city hall, and you kept pushing and pushing until I agreed to two hundred people in the Hamptons. But fine, whatever, I wanted to make you happy."

He raises a finger. "It's that you agreed to drop the Vows profile, but then decided to write about us for *Appeal* anyway. Which I also decided to let go, because I wanted to make you happy."

He raises another finger. "PDA has *never* been a thing with us, and now all of a sudden you want to start kissing in public. And again, fine, I wanted to make you happy, so I kissed you at dinner the other night…"

Another finger. "Meanwhile, I'm explicitly telling you I don't want to do a first dance at the wedding, and I'm thinking, 'Maybe he'll let me have this one thing.' And then you go and schedule a fucking *dance lesson*. It's all just—"

"It's all just what getting married *is*!" I fume. "How many straight weddings have we been to over the years? How many of your straight friends have plastered their engagement photos all over social media? How many of them have had wedding announcements published in the paper? You've never once described any of them as 'attention-seeking hurricanes.'"

"That's different," Kip claims.

"*How?*" I push.

"It just is," he says. "Straight people can do all that stuff and it's unremarkable. Gays do it and it becomes a statement. Us just existing is a statement—one that hasn't been easy for me to make, but I've learned to accept it because I love you. But all this wedding stuff takes it to another level..."

He slumps down on the couch. "And I'm not that kind of person. I'm just not. I've been trying so hard to be, for you, but it's not who I am. It's not who I want to be."

"Who even is that?" I ask.

Kip sighs and rolls his head back, as if he's looking for the answer to my question on the ceiling. But instead of finding it, he just finds yet another reason why everything is all my fault.

"You're a hypocrite," he accuses. "You've always *loved* the fact that I'm not all over social media. You're always telling me how much you admire my ability to not care about likes and shares and all that bullshit. You only want me to be out and proud in relation to you—as *your* husband—as an accessory for *your* public image."

His words hit me in the gut—which means there must be some truth to them—but I ignore the pain and force out a meek defense. "That's so not true."

"Isn't it, though?" he challenges. "You love that I'm the strong, tough one who never needs anything. Our wedding song is literally called 'Tougher Than the Rest.'"

This makes me think of what he said the other morning, about how he's always struggled with upsetting people's expectations.

It kills me to think *my* expectations have caused him so much turmoil, but I also can't help but feel like I shouldn't be blamed for taking his actions at face value. He always *has* presented himself as the strong, steady partner, so I let him be. How was I supposed to know I was playing into a lifelong people-pleasing complex?

"I just told you the other day that you don't *have* to be tough for me," I remind him. "I can handle it if you're weak. I can handle it if you're not perfect."

"You say that, but you don't mean it."

"What do you mean?"

"I mean you can't have it both ways," he says. "You can't expect me to be the man you fell in love with, and then get mad when I don't wave a pride flag around twenty-four/seven."

"It's not about waving around a pride flag!" I insist. "It's about acknowledging our relationship. It's about you not *erasing* me from your life and shoving me back into the closet—which is exactly what you do every time you let people assume straightness for the sake of avoiding point-five seconds of conversational awkwardness."

His face goes pale at that accusation, and he doesn't say anything for a minute.

"I don't have a problem acknowledging our relationship," he finally chokes out. "I've been doing it for the past six years—at least to the people who matter. My problem is you telling me to be myself, and then getting upset when *myself* is someone who doesn't like to engage in attention-seeking behavior. I'm a private person by nature, and it has nothing to do with being gay."

"Of course it does!" I tell him. "It's so clearly a result of shame."

"No," he counters. "Your constant *need* for attention—*that's* a result of shame."

"How's that?"

"Because you're always seeking evidence that you're a valid person," he says. "All I want to do is to live a normal, peaceful, *anonymous* life. I know our current culture of oversharing has you brainwashed to think that's the worst fate ever, but it's a hell of a lot more authentic than chasing likes from strangers."

"You think that's what I do?" I ask. "I never even post on social media anymore."

"It's what you used to do," he says. "Before we met. And I thought you'd gotten it out of your system, but apparently—"

He cuts himself off after getting a load of the look on my face, which I can only imagine is one of unadulterated hurt.

"I come from a different place than you with all this stuff," he redirects. "I've never needed to post my life all over social media for validation. I've always managed to get it in real life." He pauses for a moment. "But I understand that the internet is the only place where being straight *isn't* a virtue, so I get why you've always been so drawn to sharing your life on it. I do. But it's not a substitute for the real thing."

The real thing? He can't be serious. "Approval for being someone you're not is the exact opposite of the real thing."

"And what about you?" Kip asks. "You think if you write some grand love story about us for your readers, if we dance to our song together in front of a big crowd, that that's any more real?"

"It absolutely is."

"You're just as consumed with straight approval as I am," Kip scoffs. "Maybe even more so. You treat all these traditions like they're so sacred. You want our wedding to be just like the movies, just like your parents'—but you don't understand that it can't be. Even if we say all the vows and have the big kiss and the slow dance and shove cake in each other's faces, guess what? We're still two dudes. We're nontraditional by definition. I've come to accept that. Why can't you?"

"Because we don't have to accept it," I tell him. "We can rewrite the script so that it *does* include us! Can't you see that's what I'm trying to do? That's why I want to share our story, why I want to shout about our love from the rooftops."

"Shout about it to who?" he asks. "Who is this imaginary audience you're so eager to impress? The anonymous trolls of the internet? They don't care! Everybody everywhere is shouting about their lives online. Nobody's listening."

He gestures to the space between us and adds, "The whole point of a relationship is to have someone who *is* listening."

The room falls silent.

"So, then, what?" I finally ask. "What do you even want at this point? Because we have a wedding—a big gay one—in two months." Tears build behind my eyes as the next thought comes to me; I swallow them down to get it out. "And if we're gonna cancel it, we should probably start making some phone calls."

Regret floods my system as I realize I've just taken my most feared outcome of this conversation and put it on the table for Kip to consider.

He sinks into the couch and buries his face in his hands.

Several more moments pass before he can bring himself to speak up.

"I didn't say I want to cancel the wedding," he says. "I just want to…"

And now we're back to silence.

My hands are squeezed so tight, it's a miracle I don't break a finger. A flurry of words blows through my mind, but I can't steady myself enough to isolate a coherent sentence.

"What?" I manage to stammer. "What do you want?"

Kip groans. "I don't know."

The resignation in his voice is like a knife to my chest. All he had to say was something—anything—to reassure me that regardless of the identity crisis he's going through, he'd never second-guess his decision to marry me.

But it's clear that he is second-guessing it, and that makes me want to dissolve right into the fibers of this hotel carpet.

Somehow I muster the strength to shoot up from the floor and cover my pain with a shot of rage.

"Well, you need to figure it out," I hiss before slapping the security latch loose and whipping the door open. "And when you do that, please let me know."

27

I hover in the hallway outside our hotel door for several minutes, desperate for Kip to swing it open and come running after me.

The awareness that my abrupt exit was nothing more than a petulant bluff does not make me feel good. It makes me feel like the disaster of a boyfriend I used to be in my twenties, always picking drunken fights with exes. It makes me feel like the insecure train wreck I was in the weeks after Byrd cheated on me—but before he broke up with me—when I'd snap at him for the littlest things and refuse to accept his apologies, always searching for ways to make him chase after me and prove his love.

But Kip's clearly not interested in chasing, or proving, anything at the moment.

I swallow yet another rush of tears and make my way to the elevator, forcing myself to go through with my empty threat of separation. It feels like the least natural thing in the world to willingly create distance between us right now. Kip is always the one who asks for space during fights—not me—but I have no choice.

I'm in a daze as I wander around the resort, aimless and numb.

Eventually I plunk down at the indoor hotel bar, because fuck sunshine, and throw back two bourbons, neat, because fuck sugary vacation drinks.

There's an old-timey sign behind the bar that says THE COLD FEET SALOON, which nearly unravels me.

Why would a place like this have a sign like that?

As some kind of sick joke?

My throat burns with alcohol as I consider everything Kip said back in the room. What if he's right? What if I *am* being too pushy, too impatient, too selfish?

Maybe I should just offer to cancel our wedding entirely and opt for city hall instead, like he wanted to from the beginning. If it means keeping him—keeping our life together intact—it might be worth the sacrifice.

Or would it?

What if we then got married only for me to resent him for killing the dream wedding I've spent a lifetime looking forward to? Or what if Kip's pattern of molding himself after what people expect him to be runs even deeper than either of us realize—to the extent that he doesn't even know himself at all? What if he ultimately comes to realize that his true self is someone who doesn't even want to be married in the first place?

But what if our love is just as real and essential as we've both always known it to be—and the rest is just a mess of minor details that can be untangled later?

My mind circles back to the thought that it's me. I'm the problem. I need to compromise in order to be the solution.

Let Kip be as private as he wants to be.

But even if I genuinely wanted to give up on my dream wedding, the mere act of sending out cancellation notices would draw far more attention to ourselves than simply going through with it as planned.

The only real solution to Kip's grievance would be to go back in time and not insist on the dream wedding in the first place.

To go back in time and not agree to the earlymoon article.

To go back in time and not broadcast my every intimate thought and personal detail in the endless blog roll of my teens and twenties.

To go back in time and be an entirely different person.

28

~

get up and head to the beach, finally buzzed enough to stand beneath the sun and not interpret its brightness as a personal attack on my emotional state.

But halfway down the outdoor steps, the rambling outdoor pool catches my attention instead. Rows of navy-blue lounge chairs surround the rocky faux-waterfalls that jut out from every corner. A massive hot tub perches in the center of it all.

I've never understood resorts with lavish pools directly in front of the natural beauty of an actual beach, but I don't give a shit about that right now.

The only thing I give a shit about is this pool's swim-up bar, which will make it easy to continue drowning my sorrows without interruption. This trip has been an unequivocal failure—instead of strengthening my relationship, it's turned the entire thing into a question mark—and I refuse to be sober for a single second more of it.

I throw my shirt, phone, and room key on a lounge chair and dive into the chlorine. I nearly burst into tears as I order a tall can of Goose Island IPA from the swim-up bartender, momentarily forgetting that this is one of Kip's favorite beers. And again when I tell the bartender to charge it to our room, which means I have to sign Kip's name on the receipt.

I doggy paddle my way to a secluded corner of the pool, rest my elbows on the ledge, and close my eyes to the sun.

"Ray!"

The voice comes from behind and is immediately followed by the splash of a cannonball right next to me.

I open my eyes to the sight of Joley's head emerging from the water, his face half-covered in soaking-wet clumps of dark-blond hair. The canvas of ink across his chest and rib cage is now fully visible without his shirt on, and my gaze immediately glues itself to the lobster claw on his left shoulder.

"Hi," he says through a grin, water dripping from his tightly trimmed beard. "Haven't seen ya around. I wondered if you'd left."

I point at his shoulder. "I almost got one of those."

He laughs as he looks down. "A tat?"

I nod. "The lobster... I used to be a lobsterman."

His eyes widen. "A lobsterman turned internet writer? That's different."

"Well..." I'm speaking before I can even think, which is a sure sign that I'm both drunk and distressed. "My sister is a lobster boat captain here in Seabrook. My dad used to be. He wanted me to be."

"Oh," he says through a smirk. "So *you* never actually were."

"Not technically," I admit. "I went out on the boat with my sister on Tuesday, though."

"Oof. That must've been rough. I didn't even know Connecticut lobster was still a thing. At my restaurant it's always—"

"Maine," I finish for him. "I've eaten there many times."

He points to the beer in my hand. "I need one of those. Join me at the swim-up bar?"

I surprise myself by saying yes and really meaning it. I'm buzzed and sad and it feels good to not be alone, and yeah, I'll admit it, even better with the knowledge that Joley finds me attractive and would be entirely DTF if I was—even though I'm still definitely *not*.

So now I'm following behind him, studying the toothy tiger tattoo stretching across his shoulder blades. It's broad daylight, yet something about this encounter feels dark and vaguely dangerous—the kind of thing that should take place in the corner of an after-hours dive bar.

Am I leading Joley on by engaging with him right now?

Or worse—am I betraying Kip?

I push the concerns out of my head. There's nothing wrong with having a beer in the pool with a fellow gay man. I just need someone to talk to about nothing. Something to distract me until I'm ready to confront my relationship crisis again.

"You alright?" Joley asks as we approach the bar. "You seem kinda out of it."

I guzzle the remainder of my beer, slam it on the bar, and apropos of absolutely nothing, kick my legs out behind me like a merman. "I'm fine!"

He smiles and slicks a tuft of wet hair off his face. "I'm not convinced. Excuse me?" He motions the bartender with my empty can. "Two more of these, please. Charge it to Room 313."

"Oh, you don't have to get mine—"

"Please," he says. "I owe you."

"Why is that?"

"The other day," he says. "I shouldn't have been so forward. I know you're here on an earlymoon with your...mysteriously always-absent fiancé." He facetiously scans the entire pool area. "Where is he now?"

My face flushes as I realize how alone I am—or *was*, before Joley showed up—and I can't blame it on Kip being out running or me trying to work on my article over breakfast. The only thing to blame is my growing knowledge of our incompatibility.

"We had a little fight." I instantly regret being so honest. I've just opened up the stage for him to reply with the most obvious flirty response ever (*"Trouble in paradise?"*) and/or ask any number of invasive questions about the state of my relationship.

Before he can conjure one, though, I hit him with a question of my own. "Where's *your* fiancé?"

"BJ is..." He facetiously scans the entire pool area once again. "Well, he's sulking in our suite at the moment. We also had a little fight."

And then, before I can stop myself from sounding like the kind of person I'd normally hate, *I'm* the one blurting out the obviously flirty response. "Trouble in paradise?"

Joley spreads his arms wide, gesturing at the hot tub across from us, the waterfalls to our left, the beach in the distance. "Literally, right?"

He taps my beer can with his. "Here—to paradise."

Despite the word he said out loud, it really sounds more like he's toasting specifically to the *trouble* half of the phrase, which depresses me even more. I feel like crying—not celebrating.

We take a few swigs and then migrate back to the opposite ledge, closer to our lounge chairs and belongings.

"Beej is so pissed at me," Joley reveals.

"What'd you do now?" I ask, as if I've known him forever and this is the millionth time he's told me a boyfriend was mad at him.

He laughs, and all of a sudden I realize how dangerously sexual his laugh is. Deep and menacing. "You assume it's something *I* did?"

"Well..." I pretend to think for a moment. "Was it?"

He gently splashes me—basically the most flirtatious thing you can do in a body of water—and my conscience goes guilty for letting it happen.

"We have some minor trust issues," Joley says. "He snooped in my phone last night, saw the Grindr icon, had a meltdown…"

The spell of hotness he'd just had over me wanes as I envision this poor fiancé, alone in their suite, wishing he was enough for Joley to keep it in his pants.

I've been that guy before, and it's not fun.

"I don't blame him for having a meltdown," I tell him. Somehow it comes out more playfully than intended. "Why would you be on that app if you're getting married to someone who told you he wants to be monogamous?"

"I messed up," he admits. "I don't know, man. It's an addiction. Don't you ever just feel powerless against your dick?"

"All the time," I confess. "But that's one of the great things about being in a relationship. You're automatically waking up next to someone who can give your dick exactly what it wants. Why do you need to seek it out from someone else?"

He flashes dead eyes at me. "You seriously mean to tell me you never get bored of being with the same man? You never want something more exciting?"

Looking at Joley right now—a mischievous, tattooed chef who couldn't be more unlike the responsible, clean-cut doctor I've been exclusively sleeping with for the past six years—I can't deny that, sure, my body would probably really enjoy having sex with him.

But there's no way I could reconcile the carnal pleasure with the emotional betrayal. I would be physically sick with regret. Even if Kip were willing to forgive me, I wouldn't forgive myself.

"This would all be a non-issue," Joley continues, "if Beej would just agree to opening up the relationship."

"Why are you guys even getting married?" I ask. "If you're so unaligned on this fundamental question, I mean. Surely you could find some other guy who's all for a lifestyle of nonmonogamy."

"I love Beej," he insists. "I want to be with him forever. I just also want to be able to hook up with other men. Nothing more, nothing less."

"That's a very selfish version of love."

"It would go both ways," Joley says. "He could go have fun with other guys, too."

"And what about when he falls in love with one of his side flings?"

He scoffs. "That wouldn't happen."

"How are you so sure?" I ask. "It sounds to me like he's someone who attaches feelings to sex, so it would only be logical that he'd eventually—"

"You sound just like him," Joley groans. "Why do guys like you and BJ have to make sex so *complicated*? It really doesn't have to be."

"Why do guys like you have to make *relationships* so complicated?" I counter. "The idea of constantly seeking sex from strangers and dealing with their emotions and hang-ups and needs and potential diseases... That sounds a lot like work. Monogamy is simple. You have your man, and you love him, and he loves you, and that's it."

"If you say so..."

He moves closer, takes a swig of beer, and pats my chest with his free hand.

"But real talk?" he adds. "I can tell you're attracted to me. And I wanna fuck you."

I choke on my IPA as he finishes that last sentence. I have to cough several consecutive times before I can properly breathe again.

Joley smirks as his shoulders slide into an unapologetic shrug. "The only thing stopping us from being able to hook up is the fact that we're voluntarily boxing ourselves into these 1950s hetero-parroting relationship paradigms. It's ridiculous! Life is too short to deny yourself pleasure for the sake of..."

His voice trails off.

"For the sake of your partner's feelings?" I finish for him. "The partner you claim to love so much?"

"It wouldn't have anything to do with my love for him," he says. "That's what I'm trying to say."

"It would have everything to do with your love for him!" I'm suddenly overcome with an urgent need to defend the one thing I've believed in my entire life. "Are you really that self-absorbed? Everything you do needs to revolve around *yourself*? Around your direct experience of pleasure?

"Sometimes love means being selfless," I go on. "Sometimes it means you do everything you can to make your partner feel special and loved and *enough*. And the cold, hard truth is that there's simply no way to do that when you're actively seeking out sex from other people. There's a built-in implication that your partner is quite literally not enough."

As I say these words, I realize I'm indicting myself just as much as Joley.

Not that I've ever engaged in extramarital sex, just that I've hardly mastered the selflessness I'm preaching so hard. If I had, I wouldn't have immediately shot down Kip's initial suggestion of a quiet city-hall wedding. I wouldn't be so disappointed in his discomfort with my article, or with attention in general. I'd be more patient with him, grateful for the fact that he's never *once* made me feel like I wasn't special, or loved, or enough.

All my grievances with him have to do with how we present ourselves to the world—and nothing to do with the way he loves me.

Joley takes a few lifeless sips of IPA, and then a dejected laugh escapes his lips. "I guess I'm always the bad guy," he says. "I should probably just accept that I'm a piece of shit and move on with it, huh?"

"Are you trying to make me feel sorry for you?"

He makes a sad puppy face. "Is it working?"

I splash him, because somehow it fucking *is*. Goddamn him for being so adept at temporary hypnosis. "I don't think you're a terrible person. I barely know you."

He puts a hand to his heart. "Thanks."

"And I'm not saying open relationships can never work," I continue. "There are much smarter people than myself who seem to be thriving in them. Different strokes for different folks, and all that. But I will say that, judging from what you've mentioned about your fiancé, he's not one of those people. If he did agree to an open relationship, he'd be doing it as a compromise because he doesn't think he deserves what he really wants."

Joley seems bored by my response. He throws his head back and places his beer down on the ledge behind me.

Then he rises from the water and struts over to the waterfall across from us, standing directly beneath it.

It's impossible not to stare as he takes an impromptu shower, his lime-green swim trunks bunched up and drawing attention to a very conspicuous bulge. His eyes are squeezed shut as he lets the water pour over his face, and—

Oh. I didn't notice that tattoo before. A leafy vine that starts and at his left hip and disappears behind the hem of his swim trunks, right toward his—

I need to stop looking.

I need to end this encounter altogether.

I need to run back up to the room and apologize to Kip, assure him that there's nothing wrong with him, he's more than enough for me, and thank him for never insinuating that I'm not enough for him.

Because honestly? Men like Joley are a dime a dozen. I encountered them all the time when I was single—gluttons, never satisfied. Always looking for the better job and the bigger apartment and the hotter guy. Too consumed with their own desires, too afraid of missing out on something better, to ever double down on something real.

Men like Kip, on the other hand, are the rarest breed of all.

How did I allow myself to forget that? Once we fell in love, he didn't think twice about committing to me and me only. It was just a given. And that's not something I want to lose.

I'll make whatever compromises I need to make for the sake of our marriage. I still have no idea what those compromises would even look like, but I know I'm willing to put my own feelings aside to find out.

So I pull myself out of the pool and sit up on the ledge—almost knocking over Joley's half-full beer in the process—ready to dry off and go get my man.

"Wait!" Joley dives back into the water and swims back to me. "Don't tell me I scared you off again."

"I just need to get back to my room," I tell him. "And you should get back to yours, too."

"You're right." He puts a hand on my thigh, which triggers an involuntary rush of heat in my system. "But let's just finish our beers, yeah? I don't wanna leave on this weird note. I'm sorry if I made you uncomfortable."

"You didn't. It's fine." I lower myself back into the pool, primarily to conceal an imminent erection. I swear to God, I'm gonna make love to Kip *so hard* after this. Assuming he lets me back in the room and is just as eager to make up as I am.

"I'm glad," he says. "Mind if I…"

He reaches for his beer behind me, but does so in a very lascivious fashion.

All of a sudden our bodies are pressed together—chest to chest, groin to groin—and I can feel movement in his swim trunks. His stubbly cheek brushes against mine as he snakes his arm around my back, pretending he can't grip the beer that's quite easily in reach. His lips are inching closer to mine by the second.

I pull my head back, but that only seems to make him want me more.

The irony that he's coming on to me in broad daylight—willing to gay-kiss me in public like this—isn't lost on me, and it almost tempts me to just close my eyes and let it happen.

But no. This kiss wouldn't be worth it. It wouldn't be worth *anything*.

I'd take Kip in private over Joley in public any day.

Real over fake.

I snap out of the haze and begin to push Joley away, but then—

"Babe," a familiar voice booms behind me. "What the hell are you doing?"

The voice instantly unlocks a messy supercut of distant memories, but there's no way it could be who I think it is.

"Shit." Joley backs away, clutching the beer can in his hand, speaking in the guiltiest whisper of all time. "It's my fiancé."

"Fuck. *Seriously?*"

I'm suddenly reminded of a documentary I once saw about a deadly volcanic eruption on an island in Australia, where one of the bystanders managed to survive unscathed by staying entirely underwater until the storm passed.

I consider doing the same thing right now, but it's no use. *Beej* has clearly already seen the back of my head.

"It's not what it looks like," Joley says as the footsteps get closer.

"On our *earlymoon*!" BJ hisses.

How is his voice *so*—

Holy.

Shit.

My blood goes cold as I realize that it is most definitely the person I think it is.

"Ray Bruno," Joley says as I turn around and absorb the image of my long-lost ex-husband. "Meet my fiancé. Byrd Joseph Corson."

29

B yrd?"
I jump out of the pool like it's made of lava, grab the towel off my lounge chair, and frantically rub it all over my hair and face and body. As if the absurdity of this situation will somehow all make sense once I'm fully dried off.

"Ray?" Byrd reciprocates. "What the—"

"There was no funny business going on," Joley promises as he splashes out of the water himself. "I was just grabbing my beer from behind him, and we got a little smooshed."

"How do you..." Byrd growls. He hasn't aged at all since our divorce—same tanned skin, bright-blue eyes, and sweepy light-brown hair with nary a touch of gray. "What the hell is going on? You...*know* Joley? What are you even doing here?"

"Since when do you go by *BJ*?" I ask him. "I've never heard a single person call you BJ!"

He flicks his wrist toward Joley. "It's what he calls me. Why does that matter?"

"Because obviously I wouldn't have spent so much time talking to him if I'd known you were his fiancé! This is so..." I throw a hand up. "I'm engaged. My fiancé is—"

"How much time?" Byrd says.

"What?" I ask.

"You've spent 'so much time' talking? What does that even mean? Have you guys just been sneaking around behind my back all week? Is this supposed to be some kind of payback?"

"We weren't doing anything but talking!" I insist. "And I just told you I had absolutely no idea you were the fiancé he kept talking about!"

Byrd makes the face he always used to make during our arguments, which only trips me out even more. How am I having an argument with *him* right now? It's like I've fallen into a time warp and landed somewhere in 2017—as if I never even met Kip at all.

"You think I'm stupid?" Byrd asks. "Of course you knew."

"How would I know?" I ask. "I blocked you all over social! I haven't seen a single post of yours in years." I realize how defensive I sound, but I can't help it. It's absurd that he'd accuse me of flirting with Joley to get back at him for ending our marriage. As if I've just been sitting around all these years, not living my own life, waiting for the perfect time to execute my revenge plot. "I don't even know what site you're writing for these days! I didn't even know you were in a relationship, let alone engaged!"

"You expect me to believe that?" Byrd says. "I've literally watched you Google your exes before. On several occasions."

He's right in that I did used to be a chronic ex-boyfriend-Googler, but he's entirely unaware that the habit ceased entirely once I met Kip.

"It's the truth," I tell him. "I forgot that you existed! Don't blame me—"

I cut myself off upon realizing that I'm now speaking exclusively in Taylor Swift song titles.

"Let's all just calm down," Joley suggests.

"*You* need to calm down," I retort.

Dammit! I'm doing it again.

Byrd continues to grill me. "So you're telling me you just thought Joley was some random guy?"

"Yes," I answer. "The owner of the hotel introduced us."

"Why would he do that?" Byrd asks.

"Because I'm writing an article about earlymoons."

"But you had to know who each other were," Byrd insists. "I've mentioned your name to Joley a million times. He's seen our wedding pictures—"

Joley clears his throat.

And suddenly I feel like the world's biggest dumbass.

He knew exactly who I was this entire time.

30

oley suggests that we all head up to his and Byrd's suite so we can continue this highly combustible conversation in private, without making a scene.

As I follow them toward the elevator, I'm reminded of an old Monica Lewinsky interview in which she described how Linda Tripp orchestrated that whole sting operation at Pentagon City mall, prompting a slew of FBI agents to drag her up to a sterile hotel room for hours of intimidation and questioning about her sexual history with the then-president of the United States.

This feels a lot like that.

We get into their suite—a third-floor clone of Kip's and my room, minus the killer view—and Byrd slams the door shut behind him. His flimsy tank top reveals bulging veins from his chest to his neck, a sure sign of genuine anger, but his trembling facial muscles indicate a deep sadness fueling it all.

Joley grabs him by the waist. "I promise it's not what you think. I was having breakfast the other day, and the owner came up to me asking if I wanted to talk to a reporter—" He gestures at me without saying my name. "And yeah, I recognized the name. And then we met, and I recognized the face. I figured I'd just talk for a little bit, you know... I was just curious. That's all."

Byrd removes Joley's hand from his waist and steps into the living area. "Curious? About what?"

"The guy you married before me," Joley says. "I wanted to see what all the fuss was about, I guess. I don't know—"

"Please stop talking," I suggest. Our conversation at the pool suddenly takes on such a twisted implication, turning Joley from a garden variety cheater to a calculating manipulator. "How could you have talked to me all this time without letting me know you're marrying my ex-husband?"

Joley performs an insincere shrug. "I tried to tell you, but I couldn't. At a certain point it just became too late to do it without making me look like a—"

"Manipulative dirtbag?" I finish.

"You know what?" Byrd says to him. "I need to talk to Ray alone. Can you give us a few minutes?"

Joley's face flushes at the notion of Byrd and me comparing notes. "Baby, come on. Don't turn this into more than it is."

I raise a meek hand. "I should be the one to leave. This is really between you guys—"

"No," Byrd says. "You're staying. Joley is leaving."

"Beej," Joley pleads. "Calm down."

"I am calm!" he insists. "I just want to talk to Ray one-on-one. Go downstairs. I'll meet you at the cabana bar when we're done."

Joley crosses his arms. "I'm not leaving."

"Ray's not gonna tell me anything I don't already know!" Byrd snaps. "I literally just saw you thrust your body against his in the pool. I know you were trying to seduce him. That's what you do. You seduce people. I've seen you do it a million times. Now can I please have a private conversation with my ex-husband?"

Joley looks straight at Byrd, then over at me, then down at the hotel carpet. After a very long sigh, he throws his hands up.

"Whatever, fine. Just please give me a chance to talk to you afterward, okay?"

The desperation in his voice is such a stark contrast to the menacing drawl he used at the pool that I almost feel bad for him. Somehow he sounds innocent, even though he's the furthest thing from it.

"I'll meet you downstairs," Byrd promises. "Just go."

Joley disappears with his tail between his legs, and Byrd heads straight for the mini-fridge, where there's a sweaty bottle of Moët lodged diagonally across the grates.

"Champagne?" I ask. "What could you possibly want to celebrate right now?"

Byrd laughs the saddest laugh I've ever heard as he pours two glasses. "My *second* failed marriage?"

"Don't say that!" I tell him, a knee-jerk reaction. It's oddly comforting to know that despite the evidence I've recently accumulated suggesting that the concept of true love is bullshit, I'm still physiologically incapable of encouraging people to break up. "Nothing happened in the pool—or anywhere else—trust me."

"It doesn't matter what did or didn't happen," Byrd says. "This is a pattern with Joley. He's addicted to chasing sex. Chasing men. I've given him hall passes before, but it's never enough." Byrd sighs and clinks his flute against mine. "To my perfect earlymoon, in which my fiancé actively tried to fuck my ex-husband."

"I'm not toasting to that," I tell him, even though his deadpan delivery does get a small laugh out of me.

"Fine," Byrd says. "Then…to Allison Marie McBeal."

This gets a bigger laugh out of me. I'd almost forgotten about our shared love of *Ally McBeal*, and Byrd's ridiculous tendency to refer to its titular character by her full name.

"How are you in my hotel room right now?" he says after taking a swig. "This is unreal."

"Legit," I say, "unreal."

We slide down to the floor, right there in front of the mini-fridge, too emotionally exhausted to make it the ten feet to the couch.

"Sometimes I read your articles," Byrd blurts out.

Huh. "You do?"

"Mostly your old *Microphone* stuff," he says. "When you used to write about yourself... About us..."

I clear my throat before he can continue. If Byrd is about to say he misses me or regrets getting divorced, I'm gonna need a moment to process. Even though he was the one who ended things, I've never once doubted that our marriage was a giant mistake from the very beginning.

"Not because I have any regrets or anything," he clarifies, thank God. "Sometimes I just like to read the love story you wrote about us. You made us seem so happy. So perfect."

"Even though we weren't."

"Even though we weren't." His voice dips into a low, wistful hum. "We desperately wanted to be, though. That was something we had in common."

We take a few sips of champagne in silence as I think about how my relationship with Kip has been pretty much the opposite. I've never written about us on the internet, but more often than not, we have been genuinely happy together.

And isn't that way more important?

"What the hell are the odds?" Byrd finally asks.

"I know! Both of us getting remarried. Both of us going on earlymoons, here, at the same time."

"I should've known I couldn't come to Seabrook without running into you."

I laugh. "It's not like I live here."

"I wouldn't know," Byrd says. "You don't exist on social. You don't keep in touch with any of our old friends. If I had known you were engaged, I sure as hell would've avoided this hotel until after your wedding."

"What made *you* want to come here?" I ask.

"The way you and your mother always used to talk about this place," he answers through a sip of Moët. "And seeing how crushed you were before our wedding, when we looked up pricing and realized there was no way in hell we'd be able to afford to come here."

My nerves pinch at the memory. At how I eventually came to look at our lack of an earlymoon as a blessing that would allow me to have my one perfect earlymoon with Kip...

Only to end up sitting right here with Byrd anyway.

"Joley and I clearly have every issue in the book," Byrd continues. "We can't agree on anything. He compulsively lies to me. I know some people who are in open relationships and genuinely happy, but I don't even think that would satisfy Joley, really. It's the sneaking around he gets off on. The chase. But instead of leaving him, I just keep trying to change him. I really don't want to be single again. And I do love him..."

His voice wavers for a moment before he centers his breath and continues. "After you and I got divorced, the hopeless romantic in me almost died. I didn't think any relationship could ever live up to my expectations. But then I met Joley, and it was a perfect fit. We had so much fun together, and the sex was incredible. It wasn't until the past year that things became so toxic. And I don't know, I guess I thought this trip could save our future marriage. Clearly I was wrong."

My heart aches with sympathy for Byrd. I've never been engaged to a compulsive liar, but I do know what it's like to feel trapped by a fear of being alone. It was why I stayed married to *him* as long as I did.

"I don't know everything about your situation," I admit. "But if you're really not happy—or if you really don't feel valued or respected—you can leave. I know it's hard, but you *have* done it before." I tap his thigh. "To me." I tap his thigh again. "Remember?"

He attempts a smile, but it's weak, so instead he goes back to the champagne.

I follow his lead and drain my flute before he tops us off. I have no idea what to say to make him feel better, so I blurt out a random piece of self-disclosure instead.

"My fiancé isn't out to his dentist."

"What?"

"Kip," I tell him. "That's his name. He's nothing like you and me… He's never seen a single episode of *Ally*. And he's very private, which is why I've never written about us. Our relationship has taken place entirely offline."

Byrd's eyes widen. "You've seriously never written about him?"

The surprise is warranted. If Byrd had ever suggested that we take *our* entire relationship offline and just keep it between ourselves, my first thought would have been, *Then what's the point of being together?*

The fact that I've never once had such a thought about Kip tells me everything I need to know about just how much more real our love is.

"Not once," I confirm. "I've never even had the desire to, because I've never felt like I had anything to prove about our relationship. But for some reason, ever since we got engaged, I've become consumed with wanting the world to know about it. Would you believe that we were offered a spot in the *Times* Vows section?"

Byrd's eyes go even wider. "Shut up! For real? I thought you were gonna have a legit meltdown when we couldn't get in there."

"For real," I confirm. "But Kip convinced me to turn it down."

"Because he's not out to his dentist?" Byrd guesses.

"He cares too much about his Google results," I attempt. "He's a doctor and doesn't want patients finding evidence of a personal life. Nothing annoys him more than doctors who make a big show of themselves on social media."

"A wedding announcement isn't exactly a big show," Byrd says. "It's just a fact of life."

"I know! That's what I keep trying to tell him."

"So no wedding website?" Byrd asks. "No online registry?"

"It's all password-protected," I explain. "Getting him to even agree to *that* was a whole thing."

Byrd's gaze is downcast as he absorbs this information.

"Sometimes Joley gets weird about my online footprint, too," he offers. "The way we used to blog in our twenties. Editors back then were so thirsty for those way-too-confessional essays."

"The first-person industrial complex. I remember it well."

"And now our most intimate thoughts—from the ugliest decade of our lives—are immortalized forever," he says. "It's kinda fucked up, when you really think about it."

I slump against the wall. "Right? That's why I wanted the Vows piece so much. And why I agreed to write an article about our early-moon. So that I'd at least have something published to show where I'm at now in life. So people could see I'm not still that disaster of a twentysomething I was back when I chronicled my every mistake for public consumption."

"So you *do* have something to prove," he says. "Not about your relationship…but about yourself."

"That's not—"

My voice cracks as I realize he's correct. My renewed interest in online attention doesn't have anything to do at all with Kip. It has everything to do with me and my self-image. And making him an accessory to that.

"Sometimes I wonder why we're so desperate for this validation," Byrd admits. "Not just you and me, but other internet gays, too. My latest therapist has suggested it's because deep down, we fear that we're inherently inferior to everyone else. And so we constantly seek evidence to the contrary—and likes and shares are a quick and easy way to get it. Even though, ultimately, it's empty."

"So empty," I agree. "Because it's not authentic. It's not even real. And it's never enough."

"I just want someone to give me that *real-life* validation," Byrd says. "You know? I just want to feel like *I'm* enough. For once."

"You are enough," I promise him. "Deep down, I think you know that."

He wipes a stray tear from his cheek.

"I gotta say," I continue in an attempt to lighten the mood, "if someone had told me I'd be spending the third day of my earlymoon assuring my ex-husband that he's lovable...I'd have thought they were on some very potent illegal drugs."

This gets a tiny chuckle out of him. He scoots closer to rest his head on my shoulder, and I instinctively wrap my arm around him. We don't say anything for several moments, and I mentally replay the exchange we just had. Byrd admitting that he just wants someone to make him feel like he's enough.

Kip would never acknowledge such a vulnerability out loud, but what if he feels the same way? I've always thought of myself as a loving partner—and I do constantly express my love for him—but I'm also in the habit of pushing the limits of his comfort in favor of my own. Making him feel like it's not enough for him to love me and commit to me without also stepping into the public vortex of my *Appeal* article and my dream wedding.

I need to let Kip know that he's enough.

It's quite possible the whole reason he's never felt comfortable with attention is precisely *because* he's never felt like he was enough. For his father, or his ex-wife, or his patients, or me, or all the other people he's shape-shifted for over the years. Perhaps he's always feared that being his true self on too visible a stage would be a recipe for disappointment from at least a few people in the audience.

Instead of dragging him into the wedding spotlight before he's ready, my focus should first be on making him realize that he is—by any and all standards—*enough*.

Maybe if I can get him to believe that, then everything else will just fall into place.

Byrd finally springs back to life and empties the rest of the champagne between our flutes. "So do you have a picture of this mystery fiancé or what? I'm dying to see who my replacement was."

I pull out my phone and swipe to my favorite shot of us. We're at a vineyard somewhere in Tuscany, posing at the edge of a steep hill, with endless rows of grape leaves in the distance below. A fellow American tourist—who just so happened to be a professional photographer—took the picture for us, and she was very vocal with her art direction.

"Stand closer!" she'd said. "Act like you're in love."

I got nervous for a moment, worried that things were veering too close to PDA territory for Kip's comfort, but he just laughed and pulled me closer—almost like being in another country gave him permission to be someone else. I had no idea he'd be popping the question later that night on our hotel balcony.

"Oh my God," Byrd says. "He's gorgeous. And you guys look so. Damn. Happy. Why the hell are you *here*, right now, with me?"

"That's a great question," I admit. "I messed up and stormed out during an argument. I need to get back to him."

I reach for my phone, but Byrd is still staring at it.

"Do you ever look at *our* old pictures?" he asks.

"You mean like our wedding album?" I consider telling him about how I ritualistically burned it in my parents' backyard a year after our divorce, but decide it's an irrelevant detail. "Not really…"

"All our old Instagram posts," he says. "All those cringe couple selfies…"

I consider telling him about how I deleted all of them years ago, but again decide it's irrelevant.

"We had some great captions," I say instead. "People probably thought we were the happiest couple on the internet."

That last statement lingers for a moment.

"I'm not sure about that," Byrd finally says through a sad laugh. He hands my phone back to me. "The words were convincing, but the pictures always gave us away."

31

～

Kip's not in our room. My heart nearly stops beating for a moment as I contemplate the possibility that he's decided to take off altogether without so much as a note, but then I see his suitcase in the closet and heave a sigh of relief.

Where'd you go? I ask him in a text. I'm sorry for walking out before. I was hoping we could talk.

We've only been apart for a couple hours—it's possible he needs more time to collect his thoughts after the heaviness of our argument—but time isn't a luxury we have right now. We've got two nights left at the resort, and I'd like to make the most of them. I'm ready to do whatever it takes to save our marriage.

Kip views my text, starts to reply, and then doesn't.

Babe? I follow up.

Nothing.

So I expand: You were right. I got carried away with the wedding and the article and everything else, and I never stopped to think about your comfort level. I shouldn't have pushed you so much without giving you a chance to let me know where you were coming from. I know you might feel like you need to be a million things to a million people, but I need you to know that just being who you are IS enough for me. So much more than enough. I'm willing to hear you out on the wedding, on the article, on all of it. I'll meet more than halfway if I need to. I love you and I love our life and I'll do whatever I have to do to keep it.

But still.

Nothing.

My only choice is to walk the entire resort until I find him.

So I go downstairs and scan the indoor bar—nothing. I head past the pool and swim-up bar until I get to the Gull's Nest—still nothing.

As I head toward the beach, heart and feet in a race against each other, I wonder if he's made up his mind about us. I know him well enough to know that he wouldn't blow our entire life up over a single fight, but what if he's had doubts about us for a long time and has never expressed them to me?

As much as I see him every day and presume to know everything that goes on inside his head, there are so many things he's kept from me in an effort to maintain his role as the strong, steady one. What if he's been concealing a growing suspicion that our differences aren't surmountable after all?

Maybe what he wants is someone just like him. Someone whose Google results aren't a chaotic jumble of clickbait headlines and overconfessional blog posts—someone he can live a quiet, anonymous life with.

But the thing is, he *can* have that with me.

We've been living a quiet, anonymous life for the past six years, and I haven't once felt like I wanted more than what we share within the walls of our home. The differences between us—including the thing inside of me that turned me into "an attention-seeking hurricane" the second we started planning a wedding—don't have to mean we're incompatible.

They just mean we each have a little work to do to truly validate each other.

I'm willing to do my portion of the work, and I need Kip to know that.

But he's not here on the beach, and I'm running out of places to look.

Then I remember that the golf course has a driving range.

A sign directs me toward a paved pathway leading directly to the clubhouse. My plaid linen boat shoes are the last thing I should be running in, but I clomp my way through as quickly as possible—past the flower beds and benches and a surprising number of pear trees—until I get to a country-club-looking building with massive windows atop a big green hill.

I burst into the pro shop like a rocket.

A polo-clad frat bro furrows his brow at me from behind a giant display of golf accessories and Earlymoon Golf Club apparel. "You have a tee time?"

"Which way is the range?" I ask.

"Other side of the clubhouse." He points to a door leading further into the building. "You can cut through the restaurant, though."

I follow his directions and run directly into Kip at the clubhouse bar—but he's not alone. Jake and Lucy are on either side of him.

All three of them look at me like I'm a ghost. And then they look away quickly, like I'm specifically the demon from *The Ring*.

"I'll be right back," Kip tells them as he kicks his barstool out behind him.

He leads me outside to a patio overlooking the green of the eighteenth hole. I immediately gravitate toward an idle firepit in the corner with a pair of Adirondack chairs on either side, but Kip refuses to sit down.

"I'm not ready to talk," he says. "I just brought you out here to tell you that privately."

"Did you read my texts?" I ask, even though I know he did. "Why haven't you responded? And what are you doing here? With them?"

"I just told you." His gaze is focused on the green below. He won't even look directly at me. "I'm not ready to talk."

"But we need to."

"I know that," he says in a tone that can only be described as *I thought I just told you to fuck off.* "But I think it might be best if we spent the night apart first. Maybe you can go stay with your sister and I'll stay here. We can talk tomorrow morning before our tee time."

The suggestion is so extreme, I don't even register the fact that he's serious.

But then I look at him—eyes still fixated on the green—and realize he is.

"That is the most irrational thing I've ever heard," I say as calmly as possible. I really don't want to start another fight, but surely he has to understand that nothing that's happened between us warrants a measure so drastic as separating for an entire night of our vacation. "We only have two nights left here. And it's not like our fight was so—"

He cuts me off with an audible groan. "Will you just stop talking already? Christ! You're so... Dammit, Ray, I told you to leave. Just leave."

The venom in his voice is entirely foreign to me. I've never seen this side of him, and suddenly I realize it's because there's more at play than just the argument we had in the room.

A wave of tears rises from my chest to my throat to the mask of my face as I wonder what could have happened in the past couple hours to make him hate me so much.

"We saw you, alright?" he says, gesturing over at the bar we just came from. "I saw you, and so did they..."

Shit.

No.

No, no, no, no, no.

Kip takes a deep breath as he prepares his explanation, because he knows me well enough to know I won't let this go until I hear it in full detail.

"I went downstairs to look for you," he says through grinding teeth, "and you were splashing around in the pool with some tattooed guy. So I sat down at the tiki bar and watched. I was directly across from you guys—*staring*—but you were so deep in your own world that you didn't look my way once. And then Jake and Lucy showed up. Right at the moment you two kissed." He makes a tight fist and then releases it. "So, yeah, I'm thinking I could use a night to myself while I figure out what to make of all that."

I don't even know where to begin. Every organ, every nerve ending, every brain cell is ablaze with fear and guilt and regret. The thought of Kip not being able to trust me is worse than anything we've been through—today or ever. Trust has always been a given for us. And I know all too well that once it slips away, it's nearly impossible to get back.

But how can I explain the truth to him when he already thinks he saw it for himself?

"We didn't kiss!" I attempt. "He tried to, yeah, when he was grabbing his beer from behind me, but our lips didn't even touch—"

"Don't try to bullshit me," he says. "We saw you leave with him and Byrd. Literally watched all three of you get in the elevator together. When were you gonna tell me your ex-husband was here? How long did you know—" He clears his throat. "Actually? I'm not doing this. I told you I wasn't ready to talk, because I knew it would only lead to another fight."

Everything in me trembles as I reach for his wrist. "That tattooed guy is Byrd's new fiancé. We only went up to their room because Byrd insisted on the three of us talking in private. He also *thought* he saw us kissing—"

"It sure as hell looked like that's what you were doing!"

"Our faces made contact for a millisecond!" I say. "And I didn't ask for it to happen. I specifically—repeatedly—asked for it to *not* happen. He wouldn't stop coming on to me, but I pulled away the second he got too close..."

"I'm not doing this," Kip says. "It's like I was saying earlier. You and I are different. Even if what you're saying is true, maybe it's normal for you to get mixed up in a web of drama with your ex-husband and his new fiancé. But it's not normal for me. I'm an adult."

"Now I'm not an *adult*? I didn't ask to run into them this week. I didn't ask for Byrd's fiancé to relentlessly hit on me."

Kip shakes his head. "And yet somehow, it all happened."

"What is that supposed to mean?"

"It means it happened because you allowed it to," Kip barks. "Whether he was giving you attention or you saw him as a sounding board for our issues or whatever it was, you chose to get in the pool and flirt with him. At least respect me enough not to deny *that* part of it, because I know what you look like when you're flirting."

"I'm sorry," I plead. "He was just so all over me—and we had just gotten into that big fight, and, yeah, maybe I played into it just a little. It obviously feels good to be wanted. But you have to know I stopped him the second he tried to take it further. *You have to know that.*"

Kips digs his knuckles into his eyes and takes a series of shallow breaths, right as a giggly couple of earlymooners stroll onto the eighteenth green to execute their putts. I take a closer look and immediately turn my head away, realizing it's Mariah and Nicki from breakfast, clad in matching white golf skirts and blue polos.

"Let's talk about this tomorrow," says Kip. The presence of potential onlookers instantly makes him shut down. "I'm gonna hang here for a bit, then I'm gonna stay in the room and collect my thoughts."

"I can't walk away right now," I plead quietly—a feat of herculean strength when you consider that everything in me wants to scream at the top of my lungs. "It feels too much like losing you."

The dam breaks loose immediately after that last sentence, and I'm suddenly wiping snotty tears away with the sides of my hands.

Kip's face starts twitching with imminent tears of his own, but as per usual he's stronger than I am. He swallows them down and places a hand on my shoulder. I've never been so grateful for his touch. How have I ever taken it for granted?

"I'm not going anywhere," he says. "I'll be here when you get back in the morning. We'll have clearer heads and can talk everything over as rational adults. And we still have our tee time at nine."

The assurance that he intends to keep our tee time—that he's not prepared to immediately detach himself from me after whatever happens during our morning conversation—helps me to stop crying and accept his terms. This doesn't have to mean anything more than Kip's need to digest everything that's happened today before he says something he'll regret later.

I steady my breath and calm myself down with the idea that he's not doing this to tear us apart—he's doing it to keep us together.

"Alright," I finally concede. "I'll see you tomorrow morning in the room."

"Tomorrow morning in the room," Kip repeats. "Tell your sister I said hello."

32

～

"Kip says hello," I tell Stef from across the wreckage of empty fried seafood baskets and beer pitchers between us. "Can you believe that shit? It's our earlymoon, and Kip says hello! To you! Because he's at the resort, and I'm here. At the fucking *Clam Shell*. With you. During my earlymoon."

We've been going over the events of the day for nearly three hours—and as many pitchers of Coors Light—and I'm full-on slurring my words at this point.

"Dude," Stef says. "I've been keeping a tally, and this is the eighth time tonight you've reminded me that 'Kip says hello.' I'm inclined to think Kip says hello."

This gets a big, drunken laugh out of me. Stef's deadpan humor—even during otherwise bleak moments—is a gift I hadn't realized I'd missed so much before this week.

"Maybe we are too different for each other," I suggest. "Do you think we are? Tell me the truth. You've never really liked Kip, have you?"

"I never said that!"

"You literally grilled me the other night—at this very table— about whether or not I was making a mistake by marrying him."

"I didn't say mistake," she reminds me. "I said 'a resigned compromise based on your long-standing fear of dying alone.'"

"Tomato," I drone, "to-fucking-mah-to."

Stef picks at one of the disposable coasters on our table while my eyes dart around the bar—past the patchwork of neon signs and decorative buoys and draft beer handles—desperate for signs of Kip's arrival. At some point during the second pitcher, I started indulging in the fantasy that any minute now he'll realize he doesn't need any more time to sort his thoughts, he'd never even think about calling off our wedding, and he must immediately track me down to make things right. And what better place for our big reunion than here at the Clam Shell, the birthplace of my parents' grand love story?

"He's not coming," my bubble-bursting sister tells me. "He doesn't even know you're here."

"He knows about the historical significance of this place. It wouldn't be that hard to put two and two together."

"Kip is a pragmatist. You guys already made plans for the morning. It doesn't make logistical sense for him to go searching around Seabrook for you at ten at night when he knows he'll just see you in nine hours anyway. Plus, why wouldn't he just text you?"

"You don't *text* someone when you're about to make a grand romantic gesture," I explain. I know I'm being ridiculous, but something about this place makes me revert into the delusional sap my mother raised me to be. "It's all about unpredictability."

"You're expecting unpredictability from Kip Hayes?" she says.

"Well…no," I admit. "He's the most predictable man I've ever met, which is one of the things I love most about him."

"Ironic," Stef suggests. "Isn't it?"

And, well, I guess it is. If I love the reality of Kip so much, why do I bother imagining him as some kind of fictional rom-com hero? If he actually *were* to burst through these doors and profess his undying love for me, making a whole scene, I would probably be highly uncomfortable. Stef (and every other Seabrook local within these wood-paneled walls) doesn't need to bear witness to our reconciliation.

Stef adjusts her Red Sox cap and leans forward. There's a focus in her eyes that tells me she's about to either (a) give me shit, or (b) veer into a rare moment of sincerity.

"I was just busting your balls the other day," she says. "I don't think you're sacrificing who you are to be with him."

"You don't?" I ask.

She thinks about her answer for a moment. "You have changed, but I think that's just because you've grown up a little bit. All those men you dated in your teens and twenties and all those blog posts you used to write... I know you were never truly happy. No matter how much sex you had or how many likes you got, it was never enough. It wasn't until you met Kip that you finally started acting like you were enough—for the first time in your life. All the attention, all the validation you'd always craved so desperately since you were a little kid... He just gave it to you like it was nothing."

"Which is exactly why I can't lose him."

Stef flips back into no-bullshit mode at this. "Okay, I was trying to be nice, but *come on*, man."

"What?"

"That is the most pathetic thing I've ever heard!" she says. "One person can't be responsible for your *entire* sense of self-worth. At some point you need to learn how to generate some of it on your own. Otherwise you'll never be able to love Kip—and let him love you—without completely losing yourself in him at the same time. It's just like how—"

"Mom lost herself in Dad," I finish.

"Exactly," she says. "Which is the whole reason you're like this to begin with. It's all very full circle. But you can break the chain."

"Why did I have to insist on the big wedding to begin with?" I think out loud. "Why did I have to agree to the article about our trip?"

"Because you like to make things look pretty," Stef says. "Even when they're not."

"So you think Kip and I *should* break up?"

"That's not what I meant." She slugs her beer and sizes me up for a moment. "Do you remember back in the day, you must've been like ten, when you redecorated the entire house while Mom and Dad weren't home? Like, rearranged all the furniture, moved around all the pictures on the walls..."

"What does this have to do with anything?" I ask.

"Mom and Dad didn't even notice when they got home," she says. "Our house was still our house. You were determined to turn it into this Martha Stewart vision you had, but that's just not what it was. Regardless of how much you messed with the interior design, the raw materials weren't there."

"So you're saying that Kip and I are screwed?" I ask. "The raw materials aren't there? This isn't making me feel better."

"I'm saying that's how you were before you met Kip. You were always trying to project an image that wasn't real. But with Kip, I *do* think it's real. And he wants that to be enough for you—without needing to broadcast it all over the place—but you're so used to thinking the image is the thing that matters..."

She ponders for a moment before continuing. "I remember at your wedding to Byrd, you looked so sad the whole time. You were smiling and laughing, and I don't think anyone else noticed, but I noticed. And I felt so bad for you. I wished I could've gone back in time and told you not to go through with it."

"And you think I'm making that mistake again?"

"Not at all," she says. "You actually seem happy with Kip.

Granted, I barely ever hear from you, but I don't know, maybe that's *because* you're so happy—"

"I'm gonna work on that," I promise her. "This week has made me realize I should make more of an effort to incorporate people into my life who aren't Kip."

Maybe if I'd been better at doing that in the first place, this week's events wouldn't have felt so life-threatening.

"You *are* happy, right?" Stef asks me. "Or have you just gotten exceptionally better at acting since your first wedding?"

I think about my life with Kip. Randomly greeting him with names of Lilith Fair headliners. Watching *Jeopardy!* on a weeknight, playing Scrabble on a weekend, fake-dancing in the kitchen. Having drinks at our favorite bar, golfing at our local course, laughing at random shit we're positive no one in the world but the two of us would ever find funny. The olive tree in our foyer. All the boring little details that might seem insignificant when compared to the grand romantic concept of love, but the things that make up a relationship nonetheless.

And then I smile through a tear. "I'm happier than I've ever thought possible. Life with Kip is just...complete."

"Jerry Maguire over here," Stef says. "But see? There's your answer. I'm sure Kip feels the same way."

"So you don't think he's over in the hotel room right now making a list of all the reasons our marriage is destined to fail?"

She brushes me off. "What would that list even look like?"

"First bullet point: we're total opposites."

She considers this. "I don't think you are, though."

"Dude," I say in my best Stef voice. "He's a sophisticated doctor with a pristine online footprint, and I'm a trashy blogger whose penis size can literally be Googled right now."

Stef gasps. "There are nudes of you floating around?"

"No!" I clarify. "I just had to measure myself for an article once."

"Right. As all journalists must."

I respond with a bitchy glare as I take a swig of Coors Light.

"I don't think your personalities are all that different," she offers. "I know you guys thrive on the whole 'he's the strong one and I'm the weak one' dynamic, but honestly I think you're both pretty strong people. You just like to play weak so he'll take care of you."

She doesn't sound accusatory as she says this, but my first instinct is to deny it nonetheless. "I don't *play weak*."

"That was the wrong word choice," she concedes. "I'm just saying I *have* seen you be strong and independent before. After your divorce, for example, the way you rebuilt your entire life. Or when we were younger and a bee would get near you, you'd only ever freak out if Dad or I were around to 'protect' you. But I remember watching you from the window once when you were reading alone outside, a bee landed on your leg and you just calmly stayed still until it flew away. And then you kept reading!"

The way she says this—like it's the most obvious thing ever—almost betrays the revelation of it all. How have I never thought of things this way before?

Of course I'm not a chaotic, helpless train wreck at my core.

And *of course* Kip isn't a fearless, invulnerable superhero at his.

Our cores both fall somewhere in the middle. We just tend to exaggerate these extremes because that's how we've learned to function as a unit. Maybe the reason we've always felt that we have something primal in common beneath our differences is because, on a subconscious level, we do understand this.

"And don't even get me started on your online personas," Stef continues. "Those are entirely full of shit. Because whose aren't?"

This too is the most obvious revelation ever, but it also hits differently in my current emotional state.

I've always understood that everyone's online images aren't exactly accurate—it would be impossible to capture the truth of a person with whatever digital footprint they've made, either actively (like me) or passively (like Kip)—and yet I've spent the past week placing Oprah levels of importance on Kip's and mine.

Why?

Even if there was solid proof of our relationship online, it wouldn't erase the fact that the majority of Kip's search results tell the story of a straight doctor who once attended a charity gala with his wife. And the majority of mine would still tell the story of a lost teenager and twentysomething who writes self-deprecating jokes about getting STDs and dying alone.

Neither of those people is who we are. They're not even who we were at the time. As much as I used to enjoy writing about myself for the internet, the reality is that I was never *actually* writing about myself. My goal wasn't honesty; it was to gain the approval of some imaginary audience. Even if it meant turning myself into a joke by doing so.

"And by the way," Stef adds. "No one is Googling you nearly as much as you Google yourself."

Another obvious truth that I've somehow lost sight of this week. I don't need an announcement in the *Times* or an article in *Appeal* to validate Kip's and my relationship. All I need is Kip. If he'll still have me.

"You're being really nice right now," I tell Stef. I can't remember the last time we were this genuine with each other. "It's weird, but thank you."

"You're a mess," she replies through a shrug. "I'd be a shitty older sister if I didn't try to cheer you up."

"I think it's working."

There's a flash of pity in her eyes, like she doesn't believe me.

"Is this all because of what I told you about Mom and Dad yesterday?" she asks. "I swear I wasn't trying to make you blow up your relationship and make out with your ex-husband's tattooed fiancé at a swim-up bar—"

"We didn't make out! We didn't even kiss."

"Sure, Jan."

"Are they happy?" I ask. "Were they *ever* happy?"

Maybe Mom was a little delusional about how great a marriage she was in, but it couldn't have all been a lie. I lived with my parents for eighteen years. I've seen them happy. I know I have.

"I don't think they're miserable," Stef says. "I think they're just another married couple that's been together for forty years. Nothing extraordinary about it, and certainly nothing like the elaborate fairy tale Mom wanted it to be, but nothing wrong with it, either. I think they've just had a very long, typical, ordinary marriage."

"Staying together for forty years is pretty extraordinary," I suggest.

"They do know how to stay together," Stef agrees. "That's something they're good at."

The table goes quiet for a few moments. I pick at some leftover clam strips and nurse the small amount of Coors Light that remains in my pint glass.

Stef checks her phone, smiles, and bites her lip.

I'm suddenly hyperaware that we've now shared two drunken dinners together this week and have pretty much only talked about me.

"Is that Lenny?" I ask. "How are you guys doing? Are *you* happy in your marriage?"

"Of course I am," she answers in a single matter-of-fact breath. "He's my husband, I love him. And I like our life enough. I'd like it better if our traps didn't come up empty all the time."

I shift on my barstool, jolted by the reminder that Stef's biggest problem right now isn't her relationship; it's her livelihood.

"How bad is it, really?" I ask. "Do you need help?"

Stef shakes her head. "You think I'd accept help from my baby brother? Please. We're gonna be fine."

She hesitates for a moment, looks the other way, then slowly releases a breath. "We are moving, though. At the end of the summer."

"Which summer?"

"This one," she says. "Two weeks after your wedding."

"But," I choke through the whiplash I've just gotten from her admission, "you told me you were staying in Seabrook for at least another few years."

"I lied," she says. "I'm sorry! I just didn't wanna tarnish your earlymoon week with the big news. But I might as well tell you the truth now..."

"But—!"

"It's just what we have to do. Lenny's still up in Maine getting things sorted. We've got territory lined up off of Little Cranberry Island. We're renting a house."

There's an excitement in her voice I haven't heard since we were kids. She's practically beaming.

"It's going to be perfect," she continues. "Lenny was talking to his cousin who lobsters up there. We're gonna be pulling two hundred pounds a day! It'll be like this town used to be."

"So this is why you're sending me home with a box of my old shit," I say as the realization dawns on me. "You're selling the house."

She exhales. "I'm selling the house."

I take a deep breath, expecting more feelings of resistance to surface, but all I come up with is a sense of relief. I want my sister to be happy—the same way she was just telling me she wants me to be happy—and it's clear that a move to Maine is what she needs for that to happen.

"You and Kip will have to visit Little Cranberry," she says. "You'll love it. And Seabrook will always be here, even if the house isn't."

She checks her phone again. "Lenny says hello, by the way."

It's an innocuous statement from my brother-in-law, but it triggers the sense of dread that's been bubbling under my skin all night. Talking to Stef has made me feel better—and my perspective on Kip's and my relationship couldn't be clearer—but the fact remains that we've decided to separate for an entire night of our earlymoon, and I have no idea where his head is at.

"What a coincidence," I tell her as I take a final depressing swig of Coors Light. "Kip *also* says hello."

33

All those emotions I didn't feel at dinner come on at once the second I'm alone in my childhood bedroom—a quiet but deep sense of melancholy at the thought that I'll no longer have this place to come back to.

Underneath those feelings, there's a rational understanding that this really won't affect my daily life, but still. Even though I could count the number of times I've visited over the past five years on as many fingers, it hurts to lose the option altogether.

I turn the lights off, climb into bed, and scroll through my phone.

It's past midnight and I know Kip's asleep, but I can't control myself. My fingers type the words and send the text before my mind can even catch up to them: I miss you. I hate this.

My eyes grill the screen for evidence of receipt, but all I get is a notification that his *Do Not Disturb* feature is on.

I try for sleep—anything to expedite the next eight hours until we're face-to-face again—but closing my eyes doesn't accomplish anything other than turning the volume up on my thoughts.

So instead I flick the lights back on and absorb the walls of this room for what is possibly the last time. All the HomeGoods and Pier 1 relics I spent a small fortune on as a teenager, desperate to turn this room into some kind of HGTV-ish escape from the reality of my life.

The *Live, Laugh, Lobster* oar hanging above the bed actually gets a smile out of me. Even though I hated lobstering back then, I still couldn't resist it as a design aesthetic. I stand up on the bed and remove it from the wall. There's not a single room in Kip's and my house that it would make sense in, but I don't care. I'll figure out a way to work it in.

As I set the oar down, I notice a big cardboard box in the corner—the one Stef packed for me. I throw it on the bed and start digging through a mess of old books and DVDs and early-aughts fashion accessories. (Why did I have so many skater-ish wristbands? I've never even *been* on a skateboard.)

Just as I decide to trash the entire box, I find something heavy at the bottom.

My parents' wedding album.

I flip it open and take it in.

My mother's wedding dress with the train spanning eleven steps, my dad's Sonny Corleone tux. The pastel bridesmaids, mustachioed groomsmen, mile-long head table, cake higher than Willie Nelson. The looks on my parents' faces—pure bliss—as they pose in front of trees and fountains and staircases.

What if someone had told them, back then, that forty years later they'd be sleeping in separate bedrooms in some mass-produced Florida retirement community? My mom would've been crushed.

Or maybe she'd have just been thrilled to know they'd honor their vows all the way to the end, regardless of the romance that had to be sacrificed along the way.

As I flip through more of the pages, I'm reminded of the last time I held this album in my hands.

After Byrd and I got the pictures back from our wedding, Mom demanded we visit to personally show them to her.

"Why can't we just email them?" I asked. Not that I didn't

want to schedule a visit to Seabrook, but still. "I have them on my computer—"

"No!" she insisted. "I need to see them in person. You of all people should know it's all about the experience of the album."

It took months for our schedules to align, and when they finally did, I ended up making the trip alone.

"Where's your beau?" Mom asked.

I squirmed at the question. The truth was that I had just learned he was sleeping with his ex-boyfriend.

"He's on deadline for a big feature this week," I told her instead. "Where's Dad?"

"Out on the boat," she said. "You know how it is."

I felt dead inside as I handed over the heavy white book.

"Oh!" she exclaimed as she flipped through the pages. "I'm so glad you two put this thing together. You know? I'll never forgive your sister for not giving us a proper wedding portrait for the mantel."

Stef and Lenny were twenty and broke when they got married, so it was nothing more than a backyard clambake. My parents had offered to help (by taking out a loan), but Stef refused to accept.

"Well," I offer, "now you have this picture of them from *our* wedding."

I pointed at a half-page shot of Stef and Lenny in the middle of a slow dance. They were holding onto each other tight, exchanging looks of joy and mischief, like one of them had just told an inside joke. My notoriously unsentimental sister and her lobsterman husband somehow managed to display more chemistry in a single dance-floor shot than Byrd and I did in pages upon pages of staged poses and awkward candids.

"They look so happy," Mom said.

It took everything in me not to burst into tears right then. A part of me wanted to break down and tell Mom what a mess my marriage had already become—how deeply unhappy both Byrd and I were—but I was still in denial. There was no way I could say the truth of the situation out loud. Especially not to her. Our conversations about love were always shallow and rosy; acknowledging anything less than wedded bliss would be an admission of failure on my part.

"You and Byrd look so handsome," she said as she turned the final page.

"Thanks," I replied, acutely aware that she said *handsome* and not *happy*.

The wrong h-word.

"It—" she started, and then her voice shook. I almost got the sense she wanted to comfort me, like maybe she was picking up on the fact that I hated the pictures, I regretted choosing Byrd, I feared the end was near. But instead she closed the album and exhaled. "It was a beautiful day."

A beautiful day, I thought to myself, *in exchange for a lifetime of dysfunction.*

"Hey!" Mom said. "Remember how much you used to love looking at Dad's and my album? Let's bust it out."

So then she did, and it only made me feel worse.

"Look at those two," she said, staring at the wedding portrait on the cover as if it depicted Cinderella and Prince Charming themselves. "The way your father made me molt... I could cry just thinking about it."

"That metaphor doesn't even make sense," I hissed. The thought that she could be so enamored with her own wedding album so many decades into her marriage, when I hated my album from day one, was just enough to make me snap. "You're humans. Not lobsters."

Her eyes widened at my outburst. "Are you okay? What's wrong?"

"I'm fine," I lied. "I'm just saying, Dad didn't make you molt. Lobsters don't *make* each other molt. Females molt all on their own first, and *then* they attract the males. And sometimes they don't attract a male at all! Sometimes they just molt and grow a new shell and then die. Alone. Sometimes they end up in the holding tank on Dad's boat!"

"When did you become such a cynic?" she asked. "Has your sister's coldness finally started to rub off on you?"

"I'm not a cynic," I said, calming myself down. "I'm just saying that humans and lobsters aren't the same."

"Is everything alright with you and Byrd?" she finally asked.

"Yeah," I instinctively lied. But then I took a deep breath and prepared to give her a morsel of truth, filled with a sudden delusional hope that she might have some kind of marital wisdom to offer beyond a platitude. "We just…"

And then the engine of my father's truck roared outside the window. Mom sprang off the couch as if launched from a seesaw and ran out to the driveway to welcome him home from another day on the water, forgetting about me altogether.

I sleepwalked through the rest of the weekend, buried in my phone, deluging Byrd with inquisitive texts about his movements and whereabouts. Mom and I never finished our conversation, which was just as well. We'd end up having plenty of time to talk after the divorce that followed a few months later.

As I run my hand over the peeling cover of the wedding album now, I can't help but wonder how it ended up in a box of *my* things to begin with. I would have thought it would be the very first thing Mom packed when she was preparing for the move to Florida.

Maybe she finally got sick of looking at it. Maybe she was always so fixated on this fantasy wedding-day version of my father because the real one was always so absent. Maybe now that he's retired and they spend every second together, she's finally let go of the fantasy version of him altogether and accepted the real one.

Maybe it took her sixty years to grow up.

The thought should depress me, but it doesn't make me feel much of anything.

Whatever their marriage was or is—perfect or flawed, healthy or toxic, happy or resigned—it has nothing to do with me. It doesn't even have anything to do with the pictures in this wedding album. This is just a visual record of the day they got married. Nothing more, nothing less.

The reality of a marriage is all the days that come after.

saturday

34

—

Of all possible mornings to oversleep, my body chooses the one in which I'm supposed to reunite with my fiancé to discuss whether or not he still wants to be my fiancé.

I was certain I had set an alarm for six—after Stef informed me last night that she'd be sneaking out in the wee hours for another day on the boat—but it's now almost eight and I'm waking up to a series of messages from Kip.

Sorry I missed your text, he wrote three hours ago.

And another one just now: Where are you?

Shit! By the time I get ready and make it to the resort, it'll be time to golf. How are we supposed to have a big talk about our future in between tees and fairways and greens?

I give him a call as I scramble to get dressed.

"I'm so sorry! I overslept, but I'm leaving now… I can still make the nine o'clock tee time."

"We should probably cancel it at this point," Kip says. "We have too much to talk about first."

This suggestion—paired with Kip's flat delivery—triggers a surge of fear in my chest.

What if he didn't have the same revelations I had last night? What if he had revelations that were precisely the opposite of mine?

What if he doesn't want to commit to a full morning on the course because he knows he'd just have to break my heart afterward?

"No," I insist.

Everything inside of me suddenly needs to keep this tee time—as if canceling it would be akin to canceling our relationship entirely.

I know this round is the one thing Kip has been looking forward to most about this vacation. If he *is* building a case for why we're not compatible, I don't want to give him more evidence by being the sole reason he couldn't get a single hole of golf in.

And at least this will give us a guaranteed four hours together—and maybe four hours of simply being in each other's company is all Kip needs to change his mind. To remember how much he loves our life together, regardless of everything that's gone down this week.

"I really think it's more important that we talk," Kip says. "Ray—"

"I'm leaving now," I tell him. And I won't take no for an answer. "I'll meet you at the clubhouse."

35

~

Kip rolls up to the clubhouse in his Nike polo and tailored golf pants, looking so handsome it hurts. His face is a blank screen—I can't tell whether he's glad or upset to see me—but either way all I want to do is squeeze him tight and tell him how much I love him.

He greets me by saying, "We really should have canceled."

Not the best start.

"We can talk later," I promise. "I just know you really wanted to play this weekend. And it's a beautiful morning outside. We should try to enjoy it."

The starter—an athletic older man in an Earlymoon Golf Club jacket—approaches with our golf cart before Kip can further protest.

"Hayes for nine o'clock?" the starter asks.

"That's us," I answer. "Thank you."

Kip forces composure as he slides into the driver's seat.

It's an excruciatingly silent drive to the first tee, made worse by the fact that we have a freakishly long drive to get there. Usually the first hole of a course is right outside the clubhouse doors, but this place has what feels like a zillion miles worth of cart path in between. It's gorgeous, of course—lined with impeccably manicured trees and plants and even a fountain at one point—but that only makes the silence more painful.

The view is even more gorgeous when we finally arrive at the tee.

The tee box is perched on a rolling hill, with a brilliant emerald fairway stretching out in front of us and a long strip of shimmering blue water crashing against rocks behind us. The sun is hot, the sky is clear, the air is pure, and somehow this idyllic setting makes the tension between us feel even worse than it already did—like we're going against the laws of nature by not being our happiest selves.

"Sure beats our course at home," I say as Kip sets up for his first shot. My first effort to make things feel at least somewhat copacetic. "Right?"

He gives me a tight nod.

I thought he would've relaxed into his love of the sport by the time we got out here, but he hasn't. And now I'm wondering if I've made a huge mistake by forcing him to play. What if he's adding *this* to the list of reasons to leave me? *Steamrolled over my attempt to have a talk this morning.*

Because he was right. We need to sit down and have a mature conversation. Face-to-face with no distractions. Why had I instead insisted upon several more hours of this emotional murkiness? This is the exact opposite of what I actually want, which is a resolution.

I shake the regret out of my head as Kip tees off.

Any mental distress he might have right now doesn't show up in his game. He executes a razor-straight drive right out of a PGA tour stop.

"Nice!" I attempt. "You bombed it down the pipe."

"Thanks."

I creep up to the tee for my shot and try to follow his example. But instead of going straight, my ball lands on the far left side of the fairway—before pathetically bouncing into a sand trap just short of the two-hundred-yard stake.

"That would've been a decent shot," Kip says from the cart. An encouraging sign of life. "Sucks that the bunker got you."

"Of course it did," I moan.

He goes quiet again as I slide back into the cart.

We head toward the fairway, and I flinch as I consider this course's potential bee population. I haven't seen any yet, but in less than two hundred yards we've already passed several pear trees and an array of elegant flower beds dotting the cart path. I make a silent prayer that Kip remembered to throw the new EpiPen in his golf bag before leaving the room.

He drops me off at the bunker so he can ride the cart past his ball and get a better view of the green before his next shot.

I peer down into the sand and scan my surroundings for a safety check. The area is thankfully free of flowers and fruit, with nary a bee in sight. So at least I'm safe on that front.

But still. My ball is directly below the lip of the bunker, and it's going to be a bitch to hit it out.

Maybe I should give up on this hole. Actually? I should give up on this entire round—tell Kip he was right, let's go back to the room and talk instead. If he's already resolved to leave me, I highly doubt eighteen holes of emotionally fraught golf will change his mind.

But then I catch a glimpse of him out on the fairway. He just hit his second shot and is pumping his fist in the air with satisfaction at the outcome. He's finally relaxing. Allowing himself to enjoy it out here.

So...never mind. I'm going to give him this. I'm going to play my ball.

I step down into the sand, feeling a bit like Aladdin entering the Cave of Wonders, and set up for the shot.

But halfway through my backswing, a sudden bout of pure terror shoots through me. Somehow—also like Aladdin, when the cave started going berserk after he touched the lamp—I know I've just made a huge mistake.

The second my wedge hits the ball—kicking up a giant cloud of sand—all hell breaks loose.

A swarm of wasps materializes seemingly out of nowhere.

And they're pissed off.

My fear is so acute that I don't even think to scream.

I just silently drop my club and make a lightning-fast jump for the edge of the bunker, desperate to break free from the death trap I've just created.

But the wasps follow me, and before I know what's happening, my left leg—from the ankle up to the knee—burns with the pain of a sting. Probably *more than one* sting.

And now I'm just moments away from a full-blown medical emergency.

I cry out for Kip to help.

He speeds over to me, mouth opening to ask what's wrong... before looking down at my ankle, which is already turning red.

His face goes pale.

"Fuck! I left the EpiPen in the hotel room."

"What do we do?" I choke out. "We're so far from—"

"Get in the cart."

He whips his phone out and calls for an ambulance while simultaneously flooring the gas. I focus on taking deep breaths, finding as much comfort as I can in the capable sound of Kip's voice as he directs the dispatcher to the golf clubhouse.

"They're on their way," he assures me. "You're going to be alright."

"How long before I can't breathe?" I ask, grateful to be in the hands of a doctor—even though, without a pure dose of epinephrine to shoot into my thigh, he can't offer much.

"Could be a few minutes or a few hours," he says, which doesn't help to ease my panic. My brain just fixates on the first part. A few minutes. "I'm sure they have a pen in the clubhouse. Don't panic. Just breathe for me."

He rubs my back and adds, "I love you so much."

The tightness I've been carrying around in my chest for the past twenty-four hours dissipates at once, and for a moment I forget we're in a full-on race against death.

Kip hasn't changed his mind about me.

About us.

If I *can't* get a pure dose of epinephrine shot into my thigh, this confirmation feels like the next best thing.

"I love you so much," I echo back to him. "So fucking much—"

I cough through a sudden swelling in my throat.

Shit.

"Hold on," Kip says. "We're getting there. Just hold on."

He continues to speed up the cart path, past the fairway and the tee, through the meandering route back to the clubhouse.

"This thing is so damn slow," he groans to himself as he thrusts the full force of his body weight into the gas pedal. "Come on, come on, come on."

My entire leg is now on fire—absolutely covered in hives—and every breath I take seems to be exponentially more labored than the last. It's like I'm running a marathon while seated.

"Babe?" Kip asks as we pass the fountain. "We're almost there. You okay?"

I can only manage another cough in response.

"Ray?" Kip's voice is hazy and distant as we pull up to a blur of windows and siding that I assume is…a building of some kind. My head feels like a hot-air balloon. Drifting past the golf course, over the beach, out to sea. "Stay with me."

Suddenly I'm seven years old again, back on the beach with the dirty sand. My mom's eyes closed and ears covered as she listens to her book on tape. My palms burning and fingers swelling as I wail in pain.

I think of the lobsters in my dad's holding tank. How I used to envy their shells—their protection from predators, from the world—while I was stuck with my vulnerable human skin. If only I had that kind of protection.

But even lobsters don't always have that protection.

They have to molt eventually.

The next thing I know I'm in the back of an ambulance, a pair of blurry men fussing over me on the way to Seabrook Hospital.

"Raymond," a bald guy in a dark-blue shirt says. "I'm going to take this off, okay?"

He hovers over my supine body, removing an oxygen mask from my face as an aluminum roof rattles above his head.

I open my eyes wider and look down at my hands, half expecting them to be child-sized and inflamed. But instead they're the hands of a thirty-five-year-old man, and this time it's my leg that's on fire.

"Raymond?" the EMS guy repeats.

And then Kip's face comes into focus from behind him. "Ray!"

I take a deep breath—my throat irritated but not constricted—as I realize what year it is.

"What happened?" I ask.

"You passed out," the EMS guy says. "Luckily they had an EpiPen at the resort, which your friend here administered. Can you breathe alright?"

I take another deep breath to make sure the last breath wasn't just a fluke.

"Yeah," I croak through a tsunami of relief. I'm alive, I'm breathing, and the man I love is right by my side. "I can breathe."

Kip clears his throat and moves closer.

"Fiancé," he says.

The EMS guy squints in confusion. "Huh?"

"You referred to me as his friend." Kip reaches for my hand and links his fingers through mine. "I'm his fiancé."

36

After a quick intake and some questions from nurses, I'm hooked up to an IV of steroids and can already feel my symptoms fading. My ankle cools off, my throat relaxes. Kip squeezes my hand so tight I wonder if it will affect how the drugs circulate through my bloodstream.

"I'm so sorry," he says. "I should've checked that sand trap for you. I should've thrown that EpiPen into my golf bag."

"I'm the one with the allergy," I correct him. "I should've done those things."

"I should've known you wouldn't."

I take a deep breath—I can't stop taking deep, grateful breaths—and relax into the hospital bed. The sterile walls around us reflect a mosaic of jagged curtain shadows as the heart monitor next to my bed beeps in perfect rhythm.

"You called me your fiancé," I tell Kip. "In the ambulance."

He squeezes my hand again. "That's what you are."

I squeeze his hand back. "I'm so sorry for yesterday. I shouldn't have stormed out. I shouldn't have gotten into the pool with Joley."

"You don't have to apologize," Kip says. "You're allowed to talk to anyone you want. I know you told him you weren't interested. I know you pulled away when he tried to kiss you."

"You do?" I ask. "How?"

"Because you told me so," he answers.

"Still," I sigh. "I knew he was flirting with me, and I clearly flirted back enough for him to think it'd be okay to kiss me. It was just, you know, that attention. I kept thinking, 'This guy will kiss me in public, and my own fiancé won't.'"

"Babe—"

"But now I realize it doesn't matter," I continue. "I don't care if you never kiss me in public again. As long as you keep kissing me in private. As long as you keep loving me. As long as you keep administering my EpiPen when I get stung—"

"Let's hope this was a last-time-it-ever-happens situation," Kip says through a tiny laugh.

"And I know you already know this, but nothing happened in their hotel room. Joley and Byrd had a fight, and then Byrd and I had the most depressing conversation ever."

"I trust you," Kip says. "Even yesterday when I was all pissed off—deep down, I trusted you."

"And I meant every word in that text I sent you," I tell him. "If you're not comfortable with all the showy traditional stuff, we don't have to do it. We can cancel the wedding entirely and go to city hall tomorrow. As long we still get to be together for the rest of our lives, I'm willing to sacrifice whatever I need to. I'm not trying to make you someone you're not."

"I don't want to cancel the wedding," Kip assures me. "And I'm the one who should be apologizing to you, for my outburst. I don't want to go back into the closet. I don't want to be my old self. I don't want to be any version of myself other than the one I am with you."

"I love that version of you," I promise him. "And I swear it's enough for me."

"I thought a lot last night about your writing," he says. "I need you to know that I think everything you've ever done—even all that old *Microphone* content you hate so much—has been so hugely impressive to me. I honestly think it's just as important as the work I do..."

"Let's not get carried away," I tease. "You have literally saved lives."

"And maybe you have, too!" Kip suggests. "I was so wrong when I said it was all about attention seeking. Maybe that used to play a role in it, but even if it did—and even if it *still* does—your work is so much more than that. All that writing you did about your divorce from Byrd...even the silly posts about jellyfish and water sports and prostate massagers or whatever..."

"We don't need to talk about the prostate massagers," I crack.

He releases an amused breath. "Your work is the kind of thing that helps people feel less alone in the world. Feel more *seen*. I know this firsthand, because I remember reading your posts six years ago, right after we met, when I was still recovering from my own divorce and coming to terms with being gay. And all of your posts—as trivial and entertaining as they might be on the surface—made me feel less alone. They made me fall in fucking *love* with you."

I've always struggled to think about my work like this, and a part of me even wonders if Kip might be giving me a little too much credit right now—mainly because of all the hate emails and nasty blog comments I've internalized over the years. But Kip's words remind me of all the *good* feedback I've gotten over the years, too. The most important of which has come from him. The person whose opinion matters more to me than anyone else's in the world.

"That's a superpower," Kip finishes. "The way you've never been afraid to be on display—even the messiest parts of you—is something I've always envied."

"Envied?" I ask.

"Envied," he repeats. "You know I've always prided myself on being a strong person—stable and rock-solid and all that stuff. But I'm a hypocrite. If I were truly strong, I wouldn't care about being named in your article, or PDA, or anything else. I wouldn't care about patients Googling me and finding out I'm a three-dimensional human."

"You're not a hypocrite," I tell him. "You're just…well…*a three-dimensional human*. And it's like you said yesterday, some people are more private than others. It doesn't necessarily mean you're self-loathing or ashamed."

"Maybe," he says through a generous half smile. "I'll never *love* being the center of attention, and I know that's not a bad thing in itself."

"It's truly not," I confirm. "Your ability to not need so much attention is something *I've* always envied in *you*."

We don't say anything for a few moments.

"But still," Kip finally says. "I should be able to deal with a kiss, or a wedding announcement, without freaking out over what it would do to my professional image. You're not wrong about any of that stuff.

"And I know I've been saying that it's not about me being gay," he goes on, "but after thinking about it so much this week, yeah. Of course it is. My gayness is why I've developed the patterns I have in the first place. Because I got it in my head early on that the real me is flawed. So I've always needed to either hide from the world or go all in on becoming someone else entirely."

More silence as my heart monitor continues to *beep-beep-beep*. I keep trying to find exactly the right words to make him feel better, but the expression on his face tells me that's not what he wants. He's processing his feelings out loud, and I just need to let him.

"I know on an intellectual level that being gay is not nearly as big a deal as it was when I was a kid," he tells me. "The vast majority of people do not give a shit that we are two men who love each other. And in our daily lives together...I hardly ever think about any of this stuff. But running into Jake after all these years just triggered something in me. He's one of those guys who, when I look him, all I see is my father."

This is a pivot I didn't see coming. "Marshall? But you guys are so close."

Kip shrugs. "We never talk about anything beneath the surface. When I was younger, he was always so insistent that I conform. Never make a spectacle of myself..." His voice starts shaking. He's the closest to tears I've ever seen him. "It's stupid. I don't know why I even brought him up."

I press the button on the side of the hospital bed until it has me sitting in a fully upright position, facing him. "It's not stupid. I love your dad, but the man literally had the spelling of his last name changed in order to not stand out. He clearly values conformity more than most."

Kip lets out a quiet laugh.

I guess it shouldn't be surprising that his issues can be traced back to Marshall. Not only is it textbook for straight fathers to give their gay sons lifelong inferiority complexes, but I've seen how Marshall can be firsthand. I literally watched him refer to me as Kip's "buddy" at his country club.

But Marshall has changed. He apologized—not just for that incident, but for a lifetime of casually flung antigay comments—and Kip forgave him. He understood that Marshall grew up in a time and place when overt homophobia was just kind of a given. My own father was effusively supportive when I came out, but even he used to yell *fag* at the TV whenever Drew Bledsoe failed to complete a touchdown pass back in the day.

"What about that talk you guys had a few years ago?" I ask Kip.

He considers this for a moment. "It wasn't quite as deep as I

made it out to be. We said all the words we were supposed to...
Obviously he supports us and he's coming to the wedding...but deep
down I still can't shake the sense that he's disappointed in me. He
was so proud the first time I got married, and this time it feels like
he's just tolerating it.

"But maybe I'm not giving him enough credit. I don't know. I
just know that he planted a shame in me that I can't seem to kill. No
matter how hard I try to intellectualize it or let it go."

I can feel Kip's pain on a visceral level, and I'm amazed at just
how deep it goes. Outside of that one incident at the country club,
I've never heard him talk about Marshall's actions as being particularly damaging. I've always been aware of Kip's preoccupation
with Marshall's approval, sure, but I figured it was mainly a harm-
less, subconscious thing. Especially since most of his stories about
Marshall are good ones—painfully wholesome anecdotes about
baseball games, road trips, and golf lessons.

Kip seems to register my confusion and launches into a decid-
edly not-wholesome anecdote.

"When I was thirteen," he says. "My mother had just come
home from Macy's, and she'd bought my dad several packs of white
briefs. You know—the kind with the model on the box."

"I see where this is going," I crack. "The underwear-aisle gay
awakening is something we *all* have in common."

"I took it even further," Kip says. "I stole the packaging from
the garbage, took the cardboard insert out, and kept it under my
pillow..."

"Damn." When I was thirteen, the internet existed and I'd
already developed a mild addiction to gay porn. The fact that young
Kip had to make do with an underwear box is so sad but also quite
adorable. "And your dad found it?"

Kip answers with a grim nod. "And he just tore into me.

Screaming about how he refused to raise a sissy…among other slurs. He threw a full-on fit. And then he came down from it and just sulked, which was even worse. He was so cold to me, for the first time in my life, and so disappointed. He thought he was raising one kind of son, and it turned out—"

He gets too choked up to finish the sentence.

"What happened after that?" I ask.

"I told him it was just a phase," Kip says. "We never talked about it again. I became…who I became."

And now I'm the one getting choked up. The thought of young Kip enduring such a hurtful episode—ground zero of learning to become invisible—makes me the darkest combination of heartbroken and furious. Everything inside of me wants to go back in time and stop it all from happening. Maybe even kick Past Marshall in the nuts.

"I'm so sorry," I manage to get out.

Kip composes himself for the both of us and brushes it off. "I don't know why I'm rehashing all this. It was just one incident. You know I had a great childhood. A great life. Plenty of gay men have been through a hell of a lot worse than *that*."

"You don't have to diminish your pain," I tell him. "That's a formative moment, and Jesus—it explains a lot. I didn't realize Marshall was so…"

"That's the thing!" Kip says. "He's a good guy. I know he loves me. That's not who he is."

"But it is who he *was*," I say—not to indict Marshall, who I'm sure regrets that moment, but simply to validate Kip's feelings.

Kip holds back a response, and once again all we can hear is the beeping of my heart monitor. I wish I could trade places with him right now—plug my IV into his arm, pump his blood with something strong enough to dissolve all the shame that's festered inside of him all these years. I wish I could heal him. Not for my sake, or for the sake of getting to publicly brag about my perfect marriage, but for his sake. So he doesn't have to navigate such a massive gap between the person he is and the person he thinks he needs to be.

But I can't do that, so I try my best to comfort him instead.

"Maybe it is a little cliché," I start, "but there's comfort in knowing we *all* grow up with this kernel of shame deep in our core—any gay man over the age of thirty who says he didn't is entirely full of shit—which in itself should indicate that the kernel is a lie. If we were all as singularly defective as we've always feared, then how do you explain the fact that there are so many of us?"

Kip laughs. "You know what? I never thought about it that way."

"We all try to shrink that kernel in our own ways," I continue. "Some of us overcompensate by overachieving and seeking external validation. Others just want to be as unremarkable and anonymous as possible."

"But I don't wanna be anonymous anymore," Kip says. "Not if it's at your expense. That's what I realized when I saw you in that ambulance earlier. I *had* to correct that guy when he called you my friend. I needed this random stranger to know how important you are to me."

He takes a breath. "And I need to shrink this kernel. I need to fucking obliterate it."

"You will." I reach over and place a hand on his heart, which beats in perfect time with the beeps of my monitor. "And so will I."

37

~

We're exhausted and ravenous when we get back to the hotel, so we order a feast from room service and change into our pajamas (a.k.a. boxer briefs) at six o'clock. The sun is still shining in from our balcony windows and the cabana bar's sound system echoes with happy-hour yacht rock from the beach—beckoning guests to come out and join the party—but I don't give a shit.

Right now I just want to be as close to Kip as possible.

By eight o'clock, half the surfaces in our suite are covered in those shiny metal room-service lids, and we're on a sugar high. Kip forbade me from drinking due to all the steroids in my system, so we treated ourselves to the hotel's dessert special: an enormous skillet of warm chocolate chip cookie topped with twin scoops of vanilla ice cream.

"Fire round," Kip yelps. There's playful mischief in his voice—we haven't had a proper battle like this in years. "Sarah McLachlan."

"Starting with the easy ones," I tease. "Paula Cole."

"Sheryl Crow."

"Jewel."

"Ummm." Kip scratches his chin. "Natalie Merchant."

"Indigo Girls."

"Fiona Apple."

"Tracy Chapman."

"Lisa Loeb."

"Good one," Kip says. "Queen Latifah."

"Shawn Colvin." I could go all day without running out of names.

"Liz Phair."

"Erykah Badu."

"Umm... Oh! Suzanne Vega."

I nod approvingly. "Meredith Brooks."

"Who?" Kip asks.

"'Bitch,'" I explain. "She sang 'Bitch.'"

"Oh! Duh. 'Bitch.'" He strokes his chin for another moment. "Uh... Sophie B. Hawkins."

"Wrong!" I chirp. "I win."

He grimaces. "You're telling me *Sophie B. Hawkins* has never played Lilith Fair? That's impossible."

I raise a smug eyebrow. "Google it."

He does and then concedes. "'Damn I Wish I Was Your Lover' came out in 1992? I could've sworn it was later than that."

I stand up and take a bow in my underwear. Kip tugs at the waistband and pulls me back into bed. We lie there for a while, making out, tracing random shapes on each other's backs and torsos.

It's amazing how much can transpire in twenty-four hours. Yesterday I almost lost my fiancé, today I almost lost my life, and tonight I'm so grateful for both that I could burst.

"Was it lonely in here without me?" I ask Kip. "Last night?"

"Extremely," he says. "And I had the most awkward dinner with Jake and Lucy."

The mention of their names induces a full-body cringe. I'd nearly forgotten about their role in yesterday's debacle. "They must think I'm such a disaster. They must think our relationship is a fucking mess."

Ironic, really, considering the stuff that goes on in theirs.

"Screw what they think," he says. "We didn't talk about the fight all that much. You know me. But Lucy tried to bring it up. She vigorously defended you. She was so mad that I let you leave for the night."

You know what? *I love Lucy.* (Lol.)

"At least I got to see Stef again," I tell him. "Especially now that I know she's moving two weeks after our wedding."

He whips his head around. "To Maine? I thought that was five years from now."

"She lied. Didn't want to steal the thunder during our early-moon week."

"How do you feel about it?" he asks.

"I'm happy for her," I say. "She'll get to keep lobstering, which is all she cares about. And we can still visit her in Maine."

A breeze blows in from the balcony, drawing my attention to the pink-blue sky outside our window, and Kip suggests we go out and watch the sunset.

We settle into a pair of lounge chairs, holding hands across the armrests. Something about the nature around us—the water, the beach, the sky—comforts me. The way it's all so beautiful without even trying. It doesn't care if we stop and look at it or not; it just exists.

There are people on the beach, most of them with their eyes closed or buried in a phone. There are people on the patio, but they're all drinking and talking to each other. This exact view, from this exact angle, in this exact moment, will only ever be witnessed by Kip and me. I could take a picture and share it on Instagram, but it wouldn't be the same.

There's a freedom in letting the moment itself be enough.

"I'm sorry for turning into an attention-seeking hurricane after you proposed to me."

"I'm sorry for calling you an attention-seeking hurricane in the first place," Kip replies. "I didn't mean it. I promise."

"I'm gonna tell CeCe the article's off," I tell him. "Even if I do write it, I'd never be able to do this place justice."

"But you could try," he suggests. "I think you should try."

"Really?"

"Use my name, too," he says. "Maybe just don't write about the past twenty-four hours."

"You know me," I tell him. "I'll make it look pretty."

After the sun sets, back in the room, Kip starts fidgeting with the alarm-clock speaker on the nightstand. I'm about to question him on this behavior—he's one of those people who wakes up at the same time every day purely based on circadian rhythm—but then I hear the bleep of a freshly connected Bluetooth device. He scrolls through his phone for a moment, and suddenly the opening bars of "Tougher Than the Rest" fill the room.

"Dance with me?" he asks.

This request should sound ridiculous coming from a half-naked man surrounded by hotel furniture and discarded room-service plates, but instead it's the most romantic thing I've ever heard.

As I accept his outstretched hand and press my body against his, a feeling of warmth spreads through me—not quite butterflies, not quite electricity, not quite any descriptor you'd ever find in the dialogue of a Hallmark movie or the lyrics of a love song. Just a deep sense of contentment and gratitude.

"Barbara Eden would hate our technique," Kip jokes, because we have none. We're simply swaying, leaning on each other as our bodies move with the music.

"That lesson may have been a mistake," I admit. "And you

know, we really don't have to do this at our wedding. I mean it. This can be just for us."

"If we do end up doing it," he says, "I'd like to request that we at least wear clothes."

"That's fair," I admit. "Formal wear would be preferable to boxer briefs."

"Look at us," he says. "Agreeing on something."

I smile into the space between his neck and ear. We don't say anything for a few moments, and my mind drifts back to something he said during our fight yesterday—how he called me out for valuing his hypermasculine qualities just as much as everyone else in our homophobic society, the title of this song being a prime example.

"I'd love you even if you weren't tougher than the rest," I quietly tell him. "You can be weak with me whenever you need to. I promise I can handle it."

He squeezes me a little tighter and simply whispers, "I know you can."

And so we continue dancing. Holding, swaying, leaning. As if our bodies would collapse without the other one holding us up.

sunday

38

How do I know everything is back to normal? Because Kip woke up this morning and went for a run on the beach. And so of course I went down to the breakfast buffet for a final chance to get some material for my piece.

"It's just terrible," Arthur Adkins is saying. He spotted me eating alone at the same table as yesterday and came over to apologize for the wasp episode. Apparently the arrival of an ambulance on resort grounds caused quite a stir. "Our course manager has had a hell of a time trying to keep the bees under control for our guests, but there's only so much we can do. We try not to be aggressive in our efforts, given how essential they are for the environment."

This makes me laugh into my pancakes, because all I can think about is the "Against Bees" saga from a few years ago.

"The United States agricultural industry would collapse without the essential crop pollination that bees provide," I say in agreement, basically reciting one of the less vitriolic emails I received in response to that old shit-post. "And there's no need to apologize. The bees were fine. It was a sand wasp that took me down."

"Ah! Those are just useless nuisances," Arthur says. "I'll be sure to have the bunkers promptly treated." He taps the table. "How is your article coming along?"

"I've gotten some great quotes," I tell him. But not enough.

"While I have your ear, and given that you're the owner, I'm curious. What do you think makes for a successful earlymoon?"

"Hmm! That's a good one." He strokes his gray beard for several moments, careful not to rush his response. "If you're still engaged by the end of it, then it was a success."

The words sound like a joke, but his voice is serious. I have to know more. "Can you elaborate?"

A few more beard strokes, and then he speaks. "The earlymoon I took with my sweet Evelyn, sixty-some-odd years ago... We almost called off the wedding that week."

"*What*?" I pull up some of the notes I took from our first conversation. "But you said it was the most magical week of your lives. That's a direct quote."

He smiles. "It *was* a magical week. It's why this entire resort exists, after all. But it wasn't a walk in the park. It actually rained half the time, and we were trapped in our little cottage with nowhere to go, nothing to do but look at each other. Evelyn got stir-crazy one day and said, 'Arthur, what if we're too young to make this commitment?' Back then, it was common to get married at eighteen. But she was the furthest thing from common."

"So then what happened?" I ask.

"I got angry with her for questioning our decision," he admits. "Which led to a bit of a quarrel. I was a dummy. I just loved her so much, you see, and the wedding was so close. We slept in separate bedrooms that night. I was sure she'd leave me."

"Why didn't she?"

"The next morning I told her that we could cancel the wedding," he explains. "As long as we could still be together. I knew I'd never change my mind about her, but I had to accept that she needed more time to be sure about me." He shrugs. "And then we got married exactly as planned."

I know this isn't the point of the story, but it's nice to know that Kip and I are in such good company when it comes to unexpected earlymoon drama. The fact that Arthur and Evelyn went through some of their own and managed to stay married for decades afterward is a heartening indicator that we're on the right track.

"It was a very simple case of cold feet," Arthur says. "Happens to plenty of couples before the big day—oftentimes *right* before. And that's why I was so glad we had an earlymoon, to clear the aisle of all doubts and walk down it with certainty." He cracks a smile. "That's why we have that sign behind the main hotel bar."

"The Cold Feet Saloon," I respond through a smile of my own.

"That's the one!" He rises from his seat and straightens his dress shirt. "Well, Mr. Bruno, I should get back to business—much to prepare for Lobster Fest this evening. I hope to see you and your fella there."

"Thank you so much for talking to me," I say. "This place is truly special, and I look forward to writing about it."

As Arthur walks back toward the entrance, I spot the back of Byrd's head in the buffet line. No Joley—just Byrd. He's fiddling with a pair of sausage tongs, wearing the same weathered UCLA T-shirt that he used to sleep in way back when we were together.

Our eyes meet the second he turns around, and before I know it, he's joining me at the table.

"The dreaded ex-husband," he jokes.

"How does that shirt still exist?" I ask him.

"I know, right?" he says. "Those bitches at Gildan are low-key the best clothiers in the business. They make tees that could literally survive the apocalypse."

"That is...so weirdly accurate," I agree. "I have a promotional Gildan tee from one of Kip's medical conferences that has survived hundreds upon hundreds of washes."

"Where is this Kip?" he asks. "I was hoping to meet him. Is that weird? Would that be weird? Oh God. Please don't tell me you're still fighting two days later."

I fake a bullet to the chest. "Thanks for rubbing salt in the wound, asshole. We called the wedding off."

"Shut up!" he says. "Stop."

"I'm just kidding. He's on his morning run."

Byrd's eyes widen. "You ended up with a guy who runs while on vacation? Jesus. You really did do a one-eighty after our divorce."

"What about Joley?" I ask. "Where's he?"

"Sleeping off a hangover that's even worse than mine," he answers. "We guzzled two bottles of champs in the hot tub last night, so it's dehydration central in our suite."

"So you guys are...good?"

He swallows his current bite of eggs Benedict. "Well, we didn't have much of a wedding to call off in the first place. We just planned to do a quickie Vegas thing—no family or friends. But we've decided to postpone."

He doesn't sound terribly bothered by this, which makes me feel like less of a jerk for joking about a canceled wedding just now. But still, I can't help but feel for him. I know Byrd, and that couldn't have been an easy decision to make.

"I'm sorry to hear that," I offer. "Are you okay?"

He puts a hand up. "It was my idea. I'm totally fine. We're staying together and trying to make the whole 'open' thing work—with plenty of ground rules and lots of communication."

Oh. Maybe I don't know Byrd as well as I thought I did.

"But you're such a hopeless romantic!" I say and immediately regret it. This is really none of my business. "How did he convince you?"

Byrd sighs. "Honestly? He didn't. You did."

"Me?"

"Running into you here," he says. "Seeing Joley all over you in the pool—which was fucked up on so many levels, but we're working through *that*—it made me think about our marriage. And why it ended."

"Because we never loved each other," I tell him. "Not really…"

"I think I actually did love you," he says. "But you didn't love me. You loved *love*—the fantasy of it. And that was why I cheated."

If Byrd had said this to me six years ago—effectively singling me out as the reason our marriage failed—I'd have been far too defensive to receive it. But I can't deny that I was far more in love with the idea of having a husband than I actually was with him. I always just assumed the error was mutual. I never considered the possibility that he cheated not because he didn't love me, but because he knew I didn't love him.

"Joley loves me," Byrd says. "I don't even question that part of it. He also happens to be the kind of guy who's addicted to chasing sex. It's not an emotional thing for him. It's just a vice. Like how you love to drink and idealize the concept of soulmates. He loves to seduce and screw."

"And you're okay with that?" I ask.

"I just might be," he muses. "Honestly? The thought of being in a relationship but also having the freedom to sleep with a variety of men… It doesn't sound all that bad to me. It sounds like a dream, actually. I've just been so programmed to think love is this one-size-fits-all monogamy situation, but I'm starting to realize that might not be what I actually want. As long as I have a primary partner to come home to, what's wrong with having some fun on the side?"

I know myself enough to know that this is a philosophy that

could never work for me, but I'm genuinely happy for Byrd. He deserves to be happy, and it sounds like monogamy has only ever made him miserable.

"So I should thank you," he says. "Because I don't know if Joley and I would've had this breakthrough if it weren't for running into you this week."

The first response that comes to my mind is an *Ally McBeal* quote that doesn't reflect how I actually feel at all, but that I can't resist deploying nonetheless. Especially with such a perfect audience.

"It wasn't my plan to break up your marriage," I tease, "but I can't say I'm exactly thrilled to be the best thing that's ever happened to it."

He breaks into a hysterical laugh. "Season one! You know what? You really haven't changed at all. Always an Ally. These days I think I'm more of an Elaine. Just a messy bitch who embraces the drama of life."

"All this time I thought our problem was that we were two Allys," I joke. "Meanwhile, we were an Ally and an Elaine—even worse."

Byrd runs a hand through his messy hair as he smiles. "And Joley is a total Richard Fish."

"You know what? That is so spot on." Richard was the founding partner at Ally's law firm, an impish and morally bankrupt clown who somehow managed to be lovable at the end of the day.

"Who is Kip?" Byrd asks.

I've somehow never asked myself this question, but the answer comes to me immediately: "Greg Butters."

And I'm not just saying that because Greg Butters was a handsome (check) doctor (check) who Ally dated during season one. It's more because Greg had a pureness about him. He loved Ally and all of her quirks without expecting anything in return. He had a strength and stillness that served as the perfect counterpoint to Ally's ongoing neurotic chaos.

Byrd gasps at my answer.

"You ended up with a Greg?" he says. "You lucky bastard."

39

The massive indoor-outdoor event space of the grand pavilion looks like it was pulled directly from the pages of *The Knot*. A tasteful blanket of string lights hangs from the ceiling, over a shiny dance floor, surrounded by a sea of white tablecloths. Candles everywhere. A champagne fountain in one corner and a colossal raw bar made from literal ice in another.

"All this is for a Lobster Fest?" Kip asks as we settle into a round table on the perimeter, inches away from the sand. "I feel like we should be dressed for a wedding."

We're basically twinning in dock shorts and linen button-downs, but the other couples here aren't dressed any fancier.

"These aren't unheard-of ensembles for a beach wedding," I suggest.

"And yet we're requiring cocktail attire at ours…"

My vision of perfect wedding photos has always included all guests in nice dresses and/or suit jackets, but now that I think about it, maybe it's not too late to tell guests they can wear whatever the hell they want. Maybe it's not too late to change other details as well—take the emphasis away from appearances and place it more on simply having a good time.

"We can change that," I respond. "We still have time."

"Let's add it to the list of renegotiables," Kip says with a wink. He gestures at the flower arrangement at the center of the table, a towering plume of white roses and lilies. "This has got to go."

He grabs the vase with both hands and walks it over to an empty corner of the bar, where it fits perfectly into the design scheme.

"What was that about?" I ask.

"Last thing we need is a repeat sting."

"Shouldn't all the bees be going to sleep soon? It's almost seven."

He places a hand over my wrist. "I'm not taking any chances, my love."

A waiter drops off a bottle of chilled chardonnay as we peruse the prix fixe menu. Just as our glasses are being poured, a voice calls out from behind us.

"You're here!" Lucy chirps. Her hair's down in loose waves and she's wearing a flowy sundress with a whimsical lemon pattern on it. "How great is this?"

"Hey, buddy!" Jake's muscles poke out of a salmon golf polo as he gives Kip's shoulder a squeeze. "Nice spot. You expecting two more or can we join?"

"Join us," Kip offers. "Have some wine."

"What are we toasting to?" Jake asks.

"*Love*," Lucy says. "Duh."

"And marriage," I add.

Lucy inspects the menu for a moment. "Lazy man's lobster! My favorite. Who the hell has the patience to crack a shell?"

My father would be appalled at this notion, but honestly? She's correct. I've always hated all the work that goes into eating a whole lobster.

"Not me!" I respond. "Just gimme the meat."

There's a beat of silence.

"Jake," Kip says. "I swear to God, if you make a gay joke—"

Jake bursts into a laugh. "I didn't say anything! Although Ray, you did set yourself up there."

Lucy looks at me and rolls her eyes. "This is their thing now. Everything's a gay joke. You should've heard them the other night. Like children. Honestly? I think Kip coming out has made Jake realize he's a little gay himself."

Jake shoots her a middle finger, then looks at Kip and me. "No offense, guys."

Lucy flips him off right back. "Love you, honey."

The wine keeps flowing as we continue our small talk over a series of random hors d'oeuvres. Mini crab cakes, bacon-wrapped scallops, panko-crusted shrimp. All the classics. Kip and Jake are getting along like the old friends they are, Lucy and I are getting along like the old friends we feel like, and every so often the whole table erupts in laughter.

For a moment I think back to what it was like the first time we shared a table with these two—so tense and miserable—and feel so proud that Kip is an entirely different person now than he was that night.

He's *himself*.

And isn't that the real beauty of allowing yourself to be seen?

"So tell us about your wedding," Lucy is now saying. "I'm dying to know the deets."

"Honey…" Jake warns.

"What? I'm not fishing for an invite. I'm just curious."

"You guys should come if you can." I blurt this out not only because I'm starting to catch a buzz, but also because it just feels appropriate for them to be there, given the unexpected role they played in our earlymoon.

"It's going to be a beach wedding," I continue. "At a venue

basically like this, but in the Hamptons. And without the champagne fountain and ice bar." I cock my head. "Unless…"

Kip clicks his tongue. "Vetoed."

"We're keeping it very simple," I tell Lucy. "We were going to
have all the traditional bells and whistles, but now I'm thinking I
want it to be more chill. I'm gonna talk to our planner next week
and see how much flexibility we have to change things around.
Starting with the dress code—possibly none at all."

Kip flashes me a warm smile. I know he'd have been fine if we
kept everything exactly as planned, but it makes me happy to know
our wedding will now be much more of a collaboration between
our two styles.

"We're sold," Lucy says. "Jake's family has a house in Montauk,
so we won't even have to get a room."

"We'll be in East Hampton!" I tell her. "Meant to be."

The waiter comes over and takes our orders—lazy man's lobster
all around—and then the DJ takes the mic to invite all couples to
participate in a predinner slow dance. "Thinking Out Loud" by
Ed Sheeran starts flowing from the sound system as guests begin to
descend upon the dance floor.

Mariah and Nicki are front and center, so lost in each other's
arms that they don't even notice me waving from across the pavilion.

The next couple I notice are Byrd and Joley, who clearly took
a lesson with Barbara Eden at some point during their stay here.

"I wanna dance," Lucy says, tugging Jake's arm. "Come on, babe."

"To this song?" he groans. "Pass."

She crosses her arms and huffs against her chair. "You suck. I
love this song."

Kip laughs at their exchange and then does what he always does
during slow songs: picks at whatever food is on his plate (in this
instance, half a crab cake).

I could draw his attention to the fact that there are two queer couples on the dance floor right now—one of whom is doing a whole-ass waltz—and nobody is remotely fazed, but I don't. It's not about whether the people around us care, it's about whether Kip is comfortable. And if he's still not there yet, that's fine. Me pestering him about it won't make him get there any faster, and the last thing I want to do is make him feel even a little bit inadequate.

"Ray," Lucy says, throwing her napkin on the table. "Let's leave these two to eat their crab cakes and be boring together. Dance with me!"

She leads me to an empty spot in the corner and throws her arms over my shoulders, resting her hands behind my neck as I gently place mine on her waist. It's all very prom. Except for the fact that she smells amazing—like a very expensive perfume that no high schooler would ever be able to afford.

"I'm so glad you're here," she says as we sway to the music. "I felt so bad for you the other night. I kept texting you to come back to the resort, but then someone texted back with, 'Bitch, who is Ray? This is Alicia.' Did you give me a fake number?"

"No!" I say truthfully. "I must've typed it in wrong by accident."

Accident or divine intervention. Given the state I was in Friday night, if I'd seen those texts, there's a good chance I'd have come back and made a drunken scene.

"You'll have to fix it for me later," she says.

"Absolutely," I promise. "I thought about texting you myself, but I figured you were with Kip and I didn't want to put you in the middle of a whole lovers' quarrel. I'm sorry you guys had to deal with our drama at all."

"Who even was that tattooed guy you were making out with?" She whispers the next part into my ear: "He's, like, four couples away from us right now, by the way."

"We didn't make out!" I remind her. "'*It was an optical illusion.*'"

She purses her lips. "Ron Burgundy? Really?"

"I'm serious," I say. "*Camille.*"

"You know what? That's fair," she says through a giggle. "What's the deal with him, though? Just between you and me."

"He's my ex-husband's new fiancé," I answer. "Kip didn't tell you?"

Lucy gasps. "*Shut up!* No. After we saw you guys go upstairs, he didn't say a word about it. It was the elephant in the room all night."

I shouldn't be surprised that Kip kept the information to himself, even when it was obvious we were weathering a huge storm. He's always preferred to work through issues on his own, in his head, rather than seek advice from outside parties. Mainly because he understands that unless you're talking to someone who knows you better than you know yourself, advice typically says more about the person giving it than the person asking for it.

"So wait," Lucy says. "That other guy is your ex-husband?"

"He is."

"Holy shit. Did you know they'd be here this week?"

"Of course not. It was the worst coincidence of my life."

But as I say it, I realize it's not true at all. Given what ultimately came of the experience, it might actually be the best coincidence of my life.

"So what did you guys talk about all night?" I ask. "If not me?"

"You are so self-absorbed," she says. "I love it. Um. Mostly Jake and Kip were just catching up on life. Reminiscing. I was a total third wheel."

"Oh, man. I'm sorry I ruined a night of your earlymoon—"

"Not at all!" she says. "I actually want to thank you. I've seen a side of Jake this week that I never have before. He's surprised me so much, the way he's been talking with Kip. You should have heard him the other night. 'I love you, man. I respect you so much. Coming out takes balls,' and on and on. He wouldn't stop. After he got over his initial shock, it was like something clicked in him. He became totally empathetic."

As we dance through the last few bars of the song, I catch a glimpse of Kip and Jake at the table, laughing. As much as I disliked Jake at first, I do have to give the man some credit for saying the words I know Kip needed to hear. Granted, it shouldn't have taken Jake forty-five years to finally develop some empathy toward gay people, but that's the other beautiful thing about letting yourself be seen. Sometimes it can open the hearts and minds of the people you'd least expect.

"That makes me so happy," I tell Lucy. "And I know it means a lot to Kip."

"I'm happy it all worked out," she says. "You and Kip are so perfect for each other. I know I barely know you guys, but still. I can tell."

The song fades out as the DJ announces that dinner is served.

We rush back to the table—to our men and our lobster—and immediately start digging in. The perfect meal for our last night in Seabrook.

I become so swept up in the taste and all the memories and feelings it conjures that I barely notice when Arthur Adkins appears at our table out of nowhere. He's dressed like a yacht captain—pressed khakis, navy blue jacket, even one of those little hats.

After introducing himself to Kip, Lucy, and Jake, he squats by my chair.

"I met your sister today," he tells me. "What a fine young woman—and my gosh, does she take after your father! I almost thought I was buying lobster from Jim Bruno himself."

I nearly choke on my current bite. Thankfully, it's slathered in enough butter that it goes down smoothly once I push my surprise aside enough to swallow.

"You bought Stef's catch?" I ask. "Stef *had* a catch?"

"She charged a hefty premium, but I got what I could. It's our fiftieth anniversary! I had to serve Seabrook lobster." There's a wistful quality to his voice, like he'd rewind the clock fifty years right now and live it all over again if he could. "There wasn't much, but there was enough for your table."

Kip looks at me with excitement. "We're eating Seabrook lobster right now?"

"Fresh from the dock," Arthur says with a wink. "Enjoy."

"I knew it tasted different," I tell him. Even though, okay, fine, it tastes exactly the same. "Thank you so much for this. I'm sure my sister appreciated the business."

"My pleasure," he says. "Oh! And she wanted me to tell you something: 'Stef says hello.'" He shrugs. "She insisted I use that exact phrasing."

I nearly spit out my wine from the belly laugh this triggers in me. I love my sister so damn much.

"Thank you for relaying the message," I tell Arthur.

"Of course." He steps back as someone waves him toward the bar. "You lovebirds enjoy the rest of the party."

"Local lobster," Lucy marvels. "How cool is that?"

Jake shrugs. "Tastes the same as every other lobster I've ever had."

The three of us boo him in response.

As I continue eating, I tell myself to remember every last detail of this meal. The food that raised me. I make a mental note to call my parents tomorrow—first to tell them all about Arthur and the lovely gesture he made, but also simply because I don't call them enough.

After dinner, Lucy and I hit the dance floor while Kip and Jake continue to shoot the shit at the table. The DJ plays an impressive range of hits—from hip-hop to disco to eighties rock—and we go particularly hard when "Honey" by Mariah Carey comes on. Lucy moves like a legit nineties music-video vixen, and I move like an inflatable tube man at a car dealership, but somehow we have enough chemistry to keep going for several songs, bursting into laughter every few minutes or so for no reason in particular.

When we eventually return to the table, exhausted and sweat-drenched, Jake's sitting alone with an Amstel Light.

"Where's Kip?" I ask.

"Grabbing another couple beers," he says. "You two were tearing it up out there. Are you trying to steal my woman or what?"

"He already has," Lucy says before I can answer. "Your loss, bitch."

As I scan the bar for signs of Kip, the DJ comes back on the mic, telling the crowd this next song was a special request.

And then the opening drumbeat of "Tougher Than the Rest" kicks in.

Followed by a tap on my shoulder.

And there he is.

"Dance with me?" he asks.

Lucy is literally beaming on my behalf. "Awww! Oh my God!" Then she slaps Jake on the arm. "Babe, I don't give a fuck. You're dancing with me."

The four of us head to the floor and get lost amid the sea of blissed-out couples.

"You didn't have to do this," I tell Kip as we get into position—the same lazy form we took last night in our hotel room. "And we don't have to do it at our wedding."

"I wanted to." His hands against my lower back are the most natural feeling in the world. While slow-dancing with Lucy earlier was fun, this is something else entirely. This is an act of love. "Screw what anybody else thinks."

We hold each other tight, close our eyes, and move to the music. It's just like last night—both in the way we're dancing and in the way it feels like we're the only two people in the room. The only two people in the world.

"I can't wait to marry you," I tell Kip. And then something occurs to me. Amid all the tumult surrounding our impending wedding, I'd somehow lost sight of the fact that it's a miracle we're even able to get married in the first place. A privilege that had to be fought for. "You ever think about how incredible it is that we're even allowed to get married in the first place? Like, for the vast majority of our lives, our wedding would have been illegal."

"I do think about that," Kip admits. "When I got married the first time, twenty years ago, gay marriage *was* very much illegal."

"If it hadn't been, do you think you would've come out sooner?"

He thinks about it for a moment. "It's possible. Because I guess that would've meant life in general would've been easier for guys like us."

"I didn't come out until after it was legalized in Connecticut," I tell him. "Sometimes I wonder if that never happened, or if I had lived in a state where it wasn't legal, what I would've done."

"I'm one hundred percent sure you'd have done exactly what I did," Kip teases. "Purely for the sake of having a wedding."

We share a laugh and fall back into an easy silence, letting Springsteen do the talking for us. Kip is so comfortable in my arms, it's hard to believe he was so afraid of this for so long. It makes me wish I could go back and undo every slow dance we deprived ourselves of over the past six years, purely because we didn't think we deserved the same luxury of unremarkable public affection that straight people have had forever.

And I know it ultimately doesn't matter—the validity of our relationship could never hinge on something as trivial as a slow dance—but still. There's an undeniable energy of love permeating the dance floor right now, and it feels good to be a part of it. Everyone in our orbit is holding on to their person. The person who cares for and listens to and sees them when no one else does. The person who administers the EpiPen.

"I may have overestimated how big of a deal this is," Kip whispers in my ear. "I'm getting an overwhelming sense that no one around us gives a shit."

I laugh and pull him tighter. "I'm pretty sure Byrd and Joley are actively climaxing right now, and no one is batting an eyelash."

"Jake and Lucy are quite possibly conceiving their first child," Kip adds, "and nary a raised eyebrow."

"So what you're saying is that we should kiss."

"We *should* kiss."

And so we do.

epilogue

LIFE AND LOVE AT THE EARLYMOON HOTEL: INSIDE CONNECTICUT'S RESORT FOR "NEARLYWEDS"

By Ray Bruno

Two hundred acres of picturesque Connecticut shoreline. Impossibly clean beaches, gourmet restaurants, spacious suites, stunning views. A rambling pool area complete with a swim-up bar, and a meticulously designed golf course that could give even Pebble Beach a run for its money.

The Earlymoon Hotel in Seabrook, Connecticut has all this and more.

But that's not what makes it so special.

It's love.

I should mention at this point that I could be a *bit* biased. As a Seabrook native, I've always been aware of the resort's reputation as a haven for lovers. Every summer during my childhood, tourists would flock to our otherwise unremarkable lobstering community to indulge in early honeymoons (hence the resort's moniker) ahead of their tristate-area weddings. My mother so often described her own earlymoon there as the best week of her life—the perfect start to an even more perfect marriage—that she single-handedly turned her young son into a hopeless romantic. And I decided early on that the Earlymoon Hotel was the pinnacle of romance.

But I had no way to know for sure. The actual property was a mystery—its entrance hidden away by gates and hedges—which only served as rocket fuel for my fascination. Why were happily engaged couples so drawn to this place? What secrets about love and marriage did they learn within its borders? Why the focus on *early* honeymoons in the first place?

So when my now-husband, Kip, first proposed to me last year, it was inevitable that I followed up with a proposal of my own:

A stay at the Earlymoon Hotel.

We both said yes, and the getaway I'd been fantasizing about for decades was finally within reach. Five uninterrupted nights of love, romance, bliss, *perfection*.

Before I get into what ended up happening instead, some history on the resort itself.

The main hotel was built in the early seventies on land purchased by Arthur Adkins, a gregarious ex-banker with silver hair and a captain's hat, and his late wife, Evelyn. In a series of conversations over breakfast, Adkins explained that the inspiration for the resort was an earlymoon he and Evelyn had taken themselves when they were just teenagers.

"That trip changed our relationship," Adkins told me. "We just lay on the beach and played in the water and sat around our little rental cottage, but we broke through a wall. I learned things about her that I'd never known. Or even thought to ask."

And so—after striking it rich on Wall Street a decade

later—he returned to the site of that little cottage and started building.

"Evelyn had a mission with the place," he explained. "She wanted couples to leave the hotel even more in love with each other than they were when they arrived."

If the couples at the Earlymoon Hotel during my stay were any indication, it's safe to say her mission is regularly accomplished to this day. From dancing at the grand pavilion to hand-holding on the sand to admiring gazes over lobster bisque, there's an earnest sense of love in the air among the guests. A refreshing lack of self-consciousness.

"I never wanted a bachelorette party," said Mariah Hawkins, a Boston-area nurse visiting the resort with her fiancée and partner of ten years. "I want to celebrate getting married with my *love*—not with my friends."

For Hawkins and her fiancée Nicki Jameson, that celebration included things like moonlit strolls down the beach, champagne in hot tubs, and rose petals in their earlymoon suite.

"Every cliché in the book," Jameson proclaimed, "and I don't care what anybody has to say about it."

For Manhattanites Lucy Roy and Jake Meyers, the biggest gift they received on their earlymoon was simply each other's company.

"We spend so much time apart in our normal life," Roy said, noting her fiancé's long hours as a cardiologist. "Sometimes I forget how much I love him."

As for my own experience, I realized quickly that my expectations might've been a bit overblown. The setting was just as lovely as advertised, but Kip and I fought more in the first three days of our earlymoon than we had in the previous three *years* of our relationship. It was almost as if being among a sea of happy couples had shined a magnifying glass on problems we'd always silently agreed to pretend were too miniscule to even warrant examination. And it didn't help that I randomly ran into my ex-husband halfway through our stay.

But then something magical did happen.

We *talked*.

Not about our work or family or friends, or any of the mundane details that define the routines of daily life as a couple. We talked about the big, hard stuff. The kinds of getting-to-know-you-and-all-your-secrets-and-fears conversations that are more often had in the beginnings of relationships, before both parties have determined that they know everything there is to know about the other.

By the time we attended the resort's fiftieth anniversary Lobster Fest on our final night there, our relationship was on sturdier ground than it'd ever been before. My understanding of Kip—and his of me—had deepened to previously uncharted levels.

"Communication is easily the most important ingredient," Ms. Jameson said when asked about the recipe for a happy marriage. "You can't keep secrets or hold feelings inside or hope your partner is gonna read your mind. Even if they're good at it."

While this might seem obvious, it's also commonly forgotten among even the most committed couples.

Perhaps especially among the most committed couples.

"I saw a different side of Jake during our earlymoon," Ms. Roy told me a few weeks after our respective trips ended. "It was nice to know he could still surprise me. Our love is not perfect—far from it—and I know our marriage won't be either... but that trip reminded me of why I chose him in the first place."

Of course love is never perfect, because humans aren't.

Humans are selfish, insecure, sad, scared, and even mean sometimes. Putting two of them together for life is bound to require a continuous supply of compassion, compromise, and understanding on both sides. Everyone who's ever been in a serious relationship knows this, but it's amazing how quickly such knowledge goes out the window when you're consumed with trying to present the world with an image of perfection.

"If you're still together by the end of it," Arthur Adkins told me over coffee one morning on the hotel's dining veranda, "then your earlymoon was a success."

It's not the most romantic sound bite, but it is emblematic of how I've come to feel about the Earlymoon Hotel itself.

The child in me with the colossal expectations would be horribly disappointed—not that the resort doesn't live up to its reputation as a quintessential New England paradise (it does)—but that the resort is just that: a resort.

This revelation made me wonder if my mother had intentionally sold me a lie, or if she truly believed that the Earlymoon Hotel possessed an inherent magic of some kind. Was her experience there really as perfect as she'd always insisted it was? Is her *marriage* really as perfect as she's always insisted it is?

I decided to talk to her about these things when she recently visited for my wedding week.

"Our earlymoon *was* perfect," she maintained through a wistful sigh. "But our marriage sure as hell isn't."

Perhaps it was the bargain cabernet talking (we'd had plenty by then), but it was the first time in my life I'd ever heard her refer to her marriage as anything less than enchanted, so it felt like a groundbreaking admission.

"Your father has always been a great husband," she went on. "But we've had our issues, just like every other couple."

I proceeded to ask her exactly what those issues were, and whether she'd feel comfortable sharing them with the readers of this article. She considered the question carefully before relaying her enthusiastic approval. "Maybe someone out there needs to hear this."

She then explained that *her* parents openly hated each other when she was a little girl, and her coping mechanism amid the acrimony was to dream of the fairy-tale marriage that she would one day secure for herself.

"I wanted that so bad," she explained. "Not just for my own sake, but for yours. So you and your sister would know what it was like to grow up in a loving home."

But she hadn't quite bargained for the side effects of this approach—the delusionally love-obsessed son, the stubbornly cynical daughter, and the fact that she'd ultimately get so invested in her performance of a storybook love that she'd start to believe in it herself.

"There were so many times I shrunk myself down, just so I could play the damsel in distress," she revealed. "And so many times your father bottled up his feelings, just so he could be my knight in shining armor."

But of course, no person's true nature lies exclusively at one end of the fairy-tale archetype spectrum. The truth is that we all fall somewhere in between. My parents learned this lesson quickly after they retired to Florida, where they were suddenly forced to spend every waking moment together.

"Once that happened," my mom explained to me, "there was no way we could keep being who we'd always been."

So these days, they're getting to know each other all over again. Not the characters they'd learned to play for each other, but their true, full selves. Sometimes this means having deep conversations over dinner, and sometimes it means spending time apart so they can explore their own interests separately. (Apparently my father is really into pickleball, and my mother has developed a full-on obsession with Beyoncé.)

I did a double take as our conversation wound down and my mom earnestly described herself as a "strong, independent woman." And then again when she admitted that my father is *not* her Prince Charming—even going so far as to say she thinks that's a good thing.

"It's all very modern," she marveled as the last few ounces of wine were poured between us. "Certainly not the stuff of classic romance novels."

I accepted my glass and gave her a proud smile. The thought of my retired parents starting off their decades-long relationship on a brand-new foot struck me as adorable, inspiring, and—ironically—so romantic.

"But you know what?" my mom mused as she took her final sip.

"What's that?" I asked.

"I do still believe in the magic of the Earlymoon Hotel," she said through a proud smile of her own. "In fact, your father and I just booked a stay there for next week."

Reading Group Guide

1. This story begins with a personal essay written by main character, Ray Bruno, in which he reflects on his lifelong "delusional obsession with love and marriage." Did you find yourself relating to any part of Ray's essay? How much importance have you placed on the concepts of love and marriage throughout your life?

2. On the surface, Ray and Kip appear to be polar opposites, which Ray often acknowledges. Do you believe that "opposites attract"?

3. Ray and Kip are from different generations—millennial and Gen X—and at times they each epitomize certain characteristics associated with their generational labels. How accurate do you think such generalizations are? How do you feel about the way *your* generation is portrayed in media and storytelling?

4. The subject of weddings and wedding traditions looms large over this story—especially regarding how such traditions pertain to gay couples. Why do you think Ray and Kip had such vastly different feelings on this subject? Whose feelings do you empathize with more?

5. For the majority of both Ray and Kip's lives, gay marriage wasn't even legal. How do you think this affected each of them and their worldviews? How does it inform this story?

6. Two of the other couples at the Earlymoon Hotel—Jake/Lucy and Byrd/Joley—have a bit of dysfunction between them. How do these two relationships inform Ray's experience of the Earlymoon Hotel? How do they play into his character growth?

7. Mariah and Nicki are the one couple at the resort that seems to be on truly solid ground. Do you think this is because they've already been together for so long? Or for another reason? How does interviewing *them* inform Ray's experience and growth?

8. As the story progresses, Ray starts to question if he and Kip really are so different, or if they've just been conditioned to fulfill certain "roles" in their relationship. Have you ever felt like this in a relationship and/or a friendship?

9. What was your favorite thing about the relationship between Ray and his older sister Stef? Do you see them rekindling the tight bond they had as kids after this story ends, even though she's moving up north? Or will they drift apart again?

10. Kip struggles throughout the novel with the concept of letting himself be seen, whereas Ray has a history of oversharing and seeking attention. Why do you think each of them gravitate to these extremes? What is the healthiest balance, in your opinion, between maintaining a level of privacy and putting yourself completely out there?

11. The story ends with another personal essay from Ray, this time reflecting on the lessons he's learned on his earlymoon trip. How does this closing essay compare to the essay that opens the book? How has Ray grown (or not grown) from the first essay to the last?

Acknowledgments

While this is much more a story about love than it is about lobsters, I did perform a fair amount of research to ensure that Ray's background rang at least somewhat true. I was especially inspired by three books in particular: *The Secret Life of Lobsters* by Trevor Corson, *Stern Men* by Elizabeth Gilbert, and *The Lobstering Life* by David Middleton and Brenda Berry—all of which I enthusiastically recommend if you're interested in learning more about the culture and history of commercial lobstering.

This book (as with all my books) wouldn't exist without my endlessly supportive literary agent, Elizabeth Bennett, whose belief in my work has remained unwavering throughout six years of highs and lows. Thanks also to my agents Samantha Haywood and Dana Spector, along with the rest of the teams at Transatlantic and CAA. So much gratitude to my editor, Mary Altman, whose edits for this book were nothing short of brilliant (and sometimes eerily telepathic). And to the unparalleled team at Sourcebooks, including but not limited to Alyssa Garcia, Hannah Osborn, Pamela Jaffee, Katie Stutz, Paula Amendolara, Caitlin Lawler, Madison Nankervis, Molly Waxman, Diane Dannenfeldt, India Hunter, Ashlyn Keil, and everyone else on staff who has played a role in getting my books into readers' hands. Many thanks also to Julia McDowell and the team at HarperCollins Canada for your support of *The Gay Best Friend*.

This book (as with all my books) also wouldn't exist without the top-tier feedback of my trusted critique partners and beta readers. Julia Foster, I'm not even kidding, you are a storytelling genius. Steven Salvatore, your feedback and friendship is genuinely one of the only reasons this industry hasn't fully unraveled me yet. Dinah Alobeid, your early read of this story was beyond insightful, as per usual.

Endless thanks to all my fellow authors who have become friends in recent years, including but not limited to Lynn Painter, Mazey Eddings, Kate Dramis, B. Celeste, Elizabeth Everett, Susie Orman Schnall, Mia P. Manansala, Lyn Liao Butler, Annette Christie, Jenn McKinlay, Robin Lefler, Regina Kyle, Xio Axlerod, Timothy Janovsky, and every other author whose kind words have made me feel a little less alone in this industry.

I am forever grateful to the readers, booksellers, librarians, and influencers who have hosted me and/or supported my work in any capacity over the past few years—I would be nothing without you, and I'll never take your efforts for granted.

Massive thanks to the teams at Northshire Bookstore and Saratoga Springs Public Library for your support. Thank you also to Steve Rosenblum for being such a great champion of local authors and my books in particular!

I'm so lucky to be blessed with the best parents and family in all the land—thank you so much for the endless support (and patience with my writing-related disappearances) over the years. Ditto my equally supportive circles of friends—from the tristate area and beyond—y'all are the absolute best.

And to my love, Graig Williams. Pursuing this dream of mine has not been an easy path, and I don't think I'd still be on it if it weren't for your belief in me, especially on the days I don't believe in myself. Your unconditional love and support over the past decade is the reason I still am—and always will be—a romantic.

About the Author

Photo © Rob Spring

Nicolas DiDomizio is the author of the novels *The Gay Best Friend* and *Burn It All Down*, which was praised as "unforgettable" by James Patterson. He holds a bachelor's degree from Western Connecticut State University and a master's degree from NYU. He lives in upstate New York with his partner, Graig, and their shmooshy bulldog, Rocco.

Website: nicolasdidomizio.com
Instagram: @nicdidomiziobooks
TikTok: @nicdidomiziobooks